SKELETONS IN THE CLOSET

DAN O'SULLIVAN

SKELETONS IN THE CLOSET

Lulu Enterprises, Inc.

www.lulu.com

ISBN: 978-1-300-14455-7

Printed in the United States of America

Visit Dan O'Sullivan on the web at

www.dan-osullivan.com

ALSO FROM DAN O'SULLIVAN

TRAIN WHISTLE IN THE DISTANCE
A Collection of Stories

Dan O'Sullivan

ON SALE AT WWW.LULU.COM

Special thanks to my family, including Dad for genetically passing along a love for all things Twilight Zone-ish and Mom for all the work done to promote word of this book; to all friends for continued support including Trinette; and to Schroth and Lenhardt, two of my biggest supporters... I am incredibly grateful to have met you guys.

INTRODUCTION

      Halloween is by far my favorite time of the year behind Christmas, and I think that's primarily because it's the only holiday centered around storytelling. Whether it's campfire tales, urban legends, or scary movie marathons, All Hallow's Eve has been a strong symbol of spine-chilling myths and fables, and it's that essence I wanted to capture in writing this collection of stories in the vein of "The Twilight Zone" (which, eerily enough, I recently learned that my sister's fiancé's grandfather was second cousins with Mr. Rod Serling himself!) and some of my other favorite seasonal anthology films such as *Creepshow* and the more recent *Trick 'r Treat* (which I highly recommend). Thus, I present to you more than twenty frighteningly creepy tales stretching across nearly anything and everything imaginable and unimaginable, from bottomless holes to zombies, witches to Grim Reapers, and even a little something yet again from the dark bowels of my own strange dreams with the predicament that pans out in "The Last Supper". Also included in this sack of goodies for a bonus treat are two titles from earlier ventures into scary realms — the first celebrating its ten-year anniversary as of October 2012 with my smaller attempt at an anthology, "Spooky Stories That Really Aren't That Spooky But Fun Anyway", and the second celebrating its fifteen-year anniversary, "Night of the Scarecrow", which I, along with the favorable preference of an English teacher back when it was written, consider it to have for some strange reason been scribed with a tone quality that was years ahead of my time as a writer. I also remember camping down in Pennsylvania a bunch of years ago around Halloween and while rehashing the story verbally to my younger cousins one night was told by them to stop (out of their fear) and thought to myself, "Did I really write something that scary or are they just too young?" I suppose it's instances like those that reiterate the fun of storytelling around Halloween for me and what I wanted to accomplish with this collection. So check your fears at the closet door, brave readers, for once you enter that world of unlimited possibilities and unspeakable horrors, there may be no turning back.

TABLE OF CONTENTS

IF ONLY DR. DENNIS CROCKETT HAD SOME FRIENDS

Poor Dr. Dennis Crockett.

If only he had some friends.

Maybe he would finally get some rest. But there is never truly any rest for the wicked, is there? Certainly not for the heaps of teenagers he usually received on his cold, hard metal slabs down in the basement. Certainly not for the girl he had just received. They never seemed to care about rest. Never needed it. Always too busy partying all night, or popping pills to stay up late to study or do homework so they could mask the disoriented illusion to their often-concerned parents that they were trying to be good.

But not too many of them were ever really good. Isn't that what being a teenager is about? Maybe that's why Dennis Crockett liked working on them so much — it was the mystery and intrigue. It wasn't some lame, poor excuse of a middle-class suburban husband who nullified his own existence with a boring middle-age heart attack. These teenagers were full of life — full of complexity. So anxious to try, or to do, or to dare, or to want. The possibilities were endless. If only Dr. Dennis Crockett had some friends, he could create some sort of gambling pool of wages, and that way they could all have a ball at throwing in their own guesses as to how those teenagers met with the reaper.

It was usually drugs, though. Always drugs. Whether accidental at the expense of being experimental, or purposeful at the expense of being hopeful that their demise would ease their teenage-suffering mind.

Dennis Crockett slapped his other rubber glove on over his hand and pulled back the sheet, revealing the angelic naked body of a blonde goddess that nearly made him gasp in astonishment. Such a shame when he got the *really* pretty ones. She seemed like some supermodel in the making. She certainly fit the criteria, sending herself down the path of drugs early. He knew it was drugs. No doubt about that. Not only because of how they found her, but because that's how it usually was with teenagers. Why the hell couldn't kids these days handle their drugs? Why, he remembered his own experimental actions when he was their age, when it was tolerated a little more, and frowned upon a little less. Hell, when you could walk down the damn street with a lit joint in your mouth and give a friendly wave to Sheriff Bob, who would smile and stop writing the unfortunate parking ticket he was in the middle of to shake your hand and ask how your folks were doing. Nowadays you get hassled just for sparking a goddamn nicotine-light cigarette outside on the curb.

Now this girl lying on the slab was the end result of all those cautionary drug tales. Soon to be the too-soon punch line of some blonde joke at a house party. They never could handle their drugs properly. If only they had Dr. Dennis Crockett to guide them. He would've been this girl's mentor, her supplier, her friend. But they never gave a damn about his old aging ass. No, anyone over the age of twenty-five was immediately dully expendable to these damn mindless juveniles. You'd have to be a constant over-achiever to hold their short attention span. Keep something glittery or shiny dangling in front of their eyes, and you have them locked into a trance. The occasional pop music from the week's current and soon-to-be-forgotten heartthrob playing in the background is a good addition, too.

Dennis Crockett brushed a thin strand of her blonde hair from her closed eyes. That's when he noticed the craggy crack lines streaking across the backside of his hands, even through the rubber gloves. It seemed like every morning now he woke up with another one, as if any day now, the slightest bend of his fingers would break his entire hand like a shattered porcelain ballet statue. Christ, he was only in his late forties. He figured he deserved more time; after all, people seemed to be much more fit much later in life these days. He would often marvel at the physical shape of some of these people who were sent down to him, and how good they managed to keep themselves looking into their sixties or seventies.

But teenagers were always the best.

He fluttered his eyes up and down her perfectly-crafted body. You would think he was doing his initial once-over to examine the exterior for signs of struggle, bruises, conflict — but Dennis Crockett had no friends, so his eyes were on his own personal mission for him. What a goddess she was. It was amazing, how at the age of seventeen, she could have amounted such a statuesque posture and form. He skimmed his fingers over her lips. They were soft — luscious. Dennis Crockett darted his eyes up from the body and did a quick tour of the basement with them, as if searching for another warm soul lingering around. But no one ever came down there. Not this late at night, anyway. He never had a partner or anyone to jog down the stairs and greet him with a friendly cup of coffee and some bullshit late night conversation. He didn't know why he always took that second or two to check for anyone. Maybe it was cautionary habit. Maybe he liked that adrenaline rush of fearing that someone could actually be hoofing around somewhere on the floors above, working their own endless graveyard shift of turmoil, ready to come down to the basement to investigate in order to fill their own boredom and catch him in the act.

But no one ever came down. There was no reason for anyone to. And Dennis Crockett certainly didn't have any friends.

He laid his eyes back down on the girl's face. If she were alive, she wouldn't dare give him the time of day, but now she was giving him all the time in the world. All the time he wanted. Time didn't exist down

in that basement. Not for him. Not while he was down there...
"working".

A meticulously coy smile crafted upon his worn face. Dennis
Crockett began to take a tour of the girl's body — the word "body" was
much more implanted into his head because "corpse" didn't seem to serve
a proper tone for her physical wonder. He trailed his fingers down her
face and curved them around her cheek bones, tipping them at the base of
her chin. She had the smoothest skin. Teenage girls did the best job of
taking care of their faces, because that's what they cared the most about.
Perhaps they were doing it for him. He brushed more of her hair back
and guided his hand down her neck, slightly tucking it behind before
moving on to her broad shoulders. He smoothed them down her
arms — what perfect arms. He brought them to the tips of her fingers,
luxuriously investigating each digit like it was its own slender masterpiece.
He loved this part. He interlocked his fingers within hers and squeezed a
bit, closing his eyes as his jaw slightly jittered with joy. In his mind, they
could go anywhere together at that point. He often took them to the
ocean, where they trailed down white sandy beaches hand-in-hand, nude,
of course, on their own private island of wonder.

He was done with that now, easing his locked connection and
gently setting the hand which before had housed a ring or two back down
onto the cold slab. He reached down and grabbed the remaining portion
of the sheet that covered her lower half, pulling it up and off in such a
glamorous and pompous manner that made him feel like an old-time
magician unveiling a latest achievement.

And quite an achievement she was.

This girl took care of herself. He liked those ones the best. He
was given so many that appeared at first to be pretty and kempt on the
surface but underneath would always have a lazy flaw or too, like the gut
he found on the eighteen-year-old last week. She seemed so perfect and
presentable until he had lifted the blanket up and presented the notion of
one too many cheeseburgers. Funny how girls can be so good at illusion.
So many pretty faces and petite figures until you get down to the truth
beneath their clothes, and suddenly that proposed image you were holding
in your mind all those times you passed her by in the hallways at school is
shattered into a million disappointing pieces.

But this girl truly took care of herself. She was slim and slender,
yet not that sickeningly skeletal structure that the anorexic ones displayed.
Immediately Dennis Crockett knew that this one ate well, she worked out,
she took care of herself because she was above all the other girls trying to
cut corners. This girl *worked* at wanting to be noticed, and now he was
noticing her. He streaked his hand down her left leg and when he
brought it up, it shook just a tiny bit. It took a lot to get him this excited.

This girl was truly special. He glided up and down, as if her calf was some sort of pendulum he could go back and forth on eternally. He moved upward and closed his eyes as he reached the crevice between her legs, confirming his visual with his touch that she was indeed very friendly with a razor. And then he soared his fingertips back upward, bumping across the bellybutton that was once pierced but had been removed a while ago most likely due to a weekly teenage make-over boredom. He crawled his fingers over her flat stomach and up before stopping them to pull the rubber glove off as it snapped upon release. This was his favorite part of all, and there wasn't a chance in hell he would let it be ruined by a thin layer of latex. He moved his bare, age-worn fingers over the tiny speckles of hair on her skin and up to her mountainous ranges, closing his eyes once again to consume the feeling with his approaching wondrous imagination.

To say Dennis Crockett got a handful would be an understatement. Like a hungry orphan at a Thanksgiving dinner, his hands took as much as they could grab. They held, for what seemed like hours, until they were literally numb and tired. He took a long, exasperated breath and drank from the bottled water sitting on the nearby table. This girl was actually making him sweat. It took a lot for a girl to do that to him. This girl was indeed special. Special enough for him to strongly consider holding off on the initial autopsy procedures — the "gory stuff" — for another good hour or two so he could get more intimately acquainted with her. Special indeed.

Dennis Crockett drifted his eyes to the next gurney over, where another body lied covered in a white sheet, and his excitement seemed to immediately crash. That particular subject was actually work, and he always had an obsessive notion of working first and playing later, so despite the seemingly unprecedented excitement the gorgeous blonde had evoked upon him that night, he reluctantly trudged over to the second gurney, fixing the latex glove back onto his bare hand and unveiling the body of a seventeen-year-old male — decent shape, decent height, chiseled chin and chest that were the makeshift of an impending college football scholarship. They had been brought in together — a mutual overdose of euphoric teenage mistakes. Dennis Crockett sneered at the boy. It was probably his fault that the girl was lying there next to him. Girls never seemed to know any better. As implied before, they always put such a high importance of being noticed, and once they are finally recognized by those they aim for, it's an even more daunting task of keeping the attention. This girl wanted attention badly, so much to the point where her innocent mind was corrupted and steered into mortality by a mindless asshole jock simply wanting to get a piece.

Nice try, Dennis Crockett thought as he stared malevolently down at his face. *But I'll let you know how she is.*

He didn't ever tour the bodies of males like he did with the girls. He was far from finding any homosexual tendencies within himself. No, he worked on the males, and that was it. They were nothing but work for him, and this one would be easy and quick, like most. However, that didn't stop him from exacting his revenge. *That* part he enjoyed. For all the times those jock jerks back when he was in high school took the girls he wanted, the girls *he* tried to get. The ones that were so overly popular and athletically golden only to end up working in the town bowling alley or pumping gas at the interstate Mobil. *Look at you now,* Dennis Crockett could only simply say in his mind.

He walked over to the tool area and wiggled his fingers in the air over the plethora of options before settling on the basic scissor sheers. He carried them over and grabbed the sheet that curled up near the subject's stomach, lifting it up and back to look down his body. He grabbed "it" and snipped. Simple as that. It was nothing but anatomy to him. Work. Another body part. It had nothing to do with anything else but simplistic revenge. He glanced down at the stiff face of the once-thwarting quarterback. Oh, the joy of his painful screams and terror if he were still alive to experience what Dennis Crockett had just exacted upon him. Of course at this point it was redundant what the doctor had done to the body. It wasn't like the boy would ever know. But it was a simple slap-to-the-face kind of revenge that satisfied Dennis Crockett on levels he could never find the words to describe. He grabbed the other tools and started cutting, working away while occasionally glancing at his prize on the next gurney over… shooting short, small smiles to the other kind of satisfying coital revenge that waited so patiently for him to tend to.

Dennis Crockett was tired as his feet patted up the paved walkway to his well-earned house. There was still a good few hours of night darkness left, and he had earned those as well. It was the best night of his life, but it had taken a toll on him physically. Perhaps it was mostly the excitement that wore him out as opposed to the workout. As he unlocked his front door, another sly smile darted to the corners of his mouth at the thought of tomorrow night's work — what would roll downstairs to him then? What adventure would arrive on swift wings that could top the previous shift's excursion into Mecca? What if the next one was better than the last? Was it possible to top such a monumental achievement? There's always a girl more beautiful than the last. Even the pretty ones have to die young sometimes.

But he was far too tired to think or speculate anymore, and despite his sagging eyelids, he doubted he would get much quality in his slumber anyway with all the excitement still buzzing through him. He shut the door and locked it, fumbling his hand on the wall to find the light switch. He finally discovered it, but when he flipped it up, nothing happened. He twitched it and flipped it on and off, but nothing. Just pure darkness with the exception of some moonlight still shining its way through various windows. He sighed and grumbled. The power must have gone out. Perfect. An otherwise fitting wake-up call back to the realities of everyday life outside of his heavenly basement. He grabbed the flashlight sitting on the foyer's table (despite his annoyance of the situation, he was always prepared for something like it nevertheless) and clicked it on. He had briefly considered slinking down to the basement to see if a fuse had blown, but at that point, he was just too tired to care. His plan was to merely make it up the stairs with the guidance of his Double-A fueled flashlight, push open his bedroom door, and flop face-first onto the comfort of a quiet night's dreamless sleep until he could wake up to the morning glow of sunlight through his window, where he would then investigate the power outage in the comfort of full visibility and awareness.

That consideration had only lasted until he took his first step up the staircase, when the radio nearby blared on at full blast, shocking him with a startled jump that nearly made him drop the flashlight. He grabbed his chest and immediately calmed himself down, shaking the fright out of him as he took a quick moment to reflect on what had happened and hopped off the stair, burning his light onto the radio, which in turn burned the bright red digital clock numbers back at him. He grabbed the side and hit the volume, turning the loud music down — it was some teenage pop song. He hated that crap. It all sounded the same — some group of teenage guys on TV bouncing around in synchronized idiocy in some flashy room to ridiculous broken-hearted infidelity lyrics. Catchy as it might have been to the youth of the world, he knew it would only be forgotten within a matter of weeks, enjoying its Top Ten run while it could.

Dennis Crockett hit the top switch and turned the radio completely off, giving a puzzled scratch to his short, thin hair on how it could've turned on by itself, especially with the power seeming to be out. Some kind of glitch malfunction, perhaps. P.O.S. radios these days! There was always some kind of electronic bullshit download upgrade something-or-another you had to do just to keep it working, not like the quality hardware he had grown up grooving to. Strange as it might have been, stranger things have indeed happened, so he shrugged it off and headed back for the stairs while his heart continued to simmer down.

He made it to his bedroom door, turning the knob with his hand that still trembled from the musical outrage downstairs. He took a breath and clicked the flashlight off, setting it on the nightstand next to his bed as he unbuttoned his shirt and pulled off his jeans. He rubbed his nose and yawned, crawling into a much-awaited bed and under the bliss of a tranquil sea of blankets as his head soaked into the fluffy pillow.

He wasn't sure how much he had slept, if he had slept at all, because only a mere ten minutes had passed according to his old-style bedside clock when the radio downstairs had turned back on, blaring its incessant pop music at full volume once again. Dennis Crockett groaned and mumbled, pounding his fist into the mattress as he shifted his body and twisted to the side of the bed; his hands nearly knocking the flashlight over. He clicked it on and trudged out of the room, still feeling the walls of his house for guidance even with the flashlight shining before him. He bounced down the stairway and back over to the radio, wasting no time in turning it off. He uttered some confused nonsense spiced with a cuss or two and unplugged the infernal machine so that those beady red numbers on the front blacked into nothingness. He didn't care why or how it was malfunctioning. He was still too tired. The only thing he knew for sure is that he was going to enjoy granting it a trip into his trash compactor in the morning and then going out and buying an old reliable one. He hoofed back up the stairs and nearly made it back into his bed when the radio downstairs blared on full volume.

Dennis Crockett froze in place, slowly turning and creaking his aging body around to shine the flashlight out into his hallway. Impossible! Purely impossible! He had *just* unplugged the damn thing! He crept back downstairs and directed the beam of light onto the radio that sat on the foyer table with its power cord piled upon it. He picked it up and looked it over strangely as the poppy lyrics blasted. At first, the notion that it was battery-powered seemed to put his suspicions at ease, but when he turned it over to examine the bottom, that guess was put to rest when there was no apparent spot to place any within.

The radio stopped very abruptly, shutting off and the red numbers disappearing as quickly as they seemed to spring to life. He stood with a crooked face, now a bit bedazzled. And then he heard the footsteps. The footsteps that ran down the hall of the second floor balcony hallway that made him drop the radio to the floor as it broke in half. He zipped the beam of light upward; his breathing almost immediately stopping as he called out in response, "Hey! Who's there?!"

There was no reply. No footsteps. He directed the flashlight down both ends of the hallways, slowly scanning every inch from where he was standing in the foyer below. And after a long moment, he came to the conclusion that his mind was playing tricks on him. He was overtired. The radio had been giving him a ridiculous scare. He was manifesting these sounds through his fear. He was a grown man in his forties, for Christ's sake, not some little kid. *Grow up, Dennis*, he scolded himself in his head.

After scooping up the remains of the radio and disposing them in his trash, he headed back upstairs, but not before, of course, warily shining his flashlight down both ends of his hallway in suspicion of catching some prankster punk who had perhaps broken into his homestead and was the culprit behind the radio prank. He checked a closet here, a room there, a bathroom as well, before returning to his bedroom and climbing back into his bed. He had shuffled himself within the sheets and lied there for a good minute or two before realizing he was still gripping the lightless flashlight in his clammy hands. He was too wired to fall asleep now. The radio mishap had jumpstarted the beats of his heart. Besides, he was a bit concerned that if someone were indeed in his house at the moment, the fear of his safety and his possessions were of more importantly grave concern.

Until he felt the cold fingers on the back of his neck.

He gasped and froze, trying to bend his eyes back as far as he could, but to no avail, thinking that it was merely in his head. Maybe a cool draft had trickled across his neck. Maybe he was really dreaming.

No. They were fingers. They were long, slender, cold, hard fingers that intimately streamed the hairs on the back of his neck, giving him a little rub. His breath shook. He slowly began to turn, bit by bit, and in the moonlight pouring through his window, made out the naked body of his blonde goddess lying next to him, sitting slightly up as she stared at him. "Touch me, Dr. Crockett," she seductively whispered in a sweetened tone.

Dennis Crockett screamed and frantically wrestled himself out of his bed sheets, tumbling onto the floor where he dropped the flashlight. He picked it back up and fought with his fingers to click on the button, blazing the beam of light onto the bed, where only a pile of messy blankets lied. He gasped and panted out of breath; the flashlight in his hand shaking so much that he could hear the batteries inside clicking around.

He crawled onto his feet, not daring to remove the light from the bed, until he finally managed to zip it across the room, as if searching every bit of it. There was no one there. He rubbed his face. This was definitely not a good way to end a great night. He didn't know what had gotten into him. Now he was *seeing* things. *People.* Perhaps it was his tiredness. Perhaps he was coming down with something. Illnesses never seem to play nice with the human psychology. And it was in the calming notion of his breath slowing back down that he turned the light onto the open doorway of his bedroom to land directly onto the naked body of the blonde girl, who elegantly whispered within the threshold, "Touch me, Dr. Crockett."

Dennis Crockett let out a loud scream, stumbling back against the wall. The girl turned her head and watched him, adding, "Touch me, Dr. Crockett. I'm ready for you. I want you."

"Noooooo!" he hollered, shielding his eyes from the monstrosity before him.

He curled up into a ball, shaking and quivering. After long, dragging moments, he opened his eyes and peeked through the shielding protection of the fingers on his face to notice that his doorway was vacantly wide open. And that was it. That's all he could take. He didn't care why it was happening. He was getting the hell out of that house immediately. Out of the darkness that was consuming him with fear. He grabbed his keys from the pocket of his jeans and stumbled toward the door. He didn't care where he went. He just wanted to drive away from there; just drive anywhere until that comforting and warm sun came up.

He tripped in the hallway, falling to the floor where he rolled onto his back and looked up to see the face of the deceased young man from the other gurney in the morgue sneering down at him. "Hey, Doc," he grimly greeted.

Dennis Crockett gave a gasp and crawled back against the wall, taking a fuller look at the individual, who was dressed in a navy blue letter jacket, as if on his way to the latest pep rally. "I think you've got something of mine," the young man coyly murmured, reaching out with his dooming hand toward him.

"Nooooo!" Dennis Crockett screamed again through a few tears, jumping to his feet. "Go away! Leave me alone!"

He raced past the individual to the stairway, jolting down only a few steps before sharply freezing at the naked blonde girl coming up toward him as she smoothly guided her exotic fingers along the railing. "Take me, Doctor Crockett. Take me," she said.

Dennis Crockett screamed and hollered, nearly pulling what hair he had out of his head as he slumped against the wall. That's when they *all* came. Out from every door in his house, from around every corner, from every open window — all of them. All of the smirking jocks, all of the neglectful husbands, all of the naked, beautiful young women that were so much more innocent and glamorous than the previous. His eyes widened as his socked feet peddled backwards into his room. He dropped his flashlight, and it broke upon impact on the floor, blinking and fizzing out its last beams of sanctified luminance. He fell to the floor, cowering against the back wall as he watched them all begin to flood in. The young football jock reached his hand out. "I want it back," he stated.

Next to him, the beautiful blonde goddess openly extended her arms. "I'm ready for you, Doctor Crockett. Touch me. Touch me."

They came closer... closer... like an army of unwanted uncertainty filling the dark room from wall to wall. Dennis Crockett wildly shook his head as they hovered over him, reaching with impending fingers.

The obituaries stated it was a heart attack; his middle-aged stress bursting his heart like a balloon in the loneliness of his own comforting home. But he knew as it was happening what really caused it.

Poor Dr. Dennis Crockett finally got some sleep... on a gurney down in the morgue.

If only he had some friends.

SMASHING PUMPKINS

Skeletons in the Closet

Lloyd "Boney" Boggs was your average everyday eighteen-year-old American punk. He had got the nickname "Boney" on the account that his physicality had always been so thin. For as long as anyone could remember, the boy was just all "skin and bones", as his own grandfather would coin the classic term. It was most likely due from the fact that he had a high metabolism, for no matter how much he had eaten, he never seemed to gain any weight. As a matter of fact, he seemed to lose it if anything. With his height, his scraggly hair and his elongated beak of a nose, Boney was doomed for a life of nicknames from the start. There were plenty of them, originating mostly between the timeframe of middle school to junior high, scattering across the description of whatever physical abnormality he was developing into at that time. But "Boney" was the one that stuck most; the one that seemed to rightfully fit through the onslaught of other failed attempts. At one point around eighth grade, one particular kid had tried to conjure up the "Ichabod Crane" name as a replacement, seeing as how Boney was the spitting image of the classic character from famed author Washington Irving's "The Legend of Sleepy Hollow". But, as hilarious as it may have seemed to swivel around the circle of juvenile immaturity, there's the one true original nickname that always gets reverted back to, as most nicknames are unfortunately permanent in most cases.

Anyway, like most average everyday eighteen-year-old American punks, Boney had his share of hobbies, ranging from but not limited to the obvious loud rock music (which drew his parents crazy, even from the depths of the dungeon basement below which eventually became his unholy haven-of-a-bedroom), obscure horror movies, skateboarding with friends until being kicked out of the plaza parking lot by the local authorities, and of course, eating — which seemed to benefit Boney most because of his strange metabolism.

However, there's always one hobby for everyone that seems to stick out more importantly than the others. The one that people base their mundane lives around. The kind that they tweak and peak at whenever they can, itching to scratch at it in the cracks between school or work. Boney's… was smashing pumpkins. Don't ask why. At first it seems like something only young teenagers would get a kick out of, and that's how it started for Boney Boggs long ago as he entered teendom. He just simply got a pure joy out of smashing and destroying pumpkins around Halloween season. Every year, he would make a tradition of going out at night and amassing strange destruction upon people's doorsteps. In the earlier years, it was merely a bonus to him while out trick-or-treating with friends. They would ring the doorbell, collect their wrapped, sugar-coated madness, and once the unfortunate dwellers of the house had closed the door, they would pick up that pumpkin sitting next to the chair on the patio and launch it into the oblivion of the street's black paved abyss. And then they would run, laughing and cackling hysterically, being sure to skip a few houses for fear of someone actually re-opening the door behind them to discover their practical joke.

But as the others over the years outgrew trick-or-treating, toilet-papering front yard trees and smashing pumpkins, Boney continued his thwarting desire to destroy. He didn't even bother bringing a trick-or-treating bag with him anymore. If he really wanted candy, he could've just shoved some into his pocket down at the corner 7-Eleven where the old cashier struggled to focus his glasses on the newspaper he tried to read, or better yet, to reclaim some of his lost youth, would threaten some youngster to hand over their bag or permanently have their face hacked up as badly as the K-Mart mask they were wearing. But even that grew boring and tiring, for even bullying eventually loses its luster.

So Boney would make smashing pumpkins the main event every Halloween night. Lit or unlit, it didn't matter. He just got his rocks off at destroying every one in sight. Maybe it was an obsessive compulsive thing. Maybe there was some kind of repressed childhood memory involving pumpkins that he had long forgotten about. Whatever the reason, he didn't care. He would kick them, punch them, throw them, drop them — at the hand of his hand, the foot of his foot, or the bat of his bat. Of course, the lit ones were always obviously much more fun to destroy. Oh, how he loved picking those ones up and launching them through the starry nighttime Halloween sky, watching as the orange light trailed and waved in the breeze before the pumpkin smashed to the ground in a glowing pile of mush. It made him feel young again. Mindless and juvenile. It was also the excitement of doing it and not getting caught. That was just the bonus part. Most of the time, people had left them lit sitting on the porch of their dark and empty houses while they went out with their own kids trick-or-treating. That's where Boney got creative. He would deface them in some wild and whacky way, maybe checking the car in the driveway to see if it was unlocked so he could put it on top of some boxes in the driver's seat to make it look like it was driving. Or there was always the "throw and smash it against the front door" option. Once he managed to put one on a lawn gnome in the front yard, replacing its head with that of a smiling template. He didn't mind not destroying those ones as much because he received creative satisfaction out of it, but generally, most could not and would not escape his wrathful vengeance.

Boney always wore the same outfit every year on Halloween — a black shirt and black pants with a skeleton plastered on front, as if proudly embracing his nickname like a superhero going out into the night. Superhero? More like a super villain. Boney loved being bad. What were they going to do if they ever caught him? Throw him in jail for destroying pumpkins? Maybe make him write out a written apology or replace the damaged product, but they weren't going to catch him anyway.

So Boney threw on his usual ensemble that year on his eighteenth Halloween, accompanied by his best friend Wade, who was the only one out of the crew of misfits who had stuck around that long to witness and sometimes partake in the yearly traditional destruction. All of the others had graduated to seeing Halloween as more of a night to party and get drunk, and some of the lamer peers had made it a night representing a scary movie marathon. Boney was nowhere near ready to become anything like that. For all his intentions, he was ready to smash pumpkins even at a ridiculous age of eighty. Wade, however, was starting to grow tired and bored of the shenanigans. "Come on, Boney, seriously," he mumbled to Boney. "Haven't you outgrown this shit yet? You're freaking eighteen-years-old, man — going around Halloween night smashing people's damn pumpkins in their yards. I could see one or two if it were on the way to a party or something, but you set everything else in the world aside to make a damn spectacle out of it! Smashing pumpkins should never be the main event for people our age. That's just sad."

Boney would shrug him off like he always did, for every year it seemed Wade grew further and further away as his accomplice in crime. Perhaps this year, it was finally time for Wade to retire. "My night's planned, dude," Boney calmly assured him. "You can do whatever you want, but me — I'm going."

Wade huffed an unbelievable laugh. "For real? There's only one thing more lame than going out to smash pumpkins on Halloween night as an eighteen-year-old, and that's going out to smash pumpkins on Halloween night as an eighteen-year-old *alone.*"

"I'm cool with it," Boney said.

"And that's what makes it so creepy," Wade added. "Just come to the party with me. You can smash a couple on the way. Connie is supposed to be there, and Sheila told me that Jennifer mentioned she was gonna be wearing this super-sexy angel costume, with like, nothing to it. Nothing to it, dude. I know you wanna see that."

"Nah," Boney replied.

Wade rolled his eyes and shook his head. "Fag," he mumbled, turning to leave and disappointingly sulk up the basement staircase.

Boney admired himself in his skeleton clothes, shifting his body a bit to adjust to the few layers beneath that would keep him warm outside on that chilly night. And so the festivities began...

Boney Boggs skipped across the front yard of a nice house in a quiet neighborhood and soccer-kicked a lit pumpkin between two trees, shining a satisfied smile as he victoriously raised his arms. "He shoots, he scores!" he called out, cupping his hands around his mouth to make a cheering crowd noise.

He picked another up and drop-kicked it high into the air. "And we have lift off!" he said, watching as it floated up, up, up, and then finally giving into gravity as it fell and flopped into an orange mess in the grass. He chuckled and gave a quick cheer, turning to see two small kids dressed in costumes watching him from the driveway. "What are *you* lookin' at?" he called out to them. "You wanna be next?"

The kids stood there, a bit in a trance by the image of destruction they had just unfortunately witnessed. Boney growled and took a few menacing steps toward them, waving his arms as the kids took off screaming down the road. He threw his head back with a laugh, falling to the soft grass and rolling.

Smash, smash, smash, Boney had annihilated every pumpkin in sight across town, and he hadn't even begun to feel tired. His feet were ready for more walking and his fingers curled at the thought of picking up the next wonderful creation. Most of the templates that were cut into the front were generic and the same, but often times, Boney would have some fun and joke with the ones that were more creative and well-done. Very rarely did he not destroy any because he was so overly-impressed with whoever spent the time to carve a unique face by hand. But that didn't mean he would just leave it sitting on the front steps unbothered. One time, Wade had asked why it was that Boney only smashed the pumpkins on Halloween, when it was clear that people had them out at points all month long. Boney had simply replied that Halloween was the culmination point — anyone who had carved or put out a pumpkin was sure to do so by that night, or else it would slightly defeat the symbolic seasonal purpose, therefore, it was the one single night when he would have the highest amount to destroy. Aside from that, he had also mentioned that by Halloween night, most of the pumpkins that were readily sitting and waiting for days or weeks before had been seasonally weathered and aged enough to give them a perfect balance between softness and hardness. "They have to be just right. Sometimes if they're too soft, they break in your damn hands when you pick them up before you even have the chance to give them their inaugural flight," Boney explained.

But of course that never stopped him from doing it. Some were just better than others. Like a batch of cookies that had been sitting in a bowl for a while. Not every one is perfectly soft and moist; some are just better than others.

Boney wrecked destruction every which way. Every year he considered running a tally just to satisfy his personal curiosity as to how many he destroyed, but there were just far too many to keep count of! And that's the thought that made him smile most.

Later in the night, Boney had hiked his way over the hill en route to the next housing track where dozens and dozens of more victims sat lit and ready, but as he got to the top, his jaw nearly dropped to the road.

It was a field of pumpkins, all lit, all twinkling. Hundreds of them. Hundreds and hundreds! All lit and uniquely displaying some carved face. What the hell was this?! This was new! He knew his town like the back of his boney hand and had never come across anything like this before. Then he realized where he was — he was at the start of the lame haunted hayride attraction they started doing for kids a couple years before. And then he remembered reading about it in the local paper a few weeks ago. Some article mentioned that kids could have the opportunity to carve their own pumpkins for display at the attraction, and they would all be lit Halloween night. There was no tractor, nor any people around for that matter. It seemed to be closed for the night. It was pretty late, after all. But had the workers not gone and blown out all the pumpkins before leaving? *Yeah, let's leave a couple hundred lit pumpkins burning in an empty field*, Boney's sarcastic rationality laughed in his head.

Maybe they were coming back. No one was stupid enough to cause a fire hazard like that. Not in this town. Regardless, Boney was glad. Because now *he* was there... and now he would save them the trouble. He skipped into the field and found himself in his own personal heaven, kicking and throwing every pumpkin. There were so many and they were so close together, he had trouble keeping up with himself. He didn't even worry about being creative, or shouting out some stupid departing one-liner. He just *destroyed*. He wanted to cry because he was so happy. He laughed and rolled among them, cheering and looking up to the bright starry sky.

Boney Boggs destroyed them all.

It had taken him nearly most of the night, but he had decimated every single damn pumpkin in that field, and no one ever came back to put them out, either. Eventually he had left, hiking back toward his house through the woods. He was far too tired to continue on to the next housing track, even though he still had plenty of night left. The pumpkin field had more than satisfied his appetite for destruction. Besides, he knew he had to take the opportunity while he had it, for someone could have come by at any moment and caught him. He excitedly rubbed his hands at the thought of next year. Even when they come by to the field in the morning, they'll see all the pumpkins smashed and extinguished — job already well done. And even if they suspected foul prankster play, it still worked out to their advantage. Hell, maybe he could even get himself a job working the haunted hayride next year, and then when the tractor trails off into the woods carrying all those damn little idiots, he could smash as many as he could and run away, watching from afar as all the kids came back and cried over their ruined accomplishments. They would ask him what happened, and he would simply say he caught some kids smashing them and chased them off. Innocent, free and clear. Oh, what savoring satisfaction!

Boney had come across an old shack-of-a-house within the woods on the path to his own neighborhood. It wasn't one he was familiar with, but then again, probably inhabited by one of the strange outskirt hermits. And there, sitting on the rotted porch steps leading to the crooked front door, was a lit pumpkin, strangely snarling with its evil face.

Maybe just one more, Boney thought. *For old time's sake.*

It was another three-hundred sixty-five more days until he could smash the next pumpkin beneath his foot, so he figured he would take advantage of the final opportunity of the night. So he gave a quiet, small chuckle, hinted with a dash of mischievousness, and walked over to it. He picked it up, admiringly gazing at the face staring back at him. "I've seen a lot of different carvings tonight," he began to say to it, "but you are one ugly S.O.B."

He smiled and raised the pumpkin high above his head, glancing down to the dirt below with impending joy, when he heard the scratchy feminine voice behind him call out, "Hey! Who's there?"

He jolted a bit in surprise and turned to see the old lady standing on her porch, draped with dirty rags and torn shards of clothing. "Whatcha doin' there with that there pumpkin?" she then asked, taking a shaky step forward with help from her cane.

"Oh," Boney simply replied, looking down at it. "I was, uh, just, uh, admiring the craftsmanship."

"Were ya, now?" the lady suspiciously asked, taking another step. "My work you're admirin'."

"Well, then," Boney added, curving a smile. "I should say crafts*woman*ship, then."

The lady shook her cane at him. "Best be off, before I be callin' the police, boy!"

Boney rolled his eyes. Not the first time he heard that, certainly wouldn't be the last. "All right, relax, ya old hag. I'm goin'."

Boney gently set the pumpkin back down at the foot of the steps. "Plannin' on havin' some fun with that there pumpkin, were ya? Plan on destroyin' all my hard work, were ya? Go ahead."

"I said I was goin', lady, all right? Don't have a conniption fit or nothin'."

"Smash that there pumpkin and you'll have the wrath of a curse be put on ya, I say," the lady threatened, giving another shake of her cane.

She turned and waddled back into her house, mumbling some other incoherent nonsense as Boney watched and gave a small chuckle, shaking his head. "Crazy old bat," he blurted under his breath.

After she had gone back into the house, Boney turned to leave when he looked back at the pumpkin. Temptation was flirting with him, and perhaps it was the typical teenage rebellion against the maturity of the world that made him think twice as he bent over and picked it up. "Put a curse on *me*, will ya? This was the most fun I've ever had on Halloween in my life, and I'll be damned if the end of it's gonna be spoiled by the cranky likes of you, crazy old bitch."

He grinded his teeth and threw the pumpkin downward, smashing it upon the old wooden steps of the house as he gave a satisfied look toward it. He gave it the finger and turned, walking away. That put him in a much better mood. He slipped his hands in his pockets and whistled a little as he made his way through the woods, still buzzing from his anti-Halloween euphoria. But there was something uneasy breezing through the trees as he looked around. The branches shook a bit, and leaves skipped and scraped across the stony path as moonlight gave a haunting glow from the hidden sky above. Boney gave a shaky smile, continuing onward.

No one ever knew if it was in fact the old crazy hermit lady that did it. Despite Boney's account of the events, the possibilities were strange enough. Perhaps the pumpkins themselves did it out of an angering revenge, but he had woken up the next morning in his bed down in the basement and went to scratch his nose when he felt an unusually hard texture. He sat up, and his head felt a bit heavier than normal. He thought maybe he was getting a cold, but then he felt around, shifting and patting his hands against the roundness. He hurried into the bathroom, and then he screamed. There, sitting on his shoulders, where his otherwise scraggly-haired head would have been, was a large jack-o-lantern style pumpkin, carved with a small zigzag of a mouth and triangles for the eyes and nose. At first, his initial reaction was that someone was playing a gag on him, and had somehow put a gigantic pumpkin over his head, but as he tried to pry it off, it wouldn't budge. What the hell did they use to put it on? He pulled with all of his strength, but his neck was actually starting to hurt where the pumpkin portion was attached. His parents laughed at the prank while they ate breakfast, but after they couldn't get it off themselves, they grew a bit concerned as well, even to the point where they visited the village doctor later in the day.

"No logical explanation" was how he put it in terms of the pumpkin being literally attached to his neck as if it were actually a part of his body. They tried drilling and cutting it off, but Boney's screams of pain in addition to the blood coming out made them reconsider. There was actually *blood* coming out of it.

He was the talk of the town. The talk of the nation after a while, but the further the story stretched out across the country, the more people laughed at it and the less they believed it. But those around him know how sickeningly true and unexplainable his situation is. "Boney" Boggs had died. He was still very much alive, that is, but the nickname that had attached itself to his persona had soon become no more, and eventually kids and peers of all ages started cooking up many, many new different nicknames for him.

"Pumpkinhead" comes to mind.

ON SALE THIS BLACK FRIDAY
FOR THE LOW PRICE OF YOUR LIFE

"Hey!" the tall, lanky man with the mustache yelled at Deke as he joined his friend Bosco in the line. "What the hell do you think you're doing, kid?!"

Deke turned and sharply bent his eyebrows to the man in his fifties standing a few people back. "Chill out. I'm with him," he calmly assured.

"I don't care! It doesn't matter! Some of us have been waiting in this line for over three hours already!" the man with the mustache barked. "This isn't like some amusement park ride, where it's okay to join your buddy because you wanna sit next to him, or some movie premiere where there will still be plenty of seats for me to choose from. Having you jump in line ahead of me actually hurts my chances of getting what I want!"

Bosco rolled his eyes and almost wanted to smile as Deke gave him an unbelievable look. "Then let me assure you that I'm only here for movies," he told him. "So relax."

The man with the mustache huffed an agitated breath, looking around to those near him. "Movies. Ha. Yeah, right. You expect me to believe that? No one waits in a damn line a mile long all night for stupid five dollar movies."

It really was true. Deke wasn't lying. He was there solely for the movies. He had a few titles left on his wish list he wanted to beef up his collection with, and the prices were going to be out of this world. Then again, prices never seemed to stop him before, and he had never been a big fan of going out on Black Friday, especially waiting in some ridiculous line for hours upon hours, where he was sure to be trampled once those doors opened. The orderly line he had just joined was nearly a civilized mask for the absurd bloodthirsty passion of commercial humanity at its finest. Black Friday for Deke meant staying the hell home all day and not risking going out into the craziness. The worst of it was probably in the morning, because all of the best stuff would be gone fast, but that still didn't mean that good stuff wasn't available throughout the day, so he didn't feel like driving about and getting T-boned in an intersection by some crazy soccer mom trying to get to K-Mart for the one-hour special on socks.

But Bosco had convinced him to try it out that year. "A helluva experience" was how he put it. Bosco went out on Black Friday *every* year. Every year, he would do his homework, too. He would dig through the Wednesday paper the day before Thanksgiving, fishing out every single ad it had to offer with the Friday specials. He would constantly check his favorite online retailer sites every hour on the hour, adding the latest price drop change to his personally-modified chart in Microsoft Word on his computer. And then late on Thursday night, long after he had stuffed himself with the inner workings of his grandmother's Thanksgiving

Turkey Day experience, he would hit the gas in his Volvo and initiate the battle plan he had laid out just before the clock ticked to midnight.

Like any guy in his twenties, the sole purpose of his existence (other than "gettin' a piece") was being up to date on all the best in electronic euphoria. Bosco was a huge video gamer. Rather than side with one company's latest glorified technological achievement, he would join the legion of many whom were neutrally dedicated to all, making sure to buy every system out there so that when someone talked about the latest game, he wouldn't have to ever say, "Oh. That sounds dope, but I don't have a (insert system name here)."

Bosco liked choice. He lived in a world where there was plenty of it. He didn't believe in being subjected to only the things you could afford. "If you want it, go get it" was his initial life slogan outlook, followed by, "And if you can't get it, figure out a way to". If that meant selling something you didn't use anymore to head in that direction, so be it. He tried not to sell any of his video game glories, even if it was an outdated system that no one played online with anyone. Those, in his mind, were the best to play, because after hours of blasting away little kids online in the latest army death match, it was always a treat to kick back with the classics. Then he would be back playing the latest online sensation. It was a rotation of immaturity at its finest.

Now Bosco was ready for the ultimate game station — the Revolution. It was the latest and greatest in technology, far surpassing anything anyone had ever seen before. It made the current systems out there look like cheap, handheld obscenities. The graphics were supposed to be amazing, and if they looked anything like the preview videos Bosco and the other hoards of thousands waiting for its release had seen, then he had nothing to worry about.

Deke handed him the Styrofoam cup of coffee he had been fetched to get while Bosco held his place as Bosco took a sip and glared up to the red beaming logo on the side of the store's concrete building. It read, "ELECTRONIC WORLD". It was *the* premium place to buy anything you could plug in and play. Their prices were usually affordable, with the occasional door-buster sales that kept those true Black Friday hounds happy all year long. Of course, to people like Bosco, a deal was a deal, no matter where it was. He was loyal in general to this store, but he would go elsewhere to get what he wanted if that was the bottom line. His toes curled. He tried to hold back the excitement of his smile as if he were a little kid at Christmas. Perhaps that's what he liked most about spending money — he didn't necessarily like the product nearly as much as the anticipation he received from waiting for it. It was all in the excitement. And there he was, standing a good ten or so people from the front of a line headed for true super-saving electronic bliss, with the tail of it curving well-beyond the back corner of the building and into the side parking lot. The Revolution wasn't even due to hit stores for another week, but he had received the special e-mail alert that very morning on Electronic World's very exclusive deal to sell it Black Friday while the supplies lasted. The employee had already made his way down the line with the item ticket vouchers a good half hour ago before Deke had arrived with the salvation of caffeinated coffee. Bosco glanced down at his ticket, which was for his very own Revolution system. He couldn't believe he was holding it. He couldn't believe he would be one of the first people in the country to be playing, even if for only a week. He would be a god among gamers for the next seven days, gloating to all of his online friends that he was destroying monsters or other evil essences on the latest and greatest technological achievement to ever hit shelves. The predictions on the system's initial sales were to go through the roof. Many thought it would outsell anything that had ever been released before its time. Bosco couldn't believe that the ten people in line before him didn't take all the vouchers. Of course, one item per person for fairness, but still — he didn't think the store would be getting many of them. The people before him were most likely interested in flat screen high definition 3D TVs, video cameras, phones, surround sound systems — any other type of gadget that didn't make them seem as juvenile as they already were depicted to their spouses or significant others. Bosco didn't care. He would play video games into his eighties.

He looked over to Deke, who drank from his coffee as he casually scanned his eyes across the plaza to other portions of the mall that had remained closed and lifeless. Perhaps one store in the distance had some kind of pathetic line for their own deal-busters, but nothing like Electronic World. Bosco couldn't believe he only wanted movies. Damn DVDs and Blu-rays. He loved movies too, and might snag a couple while he was there, but to go on a Black Friday mission — to stand with hoards of others at quarter to five in the morning and have your main priority be movies — just seemed unnatural to Bosco. Oh, well. He was there to tag along, and Bosco was happy. In years past, he could never get Deke to join him. Deke didn't think waiting in front of a store from midnight to five a.m. seemed sane for *any* product of *any* price. So Bosco usually got his glorified deals alone with the plethora of other citywide strangers around him — his competition. But this year he had finally convinced Deke to go with him. He showed up a few hours later than expected, but he was there nevertheless. Deke had overslept. He was a family guy, and Thanksgiving for him was tiring between all of his little cousins jumping around and the older adults constantly nagging him to down more food.

"Should be any minute now," Bosco had mentioned. "Any minute, they'll open those doors and let us in."

"And that's when we get trampled to death, right?" Deke asked with an inquisitive eyebrow raised. "You've plotted and planned all these strategies for buying, but have you laid out any sort of emergency precaution plans for safety?"

Bosco blew his lips and gave a passive chuckle, shaking his head and waving him off. Every year, Deke would read about the constant accidents in the paper revolving around Black Friday and how the craziness would always seem to result in injury or perhaps, at the worst, death. He watched a video one time online that an employee was filming from within a store of the entrance doors being opened up, and the army of hungry shoppers rushing in like some sort of stampeding cattle-drive. The employees literally jumped onto the safety of the wall shelves to the side to avoid being caught up in the craziness. It was sickening to Deke. No video of anyone getting run over by a car or mutilated in some accident compared even close to that of the one he watched where he hauntingly remembered the employee jumping out of the way onto the shelves.

But he was convinced by Bosco to join him, if only for the simplistic company. Deke wasn't going to run. Not even for movies. Even if it meant the ones he was there for were gone by the time he reached that section of the store. It just wasn't worth it.

And now the time had come. A certain buzz had sifted through the air among the waiting people as the employees inside moved about, preparing to unlock and open the doors to priced-down glory. "Here we go, man," Bosco muttered with a slick smile.

The doors were unlocked, and the employee at the entrance signaled for the line to move forward. At first, it was orderly, with the people taking a few calm, shuffling steps onward, but with each step, anticipation, fear and excitement overcame the crowd, and soon those tiny steps grew bigger and faster, and the "fuck it" mentality had instantly spread throughout the crowd like a ravenous disease. They rushed in, bumping past Deke as he felt like a human pinball. He didn't understand the nature of it. Everyone had their ticket vouchers. Why were they hurrying? They were guaranteed their product. But that was the nature of man — to consume more, at any cost. They were there for cameras, or TVs, or phones, but they were going to leave with a whole lot more than planned for, and that's why they were rushing. That's what the stores wanted. They wanted them to say, "Oh, wow! Look at this price! I don't really need this, but I've gotta have it at this price!"

Deke had already lost his pal Bosco within the sea of madness. Bosco, unfortunately, was one of those mindless consumers, driven to the idealistic pleasures of owning that which you owned already. He sighed and shook his head. He was the only one moving at a smooth, calm rate.

Skeletons in the Closet

By the time he had reached the movie section, he glanced over his shoulder to see how many more brainless ants were flooding in through the entrance gates of consumable oblivion. The last of them from the seemingly mile-long line had rushed inside, and then a few employees had locked the doors. Why were they locking the doors? And even more perplexingly, why were they pulling down the shutters? They were bringing them down, locking the bottoms and blocking out the windowed view to the parking lot. Is that how it worked? They only let the line of people inside as some kind of elusive, exclusive Black Friday privilege? Other people surely had to be on their way. Weren't they open for business now in general? Deke hadn't been experienced in Black Friday functionality, but this seemed a little odd. The employees all began to gather and huddle up toward the front check-out areas. Deke looked to his side, where some people knocked over some items from a shelf and carelessly continued onward. None of the employees seemed to care. Shouldn't there have been some kind of control or order to it all? These people were ludicrous. Surely there would be employees out and about keeping order to the insanity, but there seemed to be none around. They all gathered up front and watched from afar.

Deke finally met up with Bosco, would struggled and juggled with his Revolution game system box among an assortment of other useless electronics. "What do you have a video camera for?" Deke had immediately asked him. "You don't make movies; you don't ever film anything."

"Yeah, but for this price, you'd be crazy *not* to buy it!" he said with a feverish smile.

"Whatever," Deke noted. "Look, man — something weird is going on with the employees up front. They locked the doors and pulled down the shutters."

"So?" Bosco blurted.

"So? Doesn't that seem a little weird? Aren't they open in general now? I didn't know they opened and closed right up just for the people in line? Does it work like that?"

Bosco gave a casual shrug. "Who cares. Works for me. Less people in here means more stuff left for me to buy."

Deke still felt uncomfortable as Bosco continued with his shopping rampage. It was amazing that with all the items he was managing to carry, he didn't seem to give one second of his thought time to the practicality of a shopping cart. If that didn't lay out humanity's priorities to Deke, he didn't know what would. Deke went and grabbed the movies he wanted. He got most on his list, but wasn't too concerned about the others he couldn't find. There was just something strange in

28

the air, and he wanted to pay and leave and get back home to bed as soon as he could.

Bosco and Deke were among the first to approach the registers; Bosco tumbling all of his products onto the conveyer with an exasperating breath as they waited for the employees, who all still stood huddled near the door. Bosco turned his head, looking at all of the other empty check-out lanes void of any helping hands. "Hello?" he called out. "A little service over here? Anyone working the check-out aisles?"

The employees ignored him as one or two other customers began to emerge up front with the bliss of their own treasured electronic price-steals. The man with the mustache from the line outside earlier waited in the next aisle over, tapping his hands on the counter. "Anyone gonna check us out?" he yelled to the group of employees.

They ignored him.

He looked around to the other people, who started getting a little antsy. "Hey!" he shouted in a more firm voice. "We are ready to be checked out! Quit text messaging your damn useless friends and get your minimum wage teenage ass over here to service us before I call over your manager — "dude"!"

"What the hell are they doing?" Bosco wondered with a hint of annoyance.

The man with the mustache got fed up, growling as he picked up his boxed thirty-two inch lightweight flat screen TV and trudged over to the group of employees. "Hey! Didn't you hear me?! You all deaf or something? If one of you doesn't get your ass over to cash me out, I am walking out of this store with this TV with just cause of no available service!"

The employees finally acknowledged him by all turning around and staring. They began to shake and convulse simultaneously, twitching as if going through some kind of mass seizure. The man with the mustache gave a confused look as he trailed back a few steps. "What the hell...?" was all he could manage to mumble.

The skin of their faces began to melt and burn like cheap masks. Their navy-blue uniforms tore as their muscles bulged. Their bodies enlarged. The man with the mustache dropped his jaw to the floor as he staggered back and watched the faces shape into a cross between a cat and a dragon. And then, after the employees had fully changed and morphed, they all pulled out small rods from their pockets, which shifted and constructed into large gun-like weapons.

Deke and Bosco couldn't believe their eyes as they watched from their check-out lane. The cat-like creatures stood, unflinching and unmotivated for a long moment, until the one in front finally stiffly aimed his weapon forward at the man with the mustache, pulling the trigger. A sharp blue laser blasted the TV box in his hands, disintegrating it into nothingness as he unbelievably looked at his empty grasp. His body trembling with fear, he veered his eyes back up to the creatures only to be vaporized in a bright blue melting blast.

The screams rippled through the crowd of shoppers as they began to flee. The first few that made it to the shuttered doors were met with the bright blue blasts from the guns, melting and dissolving into skeletons, which in seconds turned to ash.

"Holy shit!" Bosco hollered, ducking with Deke behind the aisle as the laser blasts seared in their direction.

Cries and hollers erupted among the other shoppers as the creatures began to pan and spread throughout the store, blasting their lasers as if working in some steady, standard militaristic formation. Bosco and Deke jetted to the TV section, taking cover behind a unit. "What the hell are these things?!" Bosco yelled.

"We've gotta try to make it to the back of the store and find a way out of here!" Deke hollered.

A woman tripped and fell to the floor at the end of their aisle, screaming as she looked back and was met with the demise of an incoming blue laser blast, melting her to nothingness. Deke looked up to see the creature approaching, and that's when he sprang forward, knocking the large flat screen TV unit over as it crashed upon it, burying it in a mess of electronic pieces. Deke noticed the weapon on the floor, free from its clawed hand, and sprang out to retrieve it.

"Dude! What are you doing?" Bosco called out.

Deke picked it up. It looked simple enough — pull the trigger and shoot. But he would only know for sure once he did. Thoughts flooded through his head — what were they? Where had they come from? Why were they doing this? Had they planned this, putting out ads and e-mails online to lure people to coming? They were just... blasting people away. Blasting them away without mercy or without strategy. Maybe that's how they operated. Ruthless beings from another world who preyed on running humans for mere sport. Deke couldn't waste time wondering about that now. Now, he had to get out of the store. Get out and find help before he and Bosco were toasted and roasted with no deserving explanation.

All he wanted was movies. Just a few movies with a discounted tag that he didn't necessarily need. If he had known this was going to be the true price, he would have never gotten out of bed. He would've stayed slumbering in his warm blankets along with half the country while the other half waited outside some lame superstore in the freezing cold. Maybe that's what most of the people there would've done if shredded dollar signs weren't coming out of their asses. He didn't see how he was going to get through the army of unsympathetic monsters. He didn't see how much cover the winding aisles of flashy electronics would give them on the way.

And he certainly didn't see the crafty creature spring out from behind the walls of flat screen TVs behind him, immediately blasting his laser gun. Bosco's eyes widened in unprecedented horror as he witnessed the gun from his best friend's hands drop to the floor when there was nothing left of him to hold onto it. He couldn't move. He was frozen in place. The creature snarled under its coarse whiskers and aimed its gun at Bosco. One of the TVs on the wall had fallen from its hinges, slapping the monster on the back and knocking it to the floor as it belted a firm grunt.

At first, Bosco watched and waited as it growled and moved about, trying to weakly free itself from the confines of the unit, but then Bosco finally snapped back to life and rolled forward, grabbing the creature's weapon and aiming. With the pull of the trigger, he blasted the cat, which let out an inhuman yelp before it dissolved into blue nothingness. Bosco panted out of breath, looking the futuristic piece of weaponry over. He turned and took a step onto a shelving unit, peeking over to cast a view of the entire store. It was chaos. Pure chaos. Plenty of countless people still ran about, flailing and waving their arms among the various blue blasts of lasers. Some managed to dodge and evade, but it was never for long. The cat-like creatures were in no hurry. They simply took step by step across the store, shooting here, blasting there, as if calmly eradicating roaches one by one. Bosco noticed the faint red-glowing emergency "EXIT" sign on the opposite side of the store. It wasn't guarded, and it certainly didn't appear to be locked down in any inescapable manner such as how the entrance had been.

He looked down at the weapon in his hand again, giving it an almost determinedly ready pat as he slammed the barrel portion into his other bare palm. He had played nearly every video game ever created. He had broken the boundaries of high scores. He had the experience of online warfare. And now he had motivation. Motivation for his own life without any resets, so that he could get out of their alive and live to see another day of playing video games — because this was now truly the biggest challenge of his life.

But it was a long way to the exit door.

THE EPIDEMIC

epidemic itineris

A farmhouse sat quiet and undisturbed among the forever-stretching green grassy plains. The skies were blue, filled here and there with a white fluffy cloud. Some bright yellow corn in a nearby field was bold and ready for the summer season, standing tall and exuberant as the plethora of lean stalks slightly swayed with each touch of gentle warm breeze. There may have been another neighboring house or two somewhere within reasonable driving distance but that wouldn't have stopped the area from being as quiet as a distant lonely planet somewhere at the edges of the solar system.

But despite the peaceful silence, colorful statements and perfect weather this particular place had to offer, there lingered some sort of eerie desolation. Something threatened this seemingly Norman Rockwell-esque lifestyle with a barely undetectable essence, maybe at first unnoticeable to the wandering eye. But if that wandering eye should continue to look, it would see no sense of fulfillment anywhere. Even at a typical three-story farmhouse in the middle of the country in the smack dab middle of nowhere there would have to be *some* sort of finely tuned atmospheric noise buzzing about, whether it was the ambience of a laughing child bouncing about as they skipped their daily outdoor chores or the melodic chirping of some breast-colored bird perched on top of the windmill.

If that wandering eye were to continue, it would slightly coast overtop the side field of the house through the growing vegetation and to the road, where a large rusted maroon tractor would be stopped and undisturbed, parked slightly askew as if it ran out of gas. And hunched over on the seat — a tall farmer wearing overalls; his hat tilting forward off his head as it rested against the steering wheel. His age would be difficult to pinpoint exactly, since the decaying process had already taken its course across his solemn face. A few flies swayed about the corpse; their buzzing being amplified as it was the only noise in the area.

That is, until the distant sound of a car approaching rattled this sound of silence. At first it was a small gray speck down the road; the sunlight beaming a bright shiny ball in its place. But it was indeed coming at a fast speed, and soon enough, without any stopping or slowing to take notice at the deceased worker, it rushed on by, void of any second thought — or even first, for that matter.

Inside the car in the driver's seat, Lander gripped the wheel tightly as he intently stared ahead. It wasn't like he had to concentrate on traffic or the weather, but his palms pumped sweat. An accruing five-o'clock-shadow was beginning to etch its way onto his twenty-five-year-old face as he scratched his messy short hair, batting away some sweat beads from his forehead in the process. He turned his attention to the passenger seat beside him, where Kaida, dressed in her navy blue flight attendant's uniform, sat twisted around as she attended to something in the backseat. She was in her mid-30's; her shoulder-length brunette hair completing her perfectly crafted face and stunning eyes to which a pair of sexy eyebrows curled over. Any guy in his right mind would only persist on staring and thinking about asking her to join the mile-high club, but Lander's insight was veered more to the situation at hand as he cocked his head over his shoulder to the backseat.

Kaida was soaking up blood from the individual lying across with old dirty rags. Her face shifted into fear and helplessness as she shook her head. She unbelievably shrugged, tossing one of the blood-soaked rags to the floor beneath her feet. She accidentally wiped a bit of it from her fingers onto her popped white undershirt collar and irrationally spoke out with, "I can't stop the bleeding!"

"Well, try harder! Push harder!" Lander told her, not knowing what to suggest other than the obvious that obviously didn't seem to work.

Kaida leaned more forward, dabbing what good was left from the rags and cloths she was using. "Jesus... we should just get him to a hospital."

"Hospital?" Lander blurted. "No way. They were saying not to go there anymore."

"For Christ's sake, we could at least drop him off!" she argued back.

Lander erratically gestured to the grassy plains around them. "Do you see any hospitals around here?" he reminded her. "Besides, who's to say that there would even be anybody there left to help if there was?"

"What the hell are we supposed to do, then?" she wondered, returning her attention to the backseat. She paused in her first aid attempts as she stared with a look of realization spreading across her face. "He's dead..." her soft voice murmured.

Lander did a double-take to the backseat, setting his eyes back on the road. "Shit," he stated with a slightly disappointed sigh.

There was a silence between them for a dragging moment or two, most likely the first breath of quietness perhaps since they had entered the car with that fateful situation. But it was when Kaida noticed the speedometer dropping drastically that she looked to their surroundings. "What are you doing?" she curiously asked as he began to pull the car to the side of the road. "Why are we stopping?"

Lander shifted the car into park, leaving it running as he unbuckled his seatbelt. "We have to get rid of him," he firmly replied.

She looked to the corpse in the backseat and then back at Lander. "N-Now?"

"Better than later. You really wanna drive around with him back there if he..."

She barely shook her head. "We don't know if that'll happen."

"The hell we don't," he told her. "I'm not taking any chances."

"But he's dead," she confirmed.

"Yeah, and that's where the problem seems to start, now doesn't it?" he briskly shot back.

He opened his door and stepped out, leaving her to think to herself for a moment before she grabbed her own door handle and exited as well. Lander opened the back door and grabbed the pair of feet wearing new white Nike shoes that were now tainted and stained bloody red. He grunted as he dragged the body out, the head whacking against the car before slumping against the hot pavement below. He only dragged it a matter of inches from the vehicle and shut the door, about to get back in when Kaida spoke out with, "You're just gonna leave him right there?" He froze in place as he grabbed his door, glancing at her on the other side. She crossed her arms. "You can't just leave him in the middle of the road like that," she continued.

He turned his head and looked both ways down the infinite stretching grayness, empty of any vehicular life. "As if anybody's gonna hit him," he sarcastically pointed out.

"You could at least have some decency."

"What? You mean drag him off to the side like a deer? Besides, in a matter of time we know what's gonna happen so it's not gonna make a difference where we put him," he explained.

She gave a barely audible huff, like a tired restless wife might signal, cocking her attention away and squinting in the sunlight. Lander rolled his eyes and sighed, flopping his arms to his sides as he turned and stepped back over to the body. He bent forward and grabbed the ankles, starting to drag it across the road with the shuffling sound of a sandpaper rub. He passed the white sideline and finally released his grip when he reached the grass. Giving his hands a smacking wipe, he perked his eyebrows back to Kaida. "There. Happy?"

"I'll be happier when we get going," she answered. "We're gonna need gas soon, too."

"Noted," Lander said with a nod, stepping away from the body. He froze when he saw her staring uneasily at it. "What? What is it?"

She crossed her arms, molding a somewhat shaky expression as she sympathetically bent her eyebrows. "I dunno, I... Should we... take his license, or something? You know, to..."

"To what?"

"I don't know. He's gotta have family somewhere. Friends," she told him, as if searching for the right way to say what her gut was telling her.

Lander closed his eyes and tiredly dropped his head. "Oh, Jesus," he murmured under his breath.

"What?" she suddenly snapped back. "Excuse me for not losing my sense of humanity even when the human race is lost. It just feels wrong leaving him here, and forgetting about him."

"We didn't even know him, and it's definitely better that way," Lander reminded her. "Look — Kaida, was it? I'm not saying he wasn't somebody. But... there's just no point. Do you honestly and sensibly think there's any point? It sucks the big one, I know. But he's dead. And that's that."

The corpse's hand abruptly snapped to life, strongly grabbing his ankle as he hollered and jumped back in horrified reaction. "Holy shit!" he managed to blurt as the corpse lifted its upper body. It opened its mouth, growling out a low sickening bellow.

Kaida's eyes widened as she staggered back against the car. Lander lost his footing and fell flat on his back to the road as the corpse used the grip on his leg to drag and pull itself closer. Lander squirmed and flopped like a doomed fish, trying to shake it off, but the corpse kept crawling upward, snarling and drooling with a fierce and hungry mucus that oozed from the corners of its mouth like draining motor oil. Its eyes were beat vein red and white, like the battered wings of a tiny insect. Lifeless. Soulless. Void. A nightmare piercing into the promising baby blues of Lander, who struggled to pull and push it away. The corpse snapped its teeth at his hands, nearly nipping off the fingers. Despite its deathly appearance, it had quite the pressuring hold on Lander, who now in the extremity of the situation shot his head back to Kaida near the car. "*Get the bat! In the trunk! Get the bat!*" he wildly screamed.

She snapped out of her frozen trance, quickly hurrying to the driver's seat. Reaching inside, she yanked the keys from the ignition and circled back to the rear of the car, scrambling through the set to find the appropriate selection. Shoving it into the slot, she turned it and popped the trunk, brushing her arm across an array of messy various items until unburying a long metal baseball bat.

The corpse had now made its way face to face with Lander, who clenched his teeth as he tried his hardest to keep it from biting him. He pushed at its neck and chin, raising it up a bit. It growled and snarled, opening its mouth wide only to get it bashed with the taste of the thick metal bat swinging forward. It released its iron grip on Lander, folding over to the pavement with a small, barely audible cowl. Lander rolled aside, heaving out of breath as he rubbed his neck and watched Kaida stand over the corpse. She curled her hands more intently around the bottom of the bat and stiffened her jaw, raising it up and heaving it down again over the monstrosity. Blood splattered across the gravel. With each sickening crunch, she continued to beat the body until its head resembled the prank of a smashed Halloween pumpkin. Its armed twitched. Its body jittered. And then it stopped moving altogether, like a broken toy whirling out of power from dead batteries.

Kaida's chest lightly heaved in and out as she stared down at her accomplishment. Lander wiped himself off and got to his feet, stepping next to her. "Thanks," he finally managed to mutter out with the scratch of his head.

"Yeah," she softly replied.

"We should go now," he urged, gently reaching down and pulling the bat from her hands. "Unless you still wanna get his license."

He walked back to the car, tossing the blood-stained bat back into the trunk and closing it. Within moments, they were back on the road, coasting through the grassy plains of nowhere as Kaida sat riding shotgun, staring out her window. "I wonder," she started to say with a dampened tone, shattering the silence between them, "if someone will question their conscience whether or not to take our licenses when we die…"

Lander looked over at her as he drove. She didn't budge. Her eyes still stared out her window to the passing solemn surroundings.

Lander's feet were beginning to hurt. He didn't know how New Yorkers could do so much walking everywhere. Of course, being a New Yorker without any personal transportation would mean being used to an easy and blister-free life. In the few times he had come there to visit, people were always moving so quickly. They would walk down the street and be some odd number of paces ahead of him. And when they got to a street crossing, they wouldn't even bother looking both ways or waiting for the signal to change. They would just charge head-on, weaving between slow moving cars as he jumped back. He was astonished at the prospect of being someone who was used to being a ruler of the road, as people are in New York.

As people *were*.

Lander and Kaida had driven nearly over two days straight to get from California to New York. And as they walked across the lumbering and historic Brooklyn Bridge via the pedestrian passageway overhead, there was no moving traffic below to remind them of the notion that no one was around. There weren't any moving cars in the entire city, for that matter. Most, if not all, had merely died out from loss of battery power with the absence of a controlling driver behind the wheel. And the drivers that were indeed still sitting behind the wheel, well... Lander didn't quite want to think about that. It was bad enough their remaining essence was beginning to creep under his nose in the early summer morning heat.

But, nevertheless, he and Kaida had no choice, as once they approached the city limits, it became harder to navigate the car through the stalled traffic all over the road. It wasn't nearly as bad as they coasted along the city on the FDR Drive toward the Brooklyn Bridge, since no one was really trying to get into the city during the chaos. The vehicles on the other side of the Drive, however, were packed bumper-to-bumper. One would need a tank to plow their way through. It was inevitable they would eventually have to ditch their car and walk the rest of the way, even on the FDR Drive North, as traffic near the bridge became too thick in spots to weave through.

There were no joggers on the Brooklyn Bridge overhead passageway. There were no bicycle riders, no tourists snapping photos, no couples making out with a beautiful Manhattan backdrop to solidify the mood. Lander and his Fiona had walked that very path back and forth a few times before. She told him it was therapeutic, if not good exercise. And now he would give anything for her to be there walking with him.

And she would be. *On the way back*, he kept thinking. Once he found her.

A large smear of blood on the path caught his eye as they walked through the second stone archway, curling around the corner and out of sight as if something had been dragged off. Kaida had spotted it as well, inching her steps cautiously closer to him. He cleared his throat, trying to get her mind off it by saying, "It's not too far once we get off the bridge." He looked to his right and gave a nod. "See that, over there? Above the roads along the water? That's the Brooklyn Heights Promenade. She lives right by it. She would take me there, especially at night. You can sit on a bench and look at the whole city lit up."

"Must be quite a sight," Kaida figured.

Lander gazed toward it for another moment before looking back forward. "Look, uh... I just wanna say... "sorry"... for, ya know, acting any way that seems..." He trailed off as she returned a glance. "I don't really act like this. I'm not like this. I'm just trying to keep a whole "cooler-minds-prevail" outlook on the situation."

"You don't have to apologize, Lander," she replied with an easy tone. "If you think you're being some kind of asshole or something, you're not. You're doing a whole lot better than most people would. Than most people *did*."

He sheepishly dug the heel of his shoe into the ground. "I just wanna get to her. Nothing else really seems sensible."

She swallowed a lump in her throat. "I'm all for that; I really am. But you just..."

Lander stopped walking, causing her to freeze as he sharply blurted, "Just what?"

"You say you're trying to be sensible. You have this commanding outlook on what to do, and what we should do. I just don't think you're preparing yourself for the sensible aspect of what you're trying to achieve here. And I'm not trying to discourage you, but Lander... I mean, the chances of her..."

"She's alive," he firmly interrupted, face edgy and stiff. "She's alive."

"I wanna believe that, and I hope to God she is, but the odds... New York City got the worst of it. And if she survived the last two or so days, there's still the issue of her staying that way," Kaida tried to explain. "There's a very fine line between hope and probability. Not acknowledging one without the other can be a very dangerous thing."

"Then why are we standing here talking?" Lander simply shot back.

Kaida was slightly shunned by this and didn't make any further verbal assessments. Lander, giving a soft sigh, slowly turned and started walking again. Kaida gave a distressed breath of her own, turning her head to look out into the lonely distance before trailing after him.

Lander pushed the door to the student housing on Clark Street open as he entered inside with Kaida. The once bustling lobby was now silent, void of the young bodies that used to come and go. Lander pulled the nine-millimeter gun out from the back of his pants — the gun he had found on the dead cop at the end of the Brooklyn Bridge. They were indoors now. And although it was still daytime, no place was safe. *They* only seemed to come out at night, but until then... they hid and waited.

He cocked the loading hammer back and glanced at Kaida. She returned a silent glare as they moved toward the front desk. It was missing the presence of the security guard, the security guard that would usually hassle him and give the visiting sign-in process a whole new meaning of "difficult". They were very strict in a place like that. Lander felt that soon enough that'd be requiring birth certificates, blood samples and a family tree history just to stay the night in someone's room. There was one guard that was cool, though, when Lander had visited the last few times. What was his name again? It began with an "s". Steve? Sam? Lander couldn't remember. No matter. There was no one there now, and despite his past accounts with them, Lander would've surely taken any security guard at that point. He moved past the electronic security turnstiles — the ones that the students used as an easy-go with their coded security cards — and led Kaida through the waist-high golden-rimmed gate. The floor was scattered with papers. A drawer behind the desk was opened, and of course — there were two bodies on the floor, which caused Lander to promptly raise his gun in a ready manner. He carefully moved toward the first body, taking a better look. It was the security guard. He had a long pencil through his eye going into his head. Lander nudged the body over with his foot and glanced at the blood-smeared gold-plated nametag on his uniform — "SAM". He figured he had turned into one of them, and someone had gotten up close and personal. They only went down permanently once you put something through their head or removed it completely. Lander darted his eyes to the other body slumped next to wall near the desk. It was mutilated beyond recognition. Kaida covered her mouth at the sight.

Lander noticed a long streaking line of blood going around the corner into the living room area where students had often filled their time on computers or playing the Nintendo Wii on the big flat-screen on the wall. Blood. It was something they were used to seeing now, and Lander certainly didn't want to see what was around the corner. He only cared about one thing, and turned to head for the elevators.

"Is it safe to use them?" Kaida wondered as he hit the button and waited.

"Should be," he assured her. "Not like it was a building problem or anything."

The elevator dinged and the door opened as they boarded. Within moments they were on the seventh floor, stepping out as Lander readily aimed his gun. "Stay behind me," he noted.

They made their way around the corner; Lander sharply drawing his gun just in case. It seemed quiet and lifeless on that particular hallway — far quieter than it normally would have if the college students that inhabited the rooms were still around. But no one was around. Anywhere. A few of the doors were open along the way, with Lander taking a quick peek inside for any signs of life before ducking back out. The rooms appeared to be empty. With as many rooms as there were on that floor, Lander figured the probability of them all being empty was slim to none. There were plenty of closed doors, some even with a faint shuffling inside that Lander and Kaida stopped to listen to for brief moments before continuing on, but they couldn't get into them if they wanted.

They reached the end of the hallway, and Lander's blood pumped as he curled his finger more readily around the trigger. He took a hard swallow and noticed that the door he was creeping toward was open, just barely enough to keep from locking. He glanced at Kaida, who returned another silent stare. Slowly, he reached forward with his free hand and pushed the door open, entering inside. "Fiona?" he softly called out. "Fiona, are you in here?"

The room was a complete mess — and not just a "college student mess". Something had happened in there. Some kind of *struggle*. Clothes were everywhere. One of the two bed mattresses was hanging off the edge of the wooden boxed frame. Items had been knocked off shelves. A computer lied in ruins on the floor. And then Lander stopped, noticing the body on the floor. Kaida froze in place beside him as well, huffing out a quick gasp and nearly bringing her hand to her mouth. A smashed nineteen-inch television set replaced the head of the body on the floor. Blood was splattered everywhere. It was a gruesome sight. Lander crouched down and looked the body over, noticing the butterfly tattoo on the left ankle. "Jesus Christ," he murmured under his breath.

"Is it... is it... her?" Kaida managed to finally ask.

"No," Lander softly replied, shaking his head. "It's Lauren — her roommate."

Kaida tilted her head, gazing upon the mess around them. "What the hell happened in here?"

Lander stood up, still staring down at the corpse. "I don't know. But here is where she isn't."

"Do you think she did this?" Kaida wondered. "I mean, somebody had to do this. Maybe she got out."

Lander picked up a picture frame. It was of him and Fiona, beautiful with her flowing golden brown hair, standing in front of a gorgeous fountain in Central Park. "That's what I'm afraid of," he added. "She's not in here safe. Which means she's out *there*. Among *them*." He took a deep breath and pulled the picture out, shoving it into his pocket. "Come on. Let's go."

The elevator dinged again as they departed back onto the lobby floor. "She could be anywhere," Kaida mentioned. "And it's gonna be dark soon."

"All the more reason to look faster," he simply stated as he walked over to the security desk.

"Which I'm all for, but you have any idea where to look?" Kaida asked.

"I already know where she is," he blurted, flipping the dead security guard Sam over as he patted him down. "Bethesda Fountain."

"What's that?"

"It's in Central Park," Lander told her, stopping to pull out and hand her the picture he had taken from the room. "It's where I told her I loved her for the first time three years ago on a school trip. I kissed her for the first time there."

"And what makes you think she's there?"

"I know she's there. I just — I know," he said. He gave a sigh, wiping a hand across his forehead. "We said for the times we were here together that if we ever got lost or separated, we would meet there."

"A little out in the open," Kaida said, perking her eyebrows as she handed the photo back. "What are you doing?"

"Seeing if he had any kind of weapon on him. It's a long walk to Central Park from here."

Kaida took a few steps past him, casually looking around. "I doubt a student housing rent-a-cop would have a gun on him, and I doubt you or I would feel comfortable using a taser against those things."

"*Look* — I'm just trying to keep my cool here," Lander snapped, but immediately sighed and rubbed his face. "I'm sorry. Jesus... I should never have let her come here for school. But she wanted to do her art thing. I just wanted her to be happy. It's done nothing but tear us apart, and now... we can't find each other."

"She's alive, Lander," Kaida tried to tell him with sympathetic assurance. "You just have to think realistically that it might take some time to find her — that we have to stop and shelter up somewhere once that sun goes down. For *her* sake."

The undead corpse popped up without warning behind her from the living room quarters, digging its mouth into her neck as she let out a scream. "Kaida!" Lander hollered, jolting to his feet.

Kaida spun and slammed the corpse against the wall as it hung on tightly. The blood poured from the wound on her neck as it kept trying to gouge more out of her. Lander aimed his gun, hesitating. "I can't get a shot!" he barked.

Kaida grinded her teeth and finally heaved the corpse off her and onto the marble-tiled floor. It growled and groaned, immediately attempting to crawl back toward her. Lander directed his gun down and blasted it in the head — and it went down for good. Kaida slammed her eyes shut tightly and slid down the wall to the floor as he rushed over, helping her yank off the jacket of her flight attendant uniform and using it to try and apply pressure to the wound. "Oh, shit. Oh, shit," was all he could mutter.

"That's how it happens, doesn't it? They just come out of nowhere. Just like the guy from the car," she said with her shaky breath. "There's just too many now out there... there's nowhere safe anymore."

"Stop talking and save your breath. You're gonna be okay," Lander briskly said.

"No — I'm not," she flatly told him, grabbing his wrist. She brought her brown eyes to his; stiff and firm, unlike they had been before, when they were kind and prompt. "We know what's gonna happen."

Lander didn't reply. He didn't know what to say in response because he knew she was right. His grip on the jacket over her shoulder loosened a bit. "Find her," Kaida said. "Find her and make sure this doesn't happen to her."

"I... I don't wanna just... leave you here," Lander softly told her.

"You didn't leave me," she said with a small cough. "You saved me. And you helped me. For as long as you could. That's why you're going to find her — because that's the kind of person you are."

Lander licked his lips and glanced down at the gun in his hand, meticulously pulling back the hammer to load it. "I can do it for you," he suggested.

Kaida's eyes slowly crept to the gun as well before returning to him. "Just make it quick. I don't even wanna know it's coming—"

Before she barely finished the sentence, Lander had directed the gun upward under her chin and fired, shutting his eyes from the sight of the blood that had been blasted up onto the wall behind her. For the longest minute, he couldn't reopen them. His jaw shook and his hand quivered as it dropped to his side. He fought the tears back. He fought them back hard. And trying to keep his eyes away from her, he slowly picked up her flight attendant jacket and covered the upper portion of her body. He sighed and calmed himself with some breaths. A part of him thought he had reacted too quickly. Perhaps they could've talked a bit more. But about what? What could there have possibly been said that hadn't already been said, or surely thought, by especially her? It was better that way. If they wasted time not acting, then who knows when she could've... changed. He didn't want to think of that happening to her. He didn't want to let it happen. She didn't deserve it. Many people didn't.

So Lander got up, staring down at her covered body and turning to walk away before freezing with a thought. He bent back down to her and reached into a pocket, pulling out her driver's license. He stared at it for a moment, safely tucking it away into his own pants as he walked forward and stopped at the doors. He pulled out the picture of him and Fiona at the Bethesda Fountain and stared down at it, rubbing his fingers over her face. It was getting dark soon, and he had a lot of ground to cover.

He was scared.

The city was awfully big without anybody walking through it.

Without anybody walking through it *yet*.

epidemic originis

Lauren couldn't hold it anymore. It wretched from her stomach, up into her throat. She thought she would just give a reflexive gag and that would be that, but this was a sure thing. Her movement seemed like slow motion, and that trip from the bed to the bathroom seemed like miles. Miles across the chaos of a small, cramped dorm room, where any mundane item or detail on the floor threatened to stretch the journey any further. She nearly tore the bed sheets apart trying to untangle herself from them, and whilst tripping in the sea of cloth she had created, her left hand smacked the screen of the nineteen-inch television that sat upon the square middle cabinet, leaving a large smudged handprint across the deep blackness. She covered her mouth, holding it in. She stammered forward, dizzily charging against the wall where her other hand prevented an otherwise hurtful impact. She bounced off, twisting and turning into the tiny white-tiled floor bathroom where she dropped to her knees in front of the porcelain toilet.

And out it came.

A miserable, unstoppable heave-of-an-upchuck that graced the posture of a sickening regurgitation too well and perfect to be true. She hacked more; her right hand bracing the lid of the seat as her left struggled to hold back her flowing dark blonde hair.

The door to the dorm room behind her opened, and Fiona stepped in to give a slightly disgusted response. "Ugh," she murmured, trying to look away.

Lauren groaned and wiped the back of her hand across her mouth, barely looking over her shoulder at her. "Perfect timing," she said.

"You're still throwing up?" Fiona asked with a hint of sympathy.

Lauren managed to slump back away from the toilet, giving a tired sigh. "Should we call Guinness yet?"

Fiona shook her head, setting her purse down on her desk outside of the bathroom. "You really need to go to a doctor, Lauren," she insisted. "You're worse than you were yesterday and worse than the day before that."

"But I look a little better, right? I mean, that's all that really counts," Lauren responded with a playful, upbeat wit. "Besides — I would need to book a reservation in advance at the rate the hospitals are filling up. I heard people are even selling their place in line."

Fiona unbelievably shook her head, tucking her soft golden brown hair behind her ear as she dug for the TV remote. "Just another prime example of what people place in their lives as priority," she grumbled.

She clicked the TV on and sat at the edge of her bed, flipping to the NY1 news. A female reporter was in the middle of rehashing facts among the chaos and commotion of downtown. "...say there is still no known origin to where the epidemic came from as it continues to rapidly spiral out of control. The death counts are rising across the country, now reportedly in the hundreds of thousands. The F.A.A. late last night officially grounded all international flights in a bold but seemingly ineffective method of containment." Footage of a hospital interior started rolling, depicting the craziness that lied within as doctors and nurses tended to the sick and injured. "Hospitals and medical centers alike are packed shoulder-to-shoulder with those seeking treatment, but there only seems to be fear in the air as every case of the infected epidemic has seemed to only result in eventual fatality." The female reporter came back on screen and extended her arm to the streets behind her. "As you can see, Tom, here in the City that Never Sleeps, people are restless and the threat of —"

Fiona clicked the TV off. "That's enough of that," she simply muttered.

"Thank you," Lauren said, shifting herself under her blankets. "Now in the absence of all my favorite soap operas from all these news reports, fill me in on what's happening with you and Lander."

"That's a few episodes-worth of explaining," Fiona mentioned, quirking her mouth as she went over to her computer desk and looked at the picture framed of her and Lander standing in front of a fountain in a park.

"Still not great, huh," Lauren figured. "Overheard you two the other night arguing on the phone."

"He wanted to come out here," Fiona told her. "He wanted to make sure I was okay, with all this flu stuff going around. I told him I was fine, and that it would just be a waste of money seeing as how I'd be home in a couple months anyway. He was just worried, that's all."

"I don't blame him," Lauren mumbled, giving a cough. "I'm living proof that this shit is everywhere."

"It's really starting to worry me," Fiona noted, twitching her nose. "All these hospitals filling up. It's scary."

"It'll blow over," Lauren added, turning again under the blankets. "He's a knight in shining armor. There aren't many of those left. You should let him rescue you just once."

"I wished we lived in that kind of world," Fiona dully noted, touching her fingers over Lander's face in the photo. "There's just so many times that so many people out there never get the chance to... get back to each other."

"Call him and tell him you love him," Lauren mumbled. "He doesn't have to be here for you to be with him."

Fiona sighed. "Maybe later. I'm gonna run across the street to the store and grab a few things. You need anything?"

"Yeah. A shopping cart full of everything in their pharmacy," Lauren joked between coughs.

"I'll see what I can do. Be back in a bit," Fiona confirmed. "Get some rest."

So Fiona headed downstairs to the lobby, where Sam, the African-American security guard, sat in his spinning chair at the front desk. Fiona shot him a smile as she approached. "Pullin' another double, Sam?" she asked.

"Hell, ain't nobody else showed up," he replied, giving a cough. "They all called in sick."

"You're not sounding too good yourself," Fiona stated with some friendly concern.

"I'll live. Only came up today. I'm sure it'll be gone by tomorrow," he told her, waving it off. "Yo — when you gonna bring down your next artistic masterpiece to show me?"

Fiona quirked her face. "My creative inspiration's been a little... out of whack lately."

"Ah. Guy troubles. That Lander's one cool dude. Don't be like the rest of these dumb bitches here and lose your guy like they lose their key cards."

Fiona gave a cute chuckle. "I'll keep that in mind. Have a good night, Sam."

"Later, girl," Sam saluted.

Fiona had run to the store across the street and did a little grocery shopping, returning in the later hours of that night back in her dorm room. It was dark, and she didn't want to disturb Lauren, who seemed silent and fast asleep buried beneath her covers. So she put the frozen food items away first and left the rest to do the next day, shaking her shoes and socks off as she slipped into her pajamas and crawled into bed. Something uneasy was in the air, and she didn't think she'd get much sleep with everything rattling in her mind until her heavy eyelids closed for the final time.

Fiona never knew how early it was because she never got the chance to look at the clock in the morning. She just knew it was simply morning because of the brightness in the room, and the noise that Lauren had been making, shuffling about and bumping into things. Fiona yawned and rubbed her sleepy eyes, giving a slight stretch. "Lauren?" she mumbled. "Are you feeling better?"

There was no direct reply, but the noises continued.

"What are you doing?" Fiona wondered, sinking her head back onto her pillow. "You're making enough noise to wake the entire floor."

A few pots crashed and clanged onto the floor, making Fiona quickly sit up. She looked over to Lauren, who had her back to her in the corner as she dug through some items near her desk. "Hey — Lauren," Fiona called out again, getting somewhat annoyed of being ignored.

Fiona swung her legs over the edge of her bed and planted her bare feet on some clothes scattered on the floor. They were everywhere. Lauren had usually been messy, but this appeared as if she were ransacking her own dressers. "You *must* still be sick if you're doing some reorganizing *this* early," Fiona added.

Lauren turned to look at her, revealing her grossly disfigured face. Fiona's jaw dropped at the awful sight. Lauren's eyes were a feverish yellow, speckled with some blue veins. Her skin was old and decrepit, paling with some bloody gouges. Her mouth slightly hung open as she growled.

"Oh my God! Lauren!" Fiona exclaimed with concern, jumping over to her and laying a hand on her arm. "I'm taking you to the hospital."

Lauren snarled and took a snapping bite toward Fiona, who managed to back away and dodge the chomping teeth in time as she strangely stared at her friend. "Lauren! What are you doing?!" she yelled.

Lauren went all-out ballistic, lunging across the room as Fiona jumped out of the way and bounced over her bed. Lauren pounced after her, nearly knocking the mattress right off of its wooden frame bottom. Fiona tried to make it to the door, but Lauren reached out and pulled her back as Fiona grabbed her computer monitor in reflex, pulling it down with her as she fell to the floor. Lauren tackled her. Fiona kicked her legs and flailed her arms, trying to bat away the ecstatic blonde. "Get off of me!" she yelled.

Lauren hungrily tried to take another bite as Fiona reached up and grabbed her head, slamming it against the TV stand. She rolled free and slapped her hands over the nineteen-inch unit, pushing it off the side as it fell and crashed over Lauren's head, sparking and bursting with electric shocks as her body jolted and shook before finally going lifeless. Fiona panted out of breath, standing over her as she stared down. Her eyes filled with tears as she covered her mouth. She felt like she was going to be sick. What had she just done? She had just killed her roommate! But it was in self defense. There was something wrong with her. Something that made her already look dead. She definitely wasn't herself.

Fiona staggered back a step or two, placing a hand across her forehead and waving it back through her golden brown hair. She felt dizzy for a moment, and the feeling passed. She darted her eyes to her cell phone on her computer desk and rushed over to grab it, nearly fumbling it out of her shaking hands as her slender fingers trembled to push buttons. She huffed an unbelievable breath, giving it a smack. The message on the screen kept reading, "NO SERVICE". "No service?" she questionably asked aloud. "How can there be no service?!"

The horror nearly made her cry. But since her cell wasn't working, her first initial reaction was to go downstairs to the security desk and have them call 9-1-1 through the landline. So she carelessly set her phone down and opened her door, going out into the hallway. There was commotion from some of the other rooms behind the closed doors. A girl screamed hysterically from one as Fiona backed against an open doorway. A boy, disfigured and bloody, growled as he jumped toward her, laying his lifeless eyes over her body as he grasped her neck and tried to bite. She screamed, struggling to push him off, and managed to cut herself loose as she hightailed it to the elevators. She frantically pushed the button, looking back to see the boy growl as he slowly rounded the corner, slugging and taking his time to get to her. "Come on! Come on!" she cried out, pushing the button over and over as he got closer and closer.

The doors dinged and opened up, and as she was about to enter, the boy had growled and yanked her back. She fought, punching him in the chest and finally kicking away as she fell back into the elevator. The doors closed, sealing her inside as she listened to the faint pounding on the other side before she started heading downward. Now she was frightened beyond belief. The same thing that had happened to Lauren seemed to happen to the boy from down the hall. Fiona's jaw jiggled as she fought back the urge to sprout more tears than she had already given.

When she reached the lobby floor, she got out of the elevators to see the commotion. Some students were running for the doors, screaming. A car driving down the street crashed into a fire hydrant in front of the building. Fiona noticed Sam, the security guard, hunched over with his back to her at the side of his desk. She was relieved that someone was there, and quickly hurried across the cold marble-tiled floor over to him. "Sam! Oh my God, Sam! Please, I need help!" she begged.

Sam turned his head to her. His eyes were bloodshot and ravenous as chunks of skin and blood hung from his mouth. Another body was on the floor by the wall, torn apart and mutilated. He had been eating it. *He had been eating it.*

Fiona began to unbelievably shake her head in a panicked fit as she backed up. Sam growled and sprang toward her as she screamed, dodging and ducking his arms as she rushed forward and slipped across a streak of blood on the floor, landing with a hard thud. She looked back to see Sam already on top of her, opening his mouth to take a bite. She noticed some long pencils and pens that had fallen to the floor next to the corpse beside the wall and reached for them, but she wasn't close enough. She grit her teeth and stretched, trying to move a few inches more beneath Sam as she simultaneously tried to keep his head up from biting her. Her fingers felt around the floor until finding the pen, but they had rolled over it too hard, sending it sliding under the desk. She let out a cry, stretching for the pencil until she finally managed to curl her fingertips around it. She fully gripped it and plunged it directly through his eye as it went into his head — and that's when he went down. He fell right over and collapsed on the floor as Fiona backed against the wall; her chest lifting up and down in a rhythmic manner. A scream came from down the hall, which electrocuted her attention as she scrambled to her feet and rushed toward the mail room. A corpse on the floor in the living room area had sprung up, spotting her as he slouched and slowly chased after. She jumped inside the mail room and slammed the door shut, locking it from within. The fists pounding on the door on the other side made her trickle some tears as she backed against a shelf, knocking some packages over. She slowly slid to the floor, huddled in the corner and burying her head in her arms.

She didn't know how long she had stayed in there, because there was no clock. She figured it must have been the majority of the day, if not longer. Perhaps even through the night. She was just too frightened to go out. And every time she had readied herself, there was some kind of strange noise or scream or cry for help on the other side that made her reconsider. Something terrible was happening. She had plenty of time to think over the possibilities, but they all led back to the strange illness that had swept across the country the past week. Had everyone gotten sick? Why was she still okay? Maybe she was immune. It was only natural in such a devastating epidemic for a small minority of people to be immune.

Then there was Landen.

She wanted him more now than ever. They had their share of problems, but now they all seemed petty and indifferent. She wished she could take back all those stupid arguments they had shouted over the phone — his belting from the golden coast while hers retorted from the east. She wanted him to be with her there; to hold her hand as they walked — even to hold her close if they were to huddle somewhere in the dark waiting for some kind of help to arrive. At this point, she would even take a two minute phone call just to hear his voice — to hear that he was safe and healthy. Everyone else had seemed to die — or come back to life — overnight of this illness, but fear was Fiona's disease now. And despite everything in her heart telling her over and over that Landen would come for her and that he was just as every bit healthy as she was —

there was still that lingering rational thought poking at her gut of something much worse.

The Bethesda Fountain. There was no way to tell him. She could've left a note, but what were the odds of him finding or seeing it? Besides, she didn't want to go back up to the room. He would find her. She knew he would. He would know to go there, because that's where she would wait for him, as long as it took. Along the way, she could find help. She could find other people to help protect her, and find out what was happening.

So she finally mustered the courage to leave the mail room, armed with only a hard cardboard poster tube — she had gone through many of the packages in search of some protecting weapon, but found nothing useful. And she hadn't heard any noises outside the room for hours upon hours.

The lobby was quiet as she meticulously walked across the floor, being wary each step along the way. Sam's corpse still lied on the floor beside the mutilated one he had been feasting upon. Early morning light was flooding in through the main entrance doors. She had definitely spent the span of the day and following night in the mail room.

Fiona sighed and pushed her way through the small gate next to the turnstiles, strolling toward the doors in her pajama bottoms and a tank top with her hair now tucked into a leisurely ponytail. The bottoms of her bare feet patted a slight smacking sound as she pushed her way out through the spinning doors.

epidemic exitus

They only really come out at night.

Then again, there really aren't many people around anymore to know for sure. No one alive, that is. You would know that, if you were to ever visit New York City now. No one except plenty of dead bodies keeping one another company around 42nd Street in Times Square. Not a single breathing soul.

You would see that all of the glimmering electronic advertisement billboards are still as flashy and catchy as they have ever been. For now, anyway. The classic electronic Coca-Cola billboard screen high above would maybe still blink and twirl the various appealing images of the bubbly drink, but eventually over time, it's sure to fail with its other electronic companions without the hands of its watchful creators.

Except no one was looking up at them. Their faces were planted lifelessly on the concrete sidewalk or crosswalk in the middle of the street, or resting hopelessly on the steering wheel of the car they had been sitting in, whether it had abruptly crashed into the rear of the one in front of it or a street pole — a taxi cab was hiked up onto the curb of a cross street and slightly riding a crosswalk sign that was still spitting out sparks from its bottom.

They had all just dropped dead, littered down the sidewalk like useless pamphlets.

Some short time ago, Manhattaners had been coughing or sneezing, but they were still going about their bustling activities, buying the latest CDs or cheap fashionable purses on sidewalk tables. Foreigners had been snapping their digital camera pictures at the glory of which was the infamous center of the city. If you were to walk down that sidewalk and step on one of those cameras, you would probably look down and notice the elderly Chinese man and woman lying motionless on the sidewalk — their faces twisted with a sickly death that had already tremendously decayed them well beyond their old years. Perhaps you would notice the man draped in robes at the foot of an electronics store entrance; his fingers curled with a death-grip around a homemade sign that read, "WE ARE ALL BEING JUDGED". Perhaps you would notice that there aren't nearly as many dead people as there should be, maybe attributed to the fact that many hundreds and thousands of them had already fled from the island when the early notions and reports flooded in stating New York had been receiving the worst of the illness.

And then there was the illness.

What kind of illness could creep over everyone across the entire country and suddenly kill everyone off seemingly overnight? You've thought about it before, but maybe you'd dash over the possibilities inside your head again — a government bio-weapon or disease that had been accidentally unleashed. Or maybe a terrorist attack, but then again, the entire world seemed to be infected, so what could that possibility gain whatever organization or individual was behind it? Then again, you might remember that you were walking through the city that once had two airplanes crash into buildings with the responsible anarchists on board well-aware of their accepted fate merely to prove a point. Or could it be simply natural? A disease that was manicured out of nowhere to naturally select human beings to be the next extinct species. Human beings and dogs, at least, for you would have surely passed a tall woman in a jogging suit back in her Brooklyn Heights neighborhood whose body had been crumpled up beside a black-barred fence with her Terrier still on its leash nearby — its paws immobile and tongue slouched out of the side of its mouth like a nightmarish cartoon.

But how would you still be alive? How could something this large, this fast, kill off nearly everything and everyone but leave you untouched? Despite the sickly coiling of your stomach when you looked at one of the dead individuals, you would still feel in premium health, untouched and unscathed by the monstrosity before you. You may remember a Stephen King movie you had seen on TV when you were younger about a plague that had ripped across the world and killed off everyone but a small percentage of immune luckies. You wouldn't remember the title and never saw the ending, but was it the same thing that had happened before your very eyes now? Or was the disease merely toying with you, buried deep and tunneling within your bloodstream until finally deciding to emerge late in the game? If *you* had survived, there had to be others. There just had to be. Especially in a place like New York, filled before with such diverse life striving to never fall asleep.

Perhaps the most perplexing thought in your wandering mind would be how those that were *not* alive were managing to come *back* alive. Maybe you would think about someone you were with before when it was all originally going down, and how they died in front of your very eyes, only to seemingly return to life in some kind of rabid rage to attack you. Even this late in the game, you wouldn't want to believe or accept the inaudible fact that the disease brought people back to life after they had died from it.

But not everyone. The few bodies that lied about the streets were inanimate and motionless. It didn't bring everybody back, because they would've come back by now. You'd know from your own witnessing eyes that it didn't take long for them to come back.

Now the only thing that mattered was staying alive. Staying alive, finding other people alive, and staying out of the dark, because that's where they are. That's where they're hiding, waiting for the sun to set against the backdrop of a city now forgotten. You would probably hide yourself for the night, taking the safe route, getting a half-assed sleep with one eye open and your hand gripped around the handle of a department store clearance metal basement bat.

Should you ever make it further uptown to Central Park around dusk, perhaps you'd see a few starting to come out, emerging from within the confines of a boat house or facilities building, or from under a pathway bridge. Maybe, perhaps, you'd even see a few aimlessly slugging their footsteps around the cool blue impending twilight sky above the Bethesda Fountain area. You'd wonder who they were in their lives before the epidemic plagued the earth — what unfortunate circumstances doomed them to their gray, decaying new existence beneath their torn and dried-bloody clothing — and you'd watch as a young man among them would mindlessly groan as he passed a once-beautiful golden-brown brunette girl dressed in her bloodied pajamas with no shoes or socks, pausing for a brief moment, maybe in some sort of lost recognition from a past life lived together. Her lifeless, bloodshot yellow eyes would trail their way to him and immediately pass without comprehensive thought as her mouth would crookedly hang torn open. You'd watch as they went separate ways among the other numbers of detriments sauntering the park.

Then it would be time for you to leave after being noticed. You would run, and even though you could easily outrun them, with every step you took into the deepening night, there would eventually be too many to run from.

So run for your life while you can — because it's all you have left.

THE LAST SUPPER

Julian squinted as the glare of the setting sun beamed directly into his eyes.

He reached up and pulled down the visor, but that didn't seem to help much. That round yellow ball was still hanging decently high among the pretty shades of pink, vanilla and purple colors in the distance. There was no escaping a setting sun. No matter which direction you were driving, it always seemed to glare into your eyes and your eyes alone, whether it was directly ahead, shining from the sides or hanging over your back in the rear view mirror. And it always seemed to last a dreadfully long time, just hanging there in the sky as if frozen like some kind of malfunctioning mechanical ball. Julian wanted it to just disappear already, if only for deleting that annoyance.

He glanced over to Rachael sitting shotgun, who pulled her visor down to not only shield her own eyes from the burning brightness, but to check her face as well. Or was she checking her make-up? Julian couldn't tell if she was wearing any. She was the type of woman who held a habit of decorating herself with just a tiny bit enough to get away with looking like she wasn't wearing any. Still, she brushed her fingertip along her eyelashes and titled her head in about forty different directions to ensure every miniscule angle of her angelic features were in pristine condition. Rachael wasn't superficial or filled with physical vanity. She didn't overdo it. She felt just as comfortable being dressed down on a couch with her darkened brown hair messily tucked into a poor-excuse-for-a-ponytail. She didn't spend hundreds and hundreds of dollars on cosmetics, although that's not to say she didn't make any dent in her budget whatsoever.

"You know you don't need to do that," Julian noted out loud, once again verbally conveying his feelings. "You're beautiful no matter what."

Rachael's finger rode her lower lip as she continued to inspect. "Trying to score points for a little motel lovin' tonight?" she coyly wondered.

"No, it's — I mean —" he stuttered, curling a small smile. "Well... if you think it'll help my chances, I can keep going."

Rachael flipped the mirror on the visor closed and turned to him, playfully rubbing his cheek with her thumb. "You've already got it in the bag," she assured him. "But only if you let me pick dinner this time."

Julian wanted to groan with disapproval, but then again, he would've liked that "Do Not Disturb" sign hanging on their door later. Still, he tried to make the proposition as mutually beneficial as he could. "Aww, really? Well, can you at least pick a place that has burgers? I've been really wanting a burger all day."

"I just told you that you're already getting buns later on; isn't that good enough?" she joked back. It sounded corny coming out, but he chuckled anyway. It was a stupid, silly banter only the best of couples in their mid-twenties could craft to perfection. "I want Italian," she simply noted.

"Really? That's so... expensive," he stated, trying to find the right word. They were already on a limited budget as it was, and had been subjected to fast food dives and dingy diners the past three days.

"It'll be a celebration," she said, trying to sound positively upbeat. "To our new lives, our new jobs, and our new home."

"It's more like a shed," he blurted. "We've been driving nearly two thousand miles to move into a shed."

"Well, when you get your promotion in six months, we'll have enough to upgrade into a garage," she sarcastically quipped, arching her arm over and resting her hand against the back of his head as she nuzzled her fingertips through his short chestnut hair. "Come on — I'm not looking for a ten-course meal at an Olive Garden," she pleaded. "This town has gotta have some kinda place that serves pasta."

Julian scanned his eyes down the stretch of Main Street as he drove into the outer limits, already noticing its lack of life. "Highly doubtful we'll find *anything*," he mumbled, perking his eyebrows. "No-Name Town Number Six-Hundred Seventy-Eight. Probably completely shuts down after six o'clock." He pulled out a pair of aviator sunglasses, slipping them on as he drew the line to becoming annoyed at the sun's constant vexation over the rolling hills in the distance. Rachael noticed and gave a smirk. He shrugged, continuing with, "What?"

"Nothin'," she answered, trying to hold back a bigger smile. "Does this trip include an in-flight movie and snacks?"

"Hey, I believe *you're* the one who got 'em for me," he reminded her. "I also believe the word you used to describe them was "sexy". Am I the only one here that's getting bothered by this stupid sun glare?"

Rachael giggled and arched her eyes over to the gages, noticing the fuel needle approaching the empty mark. "Land this plane at the next gas station. We'll ask what good places to eat at are around here."

Julian stopped at the first gas station mini-mart they came to, pulling his shiny silver Jeep Liberty up to the pumps. Rachael unbuckled her seat belt and leaned over, pecking his cheek with a kiss. "You pump, I'll pee," she said, getting out of the car.

"Thanks," Julian sarcastically perked back.

He got out and sighed, taking off the aviators since the setting sun was hidden out of sight behind some buildings. He circled around to the pumps and pulled his credit card out of his wallet, swiping it through and going through the payment procedures before unlatching the nozzle and filling his overpaid vehicle. As he stood holding the handle, he turned his head and noticed the silence that seemed to void the area of any activity. Not a soul was in sight, nor had a car passed down the street. *Forget six o'clock*, he thought to himself. *This town must shut down at noon.*

A slight chill ran through the air as he rolled his black sweater shoulders in response. Fall was no longer around the corner. It had arrived. And although it didn't feel like it, summer was a distant memory. Rachael had pushed her way out of the mini-mart. "There's no one in there," she called out to him.

He turned in place to look back at her. "What?"

"Inside," she said. "There's nobody working in there."

"Probably fell asleep in the bathroom," Julian noted.

"I checked. They weren't in there."

Julian finished pumping as it gave the signaling click that it was full, pulling the lever out and hooking it back onto the latch. "Well, there's gotta be. He's probably just... around back or somethin'. Come on; it's doesn't matter, anyway. I paid at the pump. Let's go."

"I wanted to buy a candy bar," she said.

"Why? We're just stopping somewhere in a few minutes," he reminded her.

"Something doesn't feel right," she said, looking around as she crossed her arms.

Julian gave a shrug. "So just take it, then."

She flashed a pair of firm eyes to him. "I'm not gonna just *take* a candy bar, Julian."

Julian made his way around the front of the Jeep Liberty toward the driver's door. "Then leave two bucks on the counter. That way when the hoard of police cars are behind us in a high-speed chase, we'll have security camera proof of what you had to resort to while some teenage slacker clerk was off somewhere lost in an issue of Jugs magazine."

He climbed back into the car. Rachael looked back at the mini-mart, contemplating whether to go back in or not. She didn't need the candy bar that badly. She was more curious on why someone wasn't minding the store. It was only a matter of minutes, but still — who would leave a store like that unattended? It seemed like a small town, but were they really that trusting? It shouldn't have even been an issue, but something had her concerned. Regardless, she got back into the car as Julian pulled away, and not much sooner than when he had entered the more commercial aspects of town did he spot a fast food style restaurant, adequately shaped and properly named "The Burger Barn". "Hey," he barked, drawing Rachael's attention to it. "Come on, a burger place. Let me just run in and get one, and then we'll look for some Italian. We can find some shabby motel for the night here and bring it all back there to eat in. 'Kay?"

Rachael rolled her eyes. Guys and their burgers. "Fine," she muttered.

Julian excitedly turned the wheel left, pulling into the parking lot and nuzzling next to an old beat-up Chevy. He would've much rather used a drive-thru, but since the establishment didn't have any, a quick in-and-out would've had to do. He got out, feeling his stomach rumble as Rachael joined him. He could just imagine the burgers in a place like this. They probably came in one style — humungous! He gallantly opened the door for his beautiful companion and they entered inside.

Only it was empty.

And not just empty in the sense that there were no customers, but there were no *employees*, either! The electricity didn't even seem to be on, although it was hard for them to tell at first because of all the fading natural daylight pouring in through the windowed walls surrounding the restaurant. There was no music playing. No cooking sounds. Just... silence. "Uh, hello...?" Julian called out after exchanging perplexing eyes with Rachael.

They approached the counter; Julian bending forward to get a better look back at the grill area. "Are you guys, like... closed?" he then asked.

No response.

He half-figured for some overweight manager with a bad comb-over to come out and inform them that they had to close for the day because of an electricity issue, but nobody came. Rachael took a quick look in the bathrooms, but didn't find a soul. Julian helplessly flopped his arms to his sides. "There's no one here," he simply stated.

Rachael shook her head, crossing her arms as she warily glazed her eyes across all of the empty, lonely seats. "Something weird's going on around here. It's just like the gas station," she told him.

"All right, they probably just — forgot to lock up or something," he said, trying to keep a sound mind over the situation. "Come on," he added, lightly nudging at her to follow as he headed back to the door.

Rachael paused before getting into the Jeep Liberty, turning her head. There were cars in the parking lot. Why were there cars and not people? She looked in another direction down the road. The town seemed still and frozen. There wasn't a person in sight. She climbed into the car, buckling herself in. "Something is *definitely* going on. Everyone in this town is gone," she firmly blurted.

"They're not all gone, Rachael," he retorted. "That's completely ridiculous. They probably all closed up their shops early to go to some town fair we haven't seen yet. The highlight of their year."

Julian got back onto the street, but Rachael wasn't convinced. She watched out of her window as all of the houses and stores passed. All the windows seemed dark. The doors were closed. There was no one on porches, no one jogging, no children playing. Rachael wanted to believe the feeling coiling inside her was just from all of the countless hours she had spent riding in that car the last couple days, but something else was trying to tell her otherwise. She felt like she had wandered into some bizarre Stephen King story. "Ah — there we go," Julian said with an enthusiastic spark. "Pizza Hut."

Rachael turned her attention to the Pizza Hut establishment nestled at the bottom of the hill near the center of town as Julian pulled into the parking lot. He parked right out in front and grinned, gesturing to the building. "Here's your Italian. And would ya look at that — lights are on inside. It's a corporate restaurant. Those greedy assholes wouldn't close if a meteor was about to hit earth."

Julian unbuckled his seat belt and opened his door as Rachael shifted yet another unsure face. "Let's just keep going. Let's go to the next town."

"What? I thought you were hungry?"

"Yeah, but... there's just... something weird going on around here," she shakily replied.

"Just because of an unlocked closed burger place and a missing gas station attendant? Come on, we're here. Might as well ask what's going on," he noted.

Rachael reluctantly got out, arching her head up to the large logo on the building. It looked like an older-style logo. Apparently updates were very slow out there. She took one more glance to the town that loomed behind them — some birds chased each other off a telephone pole wire. The sun was starting to make its full dip into the horizon between the rolling tree-filled hills. Julian slung an arm over her shoulders, pulling her close as they approached and entered through the door.

The couple stopped not more than four feet inside, taking a look around. It seemed to be the same situation as the Burger Barn — empty of any customers or workers and void of any ambiance like music or kitchen noises, except the electricity was fully on... and there was three people sitting in a nearby booth.

The man seemed to be an average, everyday Joe, maybe in his late thirties or early forties at the most, in decent shape and dressed in a nice thin sweater with some tan khakis. On the other side of the table, two children sat, maybe around eight or nine years old, one boy and one girl. They briefly stopped eating their pizza and drinking their soda to take notice of the new couple that had entered. Julian was first to say something in the silence when he gave a greeting nod and muttered, "Oh, uh... hey."

The trio didn't respond. They just kept staring, which made Rachael feel especially awkward. Julian slipped his hands into the pockets of his pants and looked over his shoulder, then back to the three individuals. "Are they, uh... still open? Seems a little quiet around here."

The father glanced at his children and then darted his eyes back to the couple before taking a bite from his thick slice of pizza. "No. They're not open," he merely answered with a flat tone.

"We just came from that Burger Barn place across town, and they weren't open, either," Rachael added. "There doesn't seem to be anyone around town. Is there something going on around here?"

"Everyone's gone," the father told her.

Julian and Rachael flicked their eyes to each other. "Where'd they go?" Julian then asked.

The father gave them a short stare. "You're not from around here, are you?"

"We're just passing through," Rachael said.

The father sighed and shifted himself a bit in his seat, preparing to eat more. "Then it's best you keep going while you can. Don't have much time," he noted.

"What does that mean?" Julian sharply wondered. "Where is everybody?"

"I told you — they're gone. We're the only ones left," the father briskly repeated. The kids took tiny bites from their pizza and stared at the couple. "My wife... she... she was with us, but then... she went with them. It's just us now. We're the only ones left in town. You can do whatever you want, but if you don't mind, I'm trying to have a meal with my kids. It's our last dinner together. They wanted pizza."

Julian slightly perked his eyebrows, murmuring under his breath a slightly scorched "Okay" as he tugged at Rachael's arm. "Come on, let's just go."

Rachael shook his hand off. "No. No, it's not okay. What the hell is going on around here? Where did everybody go?!"

"Rachael — it's none of our business," Julian tried to persuade her.

"They're sitting here in an empty restaurant in an empty town, Julian! That doesn't strike you as a little odd? Look at these kids! They looked scared!" she began to huff.

"You should go now," the father told them. "The sun's almost down. They're all gonna come back once it's dark."

"And what happens then?" Julian challenged.

"They'll get you. Just like they'll get us," the father dully murmured.

"If you're so worried about these people coming back, why haven't *you* left?" Rachael asked.

The father's eyes were lost in thought down on the table among the scraps of pizza and napkins. "There's no use running anymore. Maybe there was at one point, but... it doesn't matter, anyway. Eventually they get everybody. You can't hide. Not even in another town. They'll just come there, too, and it will be the same story all over again," he explained. There was something destitute and lonely about his emotions as he brought his weak eyes up to look at his children. "My kids aren't going to live that way. They're not going to live a life of fear, running from place to place. There's no hope. Nobody can save us. There's just... one... last... peaceful... family meal."

The father reached to his side, where he pulled a small six-shooter pistol out from his pocket. Julian's eyes sharpened as he took a protective step in front of Rachael, who covered her gaping mouth with a hand. "Whoa," Julian mumbled as he calmly held his palm forward. "Just take it easy, man."

The father stared at the weapon as he rubbed his thumb across the ridges of the chamber. "I only put three in here — one for each of us. You two are gonna have to worry about yourselves. Unless you leave now. Maybe you'll make it out of town and maybe you won't. But me... I've... I've got my family to take care of."

Rachael started frantically shaking her head. "No. No! Are you insane?! What is the matter with you?! You're... You can't... You can't... They're your children, for Christ's sake! You can't do that to your children! Why the hell would you even think that?!"

Julian tried to take control of her wiggling body as she stressfully fought. He turned back to the father. "Look, nobody's gonna do anything dramatic here. I don't know what you think is gonna happen when these people come, but there's always another way. This isn't the answer."

"You don't know what's happening. If you knew, you would pull the trigger, too," the father depressingly added.

"I would *never* shoot my kids! Ever!" Rachael barked.

"Look, just *tell us* what's happening!" Julian stressed. "We can help. We can go *find* help! We can all leave together. I have a Jeep Liberty outside and a full tank of gas; there's more than enough room!"

"I already told you! You can't run!" the father snapped, now seeming more intense as his eyes gleamed with water. "You'll only be delaying the inevitable!"

"Please! Just talk to us!" Julian begged.

The father looked out the window; his expression sagging and pouting as he shook his head. "It's gone. The sun's down now. It's too late. They're coming. They're on their way *right now!* I have no choice! I have no choice! Kids, come on. Out of the booth. It's time to play that game we talked about."

The children easily complied by setting their food down and shuffling out of the booth as the father did the same. "No!" Rachael screamed, stammering forward.

Julian pushed her back and threatened to charge the father, but he defensively turned the weapon on Julian, who stopped and held his hands up. "Please," the father pleaded with a tear or two now dropping as his jaw shook. "I can't use these on you. There's only enough for *us.* You have to understand that. I only brought three!"

"Don't do this," Julian said. "They're your kids. Think about that."

"I'm doing this because I love them," he noted. "Kids — turn around." The two children stood in the corner and turned with their backs facing him. The father swallowed the lump in his throat as he raised his shaking arm. He cocked back the loading hammer with his thumb. Rachael was in hysterics, quickly shaking her head as she covered her mouth again. "Everything will be okay now," he said to himself under his breath as he began to squeeze the trigger.

Julian lunged forward, grabbing the father's wrist and they wrestled about, crashing against the table and then the empty salad bar in the center as Rachael hurried over and cowered with the kids around her arms. The struggle continued for another good minute or so as Julian grit his teeth and tried to snag the gun. They crashed into a small table and landed on the floor, rolling as a gunshot erupted. Rachael gave a shriek and jolted in reaction; her eyes frozen and unblinking as the two men lied motionless for a moment. Julian was the first to mutter a noise, now in possession of the gun as he grunted and rolled off the father.

The father gasped and chomped for air, holding his hands against the bloody wound on his chest. Julian noticed, first glancing down at the gun in his hand and back to the victim. "Oh, shit," he murmured, helping the father sit up against the salad bar. "All right, just… take it easy. Just breathe. We're gonna get you some help." Julian arched his head back to Rachael and the children. "Call for an ambulance!"

Rachael took off for the kitchen area, leaving the kids as the father slumped his head back. "It's no use," he groaned in pain. "They won't answer. It won't come."

Julian whipped the tablecloth off the downed table and applied pressure onto the father's chest. "Don't talk," he calmly ordered.

Rachael held the phone up to her ear and shook her head, slamming it back onto the hook. "There's no dial tone!" she yelled.

"Use your cell phone!" Julian hollered back.

Rachael dug into her pocket and pulled her phone, dialing. The father coughed. "There won't be anybody there," he tried to convince them again.

Rachael listened and gave an unbelievable look down to her phone. "Nine-One-One isn't answering!" she said.

"What? How can Nine-One-One not answer?!" Julian bellowed.

The children took a step over to sadly glare at their dying parent. "Daddy...?" the son had whimpered with a frightened, quiet tone. It was the first thing Julian had heard from either since they had entered the restaurant.

The father hooked a bloody hand around Julian's right wrist. "P-Please. Please. Y-You have to do it now. There's only two bullets left. You have to finish it for me. Don't let them get my kids."

"Take it easy," Julian told him, holding him back. The father coughed and began to gag, losing his grip to fight. Julian gave his body a shake. "Hey. Hey! Stay with me! Come on, man, stay with me!"

But the father was gone. His eyes sunk closed and his head slightly tilted. Julian stared at him for a moment, wondering if he had only simply lost consciousness. He had never been in this situation before, so he didn't know how to handle it. He set a pair of fingers against the disheveled man's throat, but didn't feel a pulse. He was definitely dead. He glanced upward to Rachael, who hovered overhead and stared at the mess. "Oh my God..." was all she could manage.

Julian looked at the kids and then extended the tablecloth so it fully covered their father. "What do we do?" Rachael then asked.

Julian stood up, wiping his hands as he held the gun. "We gotta find someone — find the police station."

He started to make his way across the restaurant as Rachael wrapped her hands around the shoulders of the children. "Come on, kids — we're gonna go for a ride."

"Is my daddy dead?" the little girl asked, bending her head up to look at Rachael. "Who's gonna protect us from all the bad people?"

Before she could answer, she noticed Julian stop at the door and stare at something. "What? What is it?" Rachael wondered.

"There's somebody out there," he told her, trying to see within the darkness.

Rachael slightly separated herself from the kids, joining his side as she tried to identify the shape of the figure that just stood in the parking lot. "That's definitely a person," Julian added.

"What are they doing? Why are they just standing there? What do they want?" Rachael asked, now sounding a bit more frantically scared.

"Wait, wait — look. There's someone else," Julian pointed out.

Rachael noticed the second person walk up and join the first in a motionless stance. "Those are the bad people," the little boy stated, drawing a look from both Julian and Rachael.

Rachael glanced at Julian and then stepped over, crouching to his level as she laid caring hands on his arms. "Bad people? Sweetie, what do you mean?" she asked. Something caught her eyes across the restaurant as her jaw slightly went ajar. She slowly raised herself back upright. "Julian. Julian, look."

Julian turned and saw it, too. There was a plethora of people standing outside on the other side of the establishment, all lined up against the windows as they stared inside. "Jesus," Julian mumbled, shifting confused eyes. "What the hell are they doing?"

A knock came from the windowed door behind them, making them jump. Rachael clutched Julian's arm. A tall, thin man in a hooded sweatshirt stood in front of the door, hands pressed flatly against the glass. That's when Julian and Rachael noticed the assortment of people lined against that wall as if they had appeared out of nowhere. They were surrounding the entire restaurant. One by one, more came and added to their numbers, nuzzling into open spots beside the others. They seemed like everyday people, varying from teenagers to old folks. Some wore business suits, and others wore construction uniforms.

Rachael carefully backed up as the children cuddled into her sides. "What do they all want? Why don't they just come in?" she worriedly asked.

The hooded man at the door gave another knock and streaked his hand across the glass. "Pleeeeeeeease... let me in," he simply muttered.

Another boney man dressed in gray janitor overalls with long stringy black hair pressed his face against the neighboring window. "Let ussssssss in," he whispered.

"Give us the children," a woman whispered.

"Yesssssssssssssss, the children," the hooded man agreed in a quiet emotionless tone. "Give us the children and we'll let you live."

"Yesssssssssss, let you live," the woman added.

Julian lowered and waved his hand back to Rachael. "Get back," he told her as she shuffled more into the center of the restaurant with the kids. He looked back at the door and gave a nod. "What do you want?"

"We want the children," another unidentified voice replied.

"The children, yessssssssss, pleassssssse — the children," someone else added.

"We're ssssssssso hungry," a voice pleaded.

"So thirsssty," an old woman whispered.

Julian stiffened his stance and loosely aimed the gun. "I have a gun," he noted.

A *thud* came from above, causing Rachael to bend her head up. "They're on the roof," she quietly muttered. They were everywhere. The restaurant was completely surrounded.

An older, uniformed police officer with a mustache walked up to the door, giving a firm knock with his knuckles. "Let me in, son," he flatly ordered. "Just take it easy. I'm here to help," the officer assured him.

"What the hell is everybody doing here?" Julian then asked.

"I can explain everything," the officer calmly answered. "All you have to do is open the door, and everything will be okay."

The little girl looked up at Rachael. "My daddy said never to let them in," she told her.

Julian looked at Rachael. She gave her answer by shaking her head.

"Let me in," the officer repeated. "No one will get hurt."

"Fine! But just you!" Julian scuffed, aiming the gun. "No one else. Nice and slow. It's open!"

"Julian, no!" Rachael pleaded, shaking her head more.

"He's a cop!" Julian told her.

"Open it for me," the officer said.

Julian hesitated again and took a step forward, stopping to think.

"No," Rachael begged. "Please." Julian took a breath and reluctantly shook his head, taking the last few footsteps to push the door open as Rachael screamed, "*Julian, nooooooooooooo!!!*"

The officer lunged forward like an animal, hissing and flashing a pair of sharp white canines from his mouth which immediately sunk into Julian's neck as his gun flew across the floor. Rachael let out another terrified scream as her tears flew. The children whimpered and buried their heads into her, looking away from the bloody carnage. Julian couldn't put up much of a fight — maybe it was the strength of the officer or the way his physicality had angled to trap him, but he slowly fell to the tiled floor as blood spurted and poured. The army of people outside began to pour their way in through the door, one or two of them stopping to bend down and feast upon Julian's helpless bloody body as Rachael quickly sprang forward and retrieved the handgun, hopping back to defensively protect the children. The people had only come through the one entrance; the rest on the opposite side of the building marching and slugging all the way around as the inside began to fill with their snarling fangs. Rachael held the gun forward, darting her eyes to each as she was flooded back inch by inch toward the rear of the restaurant.

It all quickly became apparent to her, as unbelievable as it sounded. She was trapped inside a restaurant filling bit by bit with vampires, the seconds and space within wasting away. She was too ecstatic and bewildered to make any decisions or moves, but the possibilities rang through her mind regardless. They were vampires. They were filling a space which she had no alternate escape from.

And she only had two bullets.

She could simply use them on the first two that came after her, but what good would that have done? They were vampires — even if the bullets worked, it was redundant and useless, for she'd still have an army to deal with behind them.

She could shoot her way out through one of the windows and escape, hoping to get to the Jeep Liberty, but what of the others outside? And the kids — it would be too difficult for them to keep up. They would never make it if she started getting attacked. By herself was a different story. There was a chance. But the kids…

The unbearable thought flashed through her head. Their father's thought. She had two bullets left. Two kids. This was actually happening. Vampires. It was either die, or become one — and she wasn't sure which was worse. She wouldn't want to be one, nor would she want these innocent kids subjected to an undead blood-sucking-pale-skinned-cruelty-of-an-existence. She could make it easy and put them out of their — no! They were children, for God's sake! But then again she didn't know them. Not like they were her kids or anything.

She could put the gun to her own head. Julian, the love of her life — the man she was hoping to marry someday — was dead. She had no reason to live. But then what about the kids?! They would be left alone to that uncertain fate. Goddamn it, if only she had one more bullet!

The options pinned her back against the rear wall as the vampires slowly swarmed closer, licking their lips and snarling their unholy fangs with dreadfully playful grins.

Three gunshots were fired that night at the Pizza Hut. The first took the life of a desperate father; a helpless and grief-stricken man deluded and lost in an irremediable solution. The second two could have been any of those possibilities Rachael was quickly pressured to select from.

Perhaps only the newly-reformed townspeople know which.

THE POOR FATE OF THE PROUD AMELIA

The landing gear and flaps were down. The propellers were set to high RPM. The throttles were pulled back to idle. It was the best part of the island to land, no doubt. The corral reef surrounding its three-mile-long by one-mile-wide measurements was flat and dry at low tide around noon, a bit rocky and lacking sandy conditions — perfect for the balloon tires of her Lockheed Model 10 Electra to make a smooth enough landing. She had certainly landed on much worse.

She had been flying for more than a month.

Five hours of sleep a night.

She was completely run down.

She thought if only she could make it to Howland Island, everything would be okay. But she wasn't going to make it there. She accepted that fact already, but that didn't destroy her optimism. Right now it was about surviving; it was about landing. It was simple, professional aviation. They would come and find her. Her and Fred. It might take a little bit of time, but it was only a delay in her mind. Then she'd be back in the air finishing her record-setting journey. She had already come way too far to be defeated. She was not coming up short. It was only a matter of waiting. She was an intelligent woman, and he was an intelligent man. Between the both of them it would be nothing short of a low-quality tropical vacation.

Amelia Earhart touched the plane down with only a slight jolt and bounce on the northwest corner of the island, just past the wreck of an old freighter ship, which they had later identified with a closer look as the *S.S. Norwich City*, although neither knew of its origins or the story which fatally perched it against the coral reef. She exited the plane with an assisting hand from Fred Noonan, her trusted navigator — a hand she had taken so many times before entering or exiting her now-famous aviation glider. She wondered if at times Fred ever felt more like a servant than her partner, always there at her side as the photography continuously flashed from the press but always feeling like he was instead behind her. "Fred who?" "Excuse me, sir — could you step aside? I'm trying to get a better close-up of the gallivant Lady Lindy." Of course, she knew that Fred was well-aware she hated the celebrity aspect of it, so he had nothing to be jealous over, but she still wondered if his thoughts ever betrayed him, especially when they were lubricated by alcohol.

She expected it to come later, but almost immediately, Fred began blaming himself for the mishap up in the air. He rambled about poor bearings and direction, and she had to re-convince him that he was one of the best celestial navigators in the world and that their misfortune was due more to botched radio communications. It was probably the idea that they were stranded on that island that was no more than practically a dot from the sky, but she assured him that no expense would be spared and a rescue was a mere few days to a week away at the most.

When he had calmed down a bit, they scrounged a few basic supplies and figured to come back for the rest after they had better-determined their situation. While it was presumed that the location was most likely uninhabited by human life, they began to tour it anyway, hooking up and around the northeastern part of the island, and circling all the way to the bottom.

There were no people. No settlements. And surely no evidence that anyone had been there recently. It was even possible no one had even stepped foot onto the island for almost half a century. Regardless, they were stuck. Based upon the makeshift of the island Amelia had figuratively gathered while they circled above earlier looking for the best landing spot, the most practical area to make safe camp was in the southern bottom part of the island. Fred had agreed with this but was reluctant to be so far from the plane, especially since they would have to go all the way up and around the side they had come from, since the left side of the island was cut off by a channel connecting the ocean to its long center-island lagoon. It would've been easy to walk across, reaching only knee-height, but Fred feared sharks were prominent locals and he wanted to stay out of the water as much as he could.

The two set up camp inland, starting a fire that eased with a warm crackle and pop. Even if the rescue parties had already been disbursed, there wouldn't be any findings that night in the dark. Amelia told him to get some rest. They had already been through a lot, and they would need their strength, but like him, it wasn't easy for her to fall asleep. The rippling of the ocean waves and the insect and animal noises of the tropical jungles surrounding them provided an unnatural setting. Sleeping on the ground didn't help, either. The sand was soft but it was flat and uncomfortable. Fred's neck was starting to strain. He balled up his shirt and tried using it as a pillow, but it didn't help much. Amelia was surprised he wanted to get it dirty at all. He seemed too neat of an individual, always with his shirt tucked in and tie tightened around his neck. Neatness prompted his personality, but he always came off like he belonged more in an office than up in the sky with her.

Despite the hours fluttering away into the darkness of the island's night, exhaustion eventually caught up with the traveling pair and they drifted into a light, cautious sleep, until Amelia was woken by a slight poke across her left pant leg. She shifted herself and tried going back to sleep, then felt something brush across her foot. Something else soft and thin tickled beneath her jaw. She reflexively waved her hand across, figuring it was a piece of grass being carried by the wind.

Fred gave a scream, blasting her eyes fully open as she sat up and looked over at him. He was juggling and flailing about in the sand on the other side of the small fire, cursing and blurting incoherent words as he stood up and danced about. As Amelia prepared to question what his malfunction was, she noticed her legs by light of the fire were covered with three crawling hermit crabs. She turned her eyes to notice two more were slowly inching near where her head had been set, and like Fred, she jolted to her feet and brushed the creatures away; a slight chill rippling down her spine at the thought that they had just been crawling on her while she helplessly slept. "Bastards were pinching me!" Fred huffed.

Amelia spoke the notion that the red hermit crabs probably thought they were dead, and had no fear in curiously investigating their sleeping bodies since no humans had been on the island. Sleeping on the ground was going to be a problem, and Fred wasn't too privy to the idea of sleeping in shifts so one could keep watch over the other. Amelia had conjured the idea of using the large buka trees around them as salvation, for they could easily use the large branches as beds, granted they didn't roll off and break their necks during the night, but that could prevented with some simple tie-down rope.

"What about tree bugs? Or birds, or monkeys, or whatever the hell in God's name could be crawling up there on them?" Fred reluctantly growled.

She simply told him he could take his chances on the ground, where matters would be much worse, and used careful footing to crawl herself up onto the nearest accessible branch. Fred followed shortly after. Neither were suited to be castaways, but at least Amelia wasn't complaining about it. She didn't know much about high-class surviving on deserted islands, but she did know that the number one cause for people diminishing on them was probably the simple fact of using their thoughts to curse their bad luck instead of how to survive. "How could this happen to me?" "Why me?" "Nobody will ever find us." "I'll be here for the rest of my life." "I'll die of starvation." Amelia wasn't going to be that kind of person. She was more resilient and resourceful than that. She had been the first woman to accomplish a solo transatlantic flight, for Christ's sake.

Neither could fall back asleep after the creepy shake with the crabs. Fred had even mentioned hearing a peculiar noise from within the jungle — a rustling movement through the brush that seemed to approach closer and closer. Amelia heard it as well, but tried to convince him that it was merely the breeze floating through the grass and trees, or some small animals were up to their traditional twilight activities — or most likely, it was just an ambiance of natural sounds only heightened and sharpened to an ominous level due to their nerves being on edge. "No," he simply assured her. "There's something down there — down there in the jungle. And it's not a damn hermit crab."

They hadn't accumulated much more sleep, and by the time the sun had risen a few hours later, the unidentified sound was gone, and the jungle had returned to its daily noises of birds, bugs and other small playful critters. Fred stretched his crooked limbs after retreating down from the tree and held a hand up to help Amelia, once again mirroring their duty of boarding or un-boarding the plane.

They had to of course wait until the tide was at its lowest points in order to make the distress calls on the radio. The propellers needed to be free of water so they had the ability to spin in order to conduct power for the batteries of the radio to recharge. Amelia spent a good two hours that day on the radio, repeating her name and situation over and over. She even added the fact they were perched near the Norwich City wreck to help any possible listener with a clue of where they were. But how far could the radio signals stretch? Would anyone be listening? It was a shot into the dark. Random.

Amelia knew they wouldn't be able to call for help forever. Aside from the plane's power failing, there was also the fact that eventually the strong coral reef tide would probably pull and tear the bird apart each time it went underwater. She didn't know how long that would take. There was just simply nothing they could do about it. It was the best place to land, and they surely didn't have the means to bring it further in once they had touched down. Not that it mattered either way, though. They were practically out of gas. Soon it would be nothing more than a large paperweight. Planes could be replaced. People couldn't. And despite Fred's more dreary outlook to the situation, Amelia knew they were damn lucky to be standing on that island.

Perhaps that's what implemented their situation in stone. It was a psychological thing before — even though they couldn't use it, knowing that the plane was safely parked and waiting seemed to deliver somewhat of a comfortable sense of security. Now... there was nothing. They were officially castaways with the clothes on their backs and the limited small supplies they had managed to scrounge earlier.

Food wouldn't be a problem. There was quite the abundant ecosystem source on the island, and they wasted no time filling the empty hunger that had gnawed at their stomachs since yesterday. The hermit crabs were the easiest (it was simply a pick up job). And then there were the oysters Amelia had managed to net up, although they were difficult to pry open, so she had to forcefully smash them to collect up the insides.

Fred had also concocted a custom spear for fishing from a thick branch and a pocket knife which he had broken out of its handle.

It was the water that was going to be a problem. There was no fresh water source on the island, so they'd have to wait until it rained to collect it, and even then it would still need to be boiled in order to drink. Luckily, in fact, it did rain that second night, and they collected what they could from the bottles they had and the coconut shells that were already broken open on the island floor. The large buka trees also provided cupping gaps and crevices that captured pools of rains. Things were certainly not as bad as they seemed.

It was that third night, the Fourth of July, that really got to Fred. They had only been there three days and already the hours waned to make it feel like a week. And there certainly hadn't been any signs of rescue yet. As they lied in the large buka tree over their camp fire, Fred's eyes drifted to a beautiful starry sky that seemed lonely without any kind of celebrating fireworks. That July 4th was supposed to be the big one — the one that congratulated them across the world for their marvelous feat together. And there they were, stuck on that godforsaken island.

Stuck listening to that sound! The same sound that had repeated itself for the third night in a row — a rustling sound. A brushing sound. A movement sound. Fred tried to ignore it, but it didn't go away. He heard a sharp crack of a twig. *The breeze doesn't crack twigs in half,* he thought about saying to Amelia. Something was down there, moving around in circles, unseen in the dark, almost as if it were playing with them. Taunting them.

Fred couldn't take it anymore and didn't care what it was. He hopped and slid his way down and told Amelia he was going for a walk along the shore, despite her advising caution to the idea. There was nothing she could do to stop him, and part of her wanted to let him go so he could deal with their situation in his own way. He shuffled through the brush toward the beach in the opposite direction of the noise.

It would be the last time she'd ever see him alive.

When Amelia had woken up early the next morning, Fred was still gone. At first, she figured he was still stewing and blowing off steam nearby on the shore. Perhaps he had even fallen asleep elsewhere. But he was nowhere to be found. She called out his name and walked the beach up and down, but there was still no sign or reply from the kempt navigator. She wondered how far of a walk he had indeed taken. It was possible he trailed back up and around the north part of the island to make an attempt at retrieving more supplies from their plane, but he wasn't there, either. Amelia had spent a couple hours circling the island, but he was nowhere to be found. She went back to their campsite and waited, figuring that was the next best tactic.

Night had fallen, and she feared the worst. He would've been back already. And he surely wasn't the type mad enough to abandon her and do things on his own. Regardless, she couldn't go off searching in the dark of night. That might have been his fateful downfall. She figured to conduct a search inland at first light. After all, the island was only three miles. He had to be there *somewhere*.

She climbed into her spot in the large buka tree, burrowing herself in her little cubby bed as the nightly insects buzzed and sang their nocturnal serenades. She had nearly drifted to sleep when she heard a rustle from the foliage below. She looked down and noticed something scurry off, shaking the leaves and concealing its identity. There seemed to be more in the area surrounding the camp; creeping and shaking their way within the jungle. Amelia was definitely spooked now, but at the same time she was curious and thought that if she used a flaming branch as a torch, she could fill the void of uncertainty by getting a closer look at just what exotic creature was toying with her — and perhaps even scare it off so she could get a good night's sleep. But something unsettling kept her up in that tree. Some strange feeling that it wasn't just some muskrats or lizards. She had braved the Atlantic by herself but now here she was, hiding in a tree.

Days had passed.

Fred still hadn't come back. She made a daily routine of combing through the thicker parts of the inland surrounding the center lagoon, but still hadn't found him. At one point, she even thought she heard a plane overhead, but by the time she had scoured out of the brush and got into the open, there was nothing in the blue skies above. Perhaps it was her ears playing tricks on her, anyway. She whacked and pushed her way back into the tropical jungles, always amazed in the rear of her mind that the dense foliage made it seem like she was in the middle of the Amazon when in fact the shoreline was merely feet away.

She eventually got around to searching the northeastern part of the island, and it was when she came to a small clearing within the jungle she noticed the first traces of dried blood on the leaves. She slowed her footsteps and advanced further, covering her shocked mouth with a dirty hand.

There were pieces everywhere. Scattered and tossed pieces of Fred among the sand and brush. She thought it could've been something else at first, but the clothing and pieces of fingers the red hermit crabs were dragging off gave him away completely. She retched and almost threw up. How the hell could this have happened?! What the hell could have done this to him?! He had been completely chopped and torn to pieces! It was like someone threw him into a wood chipper. Hermit crabs and lizards don't do this, certainly not to an adult male who had one-hundred-eighty pounds of fighting capability. Even if Fred had somehow gotten injured or fallen asleep, it still didn't explain the source. Something had done this to him. Something with enough power to come out of a nightmare and deliver a gruesomely unpleasant departure.

Amelia hurried back to the campsite. She left all of his remains in place. She was alone now. Alone on that island with no answers and a spiraling fear of living the rest of her days there with something waiting to come out of the jungle for her. Still, she had to survive. She could've given up, but it was her above-average will to live, and that meant sustaining her health as best she could. She continued to catch what fish, birds, mice and turtles she could to keep her stomach at bay. She was already so small and frail to begin with. The water could've been more plentiful, but she did a fair job of rationing. It was a good week or so later that she had the idea of collecting coconuts from the trees above, since she had already scoured all of the ones that had fallen to the island floor in her area. She tried knocking them down with long branches, but they were either too far out of reach or the branches were too flimsy. She resorted to climbing. If she could climb the buka trees, she figured coconut trees would be an easy shimmy up. But she was weaker than she was before, and nearly three-quarters of the way up as she reached to knock some of the coconuts down, she had lost her footing and grip and fell, cracking and breaking her leg upon impact. She threw her head back and howled in pain. It was excruciating. And as she lied there for the next hour, the pain of disappointment and regret filled her more than the injury itself. She was done for. She would never survive now. It didn't seem like it should've happened at that height, but it did. She had landed on her leg the wrong way, and now the bones were practically sticking out through the open wound. Perhaps it was better that way. She would much rather end it than go on with the hope that help was coming to her fly-speck-of-a-new-home.

At least she would be remembered. It's not like she was an average nobody with the misfortune of marooning herself on some deserted island never to be heard from again without a second thought. She had accomplished the best she could, and in that aspect she felt a sense of pride. She hated putting her dear George through it back home, though — never knowing what became of her; never being able to see him one last time or saying the things she still had to say. Now it was only a matter of time, to which she thought she would quicken by finding the spear with the pocket knife tip and delivering herself a much more comfortable closure than the slow alternative. She couldn't find it though, and each crawl across the shore gave her a searing sense of pain she could not get used to. She lied back and temporarily gave up, nodding off for a few hours.

When she had awoken, the sun was gone, and only the ancient promise of twinkling stars in the blackness above remained. The moon was out though; casting a shine that glazed a blue tint over everything surrounding her. It was almost peaceful.

Then she heard it again. Just as she had heard it every night since arriving. The trees, bushes and leaves rustled about, moving and shaking. She could hear something approaching. It was on the ground, moving its way through the foliage with just enough noise to make itself apparent over the other standard nightly sounds of the breeze and insects. Amelia slightly cowered further back from the tree line, sliding and pushing herself with a sharp, painful grunt. Her eyes widened like saucers.

They emerged from the tree line, pushing their way out of the foliage with their front pair of claws. They were giant coconut crabs, a whole group of them, abnormally large with hard purplish blue exoskeleton-shelled bodies at about three-feet long with a series of ten legs that seemed to stretch just as far. Amelia screamed as they crawled toward her. She tried to shuffle away, but obviously couldn't, so she stretched her hand out to grab hold of a branch on the beach and sat up, whacking and hitting at them as they surrounded her. It didn't do any good as one had caught hold and snapped it in two like a twig with its powerful claw. She hollered and tried batting them away with her arm, but the group had quickly overpowered her. Two had hooked their claws around her ankles and began dragging her back into the jungle, which especially hurt considering her broken leg. Despite the pain, she flailed about and turned her body, trying to break free, but their grip was too firm. The ones on her sides hooked her arms, and now she was being carried more than being dragged. She screamed for help, but no one was there to answer. Bit by bit, she felt herself lowering into the soil.

She was being pulled underground.

She freed her right arm from the clawed grip of one of the coconut crabs and dug her fingers into the loose sand, but it did no good. She was going down into some sort of cavernous burrow crevice.

And she wasn't coming out.

SHE HAD 3YC'S AND A SICKLE

Mitch Mahoney was quite the asshole.

But oh how the women adored him!

He would flaunt his fifty and one hundred dollar bills so egotistically everywhere he went. He would always be dressed in some kind of sharp gray flashy suit that mirrored the one his wealthy day-trading father liked to wear while dispensing him hoards of cash like a human ATM. Mitch Mahoney was a modern day prince of investments. A modern day James Dean with hair that would look good even after waking in bed from his worst drunken night ever. Being twenty-six and still too young to take over the family business, he planted his interests and priorities into three things — easy women, fast cars and burnable cash. Fun was his repertoire. Power was his hunger. Attention was his goal.

And what better night to be himself than Halloween! To the young twenty-somethings of America, it was "Special-Go-Out-and-Get-Drunk-Night-of-the-Year-#45", only this time in costume. He went to that corner club downtown to meet his friends, but he could've cared less. They were all like him, anyway, shallow and bored. He was planning on leaving with someone else. It was just a matter of choosing between the girls dressed from mummies to witches to bosom-boasting nurses. What a dull choice! Always, every year, it was the same. A damn skimpy nurse costume. He was over going home with the nurses years ago. He wanted someone different this time, although in the end it's all the same, right? They all end up in bare skin.

He stood with his back to the bar counter, taking swigs from his ice cube-riddled whiskey as his cool eyes coasted across all of the hopeless monsters, superheroes, masked killers and Disney-affiliated pirates whose name will not be mentioned as they grooved and grinded on the crowded dance floor. He turned and waited for the brain-dead zombie bartender to come back down his way for a refill when the douche bag standing beside him left and unveiled the voluptuous twenty-something brunette sitting on the stool. She played with the straw in her short drink, immediately shooting Mitch Mahoney an intriguing smile as her tongue snaked across the thin plastic. She was the most beautiful creature in the entire club! Mitch Mahoney delivered his usual charming smile as he casually turned and leaned his elbow against the bar top. "Hey there, beautiful," he cunningly greeted.

"Hello," she simply answered, garnering his eyes across the sleek black shoulderless outfit she wore which empowered her inviting 34c-cup chest.

"You look like you could use another drink," he then stated, perking his eyebrows.

"No, thanks. I'm only here to take you with me," she said.

Mitch Mahoney smiled. "Ya know, I love a girl who gets right to the point. So your place or mine?"

"Neither."

"Ah, I get it. Anonymity's a great thing. Motel, then?"

She nodded toward his prompt gray suit. "A little underdressed for tonight, but saves you the trouble if you were to end up in a coffin."

Mitch Mahoney adored himself in his attire, raising his arms and giving her a three-hundred-sixty-degree modeling view. "Tonight's underrated. But look who's talking. What are *you* supposed to be?"

"The Grim Reaper," she told him.

He snickered. "Guess that's one way to do it."

She shrugged. "Ah, well, ya know, a faceless brown cloak can get so tiring day after day."

"Already a killer outfit ya got on," Mitch Mahoney noted with a smile as he took a sip of his drink. Mitch Mahoney — the only one arrogant and fool hearted enough to find humor in his own jokes. "So, you're here to take some poor soul, huh?"

"Yes. Yours, Mitch," she flatly retorted.

He sharpened his eyes, thinking twice about what she had just said. "How'd you know my name?"

"I know everything about you, Mitch Mahoney," she continued. "Comes with the job."

Mitch Mahoney kept his smile running as he leaned closer. "Oh, really?" Mitch Mahoney was already having a great time. He loved a good game! The ones that weren't the average everyday air-headed mannequins were a dime a dozen. He had really scored tonight! One of his friends probably set it up. "Okay," he presumptuously added. "So I'm gonna die, huh? How does it happen?"

"Silly, I can't tell you that," she quipped. "Then you'd be able to cheat me. And I'm not too fond of being cheated. Everybody thinks they can cheat me now after that stupid movie came out — ya know, the one with the boy, and the plane? Fuckin' Hollywood, I tell ya."

"Then why are you here now? Don't you usually show up *after* someone dies? What does that mean? I'm gonna die in here? Heart attack? Something gonna fall on me?" Mitch Mahoney was enjoying this way too much.

"I like to meet the really special ones in person early," she said. "Occupational guilty pleasure. Hitler, bin Laden, John Lennon." He gave a weird look. She winked and clicked her tongue. "All you need is love."

"And you look like this because...?"

"Because this is what fits your character profile. My little way of fucking with people. I represent all those young pretty women you conquered. The ones you chewed up and spit out. The ones you paid so many fees for at the clinic after one-night stands."

Mitch Mahoney studied her for a long moment. He had met his share of head cases, but this one was different. This one seemed a step ahead of him. Someone who could match his wits point for point. She was probably a goddess in the bedroom. He was going to use her like a ragdoll! He gave another chuckle and began bobbing his head. "All right, okay," he muttered. "But isn't there an old legend that you can challenge the Grim Reaper to a contest for the rights to your life back?"

She smiled brightly and straightened herself more promptly as her eyes excitedly widened. "Ooh! Sounds like fun! But please — no Milton Bradley. I can only gamble with people's souls over Battleship and Connect 4 so many times before it gets boring."

Mitch Mahoney cracked his fingers and waved a cool hand through his hair. "I was thinking of something a little more exciting."

She seductively curled the tip of her tongue around her straw. "I — *love* — exciting."

"Terms are simple — if you win, you get to cut me down with your fancy little steak knife. But if I win, my mortality gets a long extension, in which case..." His plotting eyes glazed down her body as he licked the edge of his lips. "...I'll be able to give *you* something of a long extension."

She dipped her eyes to his crotch and then quirked a grin. "Trust me, honey — you don't want to stick that thing anywhere in the body of someone who represents dark, decaying death. But you've got a deal." He reached his hand out for a shake. She waved an index finger at him and shook her head. "No, no, now. A handshake will give you a skeleton costume that will put all the others in here to shame. I'm good on my word."

"Very well, then," he affirmed. Mitch Mahoney could've picked any limitless contest he normally excelled at — a drinking game, trivia, darts, billiards — but he wanted something exciting! Oh, how he wanted something to get his blood rushing! "A car race," he decided with a confident grin. "A drag race. Me and you, one straight shot. I take my Porsche, but you have to take the biggest P.O.S. that's on this street."

She touched her finger to her bottom lip in thought. "Hmmmm. Now that doesn't sound too fair, Mitchell."

"Hey," he huffed with a shrug. "Neither does knowing everything about everybody, but you seem to have that advantage over me, now."

"I suppose you're right. A car race sounds just swell."

So the two left the club, and after shopping the vast selection of parked chariots down the strip, Mitch Mahoney had awarded her with the grandness of an old, white-tainted beat-up Volkswagen Beetle that could have very well been in use when Richard Nixon was still in office. But a bet was a bet, and since he was the determiner of terms, she had no say in the matter. Pit against his sleekly black custom-imported Porsche, she'd have no chance in hell! It was an easy win. If she was telling the truth, he'd safely be earning his life back. If she wasn't, he'd still win anyway, and it would only end up being a great lay story! So Mitch Mahoney and the radiant beauty lined their cars up at an intersection a few streets over, where the long stretching pavement was clear of any late-night hindering traffic. It was agreed that the change of the next traffic signal would be their start, and the next intersection a quarter mile or so down the road would be the big finish line.

The light blared green, and Mitch Mahoney stomped on the gas. His Porsche revved and roared forward, blasting down the street. At first, his opponent's laughable Volkswagen Beetle kept up, but it started to sink back bit by bit as the Porsche's speedometer erected until the Beetle's muffler loudly popped in a fit of smoke, slowing to a broken-down stop. Mitch Mahoney arched his head back and watched; his triumphant laugh growing louder and louder. Once again, he was invincible!

Though not to the pick-up truck that T-boned him from the left as he victoriously blazed through the finishing intersection. It was a hard, iron-fist-punching crash that sent his six-figure-valued car tumbling and bouncing down the road until aimlessly flailing off a bridge like a child's misguided Matchbox toy.

The driver's door to the Volkswagen Beetle down the road creaked open, and the lovely doe-eyed treat exited the smoking speed joke, starting to casually make her way step by step down the road, past the pick-up truck that had veered off its wheels while trying to turn and perched itself sideways against a park's stone wall. Blood thickly oozed from the mouth of the balled-up driver, a male in his late-forties, as he caught sight of her. "P... Help... Help... me," he miraculously managed to mutter through the broken window.

She kept walking; her eyes firmly directed forward. "I'll be helping you at the hospital in fifty-seven minutes and forty-two seconds, Jerry," she answered.

She approached the bridge and walked down the hill to the street below, where Mitch Mahoney's poor Porsche sat flipped upside down. She stopped next to the driver's side, where his mangled body hung out through the open door, watching her with blood-soaked eyes as she crouched to his level and perked her eyebrows. "You should have chosen something else, Mitch," she told him. "Otherwise I could've avoided telling you that you die in a car crash tonight."

Mitch Mahoney couldn't answer. He couldn't move. The sweet prince playboy had fallen from his pedestal. She stood back upright and placed her hands on her hips, quirking her face. "Now hurry up and die already. Halloween's a busy night for me."

THE HOLE IN THE BASEMENT OF
THE HOUSE ON BRIDGEMAN ROAD

June 1ˢᵗ was the move-in day.

It was the perfect time to move weather-wise. Not cold, but then not too hot just yet. Mason Anders carried the first of many boxes into that house on Bridgeman Road in upstate New York. It was a big house, three stories with an attic waiting for some leisurely couches, tables and a TV. He was glad he and Felicity were out of the city — out of their rickety old dirty apartment with those annoying and loud neighbors. He was finally making enough money at his boring but productive office job to move somewhere more permanent. Somewhere more permanent where he could raise the family he always wanted. Where his future kids could have a backyard to play in. Where they could play in the street without worrying about getting hit by a car, since cars didn't pass down there too often. Their new neighbors, which were older and saints compared to their previous, had mentioned that the former tenants of their proud new homestead used to have a dog that actually *slept* in the road because of its lack of activity. And speaking of traffic, it was another perk of being out in the rural country. Every morning, Mason felt as if he were immediately bombarded by the rush hour gridlock. It was suffocating and frustrating. He would gladly accept a twenty or twenty-five minute drive now. It was worth it.

Like any big move, the day consisted of a routine in-and-out lugging boxes or furniture with the help of his brother Russell and the two over-muscled movers. Occasionally Mason would cross paths with his beautiful Felicity on the way back to the truck for another load, connecting with a quick kiss. She was a goddess. His heart still pounded with that first date excitement, even after three years of marriage. All of his buddies or co-workers always told him that was he barely thirty and that the essence of flavor-losing time would eventually catch up with him, but he knew otherwise. His romantic fascinations were in it for the long haul. Besides, all of those guys were either already divorced by their mid-forties or complete morons to settle with someone they knew they weren't fully happy with at the start.

The day was aging and the sun was on its dip down as the elongated moving truck coasted away. Mason could actually see the sun setting. It was more than perfect. He wanted Felicity to come out and watch it with him from their front yard, but she insisted that there was too much work to do, and they would have plenty of sunset opportunities. She was right. Russell had quipped something about him leaving early if they wanted to get to christening their new bedroom, which got him a shove from his older brother of two years and a slightly-bashful grin from Felicity. She was working on putting things away in the kitchen as Mason and Russell carried some boxes into the laundry room, where the basement door was located. Mason told him to watch his head as he ducked on his way down.

Russell of course smacked the brim of his noggin against the backside of the steps going to the second floor above, huffing a grunt and giving a painful rub. It was a very small and thin staircase in which he had to hunch his shoulders and slightly angle his body to get down. There was already a drastic temperature drop, which was great considering the house had no air conditioning system except the basement was no place to lounge unlike the attic three floors above their heads. Mason had originally told Russell that it reminded him more of an old medieval dungeon, and Russell could now see for himself that he wasn't exaggerating. The floor was practically dirt where the thin concrete wasn't laid out, and the walls were giant brown stones. Russell felt like it should've belonged more under a barn than a house as he brushed past some drooping cobwebs. There was a septic or water tank of some sort in the corner, a fuse box and nearly half a dozen or so thin black pipes loosely stretching in different intersecting directions from the ceiling. To the right below the old wooden stairs that looked to crack with one wrong step, the wall had been broken into and filled with a powdery brown dirt. Apparently it had something to do with the foundation and additional piping when the house was expanded over the years from its original mid-nineteenth century roots, but it nevertheless gave Mason an eerie vibe and as long as everything worked well, he felt no need to go crawling around inside where some giant rat or woodchuck would jump out at him. Then there was the set of six steps leading up to the door which led to the backyard.

Mason set the box down on the floor and reached inside, beginning to pull out tools and other oddities. If nothing else, it was at least a good spot to put them all considering they were one of the only houses on that road to not have a garage. He didn't need one anyway. He wasn't the type of person to fill one with hoards of tools and fine-tuning mechanics. They began to load tools into a tall metal cabinet against the back wall that towered almost up to the ceiling; Russell pulling open each drawer and half-expecting creepy-crawlies to be weaving their way through an old human skull. He had mentioned something about seeing a girl recently, and when Mason asked about her, he shrugged the subject off as if it were secretive. Russell was always one to get into trouble. Mason knew when something was up with his brother.

Regardless, they finished in the basement and Russell went home after a nicely-cooked meal in Felicity's newly-organized kitchen. It wasn't until about a week later when Mason made the discovery. The living room ceiling fan had broke, and the heat was blistering. Having the windows open wasn't helping, so he trudged down to the basement to get some tools. He almost considered inviting Felicity down there with some chairs so they could relish the cool temperature, but she refused on the account of her arachnophobia. He pulled open one of the drawers of the tool chest as it unhitched from its rolling sliders, spilling and crashing on the dirt floor. Felicity of course gave a concerned yell from the top of the stairs, to which he grumbled an agitated affirmation in response. He sighed and returned the drawer into its proper place, picking up the tools one by one and setting them back inside. It was the wrench that caused his fall. He had taken a step to retrieve a screw driver when his foot planted on the perched wrench; it was so rusted and old it practically blended into the dirt floor. He tripped and fell back, naturally trying to grab the wall on his way down but instead managed to pull one of the smaller stones right out. The few surrounding it crumbled and gave way without support; the foundation down there was so old that it was no wonder they were loose.

But perhaps they were loose for a reason.

Mason muttered some curse words and wiped his hands across his jeans, giving a cough as he pushed himself back onto his feet and noticed the hole in the wall. His eyes cocked some confusion at first as he stepped closer to investigate. It was hollow on the other side. He stuck his hand through to make sure. There was definitely a room or area inside. He could have easily saved himself the trouble and replaced the fallen stones, but curiosity had gotten the best of him. He wanted to explore. He felt like an archaeologist. Although the outcome would probably be boring, it still would've been neat to see what was on the other side. So he snagged a crowbar from the tool chest and pried the hole into a bigger opening, being careful not to let the whole section come down on him. The stones fell easily, kicking up some dust and dirt. When it had cleared and the opening was big enough to duck through, Mason called up to Felicity about his discovery. A hole in the wall didn't seem impressive enough to drag her away from her "who's-got-the-next-singing-talent" reality show. She merely commented how it would only be more work for him to clean up. But Mason didn't care. It would give him something productive to do. He grabbed a flashlight and clicked it on, ducking through the opening. He was in a room of some sort; there didn't appear to be anything in it except something on the floor in the center. The beam of his flashlight caught a hanging chain for a light bulb. He tugged and the lone bulb above didn't illuminate, so after grabbing a new one and screwing it in, he tried again, and this time, it blared to life. The room seemed much like the rest of the basement, with old stone walls and a solid dirt floor. He didn't need his flashlight but used it anyway to highlight the door in the center of the floor, slightly elevated with a five-inch border around. The space itself appeared to be about forty by forty inches.

What was a door doing in the floor of a sealed-off room in a basement? He wondered if it was perhaps some sort of bomb shelter, or hideout, or storage space for some kind of illegal activity. What was most peculiar was the old rusted lock snapped around the handle. The room was already sealed off. Why was it necessary to lock this door within? Now his curiosity was peaked. He simply stepped back through the wall opening and grabbed a hammer. Whoever locked the door surely didn't go through enough trouble to ensure basic tools wouldn't hinder their attempt. Mason excitedly called back up to Felicity. He was practically begging. She finally trudged her way down the steps (pausing her reality show with one of those digital recorders Mason didn't even know how to operate), mustering unnerving statements about the basement's conditions before stopping at the hole in the wall to place her hands on her hips. She threatened that if there wasn't some kind of buried treasure hidden inside, she was going back upstairs. Mason took her hand with a smile that couldn't even be removed with the crowbar and hammer he was holding. She tugged back, reluctantly fighting to not subject herself to the dark confines of the hidden room, but he assured her there was nothing with more than six legs inside (which nearly got her to laugh; he was always good at that in scary situations).

Felicity finally caved and ducked through the opening with him as he gestured to the door in the floor. She told him there was probably a good reason the room was sealed and the door was locked, and he reassured her that no one would bother without something important being involved. Maybe it was her buried treasure. It slightly perked her optimism, so she let him crouch down and work at the lock without further hesitation. The lock was old and rusted, so it didn't take too much to break it off with the simple hammer and crowbar. He tossed it aside and got to his feet, grabbing the door handle as the brown rust chipped into his sweaty palm. He lifted the door as the hinges creaked and moaned, setting it back on the other side of the floor. Felicity hovered over him from behind, trying to look down as he picked up his flashlight and blared it into the black square darkness. "What is it?" she asked.

"I don't know," Mason answered with some shared confusion.

He got on his stomach and tipped over the edge, hanging his arm into the hole to shine his flashlight at nothing but pure blackness. "There's no steps," Felicity observed. "Where does it go?"

"I can't see a damn thing," he told her. "Whatever it is, it's deep."

He shuffled himself back up and looked around, stopping his eyes at the rubble of the hole in the wall. He retrieved a good sized stone and came back to the hole, getting on his knees and dropping it in to give a listen. No sound ever came. It was like an empty void, but with a small, light whistling sound, almost like wind, or a breeze. He looked back up over his shoulder at Felicity and asked if she had heard the stone hit the bottom, but she merely shook her head. He dipped his attention back into the hole and called out, hoping to make some kind of determination through the echo of his voice — but there was no echo. Now Felicity was fully submerged in curiosity. She had joined him on her knees, trying to get a better look herself. Mason suggested that perhaps they hadn't heard the rock hit the bottom because it was soft dirt. It was the most logical explanation. He wanted to take a chance and jump down, but Felicity insisted against the idea. Even if he had landed safely, they still didn't know how deep it went. There might not have been a way back up. Mason suggested it could've been a tunnel for some kind of smuggling or underground railroad for slavery, but again — there was no telling where it went or if the other end was sealed off. Mason took the next measure of investigation and dug through his tool chest to pull out one of the few flares he had been keeping for years — the flares that Felicity had always said were useless sitting in a box or a tool chest rather than in a vehicle for emergency purposes like intended. She figured it was a guy thing; just simply having them meant boasting a sense of macho character. Now Mason figured he finally had a good use for them. He snapped and cracked the top, bursting the room with a bright red shade from the blazing tip as Felicity squinted and briefly shielded her eyes. Mason dropped the flare into the hole, and the couple watched, following the red trail as it spun its way down into the black darkness, growing smaller... smaller... and smaller... until they couldn't make it out anymore. They exchanged speechless expressions.

It wasn't a tunnel.

It wasn't a storage space.

It was a hole.

And it was *deep.*

Perhaps it was the idea of not knowing an answer that filled Mason with such a sense of intrigue. For Felicity, it was simple fear. The flare's unhelpful light really put her nerves on edge. She wanted to call someone, maybe someone from the environmental protection agency or something. Maybe the fire department. She asked if Mason remembered the realtor mentioning anything about it, but he didn't. They even looked over what blueprints they had for the house, but didn't see anything about it. Mason wanted to try one more experiment before going to anyone, so he called up Russell to meet him at a home construction store. They came back to the house later with about two hundred yards worth of rope. Felicity immediately exploded into a fit about either of them going down into the hole, but Mason calmed her erratic emotions when he came in from the barn with a gray cinderblock. The three went back down into the basement, where Russell wanted to see the mystery for himself. He expected them to be playing some kind of practical joke, but his skepticism was curbed when he noticed the opening in the wall and the hole in the floor within the room. He stared down and studied it for a long moment, grabbing Mason's flashlight and asking if they had performed any kind of light test yet before chuckling it down into the hole.

"Thanks. We already tried that," Mason unbelievably mumbled.

Russell looked back down into the hole just in time to see the last bit of light from the flashlight disappearing below. Mason tightly tied one end of the rope to the cinderblock at the edge of the hole as Russell stood at the wall opening tying the other end around his waist. Very slowly, Mason begin to drop the heavy cylinder block down into the darkness, carefully sliding his hands to give the rope slack. "It's gotta have a bottom eventually," he stated.

His hands slipped and he dropped the rope as the block dropped with full gravitational force. He wasn't wearing gloves (which he regretted) and didn't want to burn his hands, so he arched back as they all watched the large pile of rope begin to unravel. The more that disappeared into the hole, the more their expressions stretched with shock. Felicity's eyes widened. The pile was getting smaller as Mason glanced back to Russell. "Let go of the rope," he told him.

Russell was still too dumbfounded by the amount that had gone into the hole and deadlocked his eyes onto the disappearing pile. "*Let go of the rope!*" Mason shouted this time, and Russell snapped back into life as he tried to untie his waist.

The force was too great as the rope caught up with him, strongly jerking his body to the floor as he slid toward the hole. Mason caught him just in time, hanging over the edge as their fingers twiddled and wiggled to undo the rope around his waist. They finally managed to free him and watched as the last tip of rope snapped over the edge and fell into the nothingness. Felicity closed her eyes and gave a sigh of relief, planting a hand over her forehead. "Jesus Christ," Russell unbelievably blurted as he stared into the hole. "How deep *is* this thing?!"

"Deeper than two football fields," Mason answered with an almost ominous tone.

Now Felicity was terrified. It was a locked door concealing a seemingly bottomless hole in a room that was sealed off. Her heart jumped into her throat every time she looked at it. "No more investigating!" she had ordered. "We need to tell someone about this!"

Mason and Russell were in the same boat. It was too dangerous to fool around with anymore. They would rather have someone of more professional standards come to evaluate the mystery. Mason went to close the hole back up with the door, but Felicity had pulled him back and scolded him to not even go near it. Mason didn't oppose her command and had added that no one should even come back into the room until they got the proper authorities there. They spent the next couple hours around the kitchen table with beers discussing the possibilities and plausible explanations. Russell concocted the idea that they had found a real black hole (in terms of gravitational field) and argued that it was a very sound and scientific notion against Mason's opposition that they were only found in outer space and not within a planet.

It was already too late, so they had agreed that calls would be made the next day after work. Russell had called early that morning and said that his car wouldn't start, so considering how Felicity and him went into work much earlier than Mason, Felicity volunteered to give him a ride. Mason had come home early later in the day, and was surprised to see Russell's jacket slouched over one of the kitchen chairs inside the house. At first he figured he forgot it when he was over the prior night, but then he heard noises coming from upstairs. Maybe Felicity had picked him up from work as well on her way home and brought him over so they could all be there when inquiring minds started arriving. But they weren't in the living room drinking coffee and chatting like a pair of casual sibling-in-laws. They weren't watching TV. They were in the bedroom. They were scrambling to put the rest of their clothes on after Mason had walked in. Shouting erupted. Tension was high. Mason felt like he had walked into some kind of sick, alternate dimension. Was this really happening to him? He couldn't believe it! He felt sick, enraged, confused and sad all at the same time. He didn't know he was capable of so many emotions at once. Russell tried to calm him down. Felicity was in tears, attempting to cover her unfaithful tracks with claims that it wasn't his fault, that it "just happened", that it "didn't mean she didn't love him".

It was like flipping a light switch off. Suddenly, Felicity was a different woman in his eyes. Mason's stomach twisted and coiled with the thought that she could be with another man let alone his own brother — his own flesh and blood, his best friend. The pair pleaded for Mason to calm down and talk about their infidelity, but he was too unbalanced. He stormed out of the bedroom and ran down the stairs as Russell took a delaying moment to call out and chase after him. Mason made his way to the basement and to the tool chest, where he grabbed a hammer. He wasn't sure what his intentions were. It's not like he wanted to kill his own brother. But he needed something. He needed something to smash something else with. Russell came to the bottom of the stairs; his button-down shirt uneven because of the quick change as he calmly waved his hands. "Come on, man, just... take it easy. Let's just talk about this. Put the hammer down. I'm your brother," he gently pleaded.

"That's right! You're my brother! You're not suppose to fuck my wife!" Mason yelled back.

Russell agreed with everything he had to say. He said he was an asshole for doing what he did, and he wasn't thinking. He deserved everything bad he had coming to him, but he also deserved for Mason to give him a chance to talk things out. He claimed it wasn't about love. Mason was already tired of hearing it. The damage had been done. Russell slowly crept closer, holding out a caring hand. Mason took a swing. Russell caught his wrist, and the two fought, spinning and turning in circles and crashing against the tool chest and hard stone walls. Punches were thrown. They hit the floor and rolled, wrestling a bit. Mason grit his teeth and dragged Russell back onto his feet as they fell through the opening in the wall. Mason threw a punch into Russell's side and clutched his neck. Russell came back with a kick, and Mason strongly flung him off as he rolled across the floor and into the hole, clutching the sides and calling out for help. Mason stared and then sprung himself back into reality. He quickly jetted over and dropped to his knees, grabbing Russell's arms as his legs freely kicked in the open darkness. At first, Mason tried to pull him up, but he couldn't get a good enough grip. His hands began to slip. Russell cried out in fear. His arms finally slipped through Mason's sweaty hands as his screams faded into the darkness below. Mason sat looking down; his jaw dropped and his eyes unblinking with an astonished freeze.

Felicity watched from the opening in the wall with her hands placed over her mouth. "Oh my God," she managed to mumble as she slowly crept in. "What have you done?" She walked over and helplessly dropped to her knees over the edge of the hole, peering down. "What have you done?" she repeated. "He was your brother!"

Mason stared down at her as she shouted for Russell into the hole. *He was your brother.* The thought rattled through Mason's mind. But as much as he felt in terrible shock for what he had just done, the anger overpowered his emotions. His breathing grew heavier. There was no forgiveness. She had hurt him in a way he never thought could've happened to him. Up until then it was only fiction in movies and television — articles in newspapers. She could easily do it again. He wouldn't live as a pushover. He deserved better than that for who he was and what he had done for her. Before he knew it, he raised his shoe and planted it against the jeans of her rear end, firmly pushing and sending her head-first down into the hole as her shriek trailed into the blackness. He collapsed against the wall and slid to the floor, eyes lost across the dirt.

He contemplated making the originally intended calls to the authorities, but now Felicity and Russell's disappearance (and possible murders) were thrown into the equation. His good conscience proposed that maybe they were okay, and informing the police could possibly help rescue them. But reality pointed to the notion that they couldn't survive a fall that deep, if there even was a bottom. He had gone past the point of no return. Things would never be the same even if he could manage to get them back.

Mason closed and sealed the door with a whole new padlock. He clicked the pull string to the light bulb off and worked all night at re-sealing the wall with the same large stones that had encased its secret to begin with, doing quite the good job at blending it in with the remaining surroundings. He shifted the large tool chest over in front of it just in case. It didn't matter, anyway. Even if someone noticed and linked their disappearances to being somewhere behind the wall, they'd only have a bottomless pit to look into.

The rest was easy. Mason started by driving Felicity's car back downtown to the parking lot of the offices where she worked while it was still dark before the sun came up. Since there was no pay required, tickets distributed or any sort of security, there would be no record of the vehicle entering or leaving. It was simply... there. Mason took a cab home and phoned the police. He informed them that he hadn't seen or heard from neither his wife or brother since they left for work the prior morning. He went on to describe how his brother had called needing a ride and she had agreed to take him (which was true!). The police in turn got back to Mason later by saying they both were seen at work as usual and left at their usual times, but Felicity's car was still in the parking lot, and then went to grill him on if they had been acting suspiciously and if he had seen anyone following them and all the like. Mason added that he suspected they were having an affair and his brother had recently told him he had met a woman and was toying with the crazy idea of leaving everything behind to run away with her (which was also true!). Through the following days, the deduction was determined by the authorities that they could have possibly run away together after work, leaving behind their vehicles, clothes and not touching their monetary assets, although Mason was sure they wouldn't disregard the notion of his own fowl play so easily. But since all of Mason and Russell's relatives were dead, and Felicity had a sister across the country she hadn't spoken with in over a decade, their missing presence would not be a pressing issue to anyone. They had enough substantial evidence to prove that they just up-and-left together, and they had no evidence to prove that Mason was necessarily involved. Mason asked one of the officers why they wouldn't take any money with them (he was trying to be convincing with the old "hide-things-right-in-the-open" tactic), and the officer explained that it was entirely possible for two people to start brand new, especially in this electronic age, with new identities. Mason was just going to have to move on with his life.

In was months later in mid-October when two detectives had rolled into Mason's driveway while he raked the colorful leaves in his front yard. His heart skipped a beat. Four months and it seemed like he had gotten away with it. But what could they possibly want after all that time of no new evidence? They flashed their badges and presented their names with titles, going on to add, "We have news regarding the disappearance of your wife and brother, if you wouldn't mind taking a ride downtown with us."

News? What news? How could they have news? It may have been Mason's first cover-up, but he was sure all the angles had been covered. He cooperated and got into the car, where they drove unable to officially divulge any information before getting downtown. Half an hour later, Mason was sitting in an interrogation room, being asked his whereabouts around a certain time on the 14th — just two days earlier. He told them he was at work, and they came back shortly after notifying him that his alibi checked out. They performed a quick bank check, seeing if any abnormal cash withdrawals or purchases had been made recently. They asked if he had gone on any trips. Now he was getting agitated. "What is this all about?" he huffed. "I thought you said you had information on my wife and brother?"

The first detective, a tall one, looked at his shorter partner and then returned his eyes to Mason. "We've identified your brother's body through the wallet in his pants. He was found in Lake Michigan. Two eyewitnesses fishing on a boat Tuesday apparently... saw him fall from the sky. They also claimed they heard or saw no plane, which could've been possible considering its altitude, but our records show nothing in the area around that time. However, the matter's still under investigation."

Mason was flabbergasted. He didn't know what to say. His eyes dropped to the table where his Styrofoam cup of aged water sat. It had been four months. *Four months.* When he finally managed to speak, he came out with, "You... You said something about my wife, too."

"If it weren't for the driver's license in her pants, we wouldn't have been able to identify what was left of her body. She also apparently fell from the sky and landed on a building in Cairo."

"Cairo? Where's that?" Mason asked.

"Egypt," the tall detective stated.

SAVE FILE AS...

There was Kyle Bernstein in Des Moines, Iowa. He downloaded it around the time the website first went live at the beginning of October. Then two days later he was hit by a bus. Then there was Chin-Lai Wan in Hong Kong, who downloaded it and got some bad take-out from a fast food restaurant; his body slowly decaying and expiring over the course of an unexplainable fast week. DeShawn Michaels in New York City downloaded it and a steel beam from a construction building accidentally fell on him. Courtney Fuller of San Diego, California, downloaded it and through circumstances crossing the street was collateral damage when she got shot by bullets meant for the police from some desperate escaping bank robbers. The beautiful temptress Estefana Consuela of Curitiba, Brazil, downloaded it and had an unfortunate mishap with the brake system of her new Porsche when she uncontrollably veered off a bridge. There was Antoine Demarco from Paris, France, who downloaded it and fatally discovered he had a faulty gas line in his apartment — only after lighting a cigarette, of course. Veronika Vladesmer of Novgorod, Russia, downloaded it and was subjected to a nasty life-ending case of some untreated tetanus when she stepped on a rusty nail in her cousin's workshop. There was Holly Muller in Redfield, South Dakota, who downloaded it and had her beautiful golden-haired head decapitated from the passing propellers of a crashing helicopter at the town's annual Halloween fair. Bernard Hoffman, Newcastle, Australia. Tom Caulier, Toronto, Ontario in Canada. Lisa Lippman, vacationing in Cancun, Mexico. Many, many others.

And now it was Grant Summers. He sat at his desk in his dorm room in Williamsport, Pennsylvania, staring at the dark computer screen with the rectangular-boxed red button in the center reading "I AGREE" in some kind of old Victorian font. "I don't know about this," he said into the cell phone pressed against his right ear and shoulder.

"Dude! Don't puss out! Just do it! And then burn it to a disc for me!" said the voice of Rick, his friend, on the other end of the line. "Come on!"

"I already told you — I'm done downloading stuff. I already got that notice from Universal Pictures," Grant firmly said.

"Seriously, man, those are nothin'. Nothin'! Just warnings. How many people other than yourself do you know who have actually gotten those things? None. It's a like a parking ticket! It means nothing! You crumple it up and throw it away. Or in this case, hit the delete button," Rick pleaded. "Come on! You're the only person I know who's gotten the e-mail invite."

"Let's just rent some movies. Some classic *good* Halloween stuff for tonight. Like that awesome haunted hayride one with those killer brothers both named Bobby. Remember that one? I mean, how good can *this* movie really be?"

"People are saying it's the best horror movie ever. It makes all the *Saw* movies look like "Sesame Street"."

"Bloodgame? Sounds like a cheesy B-movie title. If it's so good, why isn't it in theaters? Why are they only sending out these limited e-mail invites to illegally download it?" Grant argued.

"That's how they market these days. Online is the new multiplex. They get a huge following by word-of-mouth and telling you and showing you nothing about it, and it drives people crazy. Like that *Paranormal Activity* bullshit. Except *this* won't suck!" Rick explained.

Grant scratched his head and turned in his swivel chair. "Have you even been reading all this stuff online about people supposedly dying after downloading it?"

Rick gave an unbelievably groan. "Tell me you're not buying into that. Grant, it's a marketing ploy. These movie studios hire a few guys to run around on the 'net and post some bogus stories saying that anyone will die after downloading it. You go onto the movie message boards and see all these postings that are titled with things like, "My friend died after downloading this!" and "Is this movie cursed?" and it's nothin' but a way to generate buzz. Creates curiosity. All it takes is for some poor sucker to coincidentally die the next day and suddenly the studio is raking in blissful interest from a new public-created Halloween urban legend."

"They're not making any money, though. It's just a download."

"Have you been listening to a word I've been saying? You don't get it! They do this on purpose! Then after a while they'll put it into theaters and make serious ticket sales," Rick elaborated. "Now if you're not gonna download it, forward me the damn e-mail and I will."

Grant sighed. "I'll think about it," he told him. "Look, I got some stuff to finish. I'll be by your place around seven tonight."

"Bring the movie or I'll cut your dick off!" Rick barked, then hung up.

Grant set the phone down and stared at the screen. He hovered the mouse cursor over the "I AGREE" button and set his chin on his other fist, contemplating. There was a bunch of fine-print gibberish at the bottom of the page which he soared the cursor over and circled back up onto the button, shaking his head and clicking the mouse. A pop-up box sprang up on the screen with a file directory, and the task bar read, "Save file as..." with the highlighted file name "BLOODGAME.avi" already listed. Grant took a breath and clicked the "DOWNLOAD" button within the box, and the pop-up box minimized down to the bottom of his screen as it starting downloading with an ETA finish time of approximately 51 minutes and 34 seconds. He got up out of his chair and started making his Ramen Noodle lunch among other small activities while his computer chipped away at retrieving the video file.

A few hours later, after the movie had been saved to his desktop and he burned it onto a blank DVD-R for the whiney Rick, he grabbed his jacket and made his way through the building, where plenty of Halloween costume parties were raging with half-naked angel girls and toga-sporting jock guys. He made his way to the parking lot and hopped into his beat-up Sedan, soon coasting down Main Street past all of the tiny trick-or-treaters, flashing a quick reminiscing smile. Then the car started making strange noises. Grant gave a tired moan, dreading the thought of spending more countless dollars tuning the car back into passable shape. The muffler sputtered and smoke started to sift. The electronics fizzled and blinked as the speedometer began to drop, slowing him to an eventual stop as he unbelievably tossed his hands up. "Great. Just perfect," he muttered.

Then he heard the train whistle. He snapped his attention up and looked all around, noticing the red-flashing gates dropping in front and behind him. Terror filled his eyes as he saw the train engine coasting at high speed to his left. *He had stalled on the tracks.* His hands fumbled to grab the door handle, giving a pull but the door wouldn't budge. He tried hitting the unlock button, but it seemed to be jammed. Panic took over. He squeezed his thumb against his seatbelt button, but that didn't budge open, either. He tried crawling out of it, but there wasn't enough space. He shot his attention back out his window as the engine came speeding. His breaths shook. He slammed his eyes shut tightly and grit his teeth, bracing his body as the engine blasted into the car — and then everything went black.

Grant woke up with a slight gasp, trying to comprehend where he was. He was sitting in a chair in the waiting room to some office building. A few sharply-dressed receptionists answered constant calls from ringing phones at the desk in front of him. Grant cleared his throat and rubbed his eyes as the repetitive "Please hold" and "One moment, please" constantly came from the women. One wearing a headset finally looked over to him. "Mr. Summers? You can go in now," she told him.

He shifted confused eyes over to her. "What? Where am I? How did I get here?" he groggily wondered.

"Right through those doors, please," the receptionist directed him with a point before going back to her incoming calls.

Grant stood up, turning in a circle before walking over to the large doors. He opened them and entered inside, turning his head to gaze at the large office room. Long black curtains were draped over the tall windows. Some misshapen art sculptures decorated the area. A man looking to be in his mid-forties dressed in a sharp black suit with neatly-styled black hair stood up from a large chair behind an even larger desk. "Ah, Mr. Summers. Please, have a seat and make yourself comfortable," he gestured to one of the chairs in front of the desk. "Gonna be your last chance for it."

"Where am I?" Grant asked, looking around as he reluctantly sat. "Who are you?"

"Just think of it as... your new job. And I'm your new boss," the man stated. "So tell me, did you get to watch the movie?"

"What?" Grant oddly said in confusion.

"Bloodgame. Title kinda sucks and there could've been more tits, but I'm more of a torture guy, anyway," he stated. "Always a shame when I hear that someone didn't end up watching it before going. I mean, you agreed to the contract and everything; you'd think that if you're going down, you'd at least make it worth while and watch the damn thing, right?"

"Contract? What contract? I didn't agree to any contract," Grant sharply noted.

The man sat back in his chair and pulled out a cigar from a box, cutting the end off and wiping away some of the papery mess. "People these days. So eager... so anxious. Everything's click-click-click. It's so easy. It's hardly a challenge anymore. A quill pen used to be such a powerful tool. But now everybody expects everything to be free and fast. As long as you've got the hard drive space, it doesn't take long to download and it doesn't cost anything, people want it. They'll click on anything. Fake eBay e-mails asking them to sign in with their password. Bank notifications pretending to need account numbers. People have gotten so dumb it almost makes me sick."

Grant stood up out the seat and calmly waved his hand. "Look, I don't know where I am, how I got here, or who you are, but I never signed any contract, and if you're saying I did, I want a lawyer."

"You don't need a lawyer, Grant. You did such a nice job under your own willpower by agreeing to the contract. I never said you signed one. Not all contracts are signed. Some are clicked. Only people are so busy clicking, they don't care what the fine print at the bottom of the page says as long as they don't get caught downloading," the man said, sticking the cigar in his mouth as he pulled out a sheet of paper and continued by reading from it: "By clicking "I Agree", the individual downloader agrees to all terms set forth by the website moderators and relinquishes all rights to any personal, private and professional information with any associated inner body account to be collected by said moderators at a determined time and location set at their discretion."

Grant furrowed his eyebrows. "Inner body? What is that supposed to mean?"

Skeletons in the Closet

The man chewed his cigar and gave a grin. He snapped his fingers, and a single small flame of fire sparked up at the tip of his thumb, which he used to light the cigar. "Your soul," he replied.

TRINETTE GIVES EVIL THE FINGER

"I don't think you're reading the screen correctly!" the tall, slightly balding asshole barked from across the counter.

Trinette closed her eyes and sighed. Her day had been going so well, too. And she was nearly at the finish line. She didn't want to work Halloween. She had too much on her plate already to be there in the video store getting verbally bent over by a customer who couldn't tell his right from his left. He rambled on and on as the waiting customers watched. She didn't deserve this! She was intelligent. She was resourceful. She should've been out in the world somewhere, teaching or helping someone of better stock value. Instead, she was stuck at that dead-end job in her mid-twenties waiting for calls and e-mail responses that never came, getting abused every which way every day by lowly over-stressed renters who thought they were the salt of the earth. Was it too much to ask to come into a simple job every day and process a transaction without a fucking national catastrophe happening over three measly dollars?! It didn't make sense. She was a good person. She deserved better than that.

She considered letting the middle-aged crybaby have his way so she could get on with her night, but he had already slammed his intended movie rentals onto the counter, storming off with the usual, "Shove it, bitch! I'll rent somewhere else!"

She had a right to kick his ass for saying that. And if it was her last night working there, she probably would've. But alas, she wiped the insulting shoe marks off her face and continued with the next customers in line. Trinette — the human punching bag. It's not like she didn't have attitude. She did give a damn every once in a while, just out of plain respect for herself. One of the finer examples was later that night, when the two punk-thugs with the pants hanging off their asses came strolling in; the taller one cruising into the video game section while Trinette's co-worker Nate re-shelved some returns. The thug had casually slipped a copy of a Madden NFL game into his jacket while the suspecting Nate ran the old "Are-you-ready-to-check-out-with-that?" routine, to which he got the snappy reply, "No, man — I'm ready to *take* this mutha fucka! Whatchu gon' do 'bout it? Huh? I could take this, and this, and this," he cunningly stated as he blatantly shoved multiple games into his jacket. "And there ain't a *damn thing* you can do about it!"

"Uhhhh, yeah, dude, that's not cool," Nate had retorted, unsure whether the thief was joking or not.

The thug had turned (his accomplice already bolting through the exit door) and calmly walked through the security sensors, which blazed and loudly rang. Trinette, who had caught wind of the scene from behind the counter, reflexively took a hop and jumped into the thug's path as he stopped and bent intimidating eyebrows down at her short stature. "Bitch, you better get out of my way before I stomp yo' ass," he ordered.

"Happy Halloween," Trinette muttered, stepping back to grab and innocently hold out a small bowl of candy to him.

He slapped his hand up into the bowl as the candy flew everywhere and pushed his way out the door. You think she'd put her ass on the line for a few video games and the pocket-change-an-hour wages she made? Hell no! Still, it was demeaning and humiliating — having to put up with stupid things like that on a daily basis, and Halloween was when the stakes were raised with all the additional nut-jobs that came in to claim their free rental for being dressed up.

But tonight was different.

Tonight was the night she waited for all year long. It was like three-hundred-sixty-four days' worth of lame bullshit just compiling and filling her to the brim, waiting to be unleashed and explode like a volcano. Any time someone went to open their mouth, she was tempted to say, "I'm Mount Trinette! Step off or I'll blow, mother fucker!" Because tonight was her yearly tradition of *not* getting walked on by society. For one night only, she wasn't a video store clerk. She was a badass!

The store had closed early around eight that night being Halloween, and after Trinette had locked the doors and Nate coasted away in his car, she scoured the area with her eyes. It was all clear. No one was around, being that all the stores in the plaza were now closed for the night, so she hoofed over to her car and popped the trunk. She took her ugly polyester uniform off to reveal a dark undershirt that already matched her pants and slipped on a long similar overcoat, then tied back her long black hair before completing the ensemble with some black gloves. Beneath the cover flap in the trunk, she pulled out a long, silver sword and admired it with a keen grin from top to bottom as it gleamed in the moonlight. She slid it into a custom pocket sheath inside her long jacket and reached back into the trunk, clicking open a suitcase that revealed a series of knives, daggers, shurikens, liquid vials and other small objects one might think belonged to a stealthy ninja of some sort. She loaded the weaponry into her belt and array of jacket pockets, then pulled out a small container holding two contact lenses. She dipped her index finger into the solution and hooked one, plucking it into her right eye and slightly rolling it to make the comfortable adjustment. A somewhat high-tech computer screen popped onto her view, with "SIGNING IN... AGENT 1218... NYS ZONE 52-1... CODE NAME: ARWEN".

She closed the trunk. Now she was ready. She began to walk across the barren parking lot. Of course, part of her wanted to go out and party like her friends, or stay home with her dog and hand out candy to all of the little adorable tykes, but she had a job to do. Even if it didn't know it, the community depended on her tonight. She made her way out of the plaza and down the street, turning into the first residential neighborhood, where dozens upon dozens of kids ran around trick-or-treating, some with accompanying adults. She eagerly rubbed her hands together. Go time. The computerized contact lens in her right eye scanned the kids as she looked at each, highlighting them with a light green night vision-colored glow before stopping on one in the bunch whose outline flared with a bright blinking red. The tiny words "TARGET AQUIRED" sprang onto her vision as she stiffened her jaw and cracked her knuckles. "Gotcha," she murmured softly out loud.

She steadily walked toward the house and stopped at the end of the driveway as the group of excited kids were greeted at the door by an elderly gentleman who disbursed various pieces of candy into each of their waiting bags. One by one, they left, some following friends to the next house while others trailed across the street. Trinette's eyes sternly followed the kid in the werewolf costume — the one that had blinked red on her tracking screen — as he walked alone in the opposite direction from the others. She began to casually follow; her right hand smoothly reaching into her jacket as she gave a nod. "Hey — trick-or-treat, jag-off," she called out.

The werewolf turned, squeaking an "Oh, shit!" from beneath his mask as he took off running across the grass.

Trinette gallantly pulled her sword, chasing after him as he constantly looked over his shoulder to spot her gaining. He tossed his bag of candy to run more easily. Trinette jumped onto the hood of a car and quickly footed up onto the roof, taking a running leap off as she soared through the air and raised her sword. First of the night. It was always her favorite. She felt like she was in some slow motion action movie like *300*. The werewolf kid craned his neck to look back at her, pumping his fists as she swung the sword from passing above and lopped his head off, landing on her feet. The masked cranium bounced and rolled some ten feet or so down the road while the body tilted and swayed, bursting into nothingness as the remaining costume dropped to the pavement.

If she were making a tutorial video, this would probably be the part where she would calmly assure the viewer that she did not just decapitate some teenage candy collector. Instead, she thwarted a problem. A problem every All Hallow's Eve, when spineless, evil, mischievous lowlife demon dickheads came out disguised like innocent trick-or-treating children in order to steal souls! "Ever walk around on Halloween night and see pieces of costumes and lost candy sacks lying in yards or on the road?" she would probably coyly ask any watching trainee. "Those are the remains of unfortunate victims who had their souls sucked out of their Harry Potter-costumed asses by the cool Buzz Lightyear kid who claimed to only want to show them his awesome laser."

Every year, thousands of kids across the country go missing on Halloween night, but have no fear, parents — that creepy old guy inviting your child inside his house isn't a crazy pedophile. It's just a demon, that's all. And that slightly older kid with the cool-looking bloody knife going into his head isn't inviting your susceptible pre-teen children to follow him into the woods to get high on the darn marijuana — it's just an unholy lying asshole demonoid prick interested in sucking their life force through a straw like a Slurpee! That's where people like Trinette come in — agents of good employed by a secret organization to perform some low-radar ass-kicking and stop the problem before it starts! All with her sharp weaponry (silver-induced, of course, since demons can only be diminished by silver and a limited number of other things) and high-tech computer contact lens which gave a thermal readout of her targets since the body temperature of a demon was much, much higher than a human's. She had been doing it for five years now. No one knew. Not her parents, not her brother, not her friends. She had been giving up her personal fun every 31st of October for the better of the mankind. But to her, it *was* fun! It was her outlet to relieving the everyday stress of life. She always looked at it as if it were a "Superman Syndrome" — by Halloween day, she was still the helpless, dorky Clark Kent that everyone walked all over at the video store, but once night had fallen, she became Superman! Err, Super*woman*, anyway. You get the point.

A small, red digital counter in the top right corner of her eye changed from "TARGETS AQUIRED: 000" to "TARGETS AQUIRED: 001". Now the yearly tradition had been kicked off. It was like a collage of awesomeness over the next hour! Trinette had sliced and diced her way through dozens of neighborhoods across town. She jumped down from a tree in a yard onto a passing costumed demon. She had another in a headlock, using her other fist to punch his stomach over and over. She shoved another's head through a parked car's window. She ran up to a house, pushing her way past a group of kids on the porch, yelling, "Move, move!" only to stick her sword through the Grim Reaper-dressed individual giving out the candy. His body poofed into a burst of smoke as the clothes dropped. The kids all screamed, running away. At another house, she casually lied against a haystack at the bottom of the porch, sticking her leg out to trip a trick-or-treater who fell forward and impaled himself into her sword sticking up between the steps as his body disappeared into air. She walked to the next neighborhood, approvingly nodding her head as she bit into a candy bar from a sack. She beat up another kid. She chased two more down the street and flung two of her jagged-starred shurikens, easily hitting them from behind as their bodies exploded into soft smoke.

She cut another one down in front of a closed door, picking up its candy sack as an actual teenage trick-or-treater ran over and excitedly gouged his hand into the bowl of king-sized candy bars waiting at the footstep. "Hey!" Trinette firmly huffed, threateningly drawing her sword. "The sign says to take only *one*, dip-shit!" The teenager, fearing for his life, quickly dropped the pile back in and took only one, running away. Trinette unbelievably shook her head and bent down, picking up the bowl to empty it into her sack.

She took another disguised demon into a headlock elsewhere, gritting her teeth as she tried to snag his candy bag. "Gimme it! I said gimme it! I know you've got one in there! Give up the Butterfinger or I swear I'm seriously gonna get Middle Earth on your wicked ass, bitch!"

Decapitations. Dismemberments. Traps. Ass-kickings. All part of a good night's work, and it was only a little after nine-thirty. It was Friday, so this year kids would be out a little later which meant a heavier work load for her, but still, things were already beginning to wind down. Trinette had taken a small break, creaking back and forth on a wooden porch swing in the front yard of someone's uninhabited dark house as she chewed some candy and lightly kicked her feet like a content youngster. A group of five costumed kids approached down the sidewalk on the opposite side of the street, passing a heavily-decorated house. Immediately, all five bodies lit up with blinking red shades. Trinette smiled, licking some chocolate off the tip of her finger as she crumpled the wrapper and tossed the candy bag aside. They were *all* demons. Not one real kid around. It was like a sweet, tasty, chewy chocolate peanut cluster fuck of amazingly challenging work for a change. She hopped off the bench and put her gloves back on, trailing across the lawn as she pulled her sword from her jacket.

Then he came out of nowhere. The late-twenties tall guy with short frizzled hair and a neat five o'clock shadow dressed in a similar long black overcoat who pulled a sword and like he was in some kind of Jackie Chan martial arts movie, spun, twisted and jumped his way around to slice up the crew into nothing but empty costumes. Trinette stopped in her tracks and stared as her jaw hung. She couldn't believe it. She scanned her eyes across the cloth-riddled remains and looked at him. "What the fuck is *this* now...?!" she finally managed to blurt.

"Oh. Hey," the man said with a slight nod, re-sheathing his sword. "Nice night, huh? Can't get a better Halloween than *this*."

"Who the hell are *you*?" she snapped.

"Agent Zero-One-Zero-Five," he said, holding out his gloved hand for a shake which she didn't acknowledge. "I'm your replacement."

She cocked her head. "My what?"

"From the agency. I've been sent to take over your zone, NYS Fifty-Two-Dash-One. Would've come a little sooner, but had to finish up with my own zone, PA Thirty-Three-Dash-Five."

"Take over? What are you talking about? I don't need any help. Everything's under control, douche bag," she assured him.

"Not according to the agency. Seems you've been slacking the last two years. Haven't been meeting the zone quota," he told her.

"Zone quota? What zone quota? I've never heard or been told of meeting any kind of requirement quota," she said. "And if there is, it can't be right, because I've been working my ass off tonight and every other Halloween since I started!"

The man pulled out a small notepad, peering down at it. "Agent One-Two-One-Eight, code name Arwen," he said, intriguingly cocking an eye at her. "What's that supposed to mean?"

"It's an LOTR thing."

"What's that?"

Trinette gave a huff. "LOTR? Lord of the Rings? The holy trilogy? One ring to rule them all? It's a character."

The man reached into a sack and pulled out a 100 Grand candy bar, ripping it open and beginning to chew away. "You mean those movies with elves and bows-and-arrows and dancing midgets and shit? So you're one of *those* geeks, huh?"

"The correct fan term is "ringer"," she snipped back. "And who the hell are *you* to judge, anyway? What are *you* into?"

"Twilight," he noted with a shrug.

Trinette's face shifted more into surprise as she curled a smile at the corner of her mouth. "R-Really?"

"No, not really," he flatly responded as her smile dropped.

"And just what did you pick for *your* name, then?" she next asked.

"Dagger."

She crossed her arms and sourly looked away, rolling her tongue in her mouth. "Okay, so that *is* kinda cool, but regardless — why didn't the agency send me some kind of notice?!"

"You're lookin' at him," he answered. "Now if you wouldn't mind removing all forms of weaponry and setting them on the sidewalk, that would be fantastic."

Trinette sharpened her eyes; her mouth still openly ajar. "What? Dude, are you for real?"

"Section Five of Article Seven — all agents no longer in employable service must disband and disarm any agency-provided weapons immediately," Dagger promptly stated as he curiously sifted through more of a candy sack.

"Seriously, you can't do this!" Trinette whined. "Don't I get an opinion in this? Don't I get some kind of second chance, or corrective action write-up or something? Seems a little unfair to take my job away from me when I was unaware of my apparent slacking performance to begin with."

Dagger bit off a piece of a Clark Bar, wondrously admiring it up close. "You never see Clark Bars anymore. It really is a great, underrated candy bar. Who the hell around here is even giving them out? That's like going trick-or-treating for baseball cards and getting a Babe Ruth rookie card from someone," he expressed.

"Please, don't do this!" Trinette pleaded. "I need this job! You have no idea how much I look forward to this night every year! It's like therapy! Not that I need therapy or anything, but if you dealt with all the buttholes I'm subjected to on a daily basis, you'd need a form of extreme physical avocation, too!"

Dagger wiped his hands and stood back fully upright, tossing the candy sack aside as he stared and waited. Trinette sighed. There was no arguing. She carelessly tossed her sword onto the sidewalk and began purging her coat of all the smaller items like the knives and shurikens. She set the final pile onto the sidewalk, but casually sneaked one of the clear liquid vials into her palm, stepping back and giving a shrug. "That everything?" Dagger asked. "No razors hidden in your Arwen undies? You lady agents can be pretty wily."

"Would ya like to check?" Trinette asked in an almost exaggeratingly offended tone, extending her arms out for the invite.

Dagger curved a smile and bent down, starting to retrieve all the weapons and place them inside his overcoat. "Okay, Ms. Attitude — just — step on back now."

"Oh, please," Trinette muttered with the roll of her eyes as she crossed her arms. "You're acting like I'm gonna go freaking postal over losing this job."

"No..." he disagreed, shoving a knife into a custom holder. "I just didn't want you to have any of these when I told you I was really a demon."

She stiffened her eyes down at him, trying to hold back an unsure grin. "I'm sorry? Come again?"

"Yeah, I'm really a demon. All that stuff I just said about being an agent replacing you in your zone? Crap. Works like a charm, though. Humans — so gullible. You make it too easy. Five states and fourteen zones later and it's still funny," he explained.

"Because *that's* believable," she huffed. "I still have my lens in, doofus. You would've showed up on the thermal imaging as a demon."

"Every year, your agency gets better and better with your weapons and war games. Don't you think it's about time we found a way to beat some of your systems?"

Trinette took a cautious step back. She still thought he was yanking her chain, but there was something about him that was toying with her skepticism. "Look, dude — this isn't funny. You're not a demon." His face quickly morphed into a growling, hideously monstrous veneer — flat nose, bad teeth, cat-like pupils and two small horns on top of a sparsely-haired head. Trinette's eyes went wide as her mouth hung with surprise. "Oh, shit. Okay, you're a demon," she mumbled, starting to take a few slow steps backwards.

Dagger casually inched toward her. "You should've seen the look on your face when I told you the agency was replacing you. A quota system? Are you kidding me? It gets funnier every time. At least you didn't cry like that pansy I took out in Wyoming an hour ago."

"Even if you kill me, my lens has recorded everything. The agency will know who you are," Trinette told him.

"Oh, they *already* know. That actually makes it more fun. Fucking with humans is what we do best. You should know that. Besides — all the other agents I've toasted around the country tonight haven't been able to stop me," he maniacally explained. As he crept closer, Trinette's fingers subtly popped the cap off the liquid vial hidden in her gloved hand. "You're actually kinda cute, though. How 'bout it? Give up a little piece and I won't make your untimely demise as painful."

Trinette took a sharp step forward, splashing the liquid from the vial onto his face. He howled in pain, quickly covering his burning and smoking hideous features with his hands. Good old holy water! Excellent for a little demon skin singe. Trinette clenched her jaw and kicked his crotch, sending him down to the sidewalk on his knees as she took off running. "You bitch!" he yelled. "You better run!"

She made her way through the neighborhood, past some occasional trick-or-treaters as Dagger followed not too far behind. She kept throwing her head over her shoulder. She was unarmed and didn't have a plan, but if she could get away, she could contact the agency. She wondered if they had some kind of identity protection program. But it's not like he was a mob boss. He was a goddamn demon! He would find her no matter where she went or who she became. No! She had been kicking demonoid ass every Halloween for five years. He was no different than the rest of the scum she wiped off her shoe. This one just had a little more *oomph* in his attitude. All she needed was a weapon, and then it's on like Donkey Kong, yo! She pushed past some kids on a sidewalk, hearing an outraged obscenity come from one as she blazed across someone's front lawn, unintentionally running over and crushing a lit jack-o-lantern.

A tall, thin, boney teenager with long hair and a skeleton shirt stopped on the driveway and disappointedly sunk his shoulders at the sudden sight of the pumpkin mess. "Aww, maaan," he groaned, turning around to walk away.

Eventually Trinette had exited out of the neighborhood and found herself illegally entering into a carnival. It was packed with joyous Halloweeners and skater teenagers who had nothing better to do with their time. Dagger was still not far behind as she frantically looked for an escape, running past a balloon-popping gaming booth only to skid to a stop and turn back, eyes fully zeroing in on the hanging eleven-inch by seventeen-inch Lord of the Rings Legolas character poster. "No way!" she excitedly belted, reaching into her overcoat to slap a dollar onto the counter.

The booth worker gave her a set of three darts, and she quickly threw them only to have each dully bounce off the balloons in failure. "Mother *fucker!!!*" she bellowed, slamming a fist onto the counter.

Three silver shurikens spun and popped three separate balloons, jerking her attention to see Dagger casually walking toward the booth. She gasped and took off running again as he approached the counter and nodded to the worker. "I'll take the Transformers one," he decided.

The worker blankly looked up to the shurikens sticking in the wall and then reached below the counter to pull out and hand him a rolled poster. Dagger shoved it into his coat and walked onward, seeing Trinette enter a house of mirrors as he gave a grin.

She couldn't remember the last time she was in one. As she passed all of the mirrors, her body reflections inflated, then deflated, went wavy, then her head was huge, then her midsection was bloated between her tiny head and chicken thin legs. She veered and turned corners, feeling her fingertips against the glass for direction until she saw Dagger in each mirror staring at her with a devilish smile. She gasped and turned, smacking her face into a plate of glass. "Just give up, already," Dagger had called out from somewhere — but she didn't know where! "You've got no weapons. The agency won't help you. I'm not like those kiss-ass minions you've been slicing up all night. I'll find you wherever you go."

She was lost in the mirrors. It was like a scene she had viewed out of a thousand movies. Then again, she had seen demon hunting in a thousand movies, and she had lived that every Halloween for half a decade now. "Poor little Agent Arwen," Dagger had continued. "Mucking through every day of your boring life to get to one night of salvation which makes you feel so invincible. You think killing a few mindless demons makes you some kind of hero? You're just like everyone else — completely oblivious to the bigger picture."

Dagger took a few steps. Trinette gasped, reaching out and touching his reflection thinking it was his body. "Not there," he told her. "Am I here? Or am I here?" She managed to turn another corner and stopped with a surprised jolt as she faced him. He threw his head back with a laugh. "You actually thought that was the real me?" he asked. She turned her head away as his smile dropped. "It is," he firmly stated, reaching out to clutch her throat. He lifted her right off the floor; her feet freely kicking as she tried to pry his hand off her neck. "Where's your nerdy fellowship to help you out?" He threw her against one of the walls, shattering the mirrors as she thudded to the floor. "Who are you trying to fool? You would've just gone back to your mundane life tomorrow letting people walk all over you!" he said as he stepped over to her and kicked her in the stomach.

She gasped and huffed, losing her breath as she rolled on the floor. "Agent One-Two-One-Eight? More like Worthless Everyday Job Employee Zero!" he cackled, picking her up and heaving her against the opposite wall, smashing that. He tossed her up as she slammed against the mirrored ceiling, crashing more glass that rained down. He punched and shook her, shoving her back down to the floor. She coughed and groaned, picking up a piece of wood that had fallen from the structure and holding it in defense. He snickered, perking his eyebrows on his ugly face. "What are you gonna do with that? Gonna wave it and cast some kind of Lord of the Rings wizard spell on me?" Dagger taunted.

Trinette spit some blood and veered her eyes up to him. "No, dickhead — I'm gonna kill you with it."

"You dumb bitch. How did you ever make agent? I don't see a bowl of holy water for you to dip it in. And unless it's filled with silver, I'd say you're shit-out-of-luck — story of your life."

"On the contrary," she began to answer, "I'd say I'm in a pretty privileged position, considering how this entire *room* is filled with silver." Dagger's upper lip curled as his smile disappeared at the thought. Trinette raised the stick of wood. "Mirrors, mother fucker," she informed, throwing it up at the ceiling.

Dagger arched his head up, watching the wood knock the sharp piece of jagged mirror barely hanging above his head. "Shit," he softly declared, watching as it zeroed in closer and closer until he was nothing but a pile of clothes and concealed weapons among a light puff of smoke on the floor.

Trinette let out an exhausted breath, resting back on the floor for what seemed like a while. She finally got up and collected all of the weapons within the bodiless overcoat, unveiling the rolled up poster. "And Transformers sucks. Asshole," she muttered, tearing it in half.

The moon still hung high when she had tiredly reached her car in the plaza parking lot where she left it earlier. She called the agency and was debriefed over the next couple hours. They congratulated and praised her. She had thwarted the menace that tore through the country and killed off dozens of experienced agents in a matter of hours that night. She was a hero! In fact, the head honchos seemed very eager and positive about inviting her to participate in special training for the following Halloween with newly updated gear and developmental weapons that could help put an edge over the demon threat's thermal imagery avoidance. She was on cloud nine. She was on top of the world.

Then came November 1st.

Part of her felt like it was a dream. She woke up the next morning in her bedroom exhausted and overtired from her activities, drained of all her excitement and optimism. It was like a kid surpassing the pinnacle of Christmas morning and being filled with the dreadful disappointment of having to wait another year before acquiring that magical special feeling again. Trinette's brother had of course pointed out her bruises and minor injuries that morning over breakfast — "Hey, Netty! What'd you do? Hit yourself in the face playing Lord of the Rings on the Wii?" he said with a mocking laugh.

She came back with a comment on how his girlfriend put his screen name to shame on his Halo video game and she was off to work — off to work in that awful navy blue polyester uniform. She stood behind the counter at a register, boringly processing rental return check-ins as she looked down at her nametag. She wished it read "ARWEN" instead. A customer was arguing with one of the other cashiers over some ridiculous manner of supposedly being charged a fee for not rewinding a DVD. Trinette sighed. The entrance door chimed, and the punk thug from last night strolled in, barely able to walk with his drooping pants and oversized coat. He gave a nodding smile to her and made a bee-line directly to the video game section, grabbing some boxes off the shelf and fearlessly shoving them inside the jacket. He turned and headed for the exit, smirking back in Trinette's vicinity again. She stiffened her jaw. She tried to relax. She wanted to ignore it and let him walk out. But then something happened. She slammed her computer's scanner gun onto the counter and walked over to the security sensor, which had just gone off because of the thug. He stopped and swayed a little, flashing a cool expression and tossing his shoulders. "What? You want some of this? Just get outta my way, girl," he calmly blurted. When it was apparent she wasn't going to budge, he unbelievably shook his head and huffed, stepping forward and bouncing off her firm stance. "Yo, I ain't jokin'. You better think twice about —" he began to say before Trinette had grabbed his right arm, twisting it back as he let out a holler.

"Gimme the games!" she shouted. He struggled, trying to break free as she swung her foot and kicked his right leg out, making him drop to a knee on the floor. "Give — me — the games!" she strongly repeated. "Where are they?! Where the fuck are they?!" She reached inside his jacket and began yanking the game boxes out, throwing them everywhere as customers and cashiers watched in shocked silence. She punched his stomach and jabbed an elbow across his face, pulling and releasing him against the counter. She spun a kick across his face Chuck Norris-style as he dropped to the floor, grunting and crying. She grabbed his shoulders and guided him forward, drilling him head-first through the exit doors and throwing him out onto the sidewalk, where he rolled and painfully cowered into a ball. "Membership terminated — bitch!" she barked. He wept and sobbed as she went to enter back into the store, but not before stopping and turning back around to openly extend her arms out to the sides and pump her chest, giving a "What!"

CHILDREN OF THE WALLS

Skeletons in the Closet

Sable Highland was scooped up into her husband Drew's arms from her seat in the car and gently set into the waiting wheelchair.

She rolled forward a bit across the smooth dark pavement of the driveway and gazed up at the giant house. Or was it a mansion? She wasn't sure how to define it. It was just big. A big, beautiful new home with plenty of space to roll around in. Plenty of empty space, anyway. She looked over at Drew, who pulled some bags out of the car. He probably wasn't even going to be there most of the time. Part of her felt as if she was some dirty, shameful secret and the real reason for the move was so that he would have an excuse not to take care of her. She imagined the Christmas parties, or the Fourth of July cookouts, where all the other pompous men would stand tall next to their supermodel wives, and she would wheel her way over to meet the latest shark of the firm and suddenly be overwhelmed by silent and awkward sympathy, especially from the women. She would *literally* be a charity case for them. They would use her physical status to boost their self morals. In a truthful world they would say, "Look at me, look at me, I'm the pretty wife of a successful Wall Street investment broker and I can do more than screw the pool boy! I can be nice to this woman in a wheelchair! See? I can do good things!" And then her gossiping peers would say, "Oh, that Gloria! So good to the community! Look how nicely she treats that crippled lady!"

It was probably better this way. Out here in Westchester, they couldn't get to her. She'd rather be alone with no friends in a big house almost thirty miles away than have to deal with their bullshit. She wouldn't receive those "stares" that later formulated to conversations when she had wheeled out of the room.

About a year ago, a week before her twenty-ninth birthday, Sable and Drew had gone out with friends and co-workers of his to celebrate the capture of a big client. They had drinks and laughed, danced, then drank some more. Drew always held his liquor well, but that night his judgment was definitely impaired. His sleek Lexus wrapped itself around a telephone pole outside of New Jersey and Sable forever lost the use of her legs while he only earned a few minor scratches and bruises. It was devastating for her, considering she was training to be in the Olympics. Running was her life. And now... she was stuck. Stuck in that stupid wheelchair. It certainly didn't help their marriage much. It now seemed to be more handicapped than her limbs. She and Drew were drifting apart, sometimes going days only saying a handful of words between them. Drew's long hours attributed to much of that as well.

She knew that's why he was moving them out there. It was a new start. For now, he would make the hour-long commute. The money was worth it. He promised it wouldn't be for long and that he would find something more closer, but she wouldn't hold him to that. That darkened part of her suspected this was his way of dealing with their ruptured situation. He wanted to throw her in that big house and drive back to the city, where he could be overwhelmed in his world of phone calls and meetings — things he would probably welcome in place of the saddened silence he was subjected to around her.

Drew closed the doors to the car and carried the bags over to her, where he looked at the new house. "Home sweet home," he tried to say with some enthusiasm, but she knew he was making too strong of an effort.

He set the bags down and went to push her from behind, but she had muttered that she would do it herself so that he could carry the bags. His boasting gesture to take care of her had been well-worn and old. "I've been in a wheelchair for almost a year," she had recently reminded him. "You don't need to wait on me hand and foot anymore. It's time to stop feeling sorry for me and get on with our lives."

He blamed himself entirely, but he was never good with emotions. There was nothing more he could do or say. Neither of them could change things.

So Drew carried the bags as Sable wheeled herself up the ramp leading to the front door. Having such a high income gave Drew the chance to fix up the old house before they had moved in so that it could better suit Sable's conditions. He had inherited it from his old uncle two years prior, who passed away from sickly conditions. The second feature the hired hands had implemented was on the winding staircase going up from the front foyer to the second floor. It was a motorized chair lift. All Sable had to do was park herself next to it and use her arm strength to heave herself into position. Then it was just a matter of some easy electronic controls which leisurely coasted her up where a second wheelchair was waiting at the top. The house was already wide enough in each room for her to navigate through, so there really weren't too many necessary changes made.

Drew stood next to her in the foyer as she arched her head up and looked around. It was quaint and dignified, yet something rustic unsettled her nerves. A cool draft fluttered in through the open door and crawled up her back, brushing her soft brown hair up. "Like it?" Drew asked. It was her first time there. She didn't answer. Her eyes still scanned the surroundings. She wasn't used to living somewhere that big. "He had a pretty cool library. But, uh, you're only allowed to sign out three books at a time, okay?" he added with a smile than eventually dissolved from her lack of response. Nothing worked anymore. They used to laugh. And Drew's attempts were becoming few and far between.

Skeletons in the Closet

Now first nights in new houses are never easy for many people for various reasons. It could be the lack of noise for people from the city — no cars honking or ambulances or police cars wailing into the night a series of blocks over. It could be the strange room with unfamiliar walls to wake up within. For Sable Highland, the sky was the limit. It was anything and everything. She had gone through so much stress and change the past year that any reason could have easily fit for her tossing and turning that evening. Drew was sound asleep. She didn't know how he could nod off so simply. She often wondered if there were any nights since the accident when he couldn't sleep. They had their backs together so many times that there was no way for her to know. It saddened her. A married couple still so young like themselves shouldn't sleep turned away from each other.

She sighed and rested the back of her hand against her forehead. The moonlight from outside was casting the shadows of a giant oak tree's fall leaves across the ceiling, making all sorts of wavy shapes. The old grandfather clock could be heard clicking from the living room downstairs. It wasn't bothersome. She actually wanted more noise so she could fall asleep easier.

And then she got it.

It started off as a light scratching. At first, she thought it was a tree's branch being brushed against the side of the house near their bed, but as she listened harder, she determined that the scratching was from inside the wall. She sat up and brushed her hair behind her ear, listening more intently as the scratching stopped. She took a breath and softly laid back down, setting her head against the pillow and closing her eyes. The sound abruptly returned, but this time more wildly and firm, flashing her eyes back open. *Something was scratching the hell out of the inside wall!* Her heart began to beat just a little faster, and a little harder. It wasn't just scratching now — it was *clawing*. Clawing up and down, back and forth, right beside the bed as she twisted her neck to look at it. The clawing shifted into a tapping, almost as if someone's fingers were playing some kind of flat, invisible piano. It ceased for only a moment, and then there was a faint, light knuckle-induced knock. No, it couldn't have been a knock. Sable pushed herself closer to the backboard of the bed and gently set her ear against the wall, listening.

Thud! Thud! Thud!

A hard pound made her jerk back and gasp! Now she was scared. She quickly reached over and shook Drew. "Drew! Drew! Wake up!" she called out. He groaned, lightly shrugging her off as she shook him harder; her breaths growing more frantic. "Drew!" she shouted.

Drew snorted awake, a bit groggy as he mumbled, "W-What? What?"

"There something in the walls," Sable shakily informed him.

He rubbed his eyes. "What?"

"I heard a noise — in the wall. Something was... scratching. And then knocking."

"It was probably a tree or something," he said with a yawn, lying back on his side.

"No. It was *inside* the wall," she assured him.

"Mice," he simply answered. "It's an old house. They probably like to scratch around in there."

"Mice don't knock," she said. He didn't say anything. Sable gave him another shake. "Drew."

He gave an agitated groan. "What, Sable?" he asked. He flipped he top portion of the blankets off and sat up, giving a listen. "I don't hear anything," he shrugged.

"It was just happening."

"Maybe you were dreaming. It's just an old house. You're gonna have to get used to it," he briskly told her, lying back down.

Sable's nerves were on edge. She took another long, dragging moment to listen, but the sound didn't return. She cowered back down within the covers and huddled herself closer to Drew, who naturally shifted away.

Sable wasn't sure how much sleep she ended up accumulating. She woke up the next morning and Drew was already gone for work. No note, no breakfast together. That's how it had been going for months. He used to kiss her on the forehead before leaving, but she hadn't felt that in a long time. Now, for the first time, she was left alone in that house. After bathing and making herself something to eat, she figured she'd spend a good portion of the day checking out the library. It's not like she had much else to do. For the time being, anyway, she wasn't working, but wanted to find something to constructively occupy her time. Maybe an at-home job — something over the internet. There was really no rush.

She wheeled her way into the study, taking a gander. From what she gathered through Drew's recollection of his uncle, whom he hasn't seen for almost ten years, he didn't seem like much of the reading type. Perhaps with all of his wealth, he wanted to create the illusion of some kind of snobbish intellect. Sable stopped her wheelchair next to one of the tall bookshelves, craning her neck back to look at the unreachable titles high above as she gave a helpless sigh. One more project for Drew to get around to. Regardless, she had plenty of books to choose from off the shelves she could reach, so she started pulling them out one by one, reading the spines and perhaps the quick blurb in the front or back before returning it to its spot. One fell from a higher shelf above, landing on the floor next to her. She gave a strange look, then bent over the side of her wheelchair to pick it up and read the title aloud — "Hansel and Gretel."

Another suddenly fell, plopping onto the hardwood floor beside her. She looked up. That's when she noticed one of the books slowly inching toward the edge of the shelf before teetering over the side and nearly hitting her in the head. Now she was confused. She wasn't even touching the bookshelf unit nor had done anything significant to knock any off. Three more books in various spots began to slowly slide to the edge. *Almost as if they were being pushed.* They fell to the floor one by one as Sable slightly backed her wheelchair up, dodging the raining literature.

Then more books began to fall, some violently thrusting themselves through the air and colliding with the back wall. Sable's eyes widened as she wheeled herself across the room, attempting to hold one arm up to block any that came her way. When the chaos had stopped, she was left sitting and staring at the mess surrounding her with a blank face that shifted to distraught confusion when she heard the knocking coming from the walls. They started one at a time, coming from various spots and getting louder and louder, turning to pounds as she nervously escaped the study.

Sable had called Drew in a fit of hysteria. By the time he got there, nearly forty-five minutes later, the noises had long since stopped. He scoured the mess in the study with a pair of uneasy eyes and his hands on his hips. "Look at this place. You could've waited 'til I got home for me to get the ones you couldn't reach," he briskly said.

"It wasn't me!" she huffed. "That's what I'm trying to tell you! They just started... falling. And flying across the room. Like someone was throwing them."

"These shelves are old and probably uneven or something. The slightest touch to one on a lower spot could've made some of the higher ones fall," he rationally tried to explain.

"That's *not* what happened," she sternly told him. "And there were more sounds coming from in the walls. Scratching and knocking and pounding."

Drew sighed. "Sable, I left early and had to reschedule a meeting with a client. This is your emergency?"

"It was happening! I swear!" she barked back.

Drew hardly said anything after that. He just stewed and cleaned up the mess of books, and every time Sable started to say something, she stopped at the notion that he wasn't going to respond. They went to bed later, backs turned against each other as usual. Sable had a dream that night. It was the same one she usually had — she was running a one-hundred-yard dash and winning, but before she could reach the finish line, her feet tripped up, and she fell forward to get a face full of dirt and dust. Then she couldn't get up. She couldn't move her legs, no matter how hard she tried. She clawed and crawled her way toward that finish line, but it only stretched further and further away from her. She woke in a sweat, sitting up in bed. Drew was unaffected and kept on sleeping. He always did. Sable took a breath and wiped her face, running her hands through her hair. Then she heard some kind of laughter coming from the hallway outside of the bedroom — childish laughter. Playful laughter. It was quick and didn't return, so she chalked it up to her imagination, especially since the window in the room was open and there was a light whistling breeze that night.

Sable found herself getting more and more bored with each day that passed that week. She spent a lot of her time watching TV or surfing the internet on her wireless laptop, trying to find some kind of job that would suit her interests. She had never worked from home before, nor done anything business-wise on the computer, so she didn't know where to start. She took a break sometime in the afternoon, leisurely coasting through the house. She was going through the dining room when she thought she heard childish laughter again — the same tone that had nipped its way through the air a few nights prior. She stopped and listened. It was probably her mind playing tricks on her again. She did notice strange noises coming from the oddest places around the house because it was so old, but this was different. This wasn't some wood creaking, or wind whistling through an open crack. It was specific.

She wheeled her way through the foyer, and the laughter came again, this time much louder. She sharply stopped, looking up to the second floor. It was coming from upstairs. She wasn't imagining it. "Hello?" she called out. "Is anybody up there?"

A giggle came from somewhere in the dark hallway above. Then she heard something else — it was some kind of bouncing noise. She perked her ear and tried to study it, then saw the rainbow-colored rubber ball bounce its way down each curving step and onto the floor, where it finally rolled to a stop near the threshold of the study. Her eyes were deadlocked on it. It definitely didn't belong to them. "Is somebody up there?" she called out again.

There was no answer. She wheeled her way over and picked up the ball, inspecting it in her soft hands. Then came the footsteps. They were very sudden, loud and fast, running across the second floor and making her drop the ball. Now she was freaked out. Someone was up there for sure. It was a kid. They were laughing, and they certainly weren't responding to Sable's inquiries.

She called the police and told them there was an intruder, and after informing them of her condition, they instructed her to wait outside until they arrived. Drew came home shortly after, greeted by the officer at the open front door. "Mr. Highland?" he asked.

"Yeah. What's going on?" Drew wondered.

"Everything's okay. Your wife called and informed us there may have been an intruder in the house earlier, but we found no evidence of any break-in or foul play," the officer explained.

After the police had left, Drew sat at the kitchen table across from Sable, tapping his fingers on the oak. "There was someone here — in the house," she flatly repeated for the millionth time.

"But you didn't see them?"

"I heard them! As clear and plain as I hear you now. There was laughing, and they were running around upstairs," she said. "I didn't imagine it."

"I'm not saying you did. You said it sounded like kids," he added. "Maybe some kids got inside and were playing a prank or something."

"There was a ball," she went on. "It came down the stairs."

"Where is it?"

She didn't have it. Somehow, some way, it had disappeared between the time she had called the police and when they arrived, which she found to be incredibly odd, considering it was sitting on the floor of the main foyer. "I'm not crazy," she told him, shaking her head. "And I'm not just "adjusting". There's something weird with this house. I've been hearing things and now I'm seeing things."

Drew gave a helpless shrug. "What do you want me to do, Sable? Huh? Just tell me. You want to go back to the city? Is that what you're trying to tell me?"

Part of her wanted to jump at that opportunity. Things weren't much different emotion-wise there, but at least she wouldn't be creeped out by the things she had been subjected to since moving to his uncle's house. Then again, part of her didn't want to give up on that new opportunity to change things for the better.

The conversation had ended there, with Drew later that evening at dinner telling her he was staying in the city the next night for some meetings. It seemed just like him to abandon her when she needed him most. It's not like he was putting in a valiant effort to fix the broken rift between them. Now she was going to be left in that house, all alone.

The day next came and went without any incidents or occurrences, and when Sable had gone to bed by herself that night, she managed to surprisingly drift to sleep without any stress. Perhaps it was the idea that she was sleeping alone. She felt guilty and raw to think those thoughts, but it was a faint signal that she was becoming more comfortable without him. Sometime in the dead of night, she was stricken awake by the blankets covering her being tugged and pulled. She slightly turned, curling them back around her and closing her eyes. There was another tug. "Stop," she tiredly mumbled out loud as if it were a routine annoyance. Then she remembered that Drew wasn't there. There was no one sleeping beside her like usual. She slowly re-opened her eyes. The blankets kept tugging. She pushed herself up and turned, brushing the hair from her eyes to see a glowing blue child standing at the foot of her bed. "Help me," he sadly pleaded, reaching out with a small hand. "Help me."

Sable gasped and backed herself into the backboard of the bed, quickly reaching over with a fumbling hand to click on the lamplight. The child was gone. The room was empty. She panted out of breath, turning her head and scanning her eyes. Was she dreaming? Her heart pounded in her chest. She barely got any sleep the rest of the night.

Sable spent the following day juggling a notion she didn't think she could accept. The house was haunted. The thought sounded ludicrous. She never believed she could conjure such a crazy possibility. She thought of any ghost movie or ghost-hunting reality TV show she had ever watched, never assuming that one day she would be in that position. She knew she wasn't crazy. She was hearing and seeing things when Drew couldn't. Perhaps there was a reason behind that. She played around on her laptop for hours, scouring search engine sites for any kind of information on realistic house-hauntings — not the Hollywood stuff — and through her limited research, always came to the same common conclusion… that most ghosts continuously haunting a location were merely looking to be put at rest. Maybe that's why she was the only one experiencing the paranormal occurrences.

Now came the matter of what to do about it. As ridiculous as it sounded, she thought of contacting one of those ghost-hunting crews, but Drew would probably flip out. They had enough problems between them to throw childish ghosts into the mix. She was going to have to take care of this herself. As much as it frightened her, she was actually intrigued. Maybe it was because she had something worthwhile to do. She had a purpose again. She started searching websites again, first starting with that particular house. Nothing came up on it. She was sure if it had a history of haunting, then Drew would've been told about it by his uncle. Then again, maybe his uncle didn't want to lose face or rack up embarrassment with ghost stories. Or maybe the haunting had only started since she and Drew arrived there. But why? From the fleeting moments she had witnessed the child, she remembered that he was modernly dressed, so it couldn't have been a historic matter.

She found a good news article website for the Westchester area and began working her way back, sticking to missing and murdered children. The subject coiled and twisted her stomach into knots. Reading about abductions and accidents was not how she wanted to be spending her day. She did, however, manage to come across a series of related articles from about ten years earlier, when it seemed a few local children went missing. The article headlines read, "SEARCH FOR MISSING WESTCHESTER CHILD ENTERS FOURTH DAY" and "SECOND CHILD GOES MISSING" along with "POLICE — NO LEADS FOR MISSING CHILDREN". There were about five or six kids that had vanished without a trace across Westchester County in a three-month period, and a few more related articles from the outlying areas as well.

Sable was no dummy. She wondered how much Drew had really known about his uncle, other than the fact that he was wealthy and had gotten him his job in the city, as well as obviously leaving the house to him in his will. When Drew had came home later that night, she told him about the apparition she had seen in the bedroom, and then brought up all the information she had gathered. Drew was concerned. He argued that she was letting it all go to her head, and she was conducting a Nancy Drew-like mystery as a way of coping with her boredom. He assured her that as distant as he was with his late uncle, he wasn't the type to go around murdering children. "How well does anyone actually know anybody?" Sable had shot back. "You haven't seen or spoken with him in ten years! Everyone has their dark secrets."

Drew insisted for her to stop meddling. He even threatened to carry her out of the house himself and drag her back to their apartment in the city if that's what it took to get her back to normal. He told her it wasn't healthy. There was no such thing as ghosts.

Later that night, Sable had woken up to go to the bathroom. She set herself in the wheelchair beside the bed and coasted out into the dark hallway; the tiny light on the wall her only source of illuminating salvation on the way to the bathroom. There was an abruptly strong breeze that seemed to come from nowhere, blowing through her hair as she stopped turning the wheels. There were no windows nearby. To her sides, light scratching came from within the walls. Then knocking. Then she thought she heard faint voices. She curiously wheeled herself against the wall, placing her ear on it and listening. She heard soft crying and pouting. The light on the ceiling behind her blew out, startling her with a jolt. Another breeze floated past. The hallway became very cold! She could almost see her breath. Something told her to turn around — a strange feeling that something was behind her. She carefully rounded her neck to look over her shoulder as her eyes went wide. The same boy she had seen the previous night was standing at the end of the hallway, lit with a ghostly white-and-blue glow. He reached out, delicately squawking, "Help me... Please... Please help me..."

126

Sable re-faced her head forward to see a little ghostly girl standing in front of her. "Come play with me," she sweetly urged.

Sable let out a shriek, backing her wheelchair up a bit. "Hide and seek," the little girl said. "Come find us."

"Come find us!" the little boy had repeated.

Two more ghostly children emerged from out of the walls, carefully approaching her with open arms. "Come find us!" they both chimed in.

"Drew! Drew!" Sable called out.

She tried to quickly turn the wheelchair but ended up tipping over as her body spilled onto the carpeted floor. She grabbed the metal edge, trying to drag and pull herself back on as the children all approached more closely, reaching out. "You have to play to find us," one of the girls mentioned with her light echoing voice.

Sable felt their glowing hands grab her arms and begin to tug as she fought back and tried to climb onto the wheelchair. They pulled harder, now hauling her across the floor as she tried to slap their hands away. Her fingers sifted right through them as if they were air. She attempted to grab onto something, but there was nothing. "Drew!!!" she screamed at the top of her lungs! Drew groaned and slightly rolled within the blankets of the bed. How could he not hear her?!

She screamed as they pulled her closer to the edge of the stairs. They towed her down step by step as she weakly fought, eventually reaching the bottom, where they brought her to the threshold of the study and released their grip. Now free, she began to crawl away as her tears dripped to the carpet. She turned her head back and watched as they all lined up side-by-side, extending pointing arms forward into the study. "Come find us," they all simultaneously told her. "Find us."

Sable looked past them. They seemed to be pointing to the large bookshelf against the back wall. "Please," one of the little boys moaned. "I can't breathe. Help me."

The light to the main foyer clicked on, and the group of ghostly children vanished within a blink. Sable arched her head up to see Drew standing at the top of the stairs beside the light switch, rubbing his eyes as he glanced down at her. "Sable? What the hell are you doing?" he asked.

She looked back into the study and then back up to him. "I, uh..." she began to murmur, contemplating her story. "I... nothing. I just fell off the stair chair down here."

Drew bent his head down to see the motorized stair chair sitting next to him at the top. Sable noticed the flaw as well. Drew gave a weird look, then trotted down to scoop her into his arms. He asked if she was okay, and she assured him that she was fine. He brought her back to bed and retrieved the tipped wheelchair from the second floor hallway. Nothing more was said.

Sable waited until Drew had left for work the next day. She wheeled herself into the study the first chance she got and stared at the tall bookshelf against the back wall. The children were pointing at it. They were trying to tell her something. She rolled to the side and tried to pull it away from the wall, but it was too heavy, so she began to empty the lower shelves of all the books, stacking them on the floor in the corner. It was quite the daunting task considering her condition, but if one thing was to her advantage now, it was her arm strength. She went back to the side of the bookcase and began to pull it away from the wall, bit by bit as a book or two fell off here and there. After a good forty-five minutes or so, she finally managed to pull and turn the shelving unit away from the wall enough so it was bare. It was plain drywall. She was no construction expert, but it definitely seemed a bit different from the rest of the walls around the house.

If she was going to do it, she was going all the way, and she wasn't going to ask for any help. Besides, it was her house now, too, and she was going to do whatever she damn well pleased with it. She got a sizable sledgehammer from the tool shed outside and wheeled her way back into the study. It was going to be a little difficult considering how she couldn't brace herself more steadily with her legs, but she was going to work away at it, as long as it took. She gripped the sledgehammer and raised it to her side, swinging and heaving it against the wall. It made a decent crack, breaking away a small portion easily. She could do it. It was only a matter of time.

And it took her the majority of the day. She was sweaty and dirty, covered with chalky and powdery drywall dust as the sun set within the side study window. She was exhausted. She had opened up a giant portion of the wall already, revealing nothing. She didn't even know what she was looking for. Drew was going to come home from work at any moment and probably go ballistic over the mess. She didn't care anymore. And if she really was in fact going crazy enough to be put away in some kind of medicine-drooling evaluation hospital, at least she wouldn't have to worry anymore about all the stupid little things that daunted her emotions daily. Sable clenched her jaw and took another swing, breaking into the next piece of wall. After the pieces and chunks had finished raining down, she wheeled closer for a look inside when a small skeleton had tipped over and fell against the opening, allowing her to belt out a long scream as the tiny skull's jaw opened. She quickly backed up, heaving her chest up and down with frantic breaths as she stared at the remains.

It was small — the size of a small child. She raised a dusty hand to unbelievably cover her mouth. "Oh my God..." she finally managed to softly mumble out loud. A ghostly glowing girl seemed to step right through the skeleton and out of the wall, taking a few steps and stopping to silently point toward the window.

Sable turned her head. The sun's brightly setting rays poured inside and began to flood her sight with a brightness so powerful she had to squint and shield her vision. When it had receded, she opened her eyes and found herself still in the study, only it was different. Things were rearranged, and the large bookshelf was nowhere to be found. In fact, the wall in that particular spot seemed to go back further, as if it had not been filled in quite yet. Among the floor were some tools and supplies. She heard voices come from behind her. "This isn't right," the first voice said. She recognized it right away.

"It'll be done and over with and you can forget it ever happened," the second raspy voice said.

Sable turned in her wheelchair to see Drew emerge within the threshold of the study along with an older, balding man. It was his uncle. "I can't do it," Drew said, shaking his head.

"You'll do it, because if I go down, I'll take you with me," his uncle sternly told him.

"But I didn't do anything!" Drew whined.

"You can't prove that," his uncle said. He gave a sigh and laid a sympathetic hand on his shoulder. "Listen — I'm not tryin' to shake ya down, here. You're my flesh and blood, boy. My brother's son. And I can't change what I've done. What's done is done. Ain't no one gonna find 'em. *Any* of 'em. But walkin' in on me doin'... what I was doin' to 'em, well... I just need to know that you ain't gonna say nothin'." Drew hung his head, taking a deep breath. His uncle continued with, "I can set ya up with an ass-load of money and get you that shiny city job. And I'll leave ya this big ol' house in my will. You just gotta do this for me. Just a couple of times, got it? Then it's done. Done and over with. No sense in either of our lives getting ruined, right? I can't do it alone. It'll be easier and faster with some help, and better I use someone I can trust."

Drew cocked a firm eyebrow to him. "The job? And the house?"

"Yours," his uncle confirmed with a solid nod.

"I'll help you get rid of them. Nothing else. I'm not a murderer."

"That's all I ask," his uncle added with a sly smile.

The two turned and picked up a small body bag off the floor, carrying it over past Sable, who they obviously couldn't see, and to the opening in the wall. Drew's uncle crouched down and unzipped the side.

A small, tiny hand rolled out. Sable covered her mouth. Her eyes watered. She slowly shook her head.

Her surroundings faded with a bright flash of light, and she found herself back in the mess of wall rubble she had created. She slowly turned her chair to see Drew standing in the threshold staring at her. She tried to speak, but nothing came out. Finally, she managed to softly murmur, "You... You... You helped him...?"

"I just helped him hide them," he told her. "I didn't kill any of them. I would never do that."

"How... How could you do this? You helped cover up... murders. The murders of those kids. How many were there?"

Drew walked in and over to her. She slapped her hands onto her wheels, cautiously inching back as he crouched to her level. "I saw him after he had... killed one," he told her. "He threatened me. He... He got me my job. Money. The house. I... I couldn't give that up."

"They were *children!*" she barked. "Their families were left all these years with no resolution... no answers... no idea of what happened to them!"

"Sable. Sable, look at me. I did it for *us*. I did it for our future. He was right. What's done was done. They were already dead. Nothing anyone could have done would have brought them back."

"I... I can't believe you would think like that," she whimpered.

"Look — I know what I did wasn't right. But no one has to know that. We can still report it. I'll say I was doing some remodeling. The blame will fall on him, and he's dead. We can go on with our lives."

Sable took a long, hard stare into his eyes. "I don't know you anymore. You're not the man I married."

"I haven't been a good husband. But I can try. I can try harder. I can work shorter hours. I can be here for you," he insisted.

She tried to fight back the tears in her eyes. "You haven't been here for me for a while now. And now that something has come up, you're using it as an excuse to make time for me. To make empty promises."

"You have a right to blame me for putting you in that chair —" he began to say.

"This isn't about my accident!" she blurted, cutting him off. "I'm not the one who's broken! Our marriage is! And we just... we can't fix it. We can't. I thought we could, but... I can't do it."

Drew sighed. He waited a moment, then spoke up with, "So what are you gonna do? Tell the police? What are you gonna tell them? That the ghosts of some kids told you where to find their skeletons? They'll never believe you. There's no proof I had anything to do with it. Your word against mine." Sable casually eyed the glass vase on the coffee table next to her as Drew shuffled closer to her and stroked the side of her face. "Everything's gonna be okay. We'll get through this like it never happened."

As he leaned forward to give her a kiss, she grabbed the vase and slammed it against the side of his head, shattering it to pieces as he hollered and fell to the floor, rolling in dazed pain. She quickly wheeled past him as he cursed, heading for the motorized stair chair and crawling onto it as she fumbled for the switch. The chair slowly began to coast up the curved track as Drew pushed himself to his feet, patting his hair to find blood on his fingers. He growled and sniveled, walking out of the study and seeing her ascending up the stairs. She panicked, trying to get the chair to move faster. He took his time walking up the steps. Her tears dripped as she reached the top, trying to frantically get into the waiting wheelchair. If only she could get to her phone! But Drew yanked her out of the chair onto the floor. "Let me help you, dear," he coyly offered. She attempted to thwart him off with slaps and punches, but he was much bigger and had the much more obvious maneuverability advantages. "If you're not going to be with me on this one, you're just gonna have to have another accident — like a wheelchair going through an old wooden second floor railing."

He grinded his teeth and heaved her up, throwing her over the side of the railing. She crashed against the foyer desk below, feeling a sharp, jolting stab in her lower back as she rolled off and onto the debris across the floor. She groaned as Drew stared down from above. He grabbed the wheelchair and kicked away at the railing, breaking it, then threw the wheelchair below. He wiped his hands and descended toward her. "Well, a broken neck ought to do it," he decided.

Sable's eyes rolled. She was too weak to defend herself now as Drew hovered over her. Then, through the blurriness of her vision, she thought she made out some of the ghostly glowing children as they emerged from the walls and ceiling. Drew spotted them and dropped his mouth in wonder. "No. No," he mumbled, taking a step back. "I wasn't the one who killed you. I didn't kill you!"

They crept forward, extending their arms out and beginning to tug at him as he wrestled and batted them away. He started making a beeline for the front door, but above him, the ceiling light shook and gave way, falling and crashing onto his head to knock him out cold. Sable watched as the children giggled and began to float upward, waving to her before disappearing into the ceiling. She lost consciousness after, and when she awoke, Drew was still out near her. Then something strange happened. She looked down at her feet. Her big toe slightly wiggled. She was moving it. She could *feel* it!

Skeletons in the Closet

The police later escorted Drew, who had sobbingly confessed to everything, into the back of their squad car after Sable had called them from the cell phone in his pocket while he was still out. Maybe it was the sight of the ghostly children that scared him. Perhaps his guilt had finally caught up with him. An excavation team ended up finding skeletons of seven children within the walls of the study in the house. It was all over the news. Their families could finally rest knowing the truth. The children were finally free, as was Sable. She didn't want her marriage to end the way it had, but at least it wasn't for nothing. At least she could start over with a second chance.

She was free.

And now she was jogging laps around a school's circular gravel running track.

WITCH WITH A CAPITAL B

Tad just had plain old bad luck with girls.

It was as simple as that. It wasn't his looks, or his personality. He was a great guy with plenty of friends. Intelligent. Resourceful. Kind. Funny. Even a little creative. But for some reason, he just couldn't hook a girl onto his fishing line. He was only eighteen and had never been in a serious relationship, but still — after all of his attempts, one would think that he would've landed someone even decently significant by the time he was a senior in high school. "Some guys just have all the luck," seemed to be his motto. He was beginning to get discouraged. Maybe he was too nice. That's what his best friend Kirk always said. Then again, Kirk was more like that friend in those teen sex comedy movies who claimed to be a know-it-all and never held any reservations in saying what was on his mind to score a chick with a cheesy pick-up line, only to end up making a fool of himself. At least it made for a good laugh.

Tad let too many girls take advantage of his kindness. He was a push-over. One time, he was at the mall with Kirk ready to order something from the food court area when a beautiful raven-haired nineteen-or-twenty-year-old girl had approached him in line and gave some sob story about how she had dropped her twenty dollar bill somewhere and didn't have a credit card to buy something to eat. Tad thought it was destiny — a situation he could only dream of happening. A story he could tell their future grandchildren! "If she hadn't have lost that twenty dollar bill, I would've never met your grandma!" he imagined himself romantically rehashing. She claimed she would pay him back, and Tad immediately thought on his feet to take the opportunity and ask if she wanted to sit with them, but she explained that she was in a hurry, so he instead requested her phone number as an excuse to meet up with her again. She beat around the bush and dodged the question, assuring him that she worked at the pretzel stand in the west wing of the mall and he could come by any time from five to nine Monday through Thursday to talk with her. The next day, he dropped by that pretzel stand. Of course, no one there had ever heard of her.

Gullibility was Tad's middle name.

Kirk had warned him. It was just like all the flowers he had purchased for girls he liked over the years. He was always coming on too strong. Well, things were different now. Tad wasn't going to get played anymore. He was tired of getting walked on. He only had about eight months until graduation, and then it was off to college, where he could hit the reset button on his selective options — where he could start new, and maybe find some mature girls who were into genuine guys and didn't like to play games. The options at his high school had long been exhausted.

Then the new girl came. Her name was Jami, and although by first-look she wasn't his normal preference, she seemed to cast an alluring spell over all the male members of the institution. To classify her as "goth" would be incorrect. She was only on the paler side because she wasn't tanned to a golden-brown crisp like all the other girls around her. Her make-up was light, limited only to black eye-liner and an occasional dark maroon shaded lipstick. Her black hair was short on the backside and a bit longer on top — not spiked, but rather as if she slapped some hair gel into her hands and ran them straight up and through just once. Her ensemble wasn't always completely black, but definitely shaded in darker colors and a neck that was a post for close to a dozen necklaces, charms, beads and lockets. Even without all that stripped away, she was hot. Kirk compared her to a "Natalie Portman on gothic crack". It was her brown eyes that really did it. There was something about them — something enchanting yet wary.

She was different. Perhaps that's why all of the jocks began to lose interest in their eye-candy cheerleaders. No one really approached her at first when she arrived there in early October, but she definitely won the attention contest. She seemed to stick to herself, not even speaking in class. When she was accidentally bumped in the hallway by a passerby, she didn't even acknowledge their presence. She just kept on walking.

Tad's interest was peaked. Not because he was necessarily attracted to her, but because she was new. At the very least, she poised the possibility that she could make a good friend. "Always good to have chick friends," Kirk told him as if reciting some kind of rule from an unwritten dating book. "She's been here over a week and she's still eating lunch alone. Poor thing. Wish we had some kind of other emo goth girl here to be her pal."

"She's not goth," Tad insisted as he looked over to her sitting at the empty octagon lunch table in the cafeteria. "Or emo. She's too hot to be emo goth. No girl that hot could be in that category. It's just impossible. I think we should create some kind of new category."

"Fine, whatever," Kirk would muck back. "I dare ya to go talk to her. Maybe if you bring up Rob Zombie in the conversation, she'll let you into the deep, dark cave between her legs."

"Well, *someone's* gotta give her some kind of friendly welcome," Tad suggested. "I can't imagine how it is to be the new person in a town where practically everyone already knows everyone else."

With that, he got up and trekked across the cafeteria. Kirk didn't think he was actually being serious. When Tad got to the table, he stopped and gave a wave. "Hey, what's up?" he simply greeted. She flicked her eyes up at him, silently chewing her food. "So, uh... you like it here so far?" he then asked. She stared at him, scooping some macaroni and cheese up with her plastic spoon. Tad felt a bit awkward. He scratched his head. "I'm Tad," he added, reaching forward to extend his hand out for a shake and accidentally knocking over a salt shaker.

The white grains spilled next to her tray as she quickly jolted up out of her seat and stepped back. "You clumsy asshole!" she barked, giving him the finger before angrily swiping her purse-bag and trotting out of the cafeteria.

"Um... okay," Tad mumbled, watching her go with shunned confusion. "Sorry."

He made his way back to his table, where Kirk welcomed him with a soft clap. "Smooth. Very smooth, Don Juan," he congratulated. "Let me guess — she went to her locker to get her cell phone so she could put your number into it."

"It's confirmed — the new girl's a bitch," Tad said, slumping into his chair.

"What'd you expect? A girl-next-door offering to invite you over for some brownies after school?" Kirk wondered. "Your curiosity is gonna be your downfall, I swear."

Tad sighed. *You clumsy asshole.* It was probably the first thing she said to anyone since arriving, and she said it to *him*. Even when he wasn't trying to score with a girl, he had bad luck. Jami did start to bud and develop much more socially over the course of that second week. Soon her empty table at lunch was filled with guys who were trying to get into her pants and girls who were territorially keeping an eye on them. First there was Max Drumfield, the institution's prized golden quarterback boy. Tad overheard him in study hall bragging to his precious linemen protectors about how he had scored a date with her that night. "But what about Cindy?" the fat buzzed-cut right tackle had asked of Max's Barbie doll trophy girlfriend.

Guys like Max Drumfield didn't have a "girlfriend". They merely had a flavor-of-the-month club. Max might as well have plastered a Baskin Robbins logo onto his locker with some hanging applications for new tasty treats. Besides — it was the same on the other side of the fence, too. Girls like his Cindy were man-eaters, and only after finding out about Max laying the pipe to the new dark sorceress piece-of-ass-in-class and crying for five minutes would she move onto the next douche bag that would do the same thing to her in a matter of time. Only Cindy never found out about the details of Max and Jami's steamy get together, for the Tom Brady-wannabe never showed up to school the next morning. Word was that he was out sick, however, none of his friends or teammates had personally spoken to or seen him for confirmation. The information was only supplied by Cindy's gossiping girlies after she had called his house and gotten the news from his parents. She wanted to be a good girlfriend and stop over to check on him, but his parents assured her that he was in no condition to see anybody.

By the weekend, chatter had rattled and boiled to the level of concern when he didn't play or even show for Friday night's big game. And by Monday morning, three more of his best teammates were out sick as well. Apparently there was some bad flu epidemic that had unleashed itself primarily on the football team and kept students bedridden without any communication to the outside. It wouldn't have been so strange, but there wasn't even any online social communication from the missing group. At the very least in the present day and age, these guys would've been on a laptop or their smart phones texting away or posting updates on a social network website of how much staying in bed sucked, but there was nothing. Absolutely nothing. It was like they ceased to exist. Dale Rutherford was sitting at Jami's table next with his Abercrombie & Fitch-clad cronies. He was already class president, for Christ's sake. He didn't need to pull political shenanigans to get Jami's attention. Yet there she was, playfully smiling and flirting by tipping her finger under his chiseled chin.

Dale was next to catch the bug. Two or three of his buddies followed. First the football team, now the governmental branch. Shit, the whole school's structural system was falling apart. Yet it was only the male population. Tad wasn't the only one to notice this, for the official newsletter sent out by the school confirmed that the "flu" seemed to only be affecting males and there was no cause for alarm. He was, however, the only one that seemed to notice that every guy who disappeared had been last seen with Jami, whether in school or later in the day at the good ol' hangout soda shop in town.

"There's definitely something up with her," Tad briskly mentioned to Kirk.

Kirk retorted with his usual profoundly snappy rebuttal — "Ah, you're just jealous because our school finally has a slut that actually looks like one and she's giving it up to everyone but you."

"I'm serious, man — something weird is going on. You don't find it a little strange that every guy who's with her ends up getting this flu thing?"

"Oh, they're probably gettin' somethin' alright, but I doubt it's the flu," Kirk joked.

Tad wasn't amused. He didn't deny feeling some kind of hypnotic attraction to her, but he was also very skeptical of her agenda. He only seemed to ever see her with people and not by herself out and about in town. What was she doing when she wasn't in school? Where did she even live? It had been over three weeks and nobody had a clue. She had to live *somewhere*. And it's not like there had been many houses on the market before she arrived. Something definitely bugged Tad about her, and it wasn't until the fourth week was underway and half of his lunch table was out sick that he decided he wanted to do something about it. Bill was gloating how he was going out with her that night. Had her mischievousness finally reached his own table? Bill was just as "normal" of a guy as Tad was. He couldn't imagine Jami having any sort of viable interest in him. But there he was, sitting and yacking about how she invited him over to her place — "That old Buckman place in the woods off Carlton Road," he confirmed with a smiling nod. It seemed to finally be the first shred of residential proof Tad had heard, probably because the secretive information had finally reached his own circle. After all, a good twenty or twenty-five male students were now out sick with the seemingly everlasting flu, yet none of the teachers or parents were raising any large-scale concerns. She didn't have a whole heap more of quality meat to choose from. Bill slapped Kirk a smooth high-five and took a cool walk across the cafeteria to Jami's table, where he sat and was welcomed with her charming, sly smile and sparkling brown eyes.

"Fucking Bill," Kirk said with an unbelievable laugh. "What a lucky prick."

"I say we go. Tonight," Tad enthusiastically suggested. "To her house — the old Buckman place. See just what the hell she's up to."

"She's up to dirty candlelit fucking on a creaky mattress," Kirk blabbered. "You wanna bring your camera to make some kinda amateur porn, you perv?"

Tad insisted he would go himself, but it was an opportunity Kirk couldn't pass up. What the hell else was there to do, anyway? The old Buckman house had been abandoned for years. It was in the middle of nowhere in the woods, led to by a dirt road that ended at its doorstep. It was dark out. Tad and Kirk didn't bring flashlights for fear of being spotted, but Tad could see that the one-story tiny house was still in its shabby condition. He remembered being scared of it as a kid. The older kids would taunt and dare him and his friends to enter, where ghosts, goblins and other evil minions waited in slumber. The house was old. The roof was slanted and falling apart. It might as well have been made of straw. It looked like it, anyway — like some kind of house that lost kids would stumble upon in a twisted fairytale and never be heard from again. There seemed to be nobody presently home. Jami must have still been out with Bill. Bluetooth ready at the ear, Tad and Kirk approached the small ghostly manor. Since it was Tad's idea, he volunteered to sneak in and look around while his counterpart would stay outside hidden in the brush and keep a lookout.

He first tried the front door. It was locked. He circled around to the side and opened a window that was already cracked open a bit. He crawled in and gave a quick shiver. It was chilly out. A large black kettle sat in the fireplace above a small fire going in the pit, but it was dying and didn't seem to be doing much good. He peeked inside. It was empty. Nothing was cooking. Tad began to investigate. The house was very small indeed, and definitely spruced up to be inhabited, but she couldn't have lived there alone, could she? She had to be, what? Seventeen? Eighteen? Where were her parents? He already felt claustrophobic there by himself. There were plenty of oddities surrounding him — little strange knick-knacks on the tables and shelves that shared no likenesses. No posters on the walls, or make-up desk, or other girly decorations. He didn't even see a TV! What kind of a gothic hermit was this?

And then there were the frogs. At first, their constant ribbitts and croaks sounded like they were coming from outside, but Tad caught glimpse of one in a jar on a shelf by his head. Then there were the ones in the small enclosed tank on the counter. And more in jars and other sealed boxes with the necessary holes for oxygen. Around that time, Kirk had chimed in over the Bluetooth — "So, dude — any pentagrams or Ouija boards in there?"

"No — frogs," Tad replied, stepping over some clutter on the floor.

"Frogs? What do you mean?"

"I mean frogs. Everywhere. All alive. There must be over two dozen in here," he added.

"Probably for a satanic ritual," Kirk chuckled. "Hey, see what kinda panties she wears!"

Tad rolled his eyes and shook his head. Despite Kirk's brilliantly creepy suggestion, Tad crept into the bedroom anyway, where a messy bed, old dresser and nightstand sat among the wardrobe that had spilled its way out of the closet onto the floor. It seemed like a normal girl's bedroom, anyway. He was ready to leave and give up when Kirk's voice crackled over the Bluetooth — "Whoa! Incoming. Gothy bitch and Bill have arrived in car, repeat — they are here! Get out of there, man!"

"Shit," Tad flatly muttered, scurrying back into the main room. He couldn't go out the front door, or they'd see him. There wasn't a back door he was aware of, and by the time he thought about climbing out the side window, the sound of the knob being unlocked threw him into a panic. He rushed back into the bedroom, diving and sliding under the bed where he pulled in some of the clothes on the wooden floor to conspicuously conceal himself in.

Kirk's voice came through the Bluetooth, spouting, "Dude, where the hell are you?! Get your ass out of —" before Tad reached to his ear and clicked it off.

"You actually live here?" Bill could be heard saying as they came inside. "What about your parents? Th-They're not here, are they?"

"On a business trip," Jami calmly assured him.

"Oh, cool," Bill gladly responded, his voice showing optimism again. "Damn. This place used to scare the shit out of me as a kid. What is all this stuff?"

Jami edged a comfortable smile as she stepped up to him. "You wanna talk or you wanna play?"

Bill returned the smile. She curled her arms around his neck and pulled his face down to treat him to a desirable kiss. She unlocked her lips and turned, heading for the bedroom with eyes that stared back at him and told him all he needed to know. He quickly scrambled out of his jacket, following her. She wrapped her arms around his waist, kissing him more before directing him onto the bed. "You... just lie back... right there... and make yourself comfortable," she smoothly insisted.

Bill sat on the bed as the mattress weighed down over Tad hiding underneath. He cocked his eyes upward, trying to remain silent. Bill pulled his tee-shirt over his head as Jami stepped over to her dresser. "I normally don't hook up with girls like this," Bill informed her with a half-grin. "And certainly not girls like... you."

Jami pulled something out of the top drawer of the dresser and joined him on the bed. "Then tonight... you are in for a very... *very* special treat," she said.

She bent forward, pecking his bare chest with a few kisses before flatly placing her palm against his torso, gently guiding him down. She grabbed his right wrist and twisted it behind his head, slipping it through the backboard of the bed where she joined it with his left hand. She pulled out the handcuffs she retrieved from the dresser and snapped them securely in place as his expression fervidly beamed. "Damn," he muttered under his breath. "There was a rumor you were dirty, but I didn't think it was true. A lot of people thought you were just a poser."

"Oh, I'm the real deal, alright," she confirmed, sitting on his legs and grabbing one of the candles beside the bed. "Now... let's start with a little hot wax."

"Let's," Bill moaned in agreement.

"Can't forget the incantation now, either," she added, perking her eyebrows.

"Hey, I'm all up for dirty talk, baby."

She carefully began to pour some of the hot wax onto his chest as he clenched his teeth in sizzling reaction. "Rickety rockety rampa fortoo. A transformation of the legs, the arms and the head for you. What was once human, can be no more, scaly of the skin, you must crawl on all four."

Bill tried to keep a playful mind, but his shaky voice showed otherwise when he jittered, "W-What are you doing?"

"I'm turning you into a frog, silly," she told him, waving and circling the stream of wax into circles.

Tad listened with a weird face, and then his eyes shot wider at the sounds of Bill's sudden grunts and groans. He was in pain. He shook the bed. "Ah! Get off me! Get off me, you crazy bitch!" he shouted, jerking his body about. The mattress began to shake and bounce. Bill cried out, "Help me! Somebody help me!"

"No one can hear you," she calmly said. "Stop screaming and start ribbitting."

Tad was freaked out. His eyes didn't blink the entire time. This girl was out of her mind! Then the shaking stopped. Bill was silent. Tad watched as Jami's feet planted onto the floor off the bed. A frog bounced down next to them. Tad held back a gasp. *No way! No fucking way!* he thought. The frog turned and crawled, taking a hop toward him. He flicked his hand, trying to shoo it back. It hopped to the side. Jami's hand reached down and missed, then managed to capture it. "Where are you going? Get back here, you naughty boy," she playfully baby-talked it. "Time to put you with your friends."

She walked out of the room. Tad took a much needed exhale. He stayed under there for a few minutes, listening to her shuffling about in the next room before the front door creaked open and shut. Moments after that, the car outside started up and backed away before the air was filled with silence again. Tad cautiously emerged out from under the bed. The handcuffs were still locked around the backboard, but void of any attached wrists — or *body* for that matter. He walked into the main room; his eyes fearfully scanning around as they caught glimpses of all the frogs again that croaked and hopped about in their secluded confines. He stumbled back against the kitchen sink, looking down and noticing two more swimming about in clear-covered bowls. He couldn't take it anymore. His feet fumbled as he caught hold of the front door's knob and opened it, bursting his way outside into the darkness. He trailed down the driveway a bit, turning and looking back at the creepy house. When he spun forward, he nearly collided with Kirk, almost having a heart-attack as he clutched his chest. "Whoa, whoa! Bro, it's me, it's me! What the fuck happened, man?!" Kirk eagerly asked.

All Tad could do was exhale his fear.

Later on, when the two were safe and sound back in Tad's bedroom, Kirk gave an unbelievable chuckle as he spun in the chair in front of Tad's computer desk. "A fucking *witch?!* Get real," he mumbled with skepticism.

"It happened! I'm telling you, it happened! She turned Bill into a frog! That's what she's doing! All the guys that have been going out of school sick — she's turned them all into frogs and they're all in the house! In bowls, and tanks, and boxes!"

"Do you hear what you're saying?" Kirk wondered. "There's no such thing as witches. Just gothed-out wannabes who pretend to be! Like those kids who dress up like Twilight vampires. It's just dark clothes, emo attitudes and really white tans."

"What if she's dressing like that to throw everyone off?" Tad proposed.

"Yeah, and all make-up aside, she just happens to look like someone who walked off the set of a WB network teen drama," Kirk added, playing around with a bouncy ball. "Did you actually *see* Bill get turned into a frog?"

"Well — no. I was under the bed. But I heard it. She left the room alone, and when I crawled out, he was nowhere to be found. There one second, gone the next," Tad further implied. "How do you explain that?"

"I don't know, because I wasn't in there, remember? Listen, dude — I think you were just freaked out being in that scary house trying not to get caught. I bet it's not even really her house. You know that kids were always using it to party and shit back in the day. I think your adrenaline was running and two of our peers were doing some freaky shit right over your head that your straight-laced inexperienced mind couldn't comprehend so your consciousness came up with something to cope with it," Kirk theorized, tossing the ball up.

Tad stepped forward and caught it mid-air, tossing it aside. "That's really profound, Professor Kirk, but I know what happened. I know what I saw and heard. We've gotta warn somebody!"

Kirk slid out of the chair and tossed his arms up. "Yeah, and get thrown into straightjackets and mocked out of existence by the entire town in the process. Why do you always have to be so damn analytical? Why can't you just beat-off to the experience like every other normal guy? I would've given my left nut to be under that bed. I'm goin' home, man. There's some frozen burritos and a toilet calling to me. See ya tomorrow."

Tad knew that sometimes you couldn't convince people there was a fire if their hair was burning. That's why he took it upon himself to do some research. He wasn't gonna sleep much, anyway. And the next morning, he entered the school library and slapped the papers down over the book Kirk was working out of at a table. "She's here to do something," he simply said. "Prolong her life or something along the lines of that."

Kirk looked up and gave a light groan. "Aww, are you serious with this, man?"

Tad sat next to him, fluttering through the papers. "I must've gone through thirty or forty witchcraft sites reading up on it. The hardcore ones, not the Hollywood bullshit. See, right here — witches generally appear some place new under the cover of a falsified identity, allowing them to play out their agenda over the course of the calendar month — most typically October, leading up to All Hallow's Eve. That's Halloween."

"Yeah, I know that, thank you," Kirk snobbed.

"That's why witches have always been associated with Halloween — it's a sacred night in which they can complete their task. Kind of like a recharge. At the end of the night they retain their young-looking bodies and immortality for another year, but only if they can properly prepare and complete the task," Tad explained.

"You're losing me," Kirk mumbled.

"The frogs. She needs to turn young men into frogs so she can bake them in some sort of protein stew to drink on Halloween. From witch to witch, the animal or the circumstances may slightly vary, but it's all there. Read it," Tad insisted, shaking the papers at him.

"Dude — I'm saying this as your friend, but you have got way too much of a demented imagination and way too much free time to use it in," Kirk noted. "Surfing websites at night militated by sapless overweight men living in their parents' basements who can't get laid and —"

"This is serious, Kirk!" Tad barked back, trying to keep his vocal level down.

"And just what are you gonna do about it? Huh? If it was true?"

Tad flipped through the papers and showed him one in particular. "Right here. Salt. One of the few effective methods to killing a witch. Remember that day in the cafeteria when I went over to talk to her? I spilled the salt near her and she got up and freaked out."

"Because you're a spastic klutz," Kirk stated.

"It also says that forming a circle of salt around yourself can protect you against any harm or spells," Tad threw in.

"Well, I'll be sure to remember that tonight in case she gets too horny," Kirk mentioned.

Tad sharpened a pair of curious eyes. "What is that supposed to mean?"

"It means I scored a date with her. This morning. She came right up to me at my locker and started seriously dialoguing me. I think I'm gonna see what this is all about for myself."

"What? Kirk, you can't. Trust me! She doesn't want you like you think she does. She's got you under some kind of weird spell. She's got *everybody* under a spell... parents, teachers, students — she's making them believe the missing kids are at home sick. That's the only reason her plan is working!" Tad ecstatically told him.

Kirk sighed and closed his book, standing up. "Relax, bro. I'm a big boy. I can handle myself. I'll wear a rubber. We're gonna be laughing about this tomorrow."

"Kirk, wait," Tad added, trying to stop him.

Kirk smiled and gave his arm a friendly pat. "It's all good, man. You'll see. I'll call you with the details, okay?"

Kirk never called.

In fact, he didn't even show up to school the next morning. Tad was immediately concerned. He was so concerned that he left the school grounds during his lunch period and drove to Kirk's house. His mother had answered the door. "Hey, Mrs. Hoffstedt. Is Kirk around?"

"I'm sorry," she simply told him. "Kirk wasn't feeling well this morning. He's asleep in bed. I think he has that flu that's going around."

The words pierced into Tad like throbbing horror. He gave a nod and shrugged. "Oh, that's too bad. If you don't mind, I'm just gonna peek my head into his room and say hi."

Kirk's mother blocked his path in the open doorway. "I'm afraid that's not possible. He's very ill. No visitors. I'll tell him you stopped by."

"I'm not leaving until I actually see him," Tad sharply demanded.

Kirk's father, tall and muscular, approached the threshold behind his wife. "Is there a problem?" he muttered.

Tad knew he would never get through him. He could chance it, but if Jami really had brainwashed them into denying visitors to see their "ill" son, he was sure they would use all physical force necessary to keep her interests at bay. So Tad apologized and left. He considered going around to the back of the house and somehow climbing up to Kirk's window to see for sure, but who was he trying to kid? He knew there wouldn't be anyone in that bed. So he decided to go directly to the source.

It was Halloween. He figured he had until midnight to stop her — to stop her *somehow*. So later that night, while tiny costumed candy-gobblers roamed the streets and what remained of his graduating class was out at parties, Tad waited for her in the old Buckman house. She came through the front door, closing it behind her and stopping at the sight of him as she curled a playful smile and bit the tip of her fingernail. "Trick-or-treat?" she asked.

"I know who you are. And I know what you've been doing," Tad calmly told her.

"Really, now?" she inquisitively wondered, cocking an eyebrow as she stepped up to him. Her foot stopped as she slowly pulled it back and glanced down at the ring of salt that surrounded Tad on the floor.

"Ring of salt. As long as I'm in this circle, you can't do anything to me."

"Very clever," she noted.

"Turn them back," he sharply ordered.

"Turn who back?"

"The frogs. Turn them back into people."

"Frogs? What frogs?"

Tad grinded his teeth and reached behind him, where he pulled out a mini-Super Soaker water gun from the back of his pants and pointed it into her face. "All the fucking frogs in here!" he belted. "The ones you have to mix up in your batch of anti-aging stew before midnight, you psycho wicked witch bitch!"

"I don't see any frogs in here," she flatly stated with a shrug.

Tad looked around. She was right. All of the boxes, tanks and bowls were now empty. Without stepping out of his salt circle, he reached and grabbed hold of the large black kettle in the fireplace. It was still warm. He tipped it to look inside, where the last bit of liquid swished at the bottom. "B-But... you have to do it before midnight," he mumbled with some confusion.

"Exactly. *Before* midnight on All Hallow's Eve. They say breakfast is the most important meal of the day," she told him. "I liked your friend Kirk. He gave the remedy a nice little egotistical kick taste."

Tad's face flared in anger. "Then there's no reason not to waste you right here."

"With what? Water? Sweetie, this isn't the Wizard of Oz."

"No. Not water. Salt water," he corrected, squirting a stream down to her foot as it immediately sizzled.

She hopped back and held her hands up as he re-aimed it into her face. "Shit! All right! Just — wait! Hold on a second! Listen to me — what's done is done, okay? I've already rejuvenated myself until next year. So there's gonna be no more little froggies, got it?"

"That's because I'm gonna melt your murdering ass," he threatened again. "Even if no one believes me."

"That's right, Tad — no one's gonna believe you. You think you know who I am? I know all about you, too. You think it's just chance that I skipped you over? No. I've been watching you this whole time. You're different from all the others. That's why I didn't enchant you fully into being attracted to me. The difference between you and every other guy is that they know what they want when you know what you *need*."

"And what's that?" he coyly wondered.

"To be accepted. To be noticed. To be acknowledged for all the good you do that you only end up getting shit on for. We're not that different. We're both just trying to survive. I've been around for more than three hundred years. I've learned an interesting thing or two. I can do things you can't even imagine, Tad. And I can show you them all. I can *teach* you," she proposed. "Come with me."

"Where?"

"Everywhere. Anywhere. I'll make it worth your while. We can get back at all those types of girls that stepped on you and treated you like dirt just for being a nice guy. For the first time in your miserable life, *you* can be the one taking advantage. I haven't had a human tag-along in a long time. You're special. Let me show you. Just put down the gun."

Tad dropped his eyes to the gun in his hands and thought it over. She was very convincing. She did have a point. Where would his life go from there, anyway? The idea of being some kind of apprentice seemed enticing. He slowly lowered the weapon and set it on the counter. She smiled and held a hand out. He took a breath and stepped out of the circle, taking it as she pulled him into her and locked her lips onto his. She guided his hands onto her rear and caressed the back of his neck. It was the best kiss he ever had!

Gullibility had stricken Tad once again.

He wished he could tell someone how much he hated the taste of flies.

LET SLEEPING DUMMIES LIE

Miller Cronenberg coughed from the dust as his brother Ben opened the barn door.

Nobody had been in there for years. Decades, probably. Now the old house up on the hill it belonged to was being sold, and it was their one shot to investigate. It apparently belonged to some magician nearly a century ago, but one of his distant relatives who had currently owned the house had moved on and held no interest in the barn's belongings. It was being sold, and the boys wanted to stake their claim before the new inhabitants took over. "Whoever it was, they were stupid not to take a look for anything valuable before leaving," Ben had mentioned, trying to sound wise beyond his older years of being fourteen to Miller's ten.

Their mother was the realtor and had mentioned that the owner was never around to begin with. If she knew they were snooping, she'd give them an earful like always. "Maybe there's a treasure map! Like those Goonies found!" Miller excitedly hoped.

Ben wasn't as much of an optimist. He expected to find nothing but old clothes and some tractor parts. The jackpot would be hitting a mint-condition set of baseball cards! They would be millionaires!

The ground floor was just as expected. They could maybe haul some of the specific ideas out and make a good buck, but it wasn't worth it for the work, so they moved onto the second floor. Ben went first up the rickety wood-rotted stepladder, followed by Miller, who nearly fell off when his feet cracked one of the steps. He got a laugh from his always-taunting older brother followed by a helping hand up onto the platform. They perused through most of the objects — paintings, boxes of old dusty clothes, a pogo stick and teddy bear here and there; items which probably held more sentimental value than monetary. Then Ben came across the locked trunk case sitting upright on a shelf behind some other items. He moved them aside and brushed his arm through the years of stretching cobwebs to pull the box out to the edge. "What is it?" Miller inquisitively asked.

"Whatever it is, it's locked, which means there's probably something valuable inside," Ben told him as he excitedly smacked and rubbed his hands together. Ben tried pulling at the rusted padlock, but it was no use. "Look for the key," he ordered Miller.

Miller turned and looked at the stretching field of cluttered and stacked things. A key in a haystack was more like it. There was, however, some jars on an adjacent shelf filled to the brim with various knick-knacks. Miller trotted over and pulled them out, sliding over the ones with nails, screws and paper clips to find one containing some keys and buttons. He brought it over to Ben, proudly holding it up. He liked when he was able to find things over his older brother. It made him feel significant, although Ben merely snatched it from him and dug his fingers inside to start pulling out and trying the various keys. He finally found one that fit, exclaiming, "Hey! This one fits!" as he tried twisting and turning. It seemed a bit jammed as he clenched his jaw. He pulled and tugged, shaking the trunk as the lock finally clicked. The door opened, and a tuxedoed dummy flew out onto Miller as he fell back to the floor, screaming and flailing with the doll.

Ben couldn't help but throw his head back in laughter. Miller ecstatically fought with the dummy until flinging it off him and against some nearby boxes, catching his breath as he sat up and stared in shock. Ben stammered over and picked it up. "It's just a dummy, dummy!" he laughingly huffed. He gave it a once-over before turning it around and shoving his hand into its back. "It's a ventriloquist dummy," he added.

It was about three-feet-tall, sharply dressed in a black tuxedo with an accompanying black bow-tie. The oval head was more football-shaped with neatly dark slicked-back hair and a raggedly decrepit face filled with wrinkle lines and a sophisticated monocle (a small, round one-eyed glass piece) sitting on its right eye attached to a string in its front pocket that only added to its serious, flat expression — far from the usual rosy-cheeked happy-go-lucky ventriloquist stars. Ben grinned and began to work the dummy with his hand, turning its head and flapping its wooden-jawed mouth to Miller — "Hey, guys — I dunno about you, but I get the feeling that one of us here made a mess in their pants. And it wasn't the wooden guy!" he said in a playful, cartoonish voice.

Miller hated dolls. He hated them his entire decade-long life. Princess dolls, clown dolls, pull-string dolls, baby dolls, jack-in-the-box dolls — you name it. And although that wasn't too uncommon for someone his age, and they didn't have any sisters to traipse around with one in the house, the fear was still there. It had no specific origin. He just didn't like them. He always felt their eyes were on him whenever he'd pass them in a store or see some little girl playing with one. Miller abruptly got on his feet, bending some aggravated eyebrows down at his brother. "Cut it out!" he yelled.

"Oh, come on. Don't be such a wuss," Ben murmured. "It's just a stupid dummy. A really old one. Hey — we could probably get some good money for this! People pay big bucks for antique stuff like this all the time on eBay!"

Miller stepped back over to the trunk and grabbed the rusted lock. "Why was it locked up?" he curiously wondered.

"Because it's probably worth somethin'!" Ben assured him. "Or maybe someone just didn't want him to get out and run around killing people!" he added as he ran the dummy across the dusty counter.

Miller sniveled and looked away. His brother was always doing things like that to him. He supposed that's how all older brothers were, but he wished that just once he could give him a taste of his own twisted medicine. Ben wasn't afraid of anything. And Miller knew him better than anyone. The only weapon he had was making fun of him when the prospect of a pretty girl from school came up, but even that didn't seem to do much damage. He watched as Ben carelessly tossed the doll back into the trunk and snapped it shut. He wished he just would've left it there. He didn't care about the money. There was just something too creepy about it — even above his normal dummy-phobia.

On the way back home, Ben had mentioned stopping at their neighbor's house so that old man Corgan could look the dummy over and shed some kind of estimation as to how much they could get for it. He loved collecting old stuff and knew quite a bit of history. Ben was banking for something in the triple digits at the least. Old man Corgan had them sit down in the couch across from his creaky recliner as his wrinkly hands worked on opening the trunk on the coffee table between them. "Let's see what we got here," he muttered after clearing his throat of about twenty pounds of phlegm.

Ben was already bored out of his mind, perusing his eyes around the museum-like living room. Miller, on the other hand, couldn't take his eyes off the trunk in front of him. He didn't want old man Corgan opening it. He didn't want to see that stupid dummy again. Why couldn't Ben just leave the thing back at the barn? Corgan pulled the top open and took a gander at the dummy as if it was lying in its own miniature casket. "Well, I'll be," he said. "You know what you boys stumbled onto? This is Aldous Truman's ventriloquist dummy."

"Who was that?" Ben asked.

"Back in the 1920's, he was quite the magician around here. He was pretty big. Traveled the country doing his tricks and whatnot. This fella here was his main attraction for some time," Corgan explained. "But business started gettin' slow. Couldn't book a show to save his life. Folks were getting into movies more. Magic was beginning to lose its luster, especially after Houdini kicked the bucket. You can only see the same tricks so many times, ya know? Even the new ones weren't impressive. But Aldous Truman — he was a stubborn guy. Didn't wanna give it up. Became desperate. Story goes that he got into black magic in an effort to boost his ticket sales and concocted an evil spirit to possess this dummy. Guess he was tired of kids yelling that they could see his lips moving. He wanted to give them something that would knock 'em off their feet."

Miller's eyes were frozen on the dummy. He couldn't look away. "What happened to him?" his shaky voice managed to ask.

"Just up-and-disappeared one day not long after. Folks 'round these parts said there was a gypsy who claimed to be the one who helped him with the black magic and that the evil spirit possessing this doll was trying to defy his orders and take over his body. Then no one ever saw him or the dummy again. Where'd you boys say you found this?"

"In that big barn that belongs to that house on the hill," Ben noted. "My mom says the guy who owned it told her it wasn't worth the trouble of cleaning out when he sold the place."

"Ah. That would be his great-grand nephew," Corgan confirmed. "Probably didn't even know it was up there. Old ghost stories is all they really were. Campfire stuff when I was a kid. Lot of people looked for this dummy for a long time."

"Is it worth anything?" Ben asked almost eagerly. "How much do you think we could sell it for?"

"This isn't exactly the type of thing you wanna get rid of to some knucklehead," Corgan stated. "You boys bring this by the town hall, I'm sure they'd be mighty grateful. It's a historical antique. You'd be heroes."

Ben's shoulders sunk. He didn't want to be a good local patron. Or a hero. He wanted to be rich! Plus, a part of him immediately figured that there would be a whole heap of trouble rising when questions started flying about ownership. The guy gave everything in the barn up, but if this made the papers, he would probably come storming back and demand some kind of compensation. It would be a hassle. He was better off seeing how much someone would pay online for it. Miller, of course, could care less. He just wanted the thing put back into the box and taken away. After hearing old man Corgan's ghost stories, he had good reason to feel wary.

When he was making a sandwich in the kitchen later that day, Miller could've sworn he saw the dummy barely turn its head as it sat on the table. Ben had been taking pictures of it to put online and left it there. Miller wanted to shove it back into its ghostly trunk so he could feel safe that it was trapped and secure, but he knew Ben would probably give him a good punch for touching it. "This thing is an antique. Don't go playing around with it or spilling anything on it," Ben had firmly stated.

Ben knew all too well that Miller wouldn't touch it with a ten-foot pole. He just liked to remind him of his fear by harassing his brother in a method that seemed to deem he was the authority around there because their father had left years ago. Miller usually liked to watch TV in the living room around that time, but he couldn't bare constantly looking over his shoulder at the dummy on the table, so he retreated to his room where he dove into the electronic bliss of a handheld video game. Later that night, after he had been in bed sleeping, he woke up to a small sound in his room. He rubbed his eyes and tried to look around the dark atmosphere. "Ben? Ben, is that you? If you're trying to scare me, it's not gonna work," he mumbled.

There was no answer. Miller scanned his eyes another moment and gave up, lying back down and curling the covers back over him. Then he heard another noise. He sat up again, reaching beside his bed and grabbing the flashlight he had at the ready, coasting the illuminating beam through the room until stopping at his dresser. The ventriloquist dummy was sitting on top, legs hanging over the edge. Miller gave a gasp, his eyes widening. He ducked back beneath his sheets and took a breath or two, slowly peeking back over and re-directing the flashlight to see the dummy was gone. Was it even there in the first place? He thought he might have been imagining it. It was dark in there, after all. Yet something coiled in his stomach. He felt like he wasn't alone. He was too scared to reach for the light switch by his door to give him a fully bright sense of safety. He heard a small shuffle. Something moved. He jerked his flashlight to catch the small rocking chair in the corner of the room slightly tilting back and forth. There was a pitter-patter across the carpet of the floor — almost like the sound of tiny feet. Miller moved the flashlight again. His heart was racing. He started to arch over the side of his bed, clutching the blankets as he drew the light's beam to the floor. He didn't want to look under the bed. That was the *last* place he wanted to be snooping around. But he had to know. He closed his eyes. His hand was squeezing the blanket now. He counted to three in his head and jerked the blankets up, looking underneath to see — nothing. He felt relieved. He gave a much-needed exhale. He almost felt foolish. He pulled himself back up and lied down, turning on his side to see the dummy lying next to him. He screamed. He screamed *loud*.

Within moments, his mother and Ben came in, flooding the room with light. "What? What? Honey, what's wrong?" his mother asked with concern.

Miller grabbed the dummy and threw it at his brother. "You're an asshole, Ben!" he shouted.

"Hey! Language, mister!" his mother scolded. "Now what is going on?"

"He brought this stupid dummy in here and tried to scare me!" Miller argued.

Ben reached over and picked the dummy up off the floor. "I did not, you little shit," he insisted.

His mother gave his chest a light slap. "Hey! You do not talk to your brother that way!"

"He knows how much I hate dolls! He did it just to scare me!" Miller stated.

"I've got better things to do, like sleep," Ben informed him.

"Then how did it get in here?!" Miller shot back.

"Maybe it came alive and ran in so you could fondle it in bed," Ben suggested.

"All right! Stop it! Both of you! That's enough," their mother jumped in. She turned to Miller. "Sweetie, you were probably just having a bad dream."

"I wasn't dreaming! And a bad dream wouldn't bring that stupid thing into my room!" he sharply informed her.

She reached over and took the dummy out of Ben's hands, inspecting it over. "Where did this even come from? It's really ugly."

"We found it in the old barn from that big house on the hill you sold," Miller blurted. Ben grit his teeth and gave him the evil-eye.

Their mother looked back and forth between them. "You took things from that barn? It isn't yours. It doesn't belong to you."

"So? It doesn't belong to *them*, either," Ben argued, taking the dummy back. "You said the guy that owned the house and barn before was leaving them behind. So what does it matter? The new people won't know. We took it to old man Corgan's to see how much it might be worth and just got a bunch of dumb urban legends about the doll being possessed. That's probably what's making him wet the bed."

"Is not, you jerk!" Miller whined.

"You're ten years old, man!" Ben sneered. "You need to stop this stupid fear of dolls and grow up!"

"Okay! Enough!" their mother frustratingly added. "I have to be up early to show a house. I don't care what happened or who did what. Ben — take it out of here and get back to bed. Miller — go back to sleep."

Ben rolled his eyes and looked down at the dummy in his hands as he smirked and walked out of the room, giving Miller the finger. Their mother sat at the edge of the bed, tucking Miller back under the sheets and giving him a comforting kiss on the forehead. "I'll talk to him in the morning," she calmly assured him.

She headed for the door when Miller had spoken out with, "Could you leave it open a little?" like so many kids had requested before.

She flashed a smile and kept the door open a crack, disappearing for good. Miller exhaled and turned on his side. He was too shaken up to fall asleep right away, but in a matter of time, he lost his will to keep on guard and drifted into a casual slumber.

He woke about two hours later in the dead of night, groggy and surprised at how little time had passed, and almost as if he had forgotten about the incident, he trekked across his room like a lagging zombie. He patted his hand on the hallway wall, guiding himself down the stairs through the darkness and into the kitchen, where he flipped on the light and poured himself a glass of water from the sink. He chugged most of it and turned, looking into a mirror on the wall to see the reflection of the ventriloquist dummy slouched in one of the chairs at the table. He turned and coldly looked at it. Ben couldn't have played a trick on him in his bedroom — he came in right after their mother. Then again, it was dark, so maybe Miller's eyes couldn't see him escaping after placing the dummy in his bed. Though Ben was right. Miller shouldn't have been afraid. It was just a dummy. And Corgan's story was just a story.

Miller finished his water and set his glass in the sink, turning back to look into the mirror — and see that the dummy was gone. He gave a silent gasp, jerking his attention to the table. The dummy was indeed missing. But it was just there! "Ben?" he softly asked, not caring if his brother was there to scare him. But something told him that his brother was snoring back in his own bed, leg half-hanging off the side and oblivious to the dummy's whereabouts. The sound of the basement door opening around the corner caught Miller's attention next. He quickly grabbed a flashlight from the drawer and headed over, confirming the sight of the open door. *Someone* went down there. Doors don't open by themselves. Certainly not that one. He stood at the top of the stairs for a good minute or two, waiting and listening and he shined the flashlight down to the bottom. Part of him thought the idea of going down there was crazy. But then another part of him thought that his annoying older brother was right — he was ten years old. He had to stop being so scared all the time. Maybe if he forced himself to investigate, it would be like facing his fears. Ben would cut him some slack. There would be no more taunting or fighting. He could finally get some respect!

Miller took a strong breath and slowly went down the stairs. The light switch of course wasn't working, but it had been problematic before. At least he had the assuring guidance of his flashlight. He half-expected some hands to reach out and grab his ankles from under the steps, but he made it to the bottom successfully. It gave him a sense of power. Then something moved to his left, shuffling by some stacked boxes. He jerked the flashlight to see nothing. There was the pitter-patter of tiny footsteps running across the cold cement floor. Miller swallowed the lump in his throat. He was thinking the unthinkable. But dummies couldn't come to life! This one was nothing but wood, plastic and cloth. The presence ran again, knocking over a bouncy ball that rolled its way past Miller's socked feet. "Who's there?" he called out.

He waited for an answer and got nothing. Bravery was overrated. He didn't care what it was. He was retreating back upstairs to safety. He turned to go back up when a craggy, raspy voice had softly whispered through the darkness — "Miller."

The flashlight rattled in Miller's shaking hand as he craned his head back. The attack came from above — the dummy had leapt through the air off a shelf and plowed into Miller as he stumbled back into some boxes, frantically gasping and flailing his limbs. He got free of the dummy and jerked his head around, trying to find it in the darkness. It was missing again. Miller looked at the stairs and took off running, skidding to a stop when the doll had popped up from under the steps. The boy's eyes widened in horror. The dummy was moving. It was *walking*. It casually took step by step, slowly blinking its wooden eyes and turning its oval head. Miller backed up, shaking his head. "No. No, you're not alive. This isn't real. This is just a dream. This is just a dream," he tried to convince himself with a whimper. Miller backed into some boxes, nearly toppling over as he fought to keep the flashlight's beam on the dummy. "You're not real! You're not an evil spirit! It was just a story!" he blurted, trying to blink himself awake. "Aldous Truman didn't bring you to life!" Miller lost his footing and fell over.

"Kid, I *am* Aldous Truman!" the dummy snarled, its jaw flapping up and down in its custom-made wooden track as the eyes blared wide. "That no-good goddamn spirit took my body and put me into this wooden hell! I've been stuck in that box for over eighty years, waiting for someone to let me out, and I *ain't* goin' back!"

Miller grabbed a plastic Christmas candy cane yard decoration and heaved it at the approaching dummy, who growled and roared. Miller used the opportunity to race back up the stairs, but the dummy merely pushed himself back on his feet and lifted his arm, using some kind of force to *whoosh* the door shut as the boy collided into it. He shook and turned the knob, throwing his shoulder against the door. He pounded a fist. "Help! Help!" he shouted.

The dummy snarled and threw its arm down, pulling Miller and dragging him down the steps with some kind of invisible force. He dropped the flashlight as it cracked and rolled across the hard floor. Miller couldn't move. He grunted and tried to wiggle himself free of the hidden power as the dummy walked its way over. "Leave me alone!" Miller shouted. The dying luminance of the flashlight highlighted the wooden wrinkled face of the tuxedoed performer as it lurked over with its tiny steps. Miller tried to scream again but couldn't. The dummy's eyes began to glow a bright blue. Miller clenched his teeth.

The light faded and the door upstairs opened to reveal Ben as the dummy fell over. "Mill?" Ben called down. At the bottom of the stairs, Miller quickly covered the dummy with a blanket and pinned it down. "What the hell are you doing down there?" he weirdly added.

Miller arched his head up to him. "Nothing. I — nothing," he assured his brother. "I was just looking for an extra blanket."

Ben gave him a strange expression and shook his head, turning back and disappearing upstairs. Miller looked down to the blanket as the dummy started to move. "I've got you now," he noted with a firm sense of achievement.

The sun was just starting to peek over the horizon as Miller rowed the small boat to the center of the lake. He stopped and looked around. There wasn't another boat or person in sight. He reached to the floor of his boat and lifted the heavy trunk onto the other seat, opening it and adjusting one of the many bricks piled inside around the ventriloquist dummy, which was tied up and gagged. Its eyes clicked open as its head turned from side to side. "This should be enough to keep you down there and stop you from possessing someone's body," Miller told it. He gave it a pat. "Sleep tight."

The dummy murmured, trying to lightly rock in place as Miller closed the top of the trunk, sealing it with a brand new lock. He heaved it up onto the edge of the boat, almost tipping himself over before giving one strong push and sending the box into the water with a light splash. It bounced and swayed, tipping upright and beginning to sink down in a series of bubbles like a capsized ocean liner. When its top had dipped below the surface, Miller wiped his hands and grabbed the ores, starting to row away with a satisfied smile as he wondrously said to himself, "Ah... I think I'm really going to enjoy living as a kid again. I wonder if he has any good toys?"

BACK TO THE WELL

Clayton Conner loved to smack around his wife.

There wasn't a night that went by when the neighbors in the houses around the cul-de-sac didn't hear some kind of screaming or crying. Teenage Tommy Buckner next door said it was better than any reality show on TV.

And of course Jenna Conner didn't leave.

No, she was one of those "I still love him" and "he's not always like that" women, hopelessly believing their marriage was built on a more profoundly robust foundation. To call them cliché was much too erroneous; Clayton never wore a tank top and Jenna never tried to over-compensate for her bust-ups with thickly implemented make-up (although she did try, quite poorly most times), and they were far too north in Pennsylvania to be in redneck trailer park heaven down in the southern states, where they would've been welcomed with open arms and closed fists. They were quite the middle-class intellectual couple, Clayton with his construction job and Jenna with her receptionist position. Somehow, somewhere down the line, it wasn't enough. To blame it on Clayton's home life growing up was redundant. He had quite a normal childhood. Sometimes these things just happen. You marry too quickly and too forcefully, and white picket fences don't click into your repertoire. Clayton lost his way.

Clayton Conner, a bonder with the bottle.

Eventually, from one side or the other, there is always a breaking point.

It came one night when he arrived home from Sally's Bar. The dishes weren't done. Would there have even needed to be a reason? Clayton started hitting. Punching. Pushing. And then his power plummeted her against the corner of the kitchen counter, where her neck cracked upon impact. She didn't move on the titled floor. He gave her a shake. He gave her a jab. He muttered, "Quit foolin' around, you spoiled bitch. Get up!"

But she didn't.

Even in his inebriated state, he realized what had happened. He lowered himself to the floor and lifted her head. It was loose and wobbly on her neck, much like many of his action figure toys growing up. "Oh, damn," he mumbled next.

Now Clayton was smart, but only to a certain extent. He knew he would pay for this. He didn't have a good attitude track record with the police. The whole goddamned neighborhood would testify against him. He would plead that it was an accident, and he was just messin' around, but they wouldn't believe them. He would go to jail!

Perhaps now, the abuse would work in his favor. She ran away. Yeah! She was fed up and finally ran away! With, uh, that fella he suspected her of seeing behind his back. Of course, there really was no fella, but it was a good alibi that people would believe. They'd be interested in his story for five seconds and it would float out of their gossiping minds. One quick newscast about it and it would be over with! They couldn't prove anything! Not if they couldn't find the body. He went over the options — dropping her in some lake. No. With his luck any weights would break loose and she would float up to surprise some happy boating family. He could chop her up and bury her! No. Too messy. Too much work. Besides, some mangy mutt would only dig her up later. Then it came into his head. He quivered a shaky smile and trudged down into the basement, grabbing an old tattered white canvas blanket. He rolled her into it and within moments was carrying the corpse into his backyard, being careful to turn off the light first in case any of those damn nosey neighbors were still up at that hour. He made his way to the old well in the center. It was there long before they had moved in and to his knowledge might've been used before the neighborhood had switched to city water. No matter. It hadn't been used for decades. No one would ever think to look down there.

He took a cautious look around and hiked the tarp onto the edge of the stone well, unwrapping and dumping his wife's corpse as it fell to the dark abyss below. He wiped his hands and looked around, giving another coy smile. He had gotten away with it. That was the hard part. Now it was just reporting her missing and going through the motions.

Except Clayton never got the chance to do any reporting whatsoever. He woke up the next morning with a stretching yawn to the smell and sound of crackling bacon down in the kitchen and when his brain was functioning, he remembered what he had done. Who the hell was down there? Then he heard her shrill voice call up to him — "Clayton! Breakfast is ready!"

He got out of bed, dawdling down the stairs and entering the kitchen to freeze at the sight of Jenna at the stove as she slaved away. She poked the tongs into the frying pan and slapped the crisp bacon onto a plate. "C'mon, now — gonna get cold."

Clayton sat at the table, and as he journeyed through his bacon, eggs, toast and coffee, he credited the notion of what he had done the prior night to a mere dream. Just a drunken dream. It *had* to be a dream. Hell, she was alive and standing right there! But it felt so real. He wasn't *that* drunk. He tried to force it out of his mind, going through the motions of daily life and another hard shift at the construction site before retiring to Sally's Bar as usual. And as usual, his entrance home was nothing short of stumbling indignation that night. He shouted. He demanded some kind of dinner. Jenna of course made the mistake of retorting with the idea that it was well too late into the night and she had no idea when he'd be home if at all. She knew better. Maybe she wanted it. Clayton slapped and pushed her. She fought back. He grabbed her shoulders and swung her around, throwing her down the stairs. She tumbled and rolled before finally landing on the bottom, where her neck stiffly cracked.

Clayton waited for her to get up. She didn't move. The scene was eerily familiar. He hoofed down the stairs and gave her an inspection. She was dead. Immediately, he thought of the dream. He knew for sure he wasn't dreaming this time. Maybe it had been some kind of premonition. Regardless, it did lay the path for him. He went down to the basement and retrieved the same white tattered canvas blanket, carrying her out back and releasing her bruised body down the well. He was too tired to reflect and balance the logic. He went back in the house and collapsed face-first onto his bed.

He woke up the next morning — and there she was. Sleeping right next to him as if nothing had ever happened. He gave a startled gasp, quickly kicking the sheets off and getting out of the bed. He couldn't have had the same dream twice! Was he going crazy? His frantic motions had woken her. She asked what was wrong, as if she actually gave a damn. He barked a frenzy of angry questions and accusations toward her — "What the hell's going on?! What kinda game you playin', woman?!"

"What are you talking about?" she confusingly wondered.

"How'd you do it?! How'd you crawl back up outta that well?! You were dead! I saw it! I heard it!" he shouted. "Who's helping you?!"

She didn't understand. She acted completely oblivious! Clayton wasn't settling on subjecting it to some dream. She was doing it to spite him! "I'll teach you!" he huffed, pushing his way out the door and down to the kitchen. Jenna followed. He pulled a steak knife from the holder on the counter. "Try to come back after this, bitch!" he dared, raising the knife as her eyes shot wide in terror.

He struck it down into her chest. He swiped and slashed. He stabbed her — right in the heart! He slit her neck. Blood was everywhere. She lied in a pool of it by the time he had finished. He cleaned himself up and wrapped her like a tortilla in the tattered canvas blanket, keeping her in the basement until night had fallen. And again, he carried her to the well and dropped her body down. "Listen to me for once and stay down there!" his voice despicably echoed down the stone hole.

The next morning, she was back. Back to her chores of slaving away at his laziness. Now Clayton was *really* starting to think he was losing his mind. She kept coming back, and completely unaware of what had happened! No memory whatsoever! He glanced at the calendar, and then checked the news channel on TV for the date, proposing that he was somehow stuck in a nightmarish hell reliving the same day over and over like that guy in the movie *Groundhog Day* (watching it was the only time Jenna had heard him truly laugh) but the date was current. Time had been moving forward like it always eternally had. He just couldn't find or think of a rational explanation, and he sure as shit didn't want to go to anyone about it. The scientific portion of his curious mind took over. He began to experiment. Every day, he killed his wife, over and over, a different way each time, and every following morning, she would be back to normal, alive and well. He continued this for a week straight before finally approaching the idea of investigating the well in the backyard, so one night, after he had disposed of her, he set up a rickety camping lawn chair with holes in the back and broke out the twelve-pack of beer, staking out. He wouldn't sleep. He wanted to see what exactly was going on.

But this was Clayton Conner. And alcohol was his remuneration to the sandman.

He nodded off and woke up the next morning to the sound of Jenna's voice calling his name through the open back door. She queried why he was out there, and he snapped with some passive response. He missed it! He had fallen asleep. He could've tried again that night and taken some caffeine pills to stay up, but he had decided to go the whole way. After he killed her that night (the old electric toaster in the bathtub tactic), he repeated his nightly procedure of dumping her corpse into the well. Only this time, he had his rope and harness with him. He jimmied it to the top roof cover of the well and slapped his construction helmet over his head, clicking the light portion on and slowly lowering himself down inside. It was deep — much deeper than he had imagined, but he finally made it to the solid, dry bottom, where he released himself free of the harness and pulled out his additional flashlight. He turned it on. His eyes illuminated with an unspeakable mixture of horror, shock and confusion.

There, not more than a few feet away, was a pile of bodies — *Jenna's* bodies. All in different clothes and in different murdered conditions, but it was the same Jenna. Clayton couldn't speak. He trailed his helmet light and flashlight across the spilled bodies and over to some sort of tunnel which caught his perplexed attention. He began following it, having only to duck a little. Ahead, some sort of light signaled an end. He cautiously approached and entered some kind of strange, small room — it was lightly furnished with some oddities — some recognizable and others questionable — but undoubtedly inhabited. Then he saw the individual in the corner of the room, hunched over a desk with their back to him. It was small, like a midget, maybe four-feet-tall or less, dressed in some kind of raggedy brown old-fashioned attire with gray and white hair poking through the back of a triangular hat. The individual slowly turned in its chair, revealing a rigid and grotesquely brown face with an elongated pointed nose and ears that made Clayton stumble back against the wall in fear. He didn't know whether it was some kind of goblin, or troll, or elf — but it was ugly — and it wasn't fully human! It gave a creepy, half-smile and spoke out with a surprisingly deeply-toned voice — "Oh. Hello, Clayton. So nice of you to visit."

Clayton gasped and fumbled for words before finally blabbering, "Who... Who are you? What the hell is goin' on down here?"

The creature set its pencil down on its desk. "I really wish you would give me somebody else to make for a change instead of your wife," it said in a trite tone. "It gets boring recreating the same person over and over. Don't you have anybody else you want to kill? We could have a really splendid mutual partnership, you and me!"

ALWAYS BURY 'EM TWICE

Her name was Jayla.

Of course, Waylon never cared much for knowing their names in the end, but that one was special. He *had* to know that one's name. She gave him that tickle — that unique spark. A feeling that was rare, that made him question whether or not he wanted to go through with it. He always went through with it. There was no turning back at that point. Sure, he could stop and retire, and make an honest effort at getting to know her, but where was the fun it that? Knowing people was boring. Talking with them was boring. It always went in the same direction. You'd get to know somebody new and after a short time, you'd know everything there is to know about them — their past, their present and their ambitions for the future, no matter how interesting they seemed. Most of them were the same anyway, and would only end up disappointing you or screwing you over somehow. It was like watching a good movie or reading a good book — sooner or later, you knew you would reach the end and there would be nothing else. You knew you were at the peak of interest, but that thought was spoiling it bit by bit, and you could feel that special sensation molding away like bread on a kitchen counter.

Getting to know people was overrated.

Waylon would just rather stick to killing them.

He convinced himself that Jayla was no different. She'd merely be categorized under a special file in the memory of his mind, separate from all the others. He at least owed her that. He would miss the observational phase, though. It was the first one he didn't get that tired feeling from. He felt like he could keep going, every day trying to convince himself "just a little bit more, and I'll do it tomorrow." But his brain always overpowered his conscience. Dragging it on and on would only lead to trouble he didn't need or want. He just had to get it over with, and fast, before he could second guess or try to question himself. Besides, maybe he could keep one of the pictures this time. Hide it in his wall or something. No! It was against the rules. *His* rules. He couldn't possess anything that would tie him to her. He was smarter than that. That's why he hadn't been caught all those years he was doing it, even to his current point being twenty-seven.

Jayla was very photogenic, too. Every picture he snapped, whether it was outside in a park or down in a dingy subway, seemed to give her a natural glow. She was born for the camera, and not to be one of those anorexic supermodel bitches overcooked with a tan. She was like art. Like an elegant and respectable magazine pinup. Her light caramel-colored hair was perfect. She had a face that looked like it hadn't aged since she was seventeen, and it would probably remain that way well into her forties. She was short and spunky, not fitting the type that would be stuck inside some boring office job all day, but she made even *that* look good! She was never a tee-shirt and jeans girl. Well, maybe jeans, but most days it was sundresses or some kind of lightly knitted cardigan or tunic top, like the white one she was wearing that night. He was glad she looked especially nice that night. Most people could only hope to be wearing something fashionably acceptable on the day of their death. Something that presented who they were in life.

She had met a friend for coffee some place downtown. Waylon watched from the hot dog joint across the street as they sipped away at one of the outside tables on that gorgeous night, laughing and chit-chatting. It looked like catch-up talk to him. After a while, they gave their girly hug and disbursed on separate paths. Waylon trailed Jayla down the city street. He was an expert at it. Why wouldn't he be? He had been doing it for years, stalking and blending in with all of the others. He wasn't a complete hypocrite. After all, how many of those people he walked beside shoulder-to-shoulder while following his subjects were off to do their own dirty and scandalous deeds somewhere else in the city?

Waylon stopped short and watched Jayla unlock the entrance door to her tall apartment building. He had his own way inside. He always did. Everything had been meticulously planned and laid out. He knew the whole layout of the building, all of the exits, bathrooms, storage rooms, any security camera systems (which this particular complex lacked like most others) and regular habits of other tenants on her floor. He wouldn't go through with it if he wasn't prepared. Tonight... everything was in place.

He walked down her hallway, slipping on the second black glove that matched the rest of his dark ensemble. He carefully and quietly worked the lock on her door. It was too easy. At times he wished those apartment buildings would upgrade to a better system like key cards in hotels. It would give him more of a challenge. But no matter. The real challenge — the real *thrill* — was inside. He slowly pushed the door forward. If she was right there, it would have to be quick, but in most cases they never were, and that's what he loved. He loved drawing it out. Those seconds felt like hours to him, and he relished in them proudly and triumphantly. He ducked inside. She wasn't right there, which was good. He quietly closed the door behind him. He could hear the news on the TV in the living room portion around the corner. She always watched the news at that time.

Waylon inched his soft footsteps down the dark, short foyer hallway. Jayla passed across from the bathroom into the kitchen, making him slightly freeze as his eyes stiffly stared ahead. She walked out of the kitchen and headed through the living room, once again oblivious to his lurking presence. Waylon reached into his side pocket and pulled two small connected cork-like objects out as he started slinking forward again. He rounded the corner into the living room, where she was absent, and spruced his steps up a bit to enter her dimly-lit bedroom. She had her back to him, folding some shirts into her dresser drawer as he silently approached, pulling the corks apart to reveal a thin wire of twine. And then he made his move.

He quickly hooked the wire line over her head and against her throat, sharply pulling back as her eyes flashed wide and she gasped in surprise, immediately clutching her fingers to it in response. He pulled harder as she flailed her arms, trying to turn. He wanted to avoid making as little commotion as possible, which he was usually successful at. She gagged and wildly squirmed, returning her hands to her neck in attempt to claw and dig her nails into the wire. Waylon pulled tighter. Her back was against him now. He could smell how pretty her hair was. She tried calling out for help. They always did, but nothing came out. Her eyes grew bloodshot. She tried slapping behind her as Waylon spun and got better footing. Her tongue slung out of her mouth like a dying dog's. Her gasps grew raspy and desperate. She tried pulling at the wire again. Her arm weakly dropped. She raised it again; her fingernails scraping the edge before her arm dropped like a doll's. She twitched. There was another huff for oxygen.

And then her body went limp.

Waylon took a breath and gently guided her forward, setting her on the bed face-first as he pulled the wire off her neck and wound it closed, retreating it back into his pocket. Words never seemed to capture the adrenaline rush. He wished he was a poet, but once again, leaving a paper trail of his beautifully-toned experiences would be a no-no. He just simply allowed himself a moment to catch his breath and enjoy the accomplishment.

Now aside from his homicidal impulses, Waylon wasn't a genuine sicko. He wouldn't do anything weird to the bodies of his victims after or bathe in their blood or prance around wearing their undergarment wardrobe. That's how the other serial killers got caught. There was something mentally wrong with them. Waylon just liked to kill, that's all. Aside from that, he didn't look like one of those cliché fat curly-haired bug-eyed men who gave girlies drooling silent stares and he wasn't an asshole who treated people like shit with road rage or obscene shout-outs when being accidentally bumped. The phrase "it's the quiet and ordinary ones you've gotta worry about" was created for people like him. But since Jayla was more special than any of the others, he decided just that one time to limitedly divulge into his curiosity. He wasn't going to do anything to her. He didn't want to. He just wanted to... look. A short peek, that's all. And then he would carry on with the rest of his duties.

So he reached down the back of her tunic shirt and unsnapped her bra, fiddling and pulling it out altogether to toss it on the bed. He rolled her body over and leaned in a bit, being careful not to actually get on the bed for chance that he'd leave a hair behind for DNA. He pulled up the tunic and looked under. They were a lot bigger than he imagined. It was hard to tell most days with the shirts she wore, but now he had officially seen them. He felt as if finally getting to see a favorite celebrity's bosom for the first time. And although the temptation was there to cop a feel while he still could, he resisted and replaced her bra like it had never been removed. He wouldn't take advantage of her that way. He felt guilty enough just looking. Jayla was a nice girl, and he wasn't a pervert. He was a highly experienced serial killer. It was like being a seasoned bank robber or thief and not having to go around unnecessarily shooting people. It was like a sense of professionalism. He wouldn't desecrate her beautiful temple like most other jackasses would. He wanted to find the bitch out there that claimed through studies that most serial killings were from sexual impulses and slap her across the face to prove otherwise.

Waylon wasted no time. Despite having the situation locked down, there were always factors of unpredictability hovering around. He had put Jayna's five-foot-two body into a series of large black trash bags and carried it down to the end of the hall, where he dumped it down the garbage shoot that through careful experimentation beforehand he found quite large enough to fit her size. Then he retreated unseen to the basement of the complex, where he changed into a hidden tall gray jumpsuit, complete with a fake name tag. He slipped some work gloves on and pushed the large plastic garbage bin on wheels that was parked under the shoot out through the back doors and into the alley, where an old white pick-up truck he had rented sat parked. He began to reach into the garbage bin, tossing various bags into the back of the truck before heaving Jayla's body in. And after tossing a few more bags onto the accumulating pile, Waylon closed the gate of the truck and wheeled the bin back inside, coming out to close the doors and drive off like it was a routine nightly trash service.

He parked the truck on the backside of the large cemetery where no one would see it and entered through the rear gates with his key, carrying the bagged body across the lot. It was always the toughest and riskiest portion of his plan, but usually went smoothly as no one was ever around at that time of night to spot him, including kids, who never seemed to break into graveyards much anymore to cause pranks as he did when he was younger. He reached the open grave he had dug earlier that day and gently set Jayla's covered corpse onto the grass, slowly rolling her into the hole. He grabbed the waiting shovel against the tree and dug into the dirt pile, shoveling bit by bit until reaching an amount good enough to flatly conceal her completely. He wiped the sweat from his forehead and left, being a good Samaritan and purging of the garbage in his pick-up truck to the appropriate place before returning the vehicle to its rental lot. The very last thing he did that night was the hardest — disposing of all the wonderful pictures he had taken of his latest victim. It was like a tradition, standing over the stove in his apartment and cooking the photographs as if he were guiding some Jiffy Pop, one by one until the memories were nothing but ash.

The next morning, Waylon watched from his tractor as a funeral proceeded. They were all the same. Although Waylon wasn't a social butterfly and didn't have many friends or family members, his one wish would be for people to dress and come to his own funeral however they felt like attending. Black was so dreary, so boring, so traditional. People should celebrate the life of an individual with the outlook that they themselves could kick the bucket at any time in any way — for some maniacal twenty-seven-year-old serial killer could be their undoing. Waylon didn't pay attention much to the service. He sat back and read a newspaper until all of the people had eventually dissipated from the area, leaving him alone with the one or two others across the lot visiting graves. He went to work with the tractor, bulldozing and scooping dirt into the gravesite back and forth. As the soft brown dirt piled upon the casket below more and more, he couldn't help but cock a tiny smile at the edge of his mouth.

Weeks had passed. Life wasn't all that outstanding for Waylon between the times of his "hobby", but that's not to say that he didn't enjoy it. He went out and had fun, going to the movies or dinner or hanging with the humorous company of what friends he had, like any other normal person would. He never immediately itched to find his next victim. It was very much like a romantic relationship — when the time was right, he would find her. Until then, he dug graves and filled them in. He wasn't ashamed of his job. It was good pay and good security, for being in a city, there was always a steady regular count of departed patrons who needed the comfort of a dirt roof. Besides, he was still a few years from turning thirty. He had his whole life ahead of him, although being a gravedigger had it benefits. He had buried so many there already — so many corpses were beneath his feet, and then more corpses under those that he had personally contributed, never to be traced or found. That was another aspect that made him different from the others. He always gave them a semi-proper burial, instead of chopping up their limbs or disposing of them into some polluted lake. He followed the search for the missing Jayla in the papers, until the articles tired themselves out and she was feared dead. It didn't bother him that no one knew her fate. He didn't need to leave a calling card or a clue like other serial killers. If anything, he figured all of his cases were most likely catalogued under a serial *kidnapper*, for there was no outright evidence to suggest he was going around offing these people in certain methods that would coin him some kind of catchy name. He didn't need a name. Serial killers who needed names were too egotistical.

Eventually, Waylon had found his next special girl, although she didn't quite shoot off the same powerful fireworks that Jayla had supplied. It probably wouldn't happen again for a long time if at all. She was blonde, worked at a trendy clothing store and was younger at nineteen, which made it all the easier. She would have to do. Waylon started regularly snapping pictures, taking the slow but soon-to-be-rewarding time to learn her daily and nightly routines before finally reaching the culmination. He used the same method as he always had, choking her with the twine wire and smartly smuggling her body in another well-planned way to the graveyard that night where he laid her to rest beneath a shallow layer of dirt waiting for the coffin to eternally conceal her the following morning. He had come home the next day after work and fixed himself a quick TV dinner, watching some moronic sitcom when he heard the knock at his door. He turned his head in time to notice the small, square white envelope slide its way under the door across his hard wood floor. He got up and trudged over, picking it up and opening the door to look down both directions of the hallway, where no one was in sight. He slipped his index finger into the envelope and tore it open, pulling out a white hard stock card that simply read in bold handwritten capital letters, "I KNOW WHO YOU ARE".

Waylon brought his head up and looked down the hallway again. He gave a confused glance back down at the letter. What the hell did it mean? Had someone seen him kill or bury one of his victims? Impossible! Fear rattled through him as he ducked back inside his apartment and locked the door. He was always careful! He was 99.9% sure that no one was ever around when he buried the bodies. And he wouldn't slip up and kill someone with their window blinds open. He didn't make mistakes! He had been doing it way too long to fumble something up. Two thoughts managed to quickly enter his mind — either they were serious, and somehow, some way, they were onto his secret, or the note was meant for someone else in the building and was just delivered to the wrong apartment. It *was* very vague, after all. It could've meant *anything*. Waylon wasn't one to delude himself often. Deep down he knew that the note was for him specifically, and it had something to do with his killings. Rationality kicked in. He got a *note*. It wasn't the police pounding on his door. Whoever sent it didn't go to the police. Maybe they didn't have any evidence to bring them. Or maybe they did, and they wanted to blackmail him. Waylon tore the note up and tossed it in his garbage. Whatever it meant or whoever it was from, there were no further instructions on what to do next. All he knew at that moment was that he had to back off from his plans involving his latest target — a saucy Spanish girl who worked out daily on the treadmill at a gym uptown, at least until he knew who he was up against — and what he could do to remedy the hiccup.

The next day, he came home from work at the cemetery to find another white envelope, this one stuck to his door. He tore it off and looked around. Not a person in sight again. He opened it. It was another white cardstock square with the same handwriting reading, "I KNOW WHAT YOU DO". He entered his apartment and locked the door behind.

Two days later, he found a third note stuck to the door. This one read, "WHILE YOU WATCH THEM, I WATCH YOU", and this time, a small photograph accompanied the note. He unfolded it. It was of him holding a camera in a park downtown, taking a picture of his own. Now Waylon was nervous. Three notes from the same mysteriously threatening individual, and no written requests of what they wanted. It was like they were toying with him.

When he found the fourth note that had been slid under his door that read, "GO TO THE POLICE AND CONFESS", he finally took action and spoke with the superintendent of his building. He explained that someone was harassing him with threatening letters and inquired about the security of the building, and how he could find out who had entered and when, but as he came to ironically be reminded, the security in his own building was just as lax and debunked as many of the other complexes he had meticulously snaked his way into before to commit his elusive murders. The superintendent simply told him that people needed a key to enter (which Waylon knew was bullshit) or probably tailgated inside behind one of the other residents, and without any security cameras, it would be nearly impossible to get a face unless he caught them firsthand. Waylon was additionally told that if the harassment continued, he should report it to the proper authorities, which he knew damn well was not an option. He was nearly on the brink of camping out and catching the person. That's all it would take!

Despite the increasing dismay, daily life was still going on for Waylon. After work, he was downtown on his way to the subway and crossing a busy intersection with the hoard of others when someone had bumped past him going the other way. He did a double-take back and turned completely as his footsteps slowed for him to watch the backside of a short girl with caramel-colored hair heading for the other side. *Nah... it couldn't have been*, he thought to himself. He waited for her to turn just so he could prove to himself that he was a bit uppity and nervous with his eyes playing tricks, but she never did. She eventually disappeared into the rush hour platoon of citizens, and he snapped himself back to life, continuing his trek to the subway entrance.

The following day, he was enjoying a late lunch with a friend in a midtown sandwich shop. As the friend rehashed some comedic story about something funny that happened to a co-worker, Waylon bit into his sandwich and glanced out the front windows of the shop, barely catching Jayla walking past among others as her firm eyes locked onto him from beneath the bangs of her caramel-colored hair. His jaw sat askew and crooked, eyes unblinking as he quickly scrambled out of his seat and ran out the doors, leaving his friend confusingly alone. Waylon arched his head and strained his neck, trying to look through the crowd of people, but she was nowhere to be found. He took a breath and returned to his seat in the sandwich shop. "What was *that* about?" his friend wondered.

"Nothing, I... thought I saw someone," Waylon answered, taking one last look over his shoulder to the windows before picking up his sandwich as the friend continued the story.

Later that night, Waylon had a tough time falling asleep. As he tossed and turned in his bed sheets, he kept convincing himself that he was stressed. He was seeing things. It couldn't have been her. She was dead. Dead and buried; buried beneath that coffin like many of the others he had planted the graveyard with. When he finally had drifted into a light sleep, he woke up feeling the presence of someone in his room. "Who's there?" he called out, trying to adjust his eyes in the darkness. Through the cascading blue moonlight coming through his blinds, Jayla emerged from the shadows beside his bed. He let out a sharp, short gasp, squinting his eyes shut and shaking his head. "I'm dreaming. I'm dreaming. You're not here. This is just a nightmare," he said.

"You had the chance to go to the police and confess. Now you're going to pay for what you did to me," Jayla said. She snapped her hand forward and grabbed his, cracking back his index finger as he let out an abominably loud bellow.

He cried and rolled off the opposite side of the bed, hooking his hand under his armpit as he used his other to reach up to the nightstand and click on the lamplight. Jayla was gone. Gone, as if she had never been there at all. Waylon went to the hospital, shelling out some cockamamie story on how he broke his finger and within an hour or so was back on the long, lonely subway ride home with his injury secured in a splint. He popped the bottle top to the pills he was prescribed and downed a couple. The pain was still pumping, but at least it was subsiding with the medicine. He slid in his seat and rested his head against the wall, rehashing the horror he had woken up to. It wasn't possible. She was dead. *She was dead, she was dead, she was dead,* he kept reminding himself over and over. But she was there — there in his bedroom. She broke his finger. That was real.

Waylon didn't believe in ghosts. Was he being haunted? Was this how he was paying for his sinful addiction? But why just her? Why not any of the other dozens of women he had killed? Was it because she felt more special to him for some reason? The thought made his stomach turn. He needed to get away out of town for a while. He needed a break. He wanted to go anywhere. He figured he would leave as soon as he got home. He'd pack a bag and take a bus and call his employers in the morning. He had vacation time coming, and they were usually flexible with finding some immediate coverage for his absence. Maybe he wouldn't even return! Maybe he'd start his life over somewhere else. He had been in that city way too long, anyway. It was time for a change.

He turned his head and looked down the subway car, where a few others sat in silence. Among them, a girl in a sweatshirt sat reading a book; strands of her caramel-colored hair flowing out from the hood she had over her head. Waylon's eyes enlarged. His heart started beating faster. *It's not her. It's not her,* he tried to convince himself. Then she looked over in his direction and quirked her mouth into a tiny, mischievous grin as her pretty eyes met his. He got up, grabbing the handrail as the subway slowed to a stop at a station. It wasn't his destination, but he had to get out of that car. The doors opened, and he stepped out, hooking a sharp left and heading down the platform toward the stairs. As the train starting chugging along, he casually looked over his shoulder.

She was following him!

Her steps were just as steady and firm as his as she kept her head down, hands in her front sweatshirt pocket. He quickened his footing and scampered up the stairwell, nearly stubbing his toe and tripping. He trekked down the tiled hallway, throwing his head back over his shoulder to see her emerge from out of the stairwell. Now he was almost jogging. He saw the turnstile exit above and took off running, blowing his way through and not bothering to look back. He jetted up the final staircase to the street level, where a taxi cab had coasted by with perfect timing. He flagged his hand up, calling out and hurrying after it. It stopped and he ducked into the back, immediately blurting his address. The cab rolled forward. He looked out the back window. The subway exit behind was empty with no trace of any hooded girl chasing after him. He sighed and slumped his head back against the seat, closing his eyes with an exasperated breath.

Waylon didn't end up packing any bags when he arrived home. The meds had made him drowsy, and he had been through a lot that night. So despite creeping fear that Jayla's ghostly presence might float its way back into his bedroom and start cracking toes, he ended up falling asleep and woke up safe and sound the next morning. He was relieved. Maybe he *had* imagined it all. Maybe he broke his finger while getting out of bed and the stress had manifested itself into the form of his guilty pleasure. He rubbed his face and scratched his short black hair, shuffling his way out of the room and stopping dead in his tracks.

His entire apartment was trashed.

Furniture was turned over. Food and countless other items from the kitchen had been scattered about. Some art on his wall had been torn. And scribed everywhere with red spray paint was the word "CONFESS". It was on his walls. It was written across his fridge a few times. Even his smashed TV screen supplied the word at least five times. How in the hell could someone have done this while he was there? The medicine had knocked him out pretty well, so it was plausible that he could've slept through it, especially if they were quiet.

Not they. *She.* He knew exactly who it was. And ghosts could be as quiet as they wanted. It was obvious what she wanted from him. Only the thought terrified him. He always entertained the thought of his door being kicked down by a tactical unit for his capture or some equally enforcing order of law putting an end to his murderous run, but he never thought something like this could happen. Would she haunt him until the day he died if he didn't give himself up? Could she follow him wherever he went? Wherever he hid? Death row on his way to lethal injection versus being eternally haunted by this girl was more or less the same equivalency. But at least the latter option gave him his freedom. A sense of stubbornness began filling in the gap inside him formally populated by fear. He was untouchable! He gotten away for years doing what he did! And now all of the sudden that bitch was going to come at him with threats?! Ghost or no ghost, he decided not to take it anymore. Fuck going to the police! He was going to confront her if she came at him again.

A few days passed. He had since cleaned up the mess in his apartment and erased most of the graffiti, going back to work (where he did contemplate digging up the coffin in the grave he had left Jayla buried under and seeing for himself just what the hell was going on) but he didn't see or hear from her. No notes were sticking to his door or waiting on the floor. No one was following him. He didn't see her within crowds that passed. He was beginning to think he had just had a nervous breakdown, and now it was over. Maybe someone had been messing with him that looked like her; that dyed her hair the same and his mind was just mixing her up. After all, someone had to create the graffiti. That part he didn't imagine. Maybe they noticed he wasn't going to the police and gave up tormenting him after realizing they couldn't squeeze anything out of him. He felt relief.

It had been almost a week when he came home from work late one night. He opened his door and flicked the light switch, but nothing happened. He groaned, closing the door behind him. He slinked his way into the kitchen and tried digging through drawers for a flashlight, but something felt wrong. He felt a presence, like he had the night his finger was broken. He turned and saw her emerge from the darkness, illuminated lightly by strands of the moon's bright glow from his half-open window shades. It was Jayla. His eyes widened. He opened his mouth to say something, but he heard a peculiar noise, like the soft sound of a bullet being fired from a gun with a silencer. He felt the sting in his neck and reached up, pulling out the small dart and admiring it with what light he had. He immediately felt dizzy. His vision blurred. His knees grew weak as he tried to make a beeline for the door, catching himself on the edge of the kitchen counter before dropping to the floor.

Jayla took a step toward him; her familiar face still cascaded within the shadows. Waylon tried to crawl, but bit by bit, he lost function of his muscles. "You took everything away from me, Waylon," she spoke out with. "All for your fun and games. Well, I can play, too. I can plot and plan down to the T, just like you did with all of the other women. I can make your existence just as futile and unresolved as theirs. You had your chances to confess with dignity, and I would've left you alone. Since I'm smaller than you, I had to cheat a little and use alternative methods to get you to stay put," she told him, waving her dart gun. "But don't worry. I'm still gonna give you a taste of your own medicine."

Waylon's eyes rolled and swayed as he lied on his back. Things were becoming warped. Jayla hovered over him, and everything softly shifted into blackness.

Waylon had woken up sometime later, trying to sit up and whacking his head against a short, hard roof. He huffed and moved his arms, feeling the similar sides. It didn't take long for him to realize where he was. But that didn't mean he didn't panic. He started kicking and throwing his arms in his limited space, shouting and screaming for help, but his cries were muffled within the confines of his area. He felt something hard on his side, patting his hand in the darkness and feeling the handle of a flashlight. He thumbed around and located the power switch, illuminating the interior of the coffin. Perhaps the notion of actually seeing where he was made him a bit more frantic. He called out again. He could've been anywhere! He tried pushing the top open, but it was no use. He sighed. After another minute or two, he reached into the left pocket of his pants to search for keys so he could dig himself out. He was desperate, after all. But instead, he ended up pulling out a photograph, curving a weird expression as he directed the beam of the light onto it. It was simply a beat-up picture of Jayla, torn down the middle. It couldn't have been one of his. He burned them all to a crisp, and besides, she was posing and smiling directly at the camera when all of his were voyeuristic candid shots. He searched himself more, digging into his right pocket, where he pulled out another photograph.

His eyes widened as he joined the two photos together at the middle tear.

The complete photo was of Jayla, smiling at the camera as her arm slung around the shoulders of... Jayla. Another Jayla, who presented an equally-adorable smile. Realization flooded into his mind. How could he have missed something like that?! His caramel-haired goddess supplied no evidence at any point during his observations! But perhaps people show only what they want to be seen — much like him. The world can be a big enough place to disconnect some people. It certainly can be small enough to discover others.

Waylon's unbelievable breaths quickened as he tossed the two pieces of the split photo aside, shouting and hollering as he began hitting the roof of the coffin with the flashlight. He slammed and recklessly pounded it hard to the point where the flashlight broke apart; the pieces spilling over him as the light flickered and died out, leaving him in darkness as he gave a long, angry, booming scream.

HAIR OF THE DOG THAT BIT YOU

Rumors started flying, as they often did between people.

But this was almost laughable. They were calling it "The Werewolf of Westinfield". Rowan Dagmoritz half-expected the Ripley's Believe-it-or-Not van to come screeching into town with their cameras and bad make-up reenactments ready to go before the ordeal had even ended. She wanted to laugh at it herself. She wanted to laugh at the ridiculousness that poured out of people's mouths while she took down their statements. But her job as an officer of the law was to take people seriously, for there had to be *some* logical explanation behind it all.

It was the third incident reported that week, and the fifteenth that month. Four people were already dead. Slaughtered. Butchered. Torn apart. But credited to a large man-like wolf? Why did it have to happen in October of all months? It just opened up the opportunity for the townspeople to add to the rolling snowball of absurdity down the hill of gullibility. The bandwagon was gaining speed. People were blaming incidents on the beast just for connection's sake. And the teenagers — holy shit, the teenagers! As if they couldn't get enough out of their prank phone calls and toilet-papering houses, now they were vending this local fear into half-assed jokes and mockeries to anyone who would be foolish enough to give them any sort of viable attention.

It was getting out of control. And up until now, the most excitement the twenty-six-year-old Rowan had experienced as a cop the last few months was writing out some parking tickets and pulling over some D.U.I.'s. There she was, standing with her partner John Ontennio in the living room of the breaking-and-entering call they had responded to. John scratched his short spiky black hair and rustled his index finger under his bushy black mustache. Who did he think he was with that, anyway? He was the same age as her but tried to pass off some kind of age-old repertoire that all male patrol officers needed thick mustaches. It only added to his serious demeanor as a policeman. When she first transferred into town and they were paired together, he had mentioned that Rowan was too pretty to be an officer, and that crooks and hoodlums would try to take advantage of that by using it against her. She was a little more than silently appalled. She wanted to tell him that she sought the same respectable treatment as anyone else at the precinct. Besides, it's not like she was a supermodel or anything. She grew up as a brown-haired, doe-eyed girl-next-door — short as well, only five-foot-two, and waited for him to comment on that additionally, but he never did.

John took more of a cool and calm approach to the werewolf fables of Westinfield. "If it isn't some kind of animal, it's some psycho with too much time on his hands running around in some kind of Lon Chaney costume," he muttered one night. She didn't get the reference.

"How do you expect me to keep calm when I've got a damn werewolf stalking me?!" the older balding Mr. Bruggery snapped as he tried to shape his horrible comb-over.

"Did you actually see the animal, sir?" John asked, perking his eyebrows with his thumbs sticking into his utility belt.

"Not tonight, but I seen it da other night!" Mr. Bruggery stated. "In muh backyard, rummaging through muh trash cans! It was as big as a horse, for god's sake! I went to get muh shotgun and when I kicked muh way through the back door it ran off into the woods!"

Rowan silently paced through the mess of the living room. John veered his eyes around. "You have anyone that has any grudges against you? Any reason for anyone to break in and do this?" he asked.

"No! Because it ain't a person, ya jackass! Open ya damn eyes! Ain't nobody broke in here and took anythin'! This here's an animal break-in! Lookin' for food or something, I dunno, but it's this goddamn werewolf, I tell ya, and if ya people ain't gonna do nothin' about it, I'm as good as dead!" Mr. Bruggery argued.

"I already told you, Mr. Bruggery — animal control is looking into it. In the meantime, all you can do is keep your doors and windows locked and call them right away if it returns," John calmly assured him. "If you feel you're not safe here, I'd advise you to temporarily stay with a friend or relative or in a motel until things calm down, understand?"

"Safe? There ain't no safe when a goddamn werewolf is runnin' around here!" he snapped in return. "You younga kids these days know nothin' 'bout nothin'! Only the things you see in movies. Werewolves are real! And somebody here in town is changin' into one! Forget that full moon bullshit — it can happen anytime! Allergic to silver? Ha! Forget it. Silver don't do jack against 'em. You think they're just gonna feel guilty and give themselves up? Hell, some don't even remember changing into one!"

To serve and protect. Why did so many small-minded people think that every cop was the enemy, or some kind of corrupted entity? All they ever did was try to help. Rowan was beginning to learn the hard way that most people simply didn't like authority. When they had a problem and didn't know who to blame or how to handle it, they'd lash all their anger out at those trying to suggestion a resolution.

It was pushing midnight when Rowan and John left the Bruggery residence. John was finishing up with Bruggery while Rowan walked down his driveway, stopping at the fence around the front yard to greet the two small terrier dogs that happily trotted over and started licking her fingers. "Damn hicks," John had mumbled under his breath as he approached her. "They see one fatass raccoon in the dark and they spin their top looking for some kind of justifiable excuse to use their guns.

Good old Mr. Bug-Eyed-Me." The terriers cowered back and started growling and barking uncontrollably at John. He sneered down at them, adjusting his utility belt. "Even his damn dogs are pricks."

They finished the night where they normally did so many times before, at the take-out burger stand in town. John had brought Rowan's burger and fries over to her at one of the tables outside and settled down with a thickly red hunk of meat on his plate. Rowan eyed it with some disgust. "I think it's got some more time to cook," she blurted.

"I like it rare," he told her, digging in.

"If it were any rarer, it'd still be grazing," Rowan added. A Chihuahua nestled in the purse of the girl sitting behind John started wildly yapping at him. He briskly looked over his shoulder and went back to eating his meat. "What is it with you and dogs?" Rowan then wondered.

John shrugged. "Must be my cologne."

"Yeah? What is it? "Milkbone" by Calvin Klein?" Rowan asked, perking her eyebrows.

The girl with the dog evidently got up and walked away.

Rowan dropped by John's house the next night to pick him up for their shift. He yelled for her to let herself in and help herself to a drink as he finished getting ready, so Rowan casually paced his house, looking around. He seemed like a solitary man; not too many decorations on the wall or furniture filling the rooms. The door to the garage was open, and curiosity had gotten the best of her, so she helped herself to taking a peek inside. A sleek Pontiac was parked within. Rowan noticed a fridge. She went over to take him up on his offer and opened the door, only to find it completely filled with meat. Top to bottom, every shelf was stacked — and it was all raw, uncooked. It was more meat than she had seen in anybody's fridge before. Then a thought rolled through her head. A very small, almost preposterous thought —

John was the werewolf!

She stopped herself short of any further mindful implications, almost cracking a smile. And she based that on what? His love for raw meat? His uncooperative allure to dogs? Then she remembered something Mr. Bruggery had said during his rant — some werewolves don't even remember changing. A deniable sense of innocence. Could it be possible? Her own partner? It was a wild assumption based on a stray thought and little evidence. She closed the door, where John was waiting behind as she gave a light, startled gasp. He edged a hard stare at her for a second, then spoke out with, "I meant grab a drink from the fridge in the kitchen."

Rowan shimmered a shaky smile. "Sorry. Doing a little snooping, I guess."

"My fault, partially. I haven't had you over for the grand tour yet. What good is a partner if you can't connect with them personally, right?" he said. He gave a nod to the fridge. "I like to hunt."

Rowan veered her eyes to the fridge door. *Yeah. Hunt humans.*

He cocked his head. "C'mon. Let's roll."

Rowan followed him back through the door inside; her eyes barely catching the spot of gray fur on the concrete floor. *Probably just rabbit fur,* she figured.

Still, as ridiculously wild as the speculation was, it kept bugging her. It just wouldn't leave her brain. Someone — or something — was out there killing people, and they had zero leads. It could've been anyone. Why not a police officer? Why not the police officer she was partners with, riding next to her nearly every day?

Rowan wasn't sure where to stand in the whole ordeal. But the sight of Bruggery's mutilated body on his kitchen floor definitely made her question it with more concern. She only caught a brief glimpse of it when she and John had arrived on the scene. It had been called in around nine o'clock that night, and apparently, through early forensic speculation, had occurred the previous night, probably sometime after they had left, only to be reported almost twenty-four-hours later by Bruggery's ex-wife who had just stopped by the residence. No one had seen or heard him since his small rant. The house was already full with investigators and detectives aside from the men from animal control, who confirmed without a doubt that the attack appeared animalistic. The corpse had series of gashes and claw marks. Blood was everywhere. His left arm was hanging on the shoulder socket nearly by a string. And his big, bulgy eyes on his decapitated head across the kitchen were wide open with frozen horror. Mr. Bruggery, a.k.a. Mr. Bug-Eyed-Me. Rowan also overheard the detectives discussing possibilities with the animal control men on whether or not the killing could have been done by a human merely posing in a costume. "No way," one of the animal control men answered with a firm shake of his head. "If I had to make a guess flat-out, I would say bear attack. A small but lethal bear."

At that point, they had given Rowan a stingy look and one of the detectives politely but subtly suggested she wait outside and handle crowd control from the noisy neighbors. She stood in the driveway alongside John among the red and blue flashing car lights lining the street. More men tended to the shredded remains of the dogs in the front yard. The dogs. Even the damn dogs. John shook his head. "Wonder what we'll do with our nights now that Bug-Eyed-Me's gone," he blurted.

Not very professional, anyway. There was a certain layered tone to his words, almost as if he was relieved. Almost as if — he knew it was coming. Did he come back last night after their shift and silence Bruggery for good? The old man spoke like he was the werewolf expert in town. Maybe Bruggery was onto something — or someone. It occurred to Rowan that she didn't even know her partner all that well. Sure, they had plenty of nights to chit-chat with small talk where they could trade the basics, but she felt as if she still didn't know him as a *person*. He said it himself — she hadn't even gotten the official tour of his home, and she had already been there so many times over the weeks to pick him up or drop him off.

Later on that night, Rowan and John had nestled their car in the cozy confines of a speed trap under a bridge at the edge of town, where they had preyed on unsuspecting speeders so many nights before. She felt compelled to mention something about the werewolf to get him talking and possibly slip out a fact or two that would better solidify her suspicion, but she began to feel ill. It started slowly as a boiling bubble in her stomach which she passed off as bad indigestion at first, but then her chest began to ache. She felt like vomiting. John gave a question of concern, but she simply ignored him and opened her door, stepping out of the car. Her legs grew weak. She fell to her knees in the dirt. Her entire body felt as if it were on fire. It felt like something was stretching her skeleton. At that point, John had gotten out of the car and rushed over to help her. She gave a painful cry and began convulsing. Her limbs spastically shook. John grabbed the radio on his shoulder and prepared to speak into it for emergency assistance but froze at the sight before him. His eyes beamed wide. Rowan was beginning to grow larger. She was changing shape! It all happened within a matter of a quick minute and a half. She towered nearly seven feet. Dark brown and grayish hair covered her muscled body, which burst its way out of her uniform. Her nose stretched into an elongated snout, and razor-sharp fangs curved within the snarling saliva. John's mouth dropped as he stumbled back against the car in fear.

She sprang onto him, clawing and tearing as he screamed for unassisted help. When it was over, Rowan's putrid yellow eyes looked down at a mutilated mess against the front hood of the car as she wiped the blood and flesh from her mouth. A sense of guilt quickly flooded over her and she realized what she had just done. But it was so good! She wanted more. She felt alive and invincible. She felt *hungry*.

And as Rowan sprang up onto the car and crawled up to the top of the bridge to howl at the hanging moon, that thought and feeling of guilt quickly faded away, because she was sure of one thing...

In the morning, she wouldn't remember any of it anyway.

NO ASSEMBLY REQUIRED

Little Peter came rushing into the kitchen. "It's here! It's here! It finally came!" he gleefully cried out, jumping up and down.

Father put down the newspaper he was reading at the table and neatly folded his glasses into his shirt's pocket. "Well, by golly, if that wasn't fast!" he stated.

Mother wiped her hands on the dishtowel at the sink. "Now, now, Peter — calm down or you'll have yourself a spell!"

"But it's here! It's finally here!" Peter cheered.

Father stood up and slung his arm around his son's shoulders. "I suppose we ought to help those deliverymen so we can get to opening it on up, wouldn't you say?"

"Yaaaaay!" Peter triumphantly hurrahed, throwing a fist into the air.

He scurried out of the kitchen and through the living room as Father followed. They opened the door, where two men in gray jumpsuits waited with a tall silver plastic box. One of them checked his electronic clipboard and perked an eyebrow. "Wilson residence?" he asked.

"That's us," Father confirmed.

The deliveryman held the clipboard out. Father pressed his thumb against the clear plate, and the scanner read his print, giving an optimistic beep with an accompanying green flash at the top.

"Where do you want it?" the deliveryman wondered.

"Why don't you boys bring it right on into the den?" Father suggested.

The deliveryman nodded to his partner, and they wheeled the tall silver box into the house on a dolly as Father gently guided Peter back to avoid being run over. They veered the corner and went into the den, where a large metal slab table waited among some other basic furnished things like a couch, desk and bookcase. They made a team effort of picking the box up and setting it onto the slab as Peter watched with an eager smile from the doorway. When the box was neatly in place, the deliverymen wiped their hands. "All set to go," one of them noted.

Father showed them out. "Thanks, fellas. Have yourselves a good day, now," he politely said as they exited through the front door.

Peter bounced up and down, waving his arms. "Come on, come on, come on!" he excitedly called out. "Can we open it now?"

"I don't see why not," Father replied, being joined by Mother around the corner as they reentered the den. "Might as well put it to use right away."

Peter happily jittered as he stood next to the long silver box on the table. Father opened the control panel on the side and pressed a few buttons. Mother stood behind Peter, placing her hands on his shoulders.

"Remember, Peter — your Father was very fortunate to get a hold of one of these. They're aren't many left, after all," she reminded him. "Even at the clearance price, it still cost a lot, so this is your Christmas present."

"I know, I know!" Peter quickly blurted as if hearing it for the one millionth time.

Father finally got the top open, and some cold air *hissed* through the opening crack as he slid it off and set it against the wall. After the foggy blanket had cleared, Peter rolled his fingertips over the edge of the plastic box and raised himself a bit on his tippy-toes to peek inside, where the body of a five-foot-seven man lied wearing only undergarments. "Wooooow!" Peter declared, his eyes growing wide. "Look at him! He looks so real!"

"You get what you pay for," Father stated with a smile of wisdom. He reached into a side compartment, pulling out a booklet labeled at the top with the large words, "THE PERSONAL COMPANION — INSTRUCTIONS (NO ASSEMBLY REQUIRED!)".

"This is going to be so cool!" Peter added, his eyes gliding across the body's form. "We can be best friends and do *everything* together!"

"Finally... someone to do all the vacuuming, dusting and dishes around here," Mother added as she set a relieved hand across her chest.

"Let's not forget the laundry," Father threw in with a chuckle, which garnered accompanying laughs from his wife and son. "At least I won't have to worry about fiddling with the darn car when it breaks down."

"Thank you, Mom and Dad! You're the best!" Peter warmly told them.

Mother gave a comforting smile and kissed his head. "When something benefits the entire family, it's a win in *my* book," she noted.

Father flipped through the instruction book. "He's been frozen for quite some time. It says to let him warm up for a while, and then after that, he'll be on his feet in no time. What do you guys say we kill some time and get some sleep to recharge ourselves so we'll be fully alert and welcoming when he comes to?"

"What a splendid idea!" Mother contributed.

"Yeah!" Peter cheered.

The trio left the den and headed into the living room. Father slouched into his favorite lazy armchair while Mother tidily nestled herself at the end of the couch. Peter plopped himself into his fun beanbag seat on the floor. A commercial began playing on the large flat screen television panel across the wall. "Are you tired of overworking yourself hours on end to get those burdening daily house chores finished?" the announcer promptly remarked. "Don't be without the Personal Companion! It's your ticket to the easy life that you deserve! All Personal

Companions come fully guaranteed with your choice of a male or female! Human beings are in limited supply, so act now for the affordable discounted price of five-hundred-forty-thousand credits, and never overheat your android circuits again!"

Father and Mother reached into their cushions and pulled out cords. Peter reached over and grabbed the cord from the wall, lifting the side of his shirt to plug the end into the socket on his hip as he closed his eyes and comfortably lied back with a smile.

MAN MARRIES MONSTER FROM CLOSET

"Douglas Morris, but just call me Doug," the man then promptly introduced himself, holding out a hand which Will firmly shook. "So what do you do for a buck, Will?" he then asked.

"I'm an investigative journalist," Will told him.

"Whoa. Sounds seriously on the level," Doug said with an impressed tone. "Newspaper? Magazine?"

"Uh... sort of in between," Will noted as a small, shaky smile emerged. "Tabloids."

Doug perked his eyebrows, sitting back in his seat across from him. "No shit," he responded, adding a tiny smirk of his own. "You mean like "I Had Bigfoot's Baby" and "Tiny Martians Live Inside President's Brain" and all that?"

Will bobbed my head. "Unfortunately, yes. When I went to school for journalism, I didn't exactly see myself coming home from investigating a story about a woman who claimed she had three alien bodies in her possession."

Doug chuckled. "Well? Did she?"

"Nah. They were rubber dummies. Good ones, though."

"Bet you get a lot of that bullshit," Doug figured.

Will shrugged. "More often that not, you're right. But like you said — it's really for the almighty buck. Maybe someday I'll able to report on something noteworthy for a respectable publisher. I figure I'm only thirty. I've still got plenty of time. Besides — maybe I'll get lucky and actually find a supernatural story that's real for a change."

Doug broadly smiled and hiked a leg up across his other. "Well, then, Will, my friend — you are in luck. Seems we were meant to meet. I've got quite a story for you."

Will casually coasted his eyes out his window and watched as the countryside flashed by from their train. He had heard that line before. That's how everyone started their apparent claim to fame. "Really?" he asked in a somewhat tired, unenthusiastic way.

Doug's eyes caught Will's hand as he nodded and gestured toward it. "Wedding ring. What does the wife think about you traipsing from town to town investigating four-headed babies and fat gigantic cats that own twenty-three elderly ladies?"

"She's pretty understanding. She gets a kick out of the stories I write. Says she's glad she married someone who didn't have some boring, ordinary job. Then again, it's only been two years, so we'll see what she says in twenty, I guess."

Doug gave a light chuckle. "I know how that is. I'm thirty-two and I've been married almost ten years already. Feels like twenty. Wife hates it when I go on these lengthy business trips. She can be such a monster sometimes."

"Yeah, aren't they all?" Will playfully agreed.

"No, I mean my wife really *is* a monster," Doug told him. "That's the story I have for you to write, if you want."

Will smiled. "Your wife's a monster," he repeated. "What kinda monster?"

"Closet monster," Doug answered.

"Sorry, that's a new one on me. What's a closet monster?"

"Just what it sounds like. It's a monster from a closet. Didn't you ever think there was a monster in your closet when you were a kid?"

Will gave another shrug. "Sure. Every kid does, I guess."

"Well, mine was real. Most people aren't privy to the world of monsters in closets because most kids eventually outgrow their fear, and that's when the monsters lose their power — their ability to transcend from their world into ours to give a little nightly scare. But mine stuck around — kept coming back. We sorta... befriended each other. Ya know, something you'd find in an eighties Jim Henson flick or something," Doug explained.

"And you... went into wedlock with this monster," Will said.

"Well, sure. It was female, after all. And part human. All closet monsters are part human. I'm not a completely twisted freak who would marry a pure one hundred percent gruesome scaly monster. Especially a male one, at that. Anyway, the more she kept coming back, the more she kept losing her... symbiotic relationship with her own world, until she eventually became trapped here for good. She lived with me as a teenager and we tied the knot in our early twenties after college."

Will scratched his short choppy dirty blonde hair. "I gotta say, that's, uh... that's pretty original."

"Wanna see a picture of her?" Doug asked in an almost-excited tone.

"Why not?" Will blurted.

Doug reached into his back pocket and pulled out his wallet, flipping through the pictures until holding it out to Will. Will leaned forward off his seat and took a glance. "Wow... she's... actually pretty good-looking for a monster, if you don't mind me saying."

"Thanks," Doug said, taking a sentimental glance at the photo before closing the wallet back up and returning it into his pants. "Her name's Rebecca. "Becca" for short, she likes to be called. She definitely turns a lot of heads when we're out and about. A lot of people think she looks like Jennifer Garner, but I think she's more of a Keira Knightley myself."

"You have a picture of her in her, uh…" Will started to ask, searching for the right term.

"Monster form?" Doug finished. He smiled. "Sorry. Not exactly wallet photo material, if you know what I mean. She's not that scary, actually. Although, that opinion's coming from someone who's been used to seeing her true form for almost twenty-five years now. Guess that's where that phrase "Beauty is in the eye of the beholder" sits true."

"Is she... dangerous?" Will inquired.

"You bet. Got her locked up in the attic as we speak."

Will's face dropped with unbelievable shock. "Locked... in the attic. Your... closet monster wife... is locked up in an attic."

"Sure. Even after all this time, she needs a sense of control when I'm not there. Don't worry, though. I know what you're thinking. She's perfectly fine. She's got a bathroom, plenty of food and drinks and a TV."

Will rolled his tongue across his lower lip, trying not to laugh. "Okay. Um... well... let's just assume what you're saying is true. Why are you telling me this now? Why haven't you gone to a tabloid or newspaper sooner?"

"Good question, Will. Like any marriage, things after time start to feel a little... stale. Uninspired. Unexciting. Everything's still new and lovey-dovey for you now, but just wait ten years. That feeling is gonna start to creep and threaten. Of course, that's not a bad thing; doesn't mean your marriage is falling apart. It's completely normal. But you may feel you wanna try or do something new. A make-over. And that's the point where I feel we're at. I wanna get our story out there. Every couple deserves for their story to be heard. Doesn't matter if people believe it or not. And in today's economy, it wouldn't hurt to get a few dollars out of it. I've got the perfect title for it, too," Doug spoke, flashing an ingenious smile. "You can call it, "Man Marries Monster from Closet"."

Will slowly bobbed his head in agreement. "Yeah, that would do it."

Doug gave him a narrow stare in the moments of silence that followed as the train clicked and clacked along the track. "You don't believe me, do you?"

"Well..." Will groaned with a friendly leer, etching for the right thing to say not to hurt the man's feelings.

"No, no — it's cool. I wouldn't believe me either if I were in your shoes," Doug stated. "You probably get spoon-fed shit like this on a daily basis for breakfast, lunch and dinner. But I assure you — this is the one story in your entire career that will ever pan out to be completely, undeniably, absolutely true." Will gave a light sigh, thoughts racing through his head. "How 'bout it?" Doug then proposed. "Come by my place when we get back to the city and I'll introduce you. We'll take a cab from the station. My treat."

"I dunno," Will mumbled, rubbing the back of his neck. "Sounds really intriguing and all, but it's been a long trip. I really should get home and see my wife. Maybe we could... arrange something for another time?"

"This is a limited time offer, Willy boy," Doug confirmed. "Now or never. What's it gonna hurt? She cooks a great dinner. Besides — what's your worst case scenario? That I'm just another one of those money-hungry frauds who will turn the lights off and have my wife hide while I replace her with a cheap monster dummy? All that drivel you publish is bogus anyway, right? So either way you get a story. You've got nothing to lose."

Doug did make a pretty good point. The story had some ingenuity to it. It was different from the norm. But as ludicrous as it was, it was still an opportunity, and in the world of laughable crackpot tabloids, Will knew it would be unwise to pass up. So he firmly nodded and slapped his hands onto his knees. "All right. Let's do it," he agreed.

"Great," Doug optimistically stated, smacking his hands. "You'll love her. She's terrific."

The train ride didn't last much longer, and once they had arrived at the station, they gathered their baggage and hailed a cab, coasting out of the city on their way to Doug's house. Will was beginning to think twice about his decision, especially regarding his safety. There he was, riding in a cab next to a stranger he had met on a train going to his house for an apparent lead on a story which he was crazy to give any credence to — and no one knew he was going there. He would've simply made a quick call to his wife or someone at the office to let them know his whereabouts in case Doug's hospitality turned to some kind of twisted torturing abduction or worse, but the battery of his cell phone had died early during the long train ride and the charger was somewhere buried deep within his suitcase. He was overdue for a new phone, anyway. He heard about it frequently from his wife, when she couldn't get a hold of him because it was always dying shortly after a few uses. He figured it wasn't a big deal. He could merely recharge it when he got to Doug's house or better yet use Doug's phone (if he didn't get an axe in the back after entering the house, anyway).

They finally arrived. It was quite impressive, actually — a nice three story home in the countryside that was up-to-par and fairly new-looking. No chipped bricks or faded paint, no grass sprouting up through the pebble graveled driveway, and a beautiful garden in the front yard with an elegant water fountain to boot. Just another all-American couple living the white picket fence dream. Will got the impression that Doug and

"Becca" didn't need money from a stupid tabloid paper, which for a moment made him a little wary but once Doug had led him through the front door into the main foyer, he silently and calmly assured himself that any number of the strange people with their stories he had visited over the time he had been a journalist could have harmed or captured him easily, but they never did. Doug set his two suitcases next to the staircase and reached for Will's. "Here. Let me take that for you. Just make yourself at home," he warmly gestured. "Can I get you something to drink? Cold beer or soda?"

"No, I'm fine, thanks," Will answered.

Since Doug was in such a courteous mood, Will was going to ask if he could quickly use the phone to call his wife so she wouldn't worry, but Doug had beaten him to the subject. "You wanna give your wife a call? I know how they can worry," he suggested.

Will took a step toward the stairs; his eyes veering up. "My cell phone's dead, actually," he noted.

"You can use our phone if you'd like," Doug recommended. He clapped his hands together. "Better yet — why don't you see if she'd want to come here and join us for dinner? You took the cab here, so you're gonna need a ride home, anyway. If it's not too far for her to drive."

Will's curiosity got the best of him. He felt safe enough, and he was definitely built well enough to handle himself if some kind of surprising attack came, as long as he kept on his toes. He just wanted to see what Doug was razzing about. Doug had noticed his fixation on the stairs and his drifting thoughts away from the topic. "Probably just wanna get right down to business and meet the wife, huh?" he then wondered, cocking a half-grin.

"I don't want to be rude," Will mentioned, trying to keep his tone friendly.

"Not at all. Tell ya what — I'll introduce you, she'll fix a quick snack, and I'll take you home myself later on, unless you wanna call another cab. Deal?"

"Sounds good to me," Will affirmed.

"Excellent. Right this way," Doug said, hopping onto the first step and leading Will up the winding staircase to the second floor.

They strolled down the hall. Will got the impression he was passing through some kind of miniature mansion, with a statue here and there and some occasional painting on the wall that was so splattered with paint he couldn't make out its image, if there even purposefully was one. They reached a second smaller staircase, which led up to the attic door at the end of a shorter carpeted hallway, where a small wheeled tool chest sat perched. "Sorry. Been doing some work on the door," Doug noted as they passed it. "If she ever got out and couldn't control herself, I'd have a real mess on my hands." The door was secured with a series of strong protective padlocks and a slender metal-flapped slot, much like a mail drop. Doug started by crouching down and opening it, peeking through. "Hey, honey, I'm home," he said.

"Already?" Will heard a feminine voice from within respond.

"Train got in a little early," Doug added. "Are you decent?"

"Sure am," she perkily answered.

Doug raised himself upright and pulled out some keys from his pocket, beginning to unlock the series of safety mechanisms down the door. Will held back a smirk. It was a nice little touch — a gimmicky dramatic effect for everyone he probably brought up expecting to see a bogeywoman on the other side of the door. After all the slots had been unlocked and turned, Doug grabbed the doorknob and pulled open the door, revealing a nicely-furnished attic mirroring the set up of a comfortable living room, complete with a plush carpet, decorations on the wall, a table and dresser here and there, a door in the corner which Will figured to be the bathroom, and of course the TV, complete with its neighboring shelf unit of alphabetized DVDs. Will took a step forward, craning his neck to see in more, where the backside of a tall, slender woman dressed in jeans and a tee-shirt folded some clothes into the bottom drawer of the dresser. She stood upright, turning around with a gorgeous smile, and to Will's surprise, she was purely beautiful — almost supermodel beautiful, at that, with long flowing dark blonde hair. Doug was right. She definitely looked more like Keira Knightley than Jennifer Garner. She trotted forward and met Doug with a wrapping, strong hug as they exchanged a kiss. "Oooh, I missed you so much!" she romantically exclaimed.

"I hate being away from you on these stupid trips," he told her, nuzzling his nose against hers.

"Well, you're home now. Plenty of time to catch up on missed activities," she giggled in a way that paralleled most happy-go-lucky mushy couples.

Doug turned, still holding onto her and extended his arm back to Will. "Honey, this is Will. I met him on the train ride back. Will, this is my wife, Becca."

"Nice to meet you," Will said with a nod, stepping forward and shaking her hand. "You have a really nice house."

"Ohh, thank you. So nice of you to say," she politely responded. "We try to keep up on it, but who has the time anymore?"

"Will is a tabloid journalist," Doug informed her. "I thought I would bring him by to meet you, and maybe give us a chance to show him the unique aspect of our marriage to show the world, like we talked about."

Will grew another grin. "Doug told me you have a... different side of you."

"Well, that's one way to put it," Becca joked, looking back and forth between them. Doug chuckled and tickled her side as she jerked and playfully slapped his arm. She looked back at Will, continuing with, "Wow, tabloid journalist. Sounds like you never have a dull moment on the job. Probably have seen some pretty strange things, huh?"

"I've definitely seen my share of oddities," Will contested. "So, you, uh... stay locked up in here for... the whole time he's gone?"

"It's really not bad. The only bad thing about it is that I don't have my little snuggle bear to keep me company," she said, pinching Doug's cheek.

"How much did you spend this time?" Doug asked her before turning back to Will. "I should really contemplate taking the laptop out of here. She tends to get a little click-happy when she's stuck up here and can't set foot into actual stores."

"Oh, stop. You spend more than me online," she huffed.

"So... am I, uh, able to see... it... I mean — you, in your, you know..." Will wondered.

Doug looked at his beautiful wife, perking his eyebrows. "How 'bout it, honey? Feelin' up to it?"

She scrunched her face and shook her head. "I'm not sure if I'm in the mood right now," she disappointedly said.

Doug sympathetically nodded and returned his attention to Will. "Sorry, Will. This thing isn't exactly a by-the-moment thing she always has control over. Was a lot easier when we were younger but she's been out of her world for so long now... she's so accustomed to her human form."

"If you'd like to stick around for a while, I can make some coffee and desert," Becca sweetly suggested.

Will was beginning to feel a lack of authenticity. He had been down that road way too many times to not see it coming far ahead. "Thanks, anyway, but maybe I should just get going," he mumbled.

"No, no, please — stay a little while," Doug genuinely pleaded. "I realize what you might be thinking, but I promise, she's the real deal. We're not trying to play you or anything. If you stay, I promise — you *will* see it. Give us a chance."

Will sighed. His conscience was trying to tell him to leave before any more of his time was wasted, and he would've, if it weren't for that little knack — that knack of curiosity that landed him his job. That knack that kept him going with his job for as long as he had. That knack for him to ask himself those two little words — "What if?"

So Will agreed to stay, much to the delight of Becca, who immediately began brewing a pot of coffee down in the sleekly-designed kitchen. She put out a plate of some cookies and crumb cake, and the three spoke mostly of casual everyday things. Doug had especially liked rehashing stories of his earlier childhood when Becca started visiting him from out of the dark closet in his bedroom, and how he was terrified of her menacing red eyes and sharp white fangs before braving himself up to befriend her, and then those nights of terror turned into nights of conversation and joy when she shifted into her more presumptuously attractive human form to accompany him through all hours of the twilight. Will didn't get too deep into his personal life; he kept to the basic, boring facts. After all, what could top the couple's history of love? Will met his wife at a party. It was cliché and cookie-cut compared to an apparent monster transformation into love. He figured that he could possibly get something out of this after all. No matter what "monster" the couple had waiting to scare him, his employers could whip up and shape up something of more sellable value. The story had promise. He couldn't wait to tell his wife. She'd get a kick out of it and forgive him for being so late in coming home. That's when he realized that it was probably a good idea to give her a quick call, since he had been there for over an hour now. And he was just about to ask for usage of the phone when Becca had placed a hand across her stomach, slightly wobbling in place with a queasy expression.

"You okay?" Will asked.

"It's coming on," she had noted, glancing at Doug. "It's gonna happen. I'm ready to change."

Doug patted the table. "Well, Willy boy, you're in luck — looks like you're gonna see the show after all."

"Doug? Can I talk to you alone upstairs for a minute, please?" Becca then asked.

Doug helped her up from the table. "Why don't you hang here for a minute, Will? I'll be back down to get ya in a minute."

Will crafted a small smile. "Gotta touch up the costume, eh?" he coyly wondered.

"Oh, it's no costume," Doug assured him. "Trust me — you'll see it all for yourself. Be back down."

Doug led Becca out of the kitchen and through the foyer, where they ascended up the staircase. Will slightly rolled his eyes and took the last bite of his crumb cake. He was playing himself for a fool. But he *was* a professional. No matter how absurd things got, the basic line was that these people had invited him into the house and treated him with true comfortable hospitality. No matter what kind of tomfoolery they were concocting behind closed doors upstairs, he was going to act mature about it. Did they even honestly expect him to believe it? It was just fun and games. No harm, no fowl. After a few minutes, Will got up and paced into the hallway, admiring the series of framed portraits hanging on the walls — they were mostly of Doug and Becca, together or separate of varying ages, with some additional family members or friends scattered here and there. He made his way into the foyer, where Doug had come trotting down the stairs. "Everything okay?" Will politely asked.

Doug took a reclusive breath and stopped in front of Will, laying a hand on his shoulder. "Listen, Will — I really apologize, but Becca just talked it over with me. She changed her mind about the whole news article thing. She's just not ready for the world to know yet. Women... always changing their minds."

"Ah. I see," Will responded, although not too surprised. "Was it me? Something I said?"

"Oh, no, no. Not at all," Doug certified. "She just... she gets a little moody when she changes. And a little hostile. She's doesn't want to openly interact with you like that. But you can still take a peek and see her, if you'd like. Don't want you to have come out here for nothin'."

"Yeah. Yeah, I think I will, if you don't mind," Will said.

"Great. She's just ready to change now," Doug said as he began to lead Will up the stairs. "You'll be able to catch everything."

Yeah. Everything except where she puts the costume on when the lights happen to go out for fifteen seconds, Will thought to himself.

They reached the second floor and trailed up the next staircase, approaching the closed attic door at the end of the hall. "Don't worry. It's locked. She can't get out," Doug calmly assured him. Will wasn't the least bit worried. Doug gestured to the door. "Go ahead and look right through. She'll stay far back enough for you to catch it all."

Will crouched down, lowering himself as he reached for the metal-plated slot. He hesitated a brief moment, but then tipped it up and brought his face close enough to see through into the attic. Becca was nearly on the other side, still looking purely human as her steps staggered about. She grunted and groaned, jerking her body. Her hands clutched her chest, scratching about as if she were covered in ants. She threw her head back and gave a yelp, and that's when the first rip of her clothing occurred. First it was her pant leg, then it was her shirt at the hip. She was getting bigger. Will narrowed his unblinking eyes, fully immersed in her strange behavior. Then her skin darkened and became scaly. Her muscles improved. Her head and face began to reshape into something he couldn't fully describe or identify — all he could zero in on were the two blood-red eyes without pupils and the white snarling fangs that grew and snapped within her mouth. Will's eyes went wide. It was no dummy. It was no costume. There was no trickery, or illusion. *This was happening.* When the transformation had completed, all he could manage to murmur was, "Holy shit." Doug stood silently behind him. Will finally pried his attention away and looked back up to him. "You weren't kidding. You actually weren't kidding." He looked back through the slot as the monster paced and lingered about within the attic. "This is unreal. This is... This is incredible. All this time I've been traveling around dealing with fakes and wannabes and I actually found someone who was really telling the truth! You have to let me write this story! Do you realize how much money we could get if we got this on film? This isn't tabloid material — this is *national news!*"

Doug took a light breath. "I'm sorry, Will. I really am. I really wanted you to write this story. I wanted to help you. I thought we met on that train for a reason, but... it just can't happen." The alarm on Doug's digital watch began to beep as he reached down and turned it off, giving another small exhale. "Feeding time."

Will brought his face closer to the slot, pressing his hands up against the door as he continued to watch. "What do you feed her?" he wondered.

Doug reached over to the tool chest against the wall and grabbed a small lead pipe, giving a flat expression down to Will as he stood over him.

SPOOKY STORIES THAT REALLY AREN'T THAT SPOOKY BUT FUN ANYWAY

OCTOBER 2002

GHOSTS

Natasha shook her head as she stared at the rusted gates to the large abandoned house.

Turning, she looked at Josh and Faye, who stood smirking with their arms crossed. Josh was the tough type; his hair waved in a cool James Dean fashion that made him look much older than eighteen as Faye was the typical blond counterpart. After running a hand through her long brown hair, Natasha shrugged. "Guys, when I said I wanted to do something daring on Halloween I didn't mean breaking and entering."

"That's not the daring part," Josh tried to remind her. "It's what happens *after* the breaking and entering part that's daring."

"This house is not haunted," Natasha calmly assured them.

"Everyone says it is," Faye told her. "Besides, weird shit has happened to anyone who's dared to step foot inside. My cousin knew this kid who had a brother who..."

Natasha curved a smile as she began to bob her head. "...who knew a girl who had a boyfriend that was friends with a paperboy that spent the night on a dare," she finished, almost as if hearing the story a million times. "Those stories are all bogus legends. Everyone knows someone who knows someone. That's the way it works. That's the fun of it."

Josh stepped up to the gate and wrapped his hands around the cold bars. For the end of October, it was actually quite nice out that night — just a tad chilly but bearable. "I don't care about any of those weak-ass campfire tales," he sharply stated. "*I'm* here, and *I'm* going in."

Faye raised her eyebrows to Natasha. "Well, Natasha — it's either this or trick-or-treating."

"Suddenly trick-or-treating sounds a *lot* more mature," she mumbled.

Josh gave a shrug. "Fine. Stay out here. Have a nice time." He began to shake the gate, and without any trouble at all, it loudly *creaked* open. He gave a cool and sly look to the girls. "Well, I'm going in. If you hear me scream, call nine-one-one," he said. He looked at Faye. "Faye? You comin'?"

"Absolutely," she responded in a pumped manner.

The two walked through, and Natasha was left alone. It was particularly quiet in that area, which might have been one of the reasons she was starting to get spooked. And giving no hesitation, she immediately stepped forward after them. "All right, you guys — I knew I'd be babysitting your sorry asses tonight."

The three began to walk up the small hill in which the crooked house sat on. The overall establishment looked years and years abandoned. Windows that still actually existed were cracked or barely hanging on a shred of glass. The grass in the front yard was dying by the second. Maybe it was just the typical curse of the "haunted house syndrome", but this one definitely looked to take the cake in every way, shape, and form. Stepping up the front staircase, Josh came to the closed and beat-up door, turning to the girls. "Should we knock?" he wondered.

Natasha gave a strange look. "What kinda dumbass thing is *that* to do? Nobody even lives here!"

Josh turned back forward and started to knock, but as his fist hit the door, it slowly creaked open by itself. Giving a baffled expression, he looked back to Faye and Natasha. Faye almost seemed to be freaked out by the incident, and spoke her feelings with, "Ya know, Josh, whenever that happens in scary movies and the people end up going inside, they usually don't come out."

He stared at them for a long moment, and with widened eyes and the wiggling of his fingers, he made an eerie and spooky noise. When his bright smile replaced all that, he ignored her remark and simply welcomed himself right inside. Entering what appeared to be a large foyer area, he stopped and glanced all around, admiring the house and its appearance as Faye and Natasha crept in behind. The inside was just as bad at the outside, having boards lying everywhere along with the massive walls of cobwebs spread out from spot to spot. Moonlight beams shone through the cracked window boards. Dust filtered the air, and this caused Faye to cough and wave her hand in front of herself. "When's the last time you think they vacuumed?" she sarcastically murmured.

Josh grinned. "I don't think vacuums *existed* the last time this place was clean." Natasha turned her head all around as she walked over to an empty shelf. Cupping his hands together, Josh then called out, "Hello?! Any ghosts in here?"

"I think *they'd* be afraid of *you*," Natasha snickered.

Faye smiled at that and zipped her eyes to him. "Yeah, Joshy — just enough to make 'em die again."

"Screw you," he blurted. He walked forward and nodded as he admired the surroundings. "Ya know, this place would make an awesome pad. Why the hell doesn't anybody ever throw any parties in here?"

"Well, the place *is* apparently haunted…" Natasha reminded him with a smart-ass tone.

"We could get a mad little shin-dig on in this joint," he said as he placed his hands on his hips.

Suddenly, a loud echoing *thud* erupted from upstairs, causing everyone to gasp and jump in place. A wooden bowl Faye had just picked up was quickly dropped to the floor. "What the hell was that?" she wondered.

They all stood silently, and the house returned that gesture. With her blood pumping, Natasha tried to play off her frightened vibes by giving a cool shrug. "Maybe a board fell or something," she suggested.

"Or maybe a ghost pushed it over," Josh added with a devilish smile.

Faye waved her hands. "All right, weird noises in a house are one thing, but weird noises in a weird house are another," she said. She peered to Josh. "Have you had your fun yet?"

He gave her a crazy look. "Are you kidding me? Not even close to starting."

"I'm gonna have to agree with Faye and add that I'm also getting an eerie feeling from this place," Natasha spoke out.

Josh seemed to almost be getting annoyed. "Look — if you two little girlies wanna go wait outside and waste a perfectly fun night, then go right ahead. The door's right there. But me, on the other hand — well, there's only one night in the year that could even make my bones shake a little, and that's tonight, and I'm going upstairs to see what that noise was."

He stomped away toward the twisted staircase as Faye and Natasha were left to watch. As he started to step up them, Faye tilted her head toward him. "Aren't you gonna say, "I'll be right back"?" she wondered.

He looked at her. "No. Because I probably won't. It was nice knowing you two."

He turned and continued to make his way as Faye shook her head and crossed her arms. "What an ass," she mumbled under her breath.

"He's gonna go up there and realize that he was wasting his own time," Natasha pointed out.

Faye shook a finger at her. "Or, he's gonna make us think he hasn't come back, and when we go searching for him, he'll jump out and scare us."

"Can't anybody do anything original anymore?" Natasha asked.

Faye let out a small laugh. After a moment of silence, she scanned her head around the room as her spine tingled. "Ya know, I don't believe in all that kooky stuff, but you wouldn't catch *me* spending the night here."

Natasha gave an agreeing nod. "Same here. I'm surprised you're catching me here *now*."

Faye gave a quick smirk, but let it fade out as she looked toward the stairs. Letting out an overtired sigh, she then walked over to the bottom of it and leaned against the railing. "Josh?!" she yelled. There was no answer. "Josh, come on — quit being a dick. There's no one here," she pleaded. Still no answer. In a more soft and irresistible tone, she then playfully called out, "Oh, Josh? If you come down right now, Natasha and I will do something together for you..."

"What?" Natasha crazily said.

"Relax," Faye smoothly told her. "He's a guy. Hearing something like that should get his ass down here pronto." The two girls looked up the staircase, but still, no Josh. Slapping her hand on the end of the railing, Faye angrily stepped up onto the first step. "That's it — when we find him, you hold him down, and I'll punch his face in."

"Sounds good," Natasha added.

The two walked up the stairs, and when they finally reached the second floor, they stopped when faced with a hallway. Looking down both ways, there was nothing but continuous old house wreckage. "All right," Faye started, "I'll go left and you go right."

Natasha nodded, and they split up separate ways. Going down the long hallway, Natasha briefly skimmed her fingers against the wall before taking them away to see them covered with dust. Entering a room, she turned her head all around in search of any spot Josh could be hiding in. "Josh? Are you in here?" she murmured.

It didn't appear so, based on the room size, but she crept further in anyway, noticing a broken-down baby crib in the back corner. Her eyes locked on it, she steadily moved closer and closer until she finally reached it and peered inside. There, lying next to a torn-up blanket, was a baby doll. Reaching down, she gripped the doll and brought it closer to get a better look. It was beat-up and destroyed for the most part, but as she looked it over, she could almost hear the faint sound of a baby laughing. Shifting her body around, she looked at the room behind her to see it empty. But before she could do anything else, the baby noise had escalated to a slightly higher tone, and she began to nervously move her head all around to find where it was coming from.

"H-Hello?" she asked.

Her scanning eyes stopped when they reached a closed closet, and the giggling infant sounds seemed to be muffled from inside. Clutching the doll tightly, she slowly stepped inch by inch toward the closet, not daring to take her eyes off for a second. And as she approached it, a slightly trembling right hand managed to extend from her and reach for the sliding closet door, gripping the tiny hole and tugging it as it the door scraped across the floor. And giving one quick tug, she whipped the door open completely to see nothing inside. A few shelves were stacked, but that was all. Giving a sigh of relief, Natasha lowered the doll to her side as the laughing baby started up again, causing her to spin around in a startled fashion. "Josh? Josh, is that you?" she whimpered.

And through the air, a light, feathery, feminine voice could be heard whispering, "Josh? Josh, is that you?"

Natasha gasped and quickly looked all around, going all-out nervous now. Dropping the doll to the floor, she rushed out of the room and back into the hall. Growing shaky and unstable, she stumbled her way into a bathroom. Small and trashed, the toilet was nowhere to be found and the shower was just as dirty. Looking over to the cracked mirror on the wall, she turned and leaned on the sink, catching her breath for a moment. Twisting the sink knobs, she discovered the water was out, which caused her to be all the more frustrated. And as she leaned on the sink and slowly brought her eyes up to the mirror, she noticed a hideously gross zombie-like woman looking right at her from behind. Shrieking, Natasha jumped at the sight of her and placed her back to the wall, seeing no one in the room. Panting, she clutched her chest and tried to convince herself that no one was near.

Closing her eyes, she tried to convince herself by saying, "There's no such thing as ghosts, there's no such thing as ghosts. No one else was in here. I just imagined it."

Re-opening her eyes, she exited out of the bathroom and stopped in the hallway when more voices were heard saying, "No such thing as ghosts... no one else... imagine... imagine..." with the vocals changing deeper each time.

Natasha's eyes watered as she looked all around. "All right! Josh, Faye — you've scared the shit out of me! Now come out, or else I'm leaving you two here!" Neither Josh or Faye answered, and with that, Natasha was truly fed up. "That's it! I'm gone! I'm outta here! Enough of this bullshit!"

She began to stomp her way down the hall, but it was fear that was making her angry. And as she passed a room, she stopped to see Josh quickly flash by the doorway. Shooting her eyebrows down, she grit her teeth and turned into the room. "Josh, you sorry putz! I'm gonna shove my foot up your ass!"

But when she was in the room, Josh was nowhere to be found, and this confused her greatly. "Josh?" she wondered.

A *thumping* sound from the closet answered her. Figuring it was all fun and games, Natasha did her best to put on a fake, enthusiastic smile as she stammered over to the closed doors. "Nice try," she mumbled as she clutched the doors and swung them open quickly.

But what she saw inside immediately turned her smile into a gaping mouth as Josh was swinging from what appeared to be a shadowy vine. He tried to pull the strange occurrence off his neck, but it pulled tighter and tighter as his legs kicked. And, with one final swipe, his head was cut right at the neck and fell to the floor as Natasha staggered back in horror. The shadowy vines dropped his body, and the head of a ghostly figure emerged out of the closet, screaming as its mouth opened with a hole larger than the actual face. Letting out a scream, Natasha turned and ran out of the room and back into the hall, where another full-figured old woman ghost floated out of a room toward her, extending her open arms. "Darling," she began to say as her voice deepened and her face molded into a saggy devilish one, "come with me."

Natasha screamed again and ran down the hall, where she could see Faye exit a room and look at her. "Natasha?" Faye curiously asked.

"Faye!" Natasha cried out, with some tears flowing from her eyes.

But before Faye could react, a series of shadowy strings quickly flashed out from each room and each side, wrapping around her and pulling her body apart like a wishbone. Sliding to a stop, Natasha covered her screaming mouth with a hand. Her immediate reaction was to run, so she turned at the staircase and practically fell down them. When she reached the bottom, her first priority was the front door, which was closed. Running up to it, she tried to pull it open, but it wouldn't budge for some apparent reason. "Come on!" she yelled at the door. Turning her head back, she could see some ghostly figures floating down the stairs along with the eerie shadowy streams.

She pounded the door and then stepped over to a broken window, where she hollered out, *"Somebody please help me! Help me!"*

Looking back to see the figures closing in, she took off across the room and toward the kitchen, where she spotted an old-fashioned elevator laundry chute. Opening up the door, she crawled inside and tried to pull the door down shut, but that also didn't budge a bit. Some tears flew from her eyes and she pulled and pulled, being more aware of what might happen if she didn't get it closed. And when she finally thought she couldn't do it, she gave up by crouching in a ball inside the tall shaft, whimpering. And she continued to whimper and shake for another few moments, until strangely enough, everything seemed to go quiet. Bringing her head out from behind her knees, she looked forward to see nothing approaching the chute. Sniffling, she listened to the silence and cocked her head to spot no figures closing in on her. No strange moaning or groaning floating toward her to do anything like what happened to Josh and Faye. Shuffling up, she slowly clutched the walls of the chute as she managed to fully stand upright on her feet, tilting her head everywhere and listening. Still, for the longest moment, there was silence. Everything had appeared to have just gone away.

And without warning, several streaks of shadowy vines dropped down from the shaft and twisted around Natasha quickly as they pulled her up; her legs kicking as her loud scream echoed upward.

VAMPIRES

Kevin looked at the old abandoned house as he drove by.

"Creepy place," he pointed out. "Glad we're not going there."

Tracey, sitting in the shotgun seat, sighed as she rested her head against the window. "Yeah, but we *are* going to this gay party."

"What?" Kevin said in an unbelievable fashion as he looked over to her. "Are you joking? This is the biggest party night of the year, besides New Year's."

Tracey rolled her beautiful brown eyes and looked forward. "You do realize what we're going to, don't you?"

"A party," he told her again.

"No," she stated. "We're going to a massive drinking-orgy-sex fest."

Kevin chuckled and glanced over to her. "Aw... Tracey, will you have sex with *me*?" he jokingly asked.

Her face molded into a disgusted shape and she grunted. "Uggh... Now I *really* wish I went trick-or-treating. That way, I'd have a bag to barf in right now."

Kevin laughed and tapped his hands on the steering wheel. "Come on! Lighten up! This is a night of fun. Spooky gatherings, creepy incidents, scary music!"

"There was a good monster movie-marathon on TV," she told him. "We could've watched *that* and gotten trashed."

"That's no fun," Kevin told her with the shake of his head. "You do that on any *other* night. Tonight is different. The one night of the year where anything can happen."

"By anything do you mean people passing out right in the middle of the floor?" she inquisitively wondered.

"I mean having a little fun by showing up to a party where people are dressed up in who-knows-what," he told her.

She looked down at what she was wearing — typical everyday clothing. Turning her head, she scanned her eyes over Kevin's similar apparel. "This is a Halloween party, and we don't have shit on. I'm gonna feel all weird."

He shrugged it off. "Not everyone wears a costume. We could go as... bank robbers."

She raised her eyebrows. "Bank robbers? Ha, that's a good one."

"No, I'm serious. Ya know, the ones who try to get their money back from the guys who double-crossed them? Two forty-fives, lots of stuff blowing up, all that shooting in Wal-Mart?"

She shook her head, not even caring. "Didn't see that one."

Kevin took a deep breath and continued to drive. He gave another shrug. "I mean, we're eighteen. Don't you think we're getting a little too old for trick-or-treating or sitting on a couch in the dark with popcorn watching an old scary movie?"

"We didn't have to do *those* things," she insisted. "We could've done anything else."

"Like what?"

Tracey thought for a moment, but was stuck on ideas. "All right, Kevin — so I'm not great with crazy ideas. But any of my ideas would have been better than some typical teenage party."

A smirk curled on his face. "None of your ideas included this Janette girl, though."

Tracey let out a sigh and slumped her head back against her seat. "Oh my God, Kevin — you cannot be serious. That girl is a dirty whore, ya know."

"Don't call her that," he groaned with his eyebrows curved down. "She's so hot, and you know it."

"Whatever," Tracey murmured.

"Besides, how cool is she by throwing this party everyone's gonna be at?" he added. "This girl is the shit!"

Tracey rolled her eyes again as their car pulled up to a large, expensive-looking house. Numerous cars were parked down the street, and older teenagers were seen walking up to the place in costumes or without. Turning off the car, Kevin smiled as he started to get out. "The palace awaits."

Tracey stepped out as well, but gave a much stranger glance to the luxurious homestead. "And I bet they piss in gold toilets, too," she stated.

Kevin playfully shook a finger at her and briefly wrestled around. "If you're gonna be cranky, I'll have to tie you up like a mummy and throw you in the trunk."

"Please do," she insisted.

But Kevin dragged her toward the house, not letting her out of his sight. Entering through the front door, they looked around at the jumping packed homestead. The music was booming, with the base thumping. Everyone seemed to be having a great time. Kids drank and laughed hysterically. Some puffed at cigarettes while a few had already passed out in small corners of the rooms. Kevin brightly smiled as he pumped his arms in the air behind Tracey. "Yeah! Now this is what I call a party!" he excitedly said.

Tracey didn't seem to share his enthusiasm, no matter how much he tried to lighten her spirits by dancing around her. "I can't believe I'm here," she mumbled to herself.

"Neither can I," Kevin said, turning his head all around. "Now — can you see her anywhere?"

"Who?"

"Janette," he reminded her. "I wonder where she is."

"Probably table dancing," Tracey told him. "So get your one dollar bill ready. As a matter of fact, it may even be quarter night."

Kevin ignored her remarks and continued searching until they reached the boasting kitchen. And that's when Kevin stopped, staring with frozen eyes and a smile on his face. On the large kitchen table was Janette — a tall and extremely gorgeous girl with dark black hair and cunningly sexy eyes. She dipped her body and moved in a seductive fashion along with some others below her. Tracey noticed her also as she let out a soft chuckle. "Wow, I was really right," she blurted out.

But Kevin moved right past her, stuck in an unbreakable trance as he moved through the people in the kitchen. When he reached her, a cool and steady gleam seemed to shine from his face as he looked up at her. "Hey, Janette," he said. "Nice party."

Janette kept dancing and glanced down at him. "Thanks," she replied a little more softly.

"I'm Kevin," he introduced as he held his right hand up.

She lowered hers and shook it as she said, "Apparently you all ready know my name..."

Kevin smiled and gave a nod as he looked at all the dancing people around them. Janette then stopped dancing and climbed down from the table. Kevin wanted to help her, but she seemed too quick in her actions for him to do anything. Gliding across the kitchen, she opened the fridge and dug through as Kevin followed. Pulling out a water bottle, she guzzled some down and glanced at him. "You want anything to drink?" she offered.

"Nah, I'm fine. Thanks," he answered.

Janette then moved her eyes up and down him entirely, giving a light shrug of her eyebrows. "No costume?" she wondered.

Kevin looked down at himself and then chuckled. "Oh, um — I'm not really the kind for dressing up."

Janette nodded. "Me, too. I always think a person should express themselves for who they really are."

"Exactly," Kevin agreed. "I mean, although it would be fun, I just think Halloween has lost its appeal of dressing up over the years."

She curled a sly grin as she walked past him. "Come on, it's Halloween — a night of ghouls, goblins, and other mysterious monsters. Might as well blend in."

Kevin followed her as they walked into the living room. "Well, yeah... all that stuff makes Halloween, but to me, it's just gotten boring lately. I'm looking for something a bit more exciting that adds to the classic stuff."

Janette stopped and smiled. "More exciting, huh? What exactly are you looking for?"

A similar smile appeared on his face. "There *is* this party... and the host."

She raised her eyebrows. "Oh, the host? And how does the host make this party any different from the others?"

Kevin gave a somewhat bashful shrug. "She adds a lot more... sexuality to it."

Janette let out a soft chuckle and then stepped closer to him. "So you're looking to do something sexual tonight?"

"Sure."

"With me? Upstairs?" she curiously asked.

"Well, I didn't say *that*," he told her.

"You didn't have to. *I* did," she slyly replied.

Kevin then gestured toward the stairs. "So, shall we... get to know each other better?"

Janette gave a sexy grin as she started to walk past him again. She then stopped and gave a more serious expression. "Nah; you're not my type. I don't screw losers. Get a life," she flat-out mentioned with the shake of her head.

Kevin was shocked by this sudden turn of events, and all the kids standing around them gave laughs and shot-down "Oh's!" In an unbelievable fashion, Kevin shook his head and turned as he started to walk away. "Bitch," he murmured under his breath.

And suddenly, the music stopped as all the talking in the room went silent. Kevin paused in walking as he reached Tracey near the center of the room. Twisting his body all around, he noticed that half of the people in the room were just staring at him with stern faces. But Janette seemed to be the most furious of them all; her eyebrows curved way down as a light growl erupted from deep inside her and her beautiful eyes locked dead on Kevin. Kevin looked at everyone as Tracey stood a little baffled as well. And the two didn't know what to make of it for the longest time as Janette gave a cool step forward and grinned. Then, opening her mouth, she gave a loud hiss as four sharply-pointed teeth could be seen; two on top and two on the bottom. And the movement seemed to have a sudden effect on everyone in the room, as numerous people did the same thing, displaying their sharp teeth. When one boy had leapt through the air and plunged on a girl, all-out chaos seemed to break out as the fanged kids started to attack the clueless ones. One girl sunk her teeth into another's neck as thick red blood began to ooze out. Another girl tore away wildly at a boy's neck as blood splashed everywhere.

Kevin and Tracey stepped back in surprised fashions as screams started coming from some of the kids. A few tried to race toward the front door, but it was blocked off by a few fanged guys. As the bodies started to fly across the room, Kevin and Tracey staggered back and watched in complete and utter shock. A girl flashed her fangs and hissed at Kevin as she tried to attack, but Kevin managed to wrestle her away. More blood splattered onto the walls. Limbs started to join the people jumping in the air. An arm had almost hit Tracey. Grabbing her sides, Kevin quickly began to lead her through the room as more of the kids threatened to attack. Grabbing a chair, Kevin swung it down on one and cracked it as the kid fell to the floor. Moving through the kitchen, Kevin and Tracey noticed a girl struggle to get free as she was held down on the counter while numerous guys began to bite at her neck. Turning to the basement door, Kevin said, "Down here!"

Tracey wasted no time following him as they slammed the door shut behind them. Jogging down the stairs, Tracey looked around at the small and damp basement in a hysterical fashion. "Tell me that just didn't happen!" she stressed.

"You'd have to tell me *what* just happened in order for me to judge whether or not it did," he replied.

"Those were — those were — they were vampires!" she cried out.

"Vampires aren't real!" he shot back.

"Well, I'd agree with you, but after the fifth limb flew through the air, all my beliefs went out the window."

"Janette — the hottest girl in school — is a vampire. This is unreal. This can't be happening," Kevin groaned as he paced, rubbing his hands over his face. "This is some kinda joke. Or performance."

"Look — vampires or not — there is some serious and if I might add real homicidal shit going on up there, Kevin," she tended to disagree. She shook some of her reddened sleeve at him. "This isn't ketchup. This is *blood*. Okay?"

Kevin began to frantically twist his head all around the basement. "All right, all right — we need to find away out of here."

"Finally! The best suggestion you've made all night!" Tracey said, throwing her arms in the air.

210

Spotting a small window toward the ceiling on the concrete wall, Kevin quickly ran over and jumped on top of an elongated wooden box to reach it. "Look at this! I don't know if we can fit through this."

Her eyes stuck on the box he was standing on, Tracey slowly began to approach him. "Uhh... Kevin?"

He turned and looked down at her. "What?"

"Is that what I think it is?" she wondered.

Glancing at his feet, Kevin noticed what he was on and slowly began to climb down. "Holy crap," he murmured. "It looks like... a coffin." Turning her head, Tracey's mouth slightly opened as her eyes scanned all around the room. Hidden under the stairs, another long box sat undisturbed as well as one a little further from that. "Is it just me — or is this night starting to suck more and more with each passing second?" Kevin blabbered.

"Please don't use the word "suck" when we have ravaging vampires right above our heads," Tracey moaned.

Peering back down to the coffin, Kevin raised his eyebrows in an uneasy manner. "You think there's anything inside?"

"I really don't care and I'm especially really not interested in finding out," she said.

Reaching forward, he clawed his fingers under the top cover carefully. "I'm gonna open it."

Molding a crazy face, Tracey grabbed his wrists to stop him. "Are you insane? How is this helping us?" Shrugging her hands off, he continued to go forth in opening it as Tracey slowly stepped back. Finally, after raising the cover up and setting it against the wall, Kevin looked down with a horrid face to see an older man sleeping inside. "There's someone in there!" Tracey whispered in a low tone.

Backing away, Kevin's widened eyes were locked on the sleeping man. "Definitely — time — to get the hell out of here," he stated.

And suddenly, a fist pounded upward, busting through one of the other coffins as bits of wood flew everywhere. Stammering back and turning around in startled fashions, Kevin and Tracey gasped at the sight of another man sitting up out of the coffin after he had thrown the remainder of the top off. "Back upstairs!" Kevin yelled.

"Upstairs is not an option!" Tracey ecstatically said back. As she backed away, the elderly man they were previously staring at quickly sat up and moaned, clutching her wrist with a sharp grab. Letting out a scream, Tracey furiously tried to pry the hand off as Kevin helped. The elderly man *hissed* as he flashed his sharp fangs, looming in toward her arm for a big bite. As the two pounded and pounded away at the strong grip, Kevin peered down to the floor and noticed a sharp chunk of wood that had busted off the other coffin. Snagging it, he gritted his teeth and strongly plummeted it deep into the heart of the elderly man as he horrifically screamed and abruptly turned to dust.

Staring down at the pile of ashes in a surprised manner, Tracey then shot her eyes to Kevin. He quickly nodded his head. "Yeah. I'd say that was *definitely* a vampire."

Curving a scared face, Tracey then pointed behind him. "Kevin, look out!" she shrieked.

Twisting his body, Kevin practically met face-to-face with the man from the other coffin. Raising his right hand with the stake of wood in it, Kevin prepared to use it in defense as the vampire wittingly halted him from doing so. Wrestling around, the vampire then managed to throw Kevin right into Tracey as she stumbled back into a stack of boxes, knocking them all to the floor. But as Kevin got back up to continue fighting, Tracey noticed that her encounter with the boxes had revealed a closed door behind. Quickly moving them out of the way, she grabbed the handle and strongly tried to budge it open. Finally, with an old creak, she managed to expose a staircase going downward. She gaped her mouth open to get Kevin's attention but suddenly locked her eyes on the vampires starting to flood down the basement steps.

"Kevin!" she shouted as she grabbed him by the shirt. Entering the doorway, she disappeared as Kevin followed and quickly slammed the door behind him.

Standing in the pitch black darkness of the room they had flocked into, Kevin was first to point out, "I can't see *anything* in here!"

"Good observation, Einstein," Tracey murmured. "Come on; it looks a little lighter toward the bottom of the staircase. Maybe we can find some lights."

"Screw the lights; maybe we can find a way out of here," he murmured.

The two slowly stepped their way down, being careful not to fall in the endless dark that seemed to loom forever. "Jeez, how many steps *are* there?" Kevin wondered. "And what the hell is this place? It's like the basement of a basement."

"The basement of a basement in a house of vampires can't be too good," Tracey added. "You watch and see. We're gonna find some kind of light switch, flip it on, and be surrounded by a thousand coffins in a huge underground catacomb. That's how it always is in horror movies."

"We're not in a horror movie," he reminded her.

"Shucks, Kev — you're right. What was I thinking? I mean, after escaping the massacre upstairs, the two unlikely heroes run into the basement where they find coffins, open them up, *think* that the people inside are just sleeping and bam! They attack, but of course, one of the heroes gets a hold of a slice of wood and stabs the vampire, wrestles with the other while another door is uncovered, and they descend down a darkened staircase deeper and deeper," she explained. "Sounds *nothing* like a horror movie."

"Ya know, the sarcastic people always die first," he mentioned.

Feeling their feet *crunch* down on some dirt, Tracey stopped. "I think we're at the bottom."

"And still without light," he added.

Suddenly a *hiss* came from somewhere within the darkness as Tracey lightly gasped to herself. Then, smacking Kevin, she angrily said, "That wasn't funny, you dumb shit!"

"What?" he asked, as if having no idea what she was talking about.

"That hissing sound," she stated. "I can't even believe you're joking at a time like this."

"I didn't hiss," he assured her.

"Huh?"

"It wasn't me," he continued to say in his defense. And suddenly, each torch along the walls began to puff out fire, quickly illuminating the entire large room to reveal Janette along with three other vampires circled around them. The overall room looked like a much low-graded version of the upper basement, having dirt everywhere with some cartons and boxes stored here and there. A few doors were easily spotted, but no coffins this time. "Holy shit," Kevin chokingly said as Tracey hopped closer to him in a startled fashion.

"'Sup, Kevin?" Janette asked in a sly fashion as she stepped toward them. "I *did* get it right, did I? I mean, the world is full of so many guys... so many names..."

Holding his hand out, Kevin stayed close to Tracey as the vampires circled around them, stalking their prey. "Look, Janette — I gotta tell ya — it was a kick-ass party and all, but, ya know... when everybody started turning into vampires, it kinda wasn't our thing. So if you'll just let us mosey on out of here..."

She grinned and tilted her head. "Sorry, Kevin. Not that simple. Although I really wish you would reconsider. Being a vampire has its advantages. Everything pretty much except for the sun. You step outside and you'll get quite a wicked tan. But who likes tanning anyway?"

"I can't believe I wanted to hit the sack with you," he then murmured.

"Tough toodles, but the expression around here is "hit the coffin". You ever do it in a coffin? It's incredible. I highly recommend it," she said. "Now — less talk, more blood."

Lunging forward, she flashed her sharp white fangs as Kevin grabbed her arms and tried to push her away. At the same time, the other vampires had surged in, snapping toward Tracey as she screamed and smacked them away. Grinding his teeth down, Kevin managed to push her to the floor with all of his strength, and just as he turned to help Tracey, he was punched in the face by a fist and flew back into some boxes. Tracey, kicking one of the men in the groin, turned to run after him but skidded in her tracks as Janette hopped in her way, grabbing her arms and dipping her head to sink her teeth into her neck. His eyes shooting open in complete terror, Kevin stammered to his feet and yelled, "Nooooo! Tracey!"

As blood poured down Tracey's neck, Janette stopped and threw her unmoving body down to the floor, turning to Kevin as she wiped her red mouth. Grabbing boxes, Kevin started to heave them toward the approaching vampires, but it didn't seem enough to hold them off. So turning, he ran to one of the doors and easily swung it open, hopping inside and slamming it shut to find himself in a long torch-lit hallway. Hearing the *scratching* and *clawing* on the other side of the door, he breathed heavily as he started to take off the down the hall. Down one turn, around another, he ran and ran, finding himself to be in a maze of hallways. Tripping, he *thudded* onto the dirt floor and quickly jerked his head all around. He seemed to be the only one there, but for some reason, the presence of the hunting teens elsewhere seemed to *hiss* and *scratch* in the walls all around him. Panting in a nervous manner, he got back on his feet and ran down another hall, soon stopping at a small intersection to catch his breath. The scratching noises had stopped, and he seemed to lose them by finding a quiet and desolate area. His breathing growing slower and slower, he just stood at his own leisure and relaxed. And, taking one big, deep breath, he let his whole chest just sink back in with a calm tone.

Without warning, Tracey had popped up behind him, hissing loudly as she displayed her new fangs and grabbed his arms, sinking them into his neck as he strongly screamed.

ZOMBIES

Larissa, Troy and Steve walked up the jumping and jiving house, ringing the doorbell. Through the loud music and partying, the door opened up to reveal the black-haired Janette.

"Trick-or-treat," Troy dully said, holding his candy bag out.

Janette curved a smile and curled her eyebrows toward the three nineteen-year-olds. "Well, I guess you're never too old for this shit," she stated, leaning over to grab some candy.

She dumped the pieces into their bags but then suddenly paused. "Oh — almost forgot," she noted, leaning away. Coming back, she tossed a plastic pair of vampire teeth in their bags and then flickered a keen smile. "Happy Halloween."

Troy grinned and nodded. "Thanks."

She closed the door, and the three stepped down off the porch and into the front yard. All around, kids scurried and laughed as they trick-or-treated in their assortment of scary and funny costumes. But Larissa, Troy and Steve were dressed as they were — Troy in a simple brown jacket and Steve with a comfortable sweatshirt as Larissa sported a couple layers of thin long-sleeved Gap-purchased shirts. Troy wrapped his arm over her shoulder and pulled her close as the three headed across the grass toward the next house over. "Ya know, we're never too old for this shit," he murmured with a sly grin.

Lightly hitting him, she brightly displayed her beautiful, sweet smile. "Come on! Don't you guys miss doing this at all?"

"Not really," Steve mumbled as he pulled out a small pocket-sized book from his jeans. "In fact, it was dorky when I was *seven*."

"Larissa, all we're saying is that you don't see too many kids our age out asking for candy at front doors," Troy told her. "I mean, it's pretty simple — you trick-or-treat as a kid, but then you get to this certain age when you're still a kid when you think it's a pathetic thing to do — so, you lay off for a couple years, and then you reach that point again where you're a little more mature and less embarrassed. I just think you're still stuck in that stage."

She gaped her mouth open as she looked between them. "I can't believe it. You guys are no fun. You're damn right I never grew out of it. Trick-or-treating is the best part of Halloween. Maybe it's just different for girls than guys."

"This isn't puberty. It's trick-or-treating. I think I'm gonna have to agree with Troy and say that although getting free candy has its advantages, it just doesn't feel the same," Steve added as his eyes scanned through the book. "Besides — some of us have reputations to hold up."

"You're both losers," she chuckled.

Troy raised his eyebrows to her in a surprised fashion. "Even *me?*"

She giggled and tickled his sides. "Okay. You can be cool for just tonight, because it *is* Halloween." He rolled his eyes, and she supplemented that by giving him a kiss on the cheek.

Stopping at the front of the next house, Troy grumbled as his shoulders slumped. Steve was still caught up in his book. Sighing, Larissa then spoke out with, "All right, all right. I've put you boys through enough girlish trick-or-treat torment for the night. So what do you wanna do?"

"Something a little more scary," Troy suggested.

She turned to Steve. "Hey, Steve — Mr. Tough Guy Who Isn't Afraid of Anything wants to do somethin' scary. Any suggestions?" But Steve seemed too caught up in his reading to answer. Snapping her fingers in his face, Larissa repeated, "Steve! Earth to Steve!"

"Huh?" he blurted, looking up at them.

"What are you doing? That stupid book again?" Troy wondered, snatching it out of his hands.

"What book?" Larissa inquisitively asked, trying to catch a glimpse of it.

"Some "Book of the Dead" thing he's been reading all week," Troy replied, swinging his arm off of Larissa so he could use both hands in flipping the pages.

"It's some crazy shit," Steve told them. "I mean, I've read some creepy stuff but this just takes the cake."

"Where'd you say you got this again?" Troy asked.

"Some gypsy lady at that carnival that swung through town two weeks ago. You remember that?" he said.

Troy chuckled. "You actually *went* to that thing? Those people are complete freaks," he noted. "What's in this thing, anyway?"

"I dunno. Weird shit, like spells and stories; stuff for raising the dead and that hokey," he explained.

"And you actually paid money for this garbage?" Troy unbelievably wondered, curving a weird expression. "You're such a dumbass."

He handed the book back to him as Larissa sparked a curious face. "You guys up for tryin' something out of it?" she slyly asked.

"What?" Troy shockingly mumbled.

"No, I'm serious!" she tried to convince with a smile. "We should try out something. It'll be fun!"

"Honey, don't tell me you're actually buying into this bullshit."

"I'm not buying into anything," she simply assured him. "All I'm saying is that we could have a little fun. Don't you wanna do something more adventurous tonight?"

"Well, suddenly trick-or-treating sounds a lot more sane and time-worthy," Troy stated, glancing at the house as kids continuingly ran back and forth to collect their treats.

Larissa stamped her feet, displaying a puppy-face as she shook his hands. "Come on!" she whined. "Please? Pretty, pretty, pretty, pretty please? It'll be fun. I promise."

Giving a long, hesitating sigh, Troy finally answered with, "Fine. Whatever. Let's just do something other than standing in someone's front yard."

Pumped up with an thrilled and giddy mood, Larissa couldn't help but be excited for the amazing possibilities that awaited them. "So where we gonna do this?" Steve wondered.

"Duh," Larissa blurted as if wondering why she even had to tell him. "The only logical place to do *anything* on Halloween... the graveyard."

Only minutes later did the three find themselves hiking into the entrance of the large graveyard at the edge of town. The sharp-pointed fence circling the huge burial grounds was rusty and crooked at every angle. The letters on the sign arching over the entrance were falling off at the hinges. Entering through an easily accessible space in the main entrance — an open hole in the giant gate — the three stopped and stared at the eeriness that awaited them. The graveyard, although not that huge in space, seemed lonely and deserted. Because of the shifting hills waving through the ground, some of the tombstones were starting to tip or slant in a demented kind of way. Through the air, a light mist of fog sifted everywhere, creating an even more spine-chilling atmosphere. And toward the center of the graveyard, a large leafless tree sprawled its branches out like arms reaching down toward the stones.

On top of an old shed, probably used for maintenance, an owl hooted and turned its head before flapping its feathery wings and soaring off into the black sky. "I was wondering — is anybody else a little spooked right about now?" Steve asked in a somewhat nervous manner.

Troy and Larissa looked at each other and then back to him. "Nope," they simultaneously replied.

"Oh. Okay," Steve said, nodding. "I'm not. I was just asking. If you guys were."

Troy chuckled under his breath and shook his head as he started to move forward. "Careful. There's roots sticking out all over the place. The moon is giving us pretty good light but you never know when you're gonna stub your toe and go flying forward."

"Aw, so cautious and caring," Larissa jokingly muttered as she rubbed his back.

"Let's head over toward the huge tree," Troy suggested. "It looks like the scariest spot to do anything."

So they walked over toward the tree, their shoes crunching down on the cold and dying grass. Sitting down on top of a tombstone, Troy reached for the book in Steve's hands. "All right, let's take a look at this thing."

Steve pointed to where he was sitting. "Yo, dude — I don't know if you should be sitting there. That's like, disturbing the dead."

Troy glanced down at the stone and then back to him. "Oh, and something like raising people out of their eternal sleep *isn't* disturbing?"

"Come on, come on," Larissa interrupted in an eager fashion. "Less talk, more raising."

Flipping through the pages, Troy skimmed his eyes up and down, softly saying things to himself as he searched through and through. Finally, he smiled and raised his eyebrows. "Ah, here we go. The "Raising the Dead for Dummies" section."

"What does it say?" Larissa wondered, leaning in closer to see for herself.

"Well, seems like..." Troy began, reading a little. "...we've gotta say this spell or something." He shook the book toward Steve. "You wanna do the honors, bro?"

Before Steve could even answer, Larissa whipped the book out of his hands and glanced down at the page. "Hakun... navad... zappa tri-ron... kimble... zi-nano rig-rod," she read in a tone to make it sound much more professional and ancient.

Sitting in the silence of the cemetery, the three turned their heads and looked around, but nothing appeared to be out of the ordinary. "Gimme this," Troy said as he took it from her. "You probably didn't even say it right." And suddenly, the light crunching of grass and twigs could be heard coming from a short distance as Troy turned his head in response. "What the...?"

Listening, Larissa said, "What is that?"

"Shh!" Troy hushed her with the wave of his hand.

The steps and rustling started to grow closer... and closer... and closer... until, finally, a tall figure could be seen emerging out of the darkness toward them.

"Holy shit! It's a zombie!" Steve frighteningly stated, backing up as he pointed toward it.

And with that, a large flashlight clicked on and shined in their faces as they all squinted their eyes. Walking up to them and re-directing the light, a tall, late-twenties cop in a tan uniform grinned. "Not really," he told them calmly. "Well, maybe in the morning when I first get up."

Sighing, Troy seemed to ease up a bit with the rest of them. "Deputy Milner."

Milner nodded his head toward them. "Troy. Steve. Always a pleasure. What the hell are you guys doin' here?"

"You know... just a little zombie-raising, spells and Book of the Dead-type stuff," Troy told him.

"Shouldn't you guys be out toilet-papering trees or somethin'?" Milner asked.

"So that means we have your permission to do it?" Steve grinned.

"No, smart-ass. It means you guys have my permission to quit foolin' around in a dark cemetery on Halloween night. You guys know this place is off-limits after sunset."

"I was just visiting my dog. He's buried here," Troy tried to add.

"Yeah, Yeah, I'm sure *all* of your pets are buried here," Milner then mumbled with a smile as he tapped his flashlight against them. "Come on, guys — out."

The radio attached to his shoulder suddenly crackled and fizzled as a feminine voice said, "Seven-twenty, over."

Stepping back, Milner grabbed the walkie and held it up to his mouth. "Milner — go."

"Calvin, we got a couple Frankensteins down at the Quick-Mart who *claim* to have just been asking directions from some women who *claim* to only be dressed up like prostitutes," the voice said.

"All right, Debbie — I'll be there in a minute," he replied. Curving stern eyes toward the three, he then pointed a finger. "I'm serious. No more raising the dead."

"Sure thing, Dad," Troy sarcastically saluted. "We'll be inside in a minute."

Stopping as he walked, Milner paused to give them one last warning. "I mean it. I'm gonna swing by here again in a little bit. If I catch ya guys still here, you're gonna be trick-or-treating down at the station."

He then continued to walk away until he was out of sight. At that point, Troy laughed and rubbed his face. "Ohhh. What the hell are we doin'? This is dumb. Let's go home and play with a Ouija board."

"Come on, you have to admit hearing me say those ancient words was a big turn-on," Larissa smirked as she playfully tickled him.

He started to tickle her back, and the two giggled as they wrestled around with each other. Turning his back to them, Steve stepped forward a little as he said, "You guys are hopeless. I had a feeling tonight would blow. We should've just went to Food King like we do every other night, that way we would've at least —" and something from a little further away caught his attention as he narrowed his eyes in a mysterious manner. "What the hell?" he quietly mumbled to himself as he crept forward.

In front of a certain tombstone not too far away, the ground appeared to be moving, with dirt and grass carefully shifting around as if an animal were burrowing its way up from underneath. Behind him, Troy and Larissa continued to play around, unaware of what was going on. "Who feels like getting naked in a cemetery?" Larissa sang out as she nuzzled her nose against Troy's.

"Uh, hey guys?" Steve called out as he watched the ground start to break apart a little more quickly. Turning to get their attention, his own was instead diverted to another tombstone, where in fact the same thing was happening to the ground. His eyes widening, he watched as the dirt began to crumble upwards. "Uh... guys?" he repeated in an uneasy fashion.

Just as Troy and Larissa had stopped their flirting and looked to the ground, a fist had strongly busted upwards, causing them to stammer off the tombstone and back toward Steve. "What the...?" Troy mumbled as he watched the other hand emerge.

Both hands worked well with giving whoever was underneath good strength to pull themselves up through the dirt. And, in fact, a man that was heavily decayed had growled and groaned as he continued to heave the rest of himself up out of the ground. Staring with a horrified face, Larissa gripped Troy's left arm tightly. "Oh my God," she managed to spit out.

"No way," Troy said, shaking his head as if trying to convince himself it wasn't happening.

A moan came from a little further away as another person seemed to dig their way out. The three quickly turned their attention all around, where numerous people were now appearing from out of the ground. "Holy shit," Steve blurted. "It really worked."

Troy gave him a crazy look. "What do you mean, "worked"?! There's no such thing as zombies!"

"Well, what do you call *these* things?!" Steve hollered back. "What, do you think there's some massive underground cellar beneath all these graves where people are dressing up scaring us?"

A couple of the zombies had already begun to slowly move toward the three, groaning and moaning as they slumped step-by-step; their clothes shredded and hanging as one side of their body seemed to limp. "Uh... okay... how 'bout we get the hell outta here now?" Larissa strongly suggested.

"Good idea," Steve agreed.

As they prepared to move away, the zombies nearing them reached out, attempting to grab anything they could as their crooked and dusted mouths hung open. Larissa shrieked as one almost got a hold of her, but Troy grit his teeth and smacked it away. "Come on!" he then shouted, grabbing Larissa's hand and pulling her away as they ran back toward the entrance. Steve followed, ducking and dodging his way through the now flooding cemetery.

Skidding to a stop at the main gate, Troy looked back to see the dozens and dozens of zombies still in slow pursuit. Gesturing toward the open hole in the gate, Troy pushed Larissa through and then stepped in himself as Steve joined them. Ducking as he slid through sideways, Steve was about to join the already running Troy and Larissa when he noticed his shirt was caught on a part of the gate. Tugging at it fiercely, he nervously watched as the zombies neared. Stopping to realize he wasn't with them, Troy and Larissa turned and hurried back to the gate. "Come on!" Troy stressed for him to hurry.

"I'm trying!" Steve told him as he ripped at his shirt.

The zombies were now feet away, moaning as they reached their arms out. Troy tried his hardest to tug him free. "Grab him! Grab him!" he pleaded to Larissa as she helped in pulling.

"Hurry!" Steve begged.

But the zombies were now on him, grabbing and trying to pull him back in as he kicked and punched them away. And in seconds, they had easily overcome him in numbers as they groaned and managed to pry him off the fence. "Ahhhh!" he screamed as they threw him to the ground.

"Steve!" Larissa called out.

Like a herd of ravenous vultures, the zombies had enclosed around Steve, totally covering him up from Troy and Larissa's sight. Her eyes watering, Larissa helplessly watched and listened as Steve screamed. "Larissa, come on!" Troy then snapped as he grabbed her arm and pulled her away from the madness.

The two ran down a small side street, finally braking to a halt behind a building to catch their breaths. It had appeared that most of the kids trick-or-treating had now retired for the night, as it seemed like they were the only two out in the town. "They got him," Larissa said out of breath. "They got him!"

"Jesus Christ; this isn't happening!" Troy sternly stated. "It *can't* be!"

"You saw it yourself!" Larissa pointed out. "Those were one-hundred-percent real zombies."

Troy rested his hands on his knees as he bent over. "We've gotta get help."

"And say *what*? That we read an ancient spell that unleashed zombies from the cemetery?!" she added. "Who the hell is gonna believe that?"

"They don't *need* to believe it! They need to see it!" Troy snapped. "And after the first one takes a big chunk out of someone's arm, I'm sure they'll reconsider their thoughts."

"So who're we gonna tell?" Larissa wondered.

"Who else?" Troy simply put. "We've gotta find Deputy Milner."

Elsewhere in town, Milner slowly cruised down the streets in his patrol vehicle. All seemed quiet and undisturbed, until his radio *crackled* and *fizzled* with the same female voice from earlier saying, "Milner, you there?"

He reached down and grabbed the handle. "Go, Debbie."

"Remember those kids you caught egging the high school?" she asked.

"Yeah."

"Well, we got a call saying they were seen toilet-papering your house," she told him. "Just wanted to give you a heads-up."

"Those little bitches," Milner grumbled under his breath. He then sighed and went back to the radio. "Thanks, Debbie. I'll check on that."

"Oh, and one more thing — I've been getting a lot of strange calls the past fifteen minutes," she added.

"What on Halloween *isn't* a strange call?" Milner wondered with his eyebrows raised.

"I don't know, but you might wanna be on the look-out for this. Turns out we may have a couple prowlers in the area. Folks have been calling reporting seeing people digging through their garbage and wandering through their yards as if they'd lost their minds. One lady was sure she saw someone rip her dog's doghouse off the ground and go after the poor little thing," Debbie explained.

Giving a tired deep breath, Milner lifted the radio to his mouth again to say, "Thanks, Debbie. I'll check it out and see you in twenty."

Setting the handle down, he turned onto one of the main streets, not appearing happy at all. "Just what I need," he murmured to himself. "Goddamn... werewolves and monsters." Squinting his eyes, he noticed a tall, raggedy man slowly striding down the sidewalk, bumping against the store walls. "Well, what do we have here?" he wondered, flicking on the patrol lights as they flashed red and blue.

Pulling the car to the curb, he got out and closed the door, turning his head to see no one else around. Pulling his pants up a little and fixing his belt (a usual cop trademark once out of the car), he began to walk toward the approaching man. "Evening, sir," he called out.

The man kept coming, not saying anything as he bumped against the wall, walking with a slant. Watching with a curled grin, Milner rose his eyebrows and softly shook his head as he began to approach the stranger. "Had a little too much Witch's Brew to drink tonight, huh?" he wondered. Grabbing his flashlight, he then continued with, "Tell ya what. Why don't you come with me to the station? We got a nice little party goin' on down there already."

And when he turned the light on and shined it in the man's face, his expression dimmed weirdly at the sight of decaying and rotting flesh. From his look alone, Milner knew that this couldn't be the work of some costume. "What the hell?" he quietly said. The zombie moaned as he began to lift his arms and reach for the deputy. Milner, stepping back, held his hand up in defense as he put his other against his gun. "Hold it now, sir. Just back on up."

But the zombie continued to ignore his commands as he kept coming and coming, which caused Milner to finally whip out his handgun and load it with a *click*. "All right — get down on your knees and put your hands on your head!" he swiftly ordered. "Now!" Letting out a terrifying groan, the zombie kept coming. "This is your last warning. I *will* shoot you."

And the zombie's persistence was the last straw. Milner began to fire his gun, unloading the entire clip as the man seemed unaffected. When the gun clicked empty, Milner stared down at it with unbelievable eyes and then peered back up at the incoming zombie. "W-What...?" he managed to get out. From behind, another zombie seemed to come out of nowhere as it growled and dipped its head down to bite his arm. "Ahhhh!" Milner cried out in pain as he jerked himself back against the building walls. Holding his bloody arm, he looked up at the two zombies and noticed that a few more were in the vicinity coming toward him. Watching them like a frozen statue, he didn't do a thing as they cornered him and completely covered him with their attacking deteriorating bodies. His horrified and painful screams could be heard all the way down the street.

Meanwhile, Troy and Larissa had been jogging their way through town, being cautious with every step they took. As they rounded the corner of a building, they saw a zombie walking not too far away. Letting out a gasp, Larissa was quickly yanked back behind the wall for cover. "Jesus; these things are all over the town!" Troy stated. "How the hell did they get out of the cemetery so fast?"

Before Larissa could even have a chance to answer, the sound of rustling from a nearby pile of garbage caused them to turn their heads and spot Steve, who in fact looked much different than he had before. His skin was a greenish-yellow color, and his eyes sagged heavily as if he had been awake all eternity. His clothes a bit shredded, he moaned and spotted them.

"Steve?" Troy asked as he stepped forward with a familiar glance. "Is that you?"

Steve did nothing but grunt a little as he began to slither his way out of the garbage toward them. "Troy, that's not Steve," Larissa tried to convince him, tugging at his arm.

"What are you talking about? Yes, it is."

"No, it's not. Steve is dead!" she hastily reminded him.

Lunging forward, Steve went after Troy and tried to bite him as Larissa let out a scream. Cocking his head back, Steve then snapped it down to strongly bite Troy's shoulder and rip skin off some the arm as he hollered in pain. Grinding his teeth, Troy tried to wrestle him away, but Steve was much stronger than he actually appeared. Throwing him against the garbage bin, Troy turned to Larissa and shot a furious face. "*Run!*" he screamed loudly, holding his whole left side.

Larissa took off down the street, panting and breathing nervously as she saw zombies parading everywhere she looked. Growing even more scared, tears now began to fill her eyes as she ran up to a house and pounded on the door. "Help us! Somebody help us!" she hollered at the top of her lungs. "Please!"

Grabbing the handle, she entered right inside to see a zombie crouched over an elderly woman, eating away at its own pleasure. Stumbling back with terrified eyes, Larissa quickly scurried out of the house and across front lawns, turning her legs faster and faster as if racing for the gold in a marathon run. And finally, she had reached her own front steps and shot through the front door, slamming it closed behind her and locking it up tightly. Crying with tears draining down her face, she spun her head all around the darkened house and raced up the stairs into her bedroom, closing that door and locking it also. Breathing heavily in a place she found to be a bit safer, she sharpened her attention to her open window. Jolting over to it, she peered out and listened. Growls and moans could be heard all over the town. A few screams and hollers erupted from those poor souls who couldn't escape or had just realized the trueness in what they were facing. Closing the window, Larissa backed up toward her bed when she heard a noise come from her closet. Her heart thumping in her chest, she began to inch her way over; her eyes steadily open and not blinking once toward the closed door. Lifting her right hand up, she reached for the handle as her blood raced.

Thump thump thump! Thump thump thump! Thump thump thump!

And finally, taking one ready deep breath, she quickly snatched the handle with her hand and yanked the door open only to scream the loudest scream she had ever screamed.

NIGHT
OF THE
SCARECROW

OCTOBER 1997

Brad Jackson crossed his arms as he sat slumped against the hot seat of the station wagon. "I still don't understand why we just can't go with you guys," he said.

His father looked at him in the rear-view mirror. He was a man of thirty-nine-years-old, tall, strongly built, and light brown short-cut hair. "Brad, you know your mother and I have been planning this trip for months. Don't worry, Uncle Jim and Aunt Cathy will be thrilled to see you guys again."

Brad stared out the side window at the countryside, hoping to see at least *some* sign of intelligent life. He was a curious twelve-year-old boy, with green eyes and black hair, which he almost always covered with his favorite NEW YORK METS baseball cap. His parents had been planning to go on vacation somewhere in Missouri, and they were going to drop him and his sister off at their great uncle and aunt's house for the weekend in a small farming town called Wheatten in Kansas. Brad had only seen his great uncle and aunt at Christmas; they flew over every year from Colorado, which was where Brad and his family lived. It wasn't that far of a drive across the two states; the total trip would take them the whole day to get there. They had been driving non-stop, and they were almost there. Seeing there was nothing to look at out the window, Brad pulled out a stack of baseball cards and started to flip through them. "Hey, Brad," he heard someone say. He sat and looked through his cards some more, ignoring the voice. "Brad!" the voice yelled louder.

He sat and ignored it once again until his mother turned around from the front passenger seat. "Brad, answer your sister," she said.

Brad looked across the seat at his sister. Her name was Kelly; she was twelve-years-old also, his twin-sister to be exact, although they looked nothing like each other. She had long brown hair, much like her mother's, and was the person Brad was constantly annoyed with most. "What?" Brad asked.

"If you see a cow, I need it for my Travel Bingo game," she said.

Brad rested his chin on his hand and stared out the window. "Sure, Kelly — I'll tell you. Just as soon as I see another car," Brad joked.

"Oh, come on guys. It won't be *that* bad there. Uncle Jim can show you all the neat things he does on the farm, and there's bound to be some kids around somewhere," Dad had said.

"Sure thing, Dad," Brad said shaking his head. How could there be anything to do on that farm? His Uncle Jim was already sixty-three years old, which only meant that he would be mumbling on and on about *his* childhood, how hard it was back then, and how he had to walk fifty-gazillion miles to school in the snow each day. Brad didn't like it at all. He wanted to be back in Colorado playing Baseball with all his friends. After all, it *was* July.

His father peered into the rear-view mirror again and said, "We're almost there. You guys will be chasing each other in the cornfields in no time."

Dust swirled around as the station wagon pulled up to the old house. Brad and Kelly jumped out of the car and stretched their arms high into the air as Uncle Jim and Aunt Cathy strolled out the door toward them. Brad and Kelly walked over, giving them reluctant hugs and exaggerated smiles. The two elders were each gray-haired; Uncle Jim was tall and Aunt Cathy was short.

"Oh, it's so good to see you two again!" Aunt Cathy replied with a large smile spread across her face. "You've both grown so tall!"

"It's great to see you too, Aunt Cathy," Kelly said.

Aunt Cathy released her hug and said, "Now, run along inside. I've baked some cookies for you."

The two ran off inside the house while the four adults stood and chatted. Brad grabbed a cookie off the plate on the counter and shoved it into his mouth. He walked across the kitchen and stared out the back window at the large cornfield that spread for miles. "Wow!" he exclaimed. "That would make an excellent place for hide-and-seek."

Kelly walked out of the kitchen and into the living room, where she looked out another window. "Whoa, check out the scarecrow in the field," she said.

Brad, who still had his mouth full of cookie, ran in and shouted, "Where?"

Kelly pointed and said, "Out there. It looks pretty scary."

Uncle Jim and Aunt Cathy walked into the house, slamming the door shut behind them. "Your parents left," Aunt Cathy said. "I guess they're in a hurry."

Kelly shrugged as she watched the station wagon drive off in the distance. Brad, not caring, was still looking out the window. "Hey, Uncle Jim. Where'd ya get the awesome scarecrow?" he asked.

Uncle Jim walked over to the window and put his hand on Brad's shoulder. "I got it a while ago from a farming friend I used to know. He had it for years. Scared away all of the crows," Uncle Jim explained.

"What happened to him?" Brad asked.

Uncle Jim sighed and said, "Well, he, uh, was killed in a farming accident of some sort. Town's people found him all cut up into pieces in his barn one night. But you didn't come to hear that kinda stuff." He waved his arm and said, "Come on! I'll show you kids around the farm."

Kelly stood there with her mouth hanging wide open. Brad walked by her, wiggling his fingers in her face. "I bet it was the scarecrow," he said laughing.

"Shut up, Brad," she said. She followed behind him out the door, walking with them into the barn.

The inside of the large barn smelled funny, and the floor was completely covered with hay and straw. Hanging from the ceiling were dozens of knives and pitchforks, items that Uncle Jim had told them he used for farming. The barn was dusty and unevenly organized, containing piles of junk and rusted tools. A medium-sized black cat meowed as it ran by Kelly's feet. "Is that your cat?" she asked, watching the creature scurry off behind a wheel of one of the tractors.

Uncle Jim picked up a pitchfork from the ground and cleaned off the dirt with his flannel shirt. "Yes, it is," he said. "His name is Ned."

"Ned?" Brad asked. "That's a pretty funny name for a cat."

Uncle Jim let out a smile and a laugh as he put his hand on one of Brad's shoulders. "This, my boy, is the tractor for plowing the cornfield."

Brad looked up at the giant machine. It contained four big wheels and a large object connected to the front end containing about ten long sharp spikes. "Cool!" Brad said as he walked around and investigated the tractor.

"And maybe you can help me drive it once or twice, too," Uncle Jim said.

"Can I really?" Brad asked, his eyes filled with hope.

"Sure can," Uncle Jim said, smiling. He looked at his watch. "Uh-oh. We better hurry inside or we'll miss your aunt's famous chicken soup!"

Brad and Kelly followed their uncle out of the barn and back into the house. Uncle Jim led them into the kitchen where there was a large round table filled with plates, silverware, and steaming hot food. Aunt Cathy was putting the finishing touches onto her large kettle of soup when a man walked into the kitchen from the living room. "Kevin!" Uncle Jim greeted as he sat down in his favorite chair.

The man wiped his hands on a rag he had pulled out of his pocket and smiled. He was young, twenty-two to be exact, and was a little chubby with long blond hair that streaked back across his head. "Hi," he said with a low, gruff voice.

Uncle Jim held his arm out. "Kids, I'd like you to meet Kevin Malley. He lives down the street and comes down to help a lot with the farm," he explained.

"Hello," Kelly said with a smile.

Kevin sat down at the table and opened a pot. "I finished the wheat crops, Jim. I can do the plowing as soon as I come back from baseball practice tonight," he said.

Brad's eyes lit up like light bulbs. "*You* play baseball?" he asked.

"Yep," Kevin replied. "Why, do you like it?"

"I love it!" Brad shouted.

Kelly rolled her eyes. "He's a baseball fanatic. We can't go anywhere without stopping to look at something having to do with baseball," she said.

"Enough talk," Aunt Cathy said. "Sit down and eat."

The two children sat down in the oak chairs and piled food onto their plate while Aunt Cathy set down a small bowl of brown-colored soup next to them. Brad immediately shoved bread into his mouth while he looked over at his sister, who was carefully placing the food on her plate, being careful not to mix any of it together. *How stupid,* Brad thought to himself. Why did she always have to do that? Even when his family went out for fast food she *always* had to make sure that her French fries weren't touching her cheeseburger, or she would whine and whine until Dad convinced her that nothing was wrong with the food. Brad scooped up some mashed potatoes and plopped them onto his plate when he saw a figure run by the kitchen window. "Who was that?" he asked.

Uncle Jim got up from his seat and walked to the door to see an elderly man scurrying down the road. He turned around and sat back down at the table. "Well, who was it?" Aunt Cathy had asked him.

"Clyde Cliffborn," Uncle Jim said, slurping some soup into his mouth.

"You mean *Crazy Clyde?*" Kevin asked, trying to catch a glimpse out of the window.

"Crazy Clyde?" Brad asked curiously.

"Yeah," Kevin said, sitting back down. "Crazy Clyde Cliffborn. The name says it all. The guy's got one too many screws loose in his head."

"Kevin," Uncle Jim said, trying to stop him from blabbing on.

"Can't I just tell them?" Kevin asked, begging.

"No, you can't," Uncle Jim said. He looked at Brad and Kelly. "You kids stay away from that man."

Aunt Cathy sighed. "Enough rubbish-talk," she said. She stood up out of her seat. "Now, when everybody's finished, we can have dessert."

So after Kevin had wiped the cake crumbs off his face and placed his chocolate-smothered plate in the sink, he announced his eager departure by saying, "Well, I gotta go or I'll be late for baseball practice," and walked over to the screen door, opening it. "Dinner was great," he added as he walked out toward his truck.

It was dark out now, about nine o'clock, and Uncle Jim had slouched back on the reclining chair and put on his pair of slippers while Brad and Kelly lied on the floor and watched the glowing screen of the old television Uncle Jim and Aunt Cathy owned. It didn't receive that many channels and a station that played cartoons didn't come in too well, but the two kids didn't mind. An hour later, Uncle Jim had fallen asleep in his recliner and Aunt Cathy had come in and woken him up. "All right, everybody — time for bed," she said as she shook Brad and Kelly, waking them.

The two rubbed their eyes and walked into the spare bedroom, falling into the beds and drifting into a deep sleep.

Brad woke up all hot and sweaty. It was especially hot there in the summer, and they kept a window cracked to let the cool summer breeze into the room. He looked at the clock on the wall. It read 2:00 a.m.

Brad yawned and got up out of bed. He was wearing a basic T-shirt and shorts, which, in fact, kept him very cool, and he decided to go get something to drink. He strolled out of the room and stubbed his right toe on the wall, not seeing in the darkness. He stood there rubbing it for a second until the thumping stopped. He continued on his way toward the kitchen. The whole house was quiet, except for the small whistling sound of the breeze soaring through the cracks of the ancient house. He didn't bother turning the kitchen light on; he was too tired and he would probably have a hard time finding it. He strolled slowly over to the refrigerator like a zombie and opened the door. The inside of the fridge contained jugs of milk and soda, leftovers, and other typical things. He didn't want to spend all night choosing something so he just simply pulled out the large jug of milk and carefully set it on the counter next to the sink. He closed the fridge door and reached up to a cupboard to pull out a small glass. He set it next to the milk, and as he untwisted the milk jug cap, he peered outside at the scarecrow that stood in the cornfield. It wasn't too far from the house, and the bulb on the back porch shed enough light into the field so Brad could see most of the scarecrow.

He shuddered at the sight of it — how it had the long, drooping raggedy face with two empty holes cut out for the eyes. Straw stuck out of the holes and rips in the clothing. Brad guessed that it must've been a really old scarecrow. He looked at the fingers of the figure and how they were so long and creepy looking.

What a horrible scarecrow.

Brad took his eyes off the scarecrow and put them back onto the jug of milk. He carefully poured it into the glass, filling it to the top. He picked up the milk cap and fumbled with it, dropping it onto the floor. He sighed and bent down, picking it up. He screwed it back onto the jug and looked out the window at the scarecrow. And suddenly, his eyes widened in horror as he saw that the scarecrow was gone from its post. He shook his head and rubbed his eyes, praying to himself that it was just a dream. But the scarecrow was still gone. He leaned over the kitchen counter and pressed his face up against the screen, looking for a sign of anyone who might have stolen it. No way it could have run off itself.

No way.

He stood staring out the window when a sudden *thump* came from the side kitchen wall. Brad backed up and started to walk to his room. *It was just the wind,* he said in his mind over and over again. *Yeah, just the wind. It's not that stupid scarecrow. It can't be. That's impossible. I'm thinking like a five-year-old,* he said in his mind.

He backed up into his room and tumbled into his bed, pulling the thin covers up to his chin. He looked over to Kelly, who was sound asleep in her bed under the open window.

The open window!

Brad wanted to get up and slam it shut, but for some reason he was too scared. He just lied there, trembling as he watched the window. The room was quiet, and the breeze had now slowed down. Then Brad heard the sound of footsteps crunching on the grass outside. He stared at the window, seeing nothing but the outside farm. And like an eclipse over the sun, a human-figured shadow began to move across the open window. Brad gasped, hid completely under his covers, and listened more.

Silence. Pure silence.

And slowly, inch by inch, Brad rolled the blanket away from his face. Staring out the window, he saw the same thing as before — quiet farmland. Darting his eyes everywhere, Brad searched for any signs of life. Kelly snorted and turned in her sleep, a sudden sound that practically made Brad jump out of his bed. Untangling himself from the confusing twists of his blanket, Brad slapped his own face a dozen times and shook his head before finally setting foot on the floor. Then, in a quick instant, he zipped himself back into his covers, shaking. "Coward," he said to himself.

He didn't know if was going to get any sleep or not, so he just lied there, his eyes shut tightly, his mind trying not to recollect the events that had happened.

Brad woke up to the sound of a crowing rooster and emerged from under his covers. He rubbed his eyes and looked over to Kelly's bed to see her gone. He peered up at the clock on the wall, which read 8:23 a.m. Wondering if he had gotten any sleep, he slid out of bed and began walking toward the door when he suddenly remembered last night. He quickly ran through the kitchen toward the window. Aunt Cathy, Uncle Jim, and Kelly were all at the table eating breakfast. "Morning, Brad," Uncle Jim said as he read the paper.

Brad looked out the kitchen window to see the scarecrow up on its post as if it had never left. "The scarecrow's back on its post," he said.

Uncle Jim looked up from the paper. "What do you mean?" he asked.

"Last night, around two in the morning, I got up to get a drink. I looked at the scarecrow and dropped the milk cap onto the floor. When I looked again, it was gone from its post. Then, when I went back to bed, I saw a shadow approaching the bedroom window," he explained.

"It must have been a dream," Aunt Cathy said as she poured some water into a glass. "Scarecrows don't just get up and walk."

"But it *wasn't* a dream," Brad argued.

Aunt Cathy placed a plate full of bacon and scrambled eggs on the table and said, "Sit down and eat, Brad, before it gets cold."

Brad sighed. He slowly sat down and grabbed a fork. *It wasn't a dream,* he thought to himself. *It couldn't have been.* He scooped some scrambled eggs onto the fork and placed them in his mouth. Kelly was doing her usual routine of trying to eat as carefully as possible. Uncle Jim took a sip of water and folded the newspaper in half. "I'm going out to the barn to get the tractor, and then I'm going to plow the wheat field," he said as he got up out of his chair.

"Can we come and help?" Brad asked.

"Sure," Uncle Jim said with a smile.

Brad and Kelly raced toward the door behind Uncle Jim while Aunt Cathy shouted, "Aren't you going to finish your breakfast?"

"No thanks, I'm full!" Brad yelled as the screen door slammed shut.

Brad and Kelly walked alongside Uncle Jim toward the barn. It was warm out, even for *this* early in the morning. Brad looked down the street to see a house much similar to Uncle Jim's about a mile down the road. The town wasn't too far beyond that; Uncle Jim had told Brad it was only five more miles beyond that house. The three reached the giant barn door, and Uncle Jim slid it open with a big push. Light flooded the inside of the barn, revealing all of the tractors and tools. Uncle Jim walked over to the tractor and inspected the wheels while Brad and Kelly looked around. Brad saw a funny-shaped tool hanging on the wall, and went over to look at it when he heard Kelly scream. Uncle Jim jumped away from the tractor and hurried to the other side of the barn with Brad following behind. "What is it?" Uncle Jim asked. Kelly covered her mouth and pointed a couple feet in front of her. Uncle Jim stepped back. "Oh my God," he said.

Brad looked closely to see a small black cat speared flat to the ground with a pitchfork, blood and fur lying everywhere. He felt sick, the sickest he had ever felt, and looked up at Uncle Jim.

"*Oh my God,*" Uncle Jim had repeated.

Uncle Jim carried the brown bloody sack in which he put the dead cat inside the house and set it on the table. Aunt Cathy wiped the tears off her face and said, "I just don't understand how this could have happened. Poor Ned."

"It was an accident. He was probably crawling around when the pitchfork fell from the wall," Uncle Jim suggested.

"Uncle Jim, wasn't that pitchfork on the wall on the other side of the barn with all the other pitchforks?" Brad asked.

Uncle Jim sighed. "Well, something happened," he said.

Aunt Cathy sighed. "Kids, go outside and play while your uncle and I clean up. Be back in time for dinner tonight."

Brad and Kelly nodded their heads and went out the screen door. Brad kicked some dirt and put his hands into his pockets. "Something *very* weird is going on here, Kelly," he said.

Kelly gazed at the wide open distance, thinking. Not a cloud was in sight to cover the sun, making temperatures rise to the high eighties. It was late afternoon now. Kelly wanted to go home. She didn't like it there. She didn't like it there at all. Brad then spotted something and knelt down to pick it up. "Kelly, look at this," he said.

Kelly walked over to him and knelt down beside him. He was holding a long thin piece of straw in his fingers. Kelly knew *exactly* what he was thinking. "No way," she said shaking her head.

"But Kelly, how else could it have gotten all the way over here? There's been no heavy wind to blow it in days," Brad said.

"That's impossible. A scarecrow just can't come to life. You know that," Kelly said.

"I know, but something killed the cat," Brad said. "*I know* it wasn't an accident."

Suddenly, a large shadow cast over them, and they both spun around to see a tall elderly man standing over them. "You're right; it wasn't an accident," the man said. "And it will happen again tonight. Last night was only the beginning."

Brad and Kelly stood up to completely see the man. It was Clyde Cliffborn. *Crazy* Clyde Cliffborn. "What do you mean?" Brad asked, squinting his eyes.

Clyde started to walk away. "Come with me. I have a lot of explaining to do."

Kelly sipped the ice-cold lemonade from her tall glass. She looked over at Clyde Cliffborn. She still wondered if it was a good idea to go there. But Brad had insisted. She just hoped that this Clyde Cliffborn wasn't as crazy as everyone said he was. She listened as he began talking: "I heard about what happened to your uncle and aunt's cat. I want to tell you what happened to it," Clyde explained.

"What?" Brad asked.

"The scarecrow out in your uncle's cornfield. It did it. And it's going to do it again. Tonight."

"What are you talking about? Scarecrows can't come alive," Kelly said.

"This one can," Clyde began. "Did your uncle tell you where he got that scarecrow?"

"Yes, as a matter of fact he did," Brad said.

"Well then, as you already know, the man he got the scarecrow from was killed in a terrible accident. But it was no accident," Clyde began. "The scarecrow killed him."

Brad's eyes widened in horror. "Somehow, I believe you."

Clyde didn't argue with him. "Legend has it, that scarecrow out in the cornfield comes alive every five years to kill."

"But why?" Kelly asked, jumping back into the conversation.

"No one knows. Some think a curse was put on it. But, as part of the legend, the scarecrow must kill one animal the night before it kills its owner," Clyde said. "And anyone else on the farm."

"*I* don't believe you," Kelly said, staring at him with stern eyes.

"Think about it!" Clyde yelled with his arms spread in the air. "Did you hear the scarecrow last night? Did you perhaps notice *anything* weird going on?"

"Well, yeah," Brad began, "when I woke up in the middle of the night to get a drink, I saw from outside the kitchen window that the scarecrow was gone."

Kelly looked at her watch. "We should start heading back," she suggested.

Clyde sighed. "Just be careful tonight," he said. "It will start the killing as soon as night falls."

Kelly and Brad walked down the road, not able to stop thinking about what Clyde had told them. "Do you think Clyde was telling the truth?" Brad asked.

Kelly shook her head. "You actually believed him?" she asked. She began to break out laughing.

Brad shrugged. "Well, no, not really," he said. "In fact, I think he's as crazy as people say he is."

They walked up to the house and Brad pulled open the screen door. The two of them walked in, finding that the house was empty and quiet. "Uncle Jim? Aunt Cathy?" Kelly shouted.

No reply.

They split up, searching different rooms of the old house. They soon met up in the living room and stood there, speechless. Brad looked up at the old wood-cracked clock on the wall. It read 5:15 p.m., and Brad was beginning to wonder where his aunt and uncle could have gone. They were supposed to be having dinner around this time, and Brad had noticed earlier when he walked through the kitchen that no food or cooking materials were out on the counter. "Where could they have gone?" Kelly asked Brad.

Brad walked over to the living room window and peered out. "Maybe they're in the barn or out back somewhere," Brad suggested as he started for the back door.

"And where is Kevin?" Kelly asked. "I haven't seen him since last night at dinner."

Brad, who opened the back door and went outside, replied with, "Oh, he went to one of his friends' house after baseball practice. He's spending all of today there and then he's going to his baseball game tonight. He told me he wouldn't be back until ten o'clock or so."

Kelly shrugged and followed Brad as he walked into the entrance of the cornfield. It was large, spreading for what looked to be miles, with the stalks rising at least seven feet in the air, keeping anyone well-hidden in the dozens of thin pathways. Brad pushed aside some stalks and began to follow one of the trails. Flies buzzed around his head as a mosquito landed on his arm. He smacked it away, continuing through the dense crops. He pushed another out of the way as it flung back up behind him and whacked Kelly in the shoulder. "This is a good place to get lost," she said.

"But an excellent place for hide-and-seek," Brad said. "That is, if you're not too scared to come out here at night."

Kelly laughed. "You're a funny kid, Brad. But I'm not the one who's scared of a dumb scarecrow."

"Me? Scared? Yeah, right," Brad said courageously. "I just wasn't too sure what happened to the scarecrow last night, that's all."

"Nothing happened," Kelly began, "because it was a dream. Just last week you thought the dog had wings, remember?"

"I told you *that* was a dream, but this wasn't. I'm telling you. I was wide awake," Brad told her. Brad was starting to face the fact that it was a dream. Either that or he was going crazy. Or the scarecrow really *was* walking.

After long, hard walking through the cornstalks, they finally managed to reach the other side. They were not too far from the barn now, and Brad saw that the doors were shut. Where could they be? Kelly began to get intensively worried now, when she heard the sudden yelling. "What was that?" she asked.

Brad placed his index finger on his lips and whispered, "Quiet, I'm listening."

There was silence for a moment, and then the yelling began again. Brad raced across the edge of the cornfield, seeing the top of the scarecrow's head through the tall stalks. He was glad they circled around it; he didn't want to go near that hideous thing. The two reached the edge of the cornfield and looked at the house to see Aunt Cathy leaning out the door and waving her arm in the air for them to come back. They ran toward the house, and when they reached it, met up with Aunt Cathy at the doorway. "There you kids are," she said. "I was starting to worry. Dinner's almost ready."

Brad shook his head as she turned around and walked into the house. *Grown-ups worry too much about kids*, he thought. *They should worry about more of their own problems.*

Uncle Jim was at the table reading the newspaper as usual while Aunt Cathy went back to finish up her cooking. Brad could smell the sweet aroma of turkey boiling in one of the pots and he could see freshly buttered steaming corn lying in stacks on a plate on the table. Brad and Kelly sat down. The clock on the wall now read 5:45. Brad was finally glad they were out of the cornfield.

And away from the scarecrow.

Uncle Jim folded his newspaper and took a sip of his coffee. "Where were you guys?" Kelly asked.

"Where were *we?*" Uncle Jim asked. "Where were *you?* We were looking all over for you kids."

"Well, first we went down to —" Brad began but was nudged in the hip by Kelly. Brad realized that if he told Uncle Jim and Aunt Cathy they were down at Clyde Cliffborn's house, they would both be in big trouble. He remembered what Uncle Jim said before about not going near Clyde. "Um, we went down to the cornfields," Brad finished.

Uncle Jim popped up an eyebrow. "Well, you kids just make sure to tell us where you're heading next time."

Aunt Cathy set down the large pot that contained the turkey and sat, loading everyone's plate. Brad crunched down on his corn and said, "Hey, Uncle Jim. Do you think we can play catch tomorrow?"

Uncle Jim smiled. "Sure. I've got an extra mitt down in the basement. After dinner you can go down looking for it so we'll have it ready tomorrow," he said.

"Now," Aunt Cathy began, "let's eat."

Brad grabbed the doorknob to the basement and twisted the handle, opening the door with a loud creaking noise. He wasn't sure if he could move. He had filled himself up with dinner and had three fairly good-sized pieces of cake while the four played a game of checkers.

He reached inside and flicked on the light switch. He started walking down the old staircase, and he stopped to look around when he reached the bottom. The basement was small, made with a concrete floor and concrete walls, and was filled from floor to ceiling with boxes and old junk of the sort. *Wow,* Brad thought. *This stuff is probably older than I am.*

He began to search through the boxes, blowing dust and cobwebs off the top. He pulled out an old photo book, flipped through it, and tossed it aside. He searched through another box and pulled out an old flashlight. That reminded him. He peered up at a small window that lay wedged between the concrete wall. It was dark out now, and he and Kelly were supposed to go outside and play hide-and-seek soon. But did he really want to? What if what Clyde had told them was true? But how could it be? He snapped his thoughts back to the basement and searched through it more. He wanted to find that mitt. He focused his eyes on all parts of the room, until he stopped at a shelf, where he spotted the baseball glove. It was sitting on the very top of the shelf, along with some other dusty items. Brad walked over to the shelf and jumped up, trying to snatch the mitt. But it was too high up, so he decided to step on the second layer of the long metal shelf and climb up to retrieve it. He extended his arm up and knocked down a stack of plastered frames. He watched as they fell to the floor, and squinted his eyes at what was inside them.

He jumped down from the shelf and knelt down on the floor, picking up the one of the frames. The inside contained an old newspaper, dating July 14, 1992. He looked at the headlines of the newspaper and widened his eyes as he read it. The headline, in bold letters, read, "TONIGHT MARKS FIVE-YEAR ANNIVERSARY OF MYSTERIOUS FARM ACCIDENTS".

He continued to scan the article; his eyes flickering back and forth as he read each sentence. The article read:

Skeletons in the Closet

- July 14, 1992. Today marks the anniversary of what is known as the mysterious farming accidents that have happened for the past twenty years, going in five-year spans. Five years ago, 54-year old Ted Norman, a local farmer, was found dead in his barn on the morning of July 14, 1987. His body contained slashes and cuts that were believed to be from a pitchfork. There were no traces of a murderer, police said, after scanning the area for a culprit. Mysteriously, five years before that, the same thing happened to 62 year old Bill Hesser, and five years before that, to 43-year old Vernon Bermac. How are these mysterious killings related and who is behind them? For now, police are baffled. -

Brad set down the frame as a sudden fear rushed through him. *Farming accidents,* he thought to himself. *Clyde Cliffborn had said that the scarecrow killed every five years on this date. It's true. It's completely true.*

Brad ran up the stairs, slamming the basement door shut behind him. He ran into the living room, where Aunt Cathy sat in the large rocking chair in front of the TV alongside Kelly. She was asleep, and Brad didn't want to wake her. He walked over to Kelly, who was lying on her stomach watching TV, and grabbed her shoulder. She spun her head around and said, "Oh, Brad. You ready to go outside and play hide-and-seek?"

He didn't know what to tell her. But when he managed to open his mouth she sprung out from the floor, ran into the kitchen, grabbed a flashlight, and ran out the back door. "Kelly!" Brad yelled. "Don't go out there!"

But it was too late. She was already outside running toward the cornfields. Brad didn't want to go outside tonight. But now he *had* to. He pushed open the back screen door and strolled out into the darkness. He flicked on his flashlight and pointed the beam around. It actually wasn't *that* dark; the light from the house made the backyard look like a baseball field at night, and the large blue-lit bug-zapper near the back door illuminated the back porch. Brad darted his eyes back and forth, searching for any sign of his sister. "Kelly?" he called out. After a moment of no reply, he moved closer to the cornfield and yelled out "Kelly!" once again.

There was still no reply.

Where could she have gone? He turned in a complete circle, and yelled, "Come on, Kelly, this isn't funny!"

Actually, it was dangerous. He didn't want her out there alone.

Then he heard the sound of the cornstalks rustling back and forth, as if someone were approaching him. Brad took a few steps back and pointed the beam of light into the field. The rustling sound began to move closer and closer now, and Brad could see the stalks bending back and forth. And he heard loud breathing — a terrifying sound. The cornstalks bent forward as Brad gripped his flashlight tightly, his hands trembling. The figure emerged from out of the field. "Found ya," the figure said.

It was Kelly, and she directed the flashlight onto Brad's face, making him turn his head away from the blinding glare. She then turned the beam away, letting Brad see the smirk on her face. No matter, he didn't care about that right now. He walked closer to her so he wouldn't have to shout. "Kelly, listen to me," he said. "I found some old newspapers down in the basement. There were some articles on the farm accidents that happen every five years. Every five years, Kelly. Ring a bell?"

Kelly put her finger on her chin and looked up to the night sky. "Hmmm," she thought. "You're not believing what Clyde told you, are you?"

Brad grabbed her arms. "That's *exactly* what I'm believing. You see, Kelly, it's all true!"

Kelly sighed and shook her head. Brad didn't feel like standing there all night and talking to her. He wanted to prove to her that it was true. He started to run into the nearest pathway. "Where are you going?" she asked.

Brad turned around and went back to the entrance. "Come on!" he said as he waved his arm for her to follow him. "I'm going to show you that the scarecrow's alive."

She ran into the pathway, trying to catch up to her running brother. Brad didn't want to have to go near the scarecrow, but it was the only way he could prove to her that it was alive. Maybe he could even stop it. He just hoped he wasn't too late. He darted in and out of the winding turns, glancing back every now and then to see Kelly trying to keep up with him. He finally managed to find the right pathway, and entered a large open area that seemed to be the center of the whole cornfield. All of the pathways emptied out into this area. Kelly, who was panting out of breath, finally caught up to him. "Well?" she asked.

Brad couldn't say anything. Words wanted to jump out of his mouth, but couldn't. He just stood there and stared. "Brad! Earth to Brad!" Kelly yelled, waving her arms in front of his face.

She took her eyes off of her mesmerized brother and looked at the scarecrow pole in the middle of the circle. Her mouth dropped wide open.

The scarecrow was gone from its post.

"No way," Kelly exclaimed as she stared at the empty post. "It can't be alive. Maybe Uncle Jim took it down."

Brad finally snapped out of his silence and said, "Or maybe it's out for a late night stroll."

"Brad, we've got to get back to Uncle Jim and Aunt Cathy!" Kelly said. But before they both could take a step, there was a sharp *cracking* of a cornstalk nearby. "What was that?" Kelly asked, terrified.

"I don't know and I don't want to stay here to find out," Brad said as he dashed to a pathway across the circle. Kelly quickly followed behind.

They entered the pathway and ran through it, pushing aside the tall stalks. Brad was pretty sure he knew where he was going. He had *prayed* that he was going the right way. Kelly, who was right behind him, tripped and fell to the dirt ground; her flashlight fleeing into the corn stalks. Brad grabbed her hand and pulled her up, forgetting about the flashlight. They began running again, and Brad had glanced back behind them to see cornstalks cracking and rustling.

Something was chasing them.

Brad, being the quick-thinker that he was, took Kelly and dove into the nearest turn of another path. He signaled Kelly to be quiet and he camouflaged them with dead stalks. They could hear footsteps quickly approaching them now, and Brad saw the shadow of feet coming up to their hiding spot. The feet stopped in front of them, and turned in different directions, as if searching for where the two kids had gone. Brad stared at the feet. Although he couldn't see them too well, he could see the straw pouring out of the pant leg.

It *was* the scarecrow that had been chasing them. The scarecrow *was* alive.

Brad was silent, and Kelly almost screamed. He quickly covered her mouth with his hand and watched as the figure ran away. *Good,* Brad thought. *It hadn't seen them.*

He waited a few moments and then helped Kelly from out of the stalks and back into the pathway. Brad had left his flashlight in there, and there was no time to go back in and retrieve it now. Now they had to run. And they did, until they reached the exit of the cornfield. They were right in front of the house now, and Brad and Kelly didn't hesitate to run inside. Brad slammed the screen door shut as he yelled, "Aunt Cathy? Uncle Jim?"

The TV was still on in the living room, and Brad could see that Aunt Cathy was still lying in her recliner. He gave a sigh of relief as he walked up to the chair. "Aunt Cathy, we're so glad you're still here," he said as he walked in front of the chair.

Brad and Kelly froze as they looked at their Aunt. She was lying there were her eyes open, just staring toward the TV. "Aunt Cathy?" Brad said as he waved his hand in front of her face. The old lady still just sat there with a blank stare, as Brad grabbed her shoulder and shook. "Aunt Cathy?" he asked once again.

He shook so hard that she rolled right out of the recliner and onto the floor, and Kelly screamed as she stared at the bloody knife that was plunged into her back.

"Oh no," Brad said as he covered his mouth. His own aunt, murdered! "Come on!" Brad shouted as he grabbed Kelly's hand. "We've got to find Uncle Jim!"

They ran out the house and were soon in the backyard. Brad looked all around and saw that the barn light was on. "This way! In the barn!" he shouted. "He's gotta be there!"

Before Brad could move, a blue pick-up truck rolled into the side driveway. The headlights flicked off, and the engine went silent. The driver's door opened and out walked Kevin. He was in his baseball uniform; it was covered in dirt that he had slid in during his baseball game. "Kevin! Over here!" Brad shouted, waving his arms to try to get his attention.

Kevin looked up and shouted, "Hey guys! Tired of hide-and-seek already?"

"Kevin, get over here, quick!" Brad yelled, ignoring Kevin's question.

Kevin jogged over, carrying his bag of bats and baseballs over his shoulder. "What is it?" he asked.

"Aunt Cathy, she's dead!" Brad yelled, even though Kevin was standing right in front of him.

"What do you mean?" Kevin asked, raising an eyebrow.

"I mean, *she's dead*," Brad repeated. "And if we don't hurry, Uncle Jim could be, too."

"Wait," Kevin said. "Slow down. Where is she?"

"In the house!" Kelly said, grabbing his hand and leading him into the house. She showed him the dead body on the floor, and he knelt down and inspected the knife stuck in her back. "How did this happen?" Kevin asked.

"It was the scarecrow!" Brad yelled. "It's alive, and we've got to stop it before it gets to Uncle Jim!"

Kevin closed his eyes tightly. "Wait a minute — a scarecrow could not have done this, guys," he said. "Where's Uncle Jim?"

Brad sighed. "I saw a light on in the barn. I think he might be in there."

Kevin got up and ran out the door with Brad and Kelly following closely behind him. They reached the barn and Brad swung the large door open. He stepped over the threshold and onto the thick dirt that covered the barn floor. "Uncle Jim?" Kelly shouted as she entered in after him.

Kevin was last to enter. There was silence. Nothing moved. Nothing chirped. Silence. Brad knew he wasn't in there. Uncle Jim told him he didn't leave the barn light on at night. Kevin passed Brad and looked around the barn. "Jim? Are you in here?" he called out. The three of them were in a corner now, where they spotted a piece of clothing lying on the floor. Kevin, along with Brad and Kelly, knelt down a looked at it. "I think this was Jim's," Kevin said as he held the piece of cloth between his fingers. He rubbed the soft fabric.

"How can you be so sure?" Kelly asked.

"Well, for one thing —" Kevin began.

But before he could finish, Brad had looked under the plow tractor and saw the approaching feet. The same hay-filled feet he had seen before with Kelly in the cornfield. "Uh, guys," he said.

Kevin and Kelly both spun around to the see the giant scarecrow approaching them. It walked in a slow manner, like a zombie would, dragging its feet while hay spilled out of the holes in its shirt. This was the first time Brad had seen the scarecrow up close, and it was a time he would never forget. The mouth was sown shut and the eyeholes, like Brad had noticed before when he looked at it through the kitchen window, were two empty black holes. Kelly screamed as it reached out with its raggedy arm to the wall and grabbed a small-sized pitchfork. It took a couple more steps toward the three, who were huddled up and trapped in the corner. The scarecrow raised the pitchfork over its head as Brad closed his eyes shut.

Then there was the sound of firing. Brad re-opened his eyes to see the scarecrow standing still, and then it fell back to the ground. Standing in the doorway was Clyde Cliffborn, holding a shotgun in his hands. The barrel was still smoking. "Take that, you stupid scarecrow!" he said smiling.

Brad, Kevin, and Kelly got up from their huddled spot in the corner and walked over to Clyde, stepping over the immobile scarecrow. "Wow, thanks," Kevin said as he, along with Brad and Kelly, were relieved to be alive.

"I told you it was alive!" Brad said to Kevin.

"Wow," Kevin said as he ran his fingers through his hair. "I can't believe it. I can't believe it."

"Everybody okay?" Clyde asked as he looked at each.

"Yeah," they all replied at once.

Clyde gave them a sad look. "I saw your aunt in the house. I stopped by to see if everything was okay, and then I saw the barn light on.

I figured everyone was in here, so I ran over. Lucky I brought my shotgun," he explained.

The four began talking as Brad smiled to himself. *It was over. It was finally over.*

And that's when he saw the leg of the scarecrow move. At first, he thought it was an illusion, but then he saw the left arm move, too. Little by little, the scarecrow was beginning to remobilize. "Uh, guys, I hate to dim the light on the celebration, but you better have a look at this," he said to them.

The three peered down as the scarecrow began to slowly get back up from the ground. "What the...?" Clyde replied as he stared at the body.

"Come on!" Kevin yelled as he grabbed Brad and Kelly and raced out the door. Kevin looked back at the barn door. "Clyde, move it!"

Clyde just stood there, staring. "No! No! You can't be alive!" he shouted as he loaded his shotgun at the standing scarecrow. He pulled the trigger back and sent the first shell flying into the scarecrow's right arm. It kept coming toward him, and Clyde shot again, this time hitting it straight in the chest. Again, nothing happened as the scarecrow surged toward him.

Clyde pulled the trigger, but the gun clicked. He reached into his shirt pocket and pulled out three more shells, fumbling with them as he tried to insert them into the gun. But he couldn't do it quickly enough. The scarecrow pulled a large knife off the wall and knocked the shotgun out of Clyde's hands. It raised the knife back and swung, slicing through Clyde's chest. He screamed in excruciating pain as he stumbled back against the wall. The scarecrow lifted the knife again, and this time swiped across Clyde's eyes. Clyde grew dizzy, and stumbled out the door onto the grass. Little by little, spots were beginning to fill his eyesight, until he couldn't see a thing.

He was blind.

He didn't know where the scarecrow was now, until he felt the searing pain throughout his right leg. He reached down, only to find out that there was nothing there. He screamed as the scarecrow swiped again. He just wished it would all end soon.

Kevin, Brad, and Kelly ran toward the nearest entrance to the cornfield. "Why are we going in here again?" Brad asked.

"Because it's the quickest way to get to the windmill," Kevin said. "We'll probably be safe there."

They ran in, swishing the cornstalks to their sides. Kevin was pretty sure he knew what he was doing. And he knew that they must be *way* ahead of the scarecrow now. Again, like Brad and Kelly had done before, they swerved through the tall stalks deeper into the field. Brad had no idea what time it was now. It seemed like they had been running from the scarecrow forever. He just wanted to go home. Back home, where there were no scarecrows. What was he going to tell his parents? He didn't want to think about the answer to that right now. They were running at full speed through the pathways with Kevin in the lead. Every now and then, he would take a quick glance behind them in search for the scarecrow. Each time he looked, he didn't see it, and although that gave him a good feeling, he had something inside himself tell him that the scarecrow was not infact behind them, but *ahead* of them. They ran through the pathway until they reached the small open area in the middle of the cornfield. Kevin's mouth gaped at the sight in front of them. There, hanging on the scarecrow post, was Uncle Jim. He had in fact been hung; a wire was wrapped around his neck and tied to the top of the wooden post. "Looks like the scarecrow got him!" Brad said.

Kevin turned his head his away, feeling sorry for the man he had known for years. "Come on," he said softly. "Let's get to the windmill."

The three turned around and headed back into the pathways. As they were running, Kevin thought to himself, *Where was the scarecrow?* It had to be at least closer to them now that they had stopped for a moment at the small clearing. They were lucky not to run into it. They had finally reached the end of the cornfield. The windmill wasn't too far from the field, so it wouldn't take them long to get there if they didn't stop running. After about a minute and a half, the three reached the front of the giant windmill. It was huge, with giant vanes spinning at about the speed of forty miles-an-hour. It reminded Brad of a giant fan, spinning round and round. Kevin grabbed the handle to the door and tugged, but it didn't budge open. "I think it's locked," Kevin said as he shook the tingling feeling from his hands. He lifted his foot up and kicked at the door, but still, the door didn't move.

A loud rustling sound came from the direction of the cornfield as the three turned around and saw the scarecrow coming out of the field. Kevin quickly decided that their only option was to climb up on the roof. He ran over to the side of the windmill and looked up. There were rows of little steps that they could use to climb onto the top, where the roof was long and flat. "Okay, climb to the roof!" Kevin said as he helped Brad and Kelly up the steps.

Foot by foot Brad climbed onto the steps, being careful not to slip and fall. Kelly was under him, hoping he wouldn't drop and knock her down. And Kevin was last, about the first three steps up when he saw the scarecrow coming toward them. "Hurry!" he yelled.

Brad climbed and made it to the top, pulling Kelly up with his hands. When they were both on the roof, they lied on their stomachs. "Kevin, go! The scarecrow's right below you!" Kelly yelled.

The scarecrow was under Kevin, and still carried the large knife in its hand. Blood trickled from the edge as the scarecrow swung at Kevin's feet but missed. Kelly reached her hand out and said, "Kevin, grab my hand!"

Kevin was only five steps away from the roof (the steps were about six inches apart) when the scarecrow swung from below and lopped his right foot off. Kevin screamed as he let one hand go, leaving him swinging with one arm dangling in the air and one hand gripping the next step. "Kevin!" Brad shouted.

The scarecrow, who was also climbing the steps, took another swing and completely took off Kevin's right leg. Blood gushed everywhere as Kevin finally let go. Brad and Kelly watched with frightened eyes as he tumbled down to the ground nearly fifty-five feet below. The scarecrow ignored the falling body and focused his eyes on the two kids, climbing up the steps. Brad and Kelly got up and ran to the other side of the roof, waiting for the horrifying moment when the scarecrow would climb up over the edge.

There was nothing they could do now, Brad thought over and over. *They were alone.*

The scarecrow slammed its straw hand over the edge of the roof and dragged the rest of its body upward. It got up on its feet and started slowly walking toward them. Kelly screamed once again as the scarecrow lifted the knife back into the air above its head. It brought the knife down fast, and Kelly and Brad dove out of the way. Brad looked around at the roof. There was nothing but them on it. What could he use to stop the scarecrow? The only thing would be to... yes! He had to get over to the vanes. They were spinning at over forty miles-an-hour, perfect to slice up that scarecrow. He would somehow have to lure it over there, but how? The scarecrow had to be too smart to stay away from the vanes. He then heard Kelly scream as the scarecrow swiped at her with the knife. She moved out of the way in time to get only a slight slash through the arm, nothing too serious. Brad then had an idea. He ran over to the edge of the roof where the vanes were and stood there waiting for the scarecrow. "Hey! Hey! Over here! Hey!" he yelled, jumping up and down while waving his arms.

The scarecrow turned and looked at him, then twisted back around only to see that the girl was gone. It turned back and faced Brad now, who was joined by Kelly. Determined, it started to head toward them; its knife ready to slice anyone that got in the way. Brad stood ready, waiting for it to come closer. It nearly reached him now, and Kelly backed out of the way. When she saw that Brad was not moving, she yelled, "Brad, what are you doing? Move!" Brad still stood there, waiting as the scarecrow approached him. It stopped right in front of him and lifted its knife once more. "Brad! Get away!" Kelly yelled as she watched him stand there.

This is it, Brad thought. *This has to work.*

The scarecrow swung the knife down toward Brad's head, and Brad quickly ducked straight down just as it cleared him. The scarecrow stumbled forward a little, and Brad kicked its legs, causing it to fall forward. The large knife flew out of the scarecrow's hands and right through the spinning blades of the vanes. Brad reached over and ripped both of the scarecrow's arms off, throwing them into the vanes and watching as the hay chopped up into pieces. He dove to the scarecrow's legs and grabbed them. "Kelly, come help me push it in the vanes!" he shouted.

Kelly ran over and started to push, with the scarecrow struggling to get free. It had no arms to grab them, so it was useless. They pushed it all the way to the edge of the rooftop, with the scarecrow's head almost touching the vane blades. "Give my regards to the Wizard of Oz, you freak," Brad replied as he gave one final push.

The scarecrow fell over the edge and into the vanes, getting chopped up into millions of pieces. Hay and strands of old clothing flew everywhere as Brad and Kelly sighed and sat back. After a few moments they walked to the edge of the roof where the steps were and climbed down carefully. The two kids stood watching the blades of the windmill spin and pieces of hay float down. "I wanna go home now," Kelly said.

"Yeah, me too," Brad replied as they started walking back toward the house. "I'll call the police and they can contact mom and dad when they get here. They'll never believe a story like this."

A sad look grew on Kelly's face. "I just can't believe they're all dead," she said. "They didn't deserve to die."

"I know," Brad said, resting his hand on her left shoulder. "I know."

"At least it's over," Kelly said as she slid her hands into her pockets. "If I see a scarecrow this Halloween, I'll freak out." A large smirk curled around Brad's face as they walked along. Kelly looked at him and added, "Don't even think about it, Brad."

ABOUT THE AUTHOR

Award-winning writer Dan O'Sullivan was born and raised in upstate Rochester, New York, home to giant film-processing corporation Kodak. A scribe of feature length screenplays and stories widely stretching across every single genre, he attributes his natural use of wordplay from his mother's scholastic English-teaching roots and his fascination for the science fiction genre in particular from his father. His personal inspirations stem from the work of John Hughes, Quentin Tarantino, Kevin Smith, Stephen King and Kevin Williamson.

O'Sullivan is a graduate of both the New York Film Academy and Brooklyn College in New York City for film production and screenwriting.

Most of his work can be found readily accessible on his official website at www.dan-osullivan.com.